AMERICAN GOD

ORDER OF THADDEUS • BOOK 4

J. A. BOUMA

EmmausWay
P R E S S

PROLOGUE

The man was pushing his steed of pure white to its limits, a faithful and true companion since escaping from that Boone County prison. A cloud of dust plumed behind him as they raced toward Zion, the home of his people, the chosen ones.

It had been a tumultuous several days filled with the threat of war by roving militias; the accursed accusations of thievery, murder, and the treasonous offense of establishing a kingdom within America; that blasphemous prosecution damning him to imprisonment.

The work of the Devil, it was, and the apostate Church!

His steed grunted in protest as the man continued pushing him homeward. It had been less than ten hours since his departure from that accursed place, and the enemy was surely not far behind. He had to reach the Saints at Far West. He hoped it was not too late.

In the distance, he caught sight of the location that had led him to the holy site in the first place. His heart leaped with joy, he grinned with satisfaction for arriving at the Promised Land. For years his people had wondered where God would build Zion, where its location would be revealed. He had received a series of prophetic visions, culminating in the final revelation on June 7, 1831: *"Ye shall assemble yourselves together to rejoice upon the land of*

2 | J. A. BOUMA

Missouri, which is the land of your inheritance." It was the ideal location to build God's kingdom, for it could provide peace and safety for the Saints and it was situated along the borders of the Lamanites, a vital end-times necessity.

He steered the white horse toward a bluff overlooking the blessed lands, navigating him along a rocky path toward the outcropping that had given him vision for what he had created not more than a year ago.

There it is...

He pulled up his steed alongside a rock formation commanding the center of the bluff overlooking the territory, an altar from ancient times that surely had been used by the ancestors of those great lands to offer up sacrifices and supplications before Elohim. He gazed upon those rocks, recalling the revelation that had filled his soul at first sight.

The man had announced before his people that the ruins were indeed an altar, built by none other than the first man whom Elohim had crafted from the dust of the earth—Adam. It was in that very spot that Adam and Eve had fled after being expelled from the Garden of Eden for their disobedience against their Maker.

He could feel the skepticism radiating from the faithful ones, but he reminded them of what he spake to them heretofore regarding the location of the legendary Garden in Jackson County. He exclaimed that now they had discovered where the first human couple had settled after their expulsion. It was nothing less than a divine miracle! The Saints had been led there by Providence!

"It is from this very spot," he had prophesied, "that Adam will be returning in fulfillment of prophetic utterances relating to the second coming of Jesus Christ. Here is where Zion will rise!"

He went on to teach them many things concerning the first ancestors of the ones who had fled Canaan in search of safer ground. How Cain and Able, Enoch and Methuselah all settled and lived in the Missouri territory. How Noah had transported the survivors of the Great Flood across the Atlantic—

A sound interrupted his recollection. He whipped his horse around, the steed whimpering in protest and his breath catching in his throat.

How could he have been so careless! Had he been followed the entire way? Was he now trapped, ready to be bagged by bounty hunters who would surely collect a pretty price for his head? He scanned the bluff looking for the source—

There it was again. Louder, heavier, more purposeful.

He withdrew the pistol he had absconded from the deputy passed out from the jug of whiskey he and his older brother Hyrum had bribed the Sheriff with in the early evening hours, ensuring he and the other Church leaders wouldn't be doomed to a life of imprisonment.

The breaking of branches echoed through the path he had just ascended. He cocked back the hammer. A chilly spring breeze rustled through the bluff and carried along the scent of something burning off in the distance as he took aim.

He came up quick and with purpose, as if he had known exactly where to go, having ascended those heights a hundred times before.

The man nearly set off his firearm, but sighed instead at the sight of the buck, its full set of antlers rising through the pathway— challenging and menacing and awe-inspiring all at once. He slowly lowered his arm and holstered his weapon.

The beast stopped short, startled to have come upon the man as much as he was to find the animal coming upon him. The breeze carrying the scent of burned wood and fields must have shielded his scent from the deer's approach.

The two stared at each other for a good few seconds. Then the beast darted back down the path as quickly as he had arrived.

The man took a deep breath and gave a short chuckle at his hammering heart, thinking that he was about to be apprehended by those heathen authorities who had laid hold of him and his brethren those many days ago. It all started with those dissenting apostates who had dared challenge him and his teachings. They were good for nothing, except to be cast out and trodden under the foot of men, as he had thundered before his flock.

He had dispatched with haste the commander of his Destroying Angels, Sampson Avard, to cleanse the Church of the very great evils which had hitherto existed among them inasmuch as they could not be put to right by teaching and persuasion alone. Although Avard and his band of brothers had succeeded in driving away the dissenters, the man on the horse had not fully considered the Missourians and their ill intent to dispatch him and the Saints with fury. Neither had he considered the possibility of a traitor in their midst.

Avard...

He set his jaw tight and clenched his fists around the leather reins of his horse, recalling the moment the man stepped into the courtroom during his hearing, bearing the blasphemous testimony of spilled secrets and holy plans. The wretched soul had even quoted words from another of the Apostles, Thomas Marsh:

"The plan of said Smith, the Prophet, is to take over this State, and he professes to his people to intend taking the United States and ultimately the whole world. This is the belief of the Church."

The man spat out over the bluff at the memory and the words that had sealed his fate.

That smell returned, carried along again by that breeze. The man swallowed hard and pulled on the reins, guiding his steed toward the vista. He looked below and scanned the horizon seeking—

Wait...Doth my eyes deceive me?

Billowing on the horizon beyond was a cloud, a mixture of menacing black and dusty brown. The man's face twisted with a mixture of fright and indignation at the sight. He pulled on the reins again, swinging his horse back toward the path from whence he came.

"Git!" he called out while kicking his steed in the ribs, urging him to make haste.

As the horse galloped forward, so did his heart. He knew the Missouri militia had marched against Far West, attempting to intimidate the Saints by making a show of picking their flint and priming their guns, as if they were making ready to fire. But he had been told the war was over before it started, that the general, that apostate Lucas, had spared his people.

But what was the meaning of this dreadful sight before him?

The closer he approached, the more easily he could discern two separate clouds: one of smoke and ash, the other of dust and dirt.

Soon, he came upon the very road he had trodden the March of last year, the one that led him to the thriving settlement firmly established by the Saints while he had been in Kirkland, Ohio—another blight on his ministry after having been driven from that first holy land, after having been proclaimed depraved.

The smell was far stronger and more wretched now, of burned buildings and foliage and crops, even the flesh of man or beast, though he couldn't discern which. When he rounded the bend, he pulled back hard against the reins and gave a cry.

Far West had been gutted. Smoldering ruins, black and wicked, were the culprit of the smoky stench. The flames had been put out, but the husks of the former town remained as a testament to the holy settlement.

God's chosen city lay in ruin, like Jerusalem of old, besieged by Babylon...

He sent his steed trotting forward. It was only as he approached closer that he understood the true gravity of the hour. Zion had not only been burned, it had also been abandoned. There wasn't a soul in sight. Which, for a town of thousands, sent the man into a panic. Now he understood the secondary cloud of beige: it was the remnants of the Saints as they departed.

He kicked his steed forward and rode hard through the center of town, coming upon abandoned storefronts and overturned carts. And then he saw it...

The temple, leveled to the ground in a heap of charred remains and blackened stone!

He pulled up hard to a stop at its threshold, his face twisting with rage at the wickedness that had befallen the holy building. He leaped off the steed, rushed inside the ruins, and stood among the charred remains of his upstart religion, falling to his knees crestfallen. He wanted to scream with rage at the desecration, but a shout from the street caught his attention.

"Prophet Joseph? Is that you?"

The man spun around to find a portly man with long hair and beard bearing the reins of a sickly horse drawing a cart of household goods, his wives and children close behind.

"Jedediah? Is that you?"

"Yes, brother Smith. You've returned! And just in time to join the last group of Saints heading for the Mississippi."

The prophet shuffled out of the ruined husk of the temple and ran to embrace his brother in the deadened street.

"But I don't understand," Jedediah continued. "We received word you were doomed to incarceration."

"As with the apostle Peter, the Lord hath brought me out of prison in might and power. Now, tell me, what has befallen our blessed New Jerusalem?"

The man's face fell, his features growing dark and eyes welling with emotion.

"Speak of what has transpired here," the prophet said lowly.

Jedediah cleared his throat, and said, "General Clark had assembled every one of our male Saints into the town square, informing us that the governor himself had ordered our extermination. Instead, the man urged us to become as other citizens, lest by a recurrence of their malicious events we bring upon ourselves a recurrence of the militia and irretrievable ruin upon ourselves. He spared our lives, but his troops looted and laid siege to our buildings and crops."

Smith asked him in haste, "Where is the medallion I sent ahead, the one bound by my letter of exhortation?"

Jedediah's face fell further. He looked off toward the smoldering temple and nodded.

Prophet Joseph's heart sank. But he knew what he needed to do. He gave his greetings to the wives and children, then bid Jedediah farewell. He mounted his steed of white once more and rode to meet the train of Saints departing Far West for its new home, the next New Jerusalem.

The prophet looked back over his shoulder at the remains of his Zion. One end of his mouth curled upward, believing that one day the truth buried in those smoldering ruins would rise again according to God's providence to accomplish a mighty miracle.

For he had foreseen that a time was coming when the Constitution of those American lands, forged in the soil first trodden by God's chosen ones, would be torn and hang as it were by a thread, nearly destroyed. At a crucial time, the righteous of his country, the Latter-day Saints, would be rallied with gathered strength and send out an Elder to gather the honest in heart to stand by the Constitution of the United States, stepping forth to rescue it from utter destruction above all other people of the world.

And that medallion would be the catalyst for such a revolution...

By Elohim's command, Joseph Smith will have the last word against the apostate Church and its State!

CHAPTER 1

No one goes to grad school to become an ex-professor. Yet there was Silas Grey, box in hand, packing up his Princeton University office. As a professor of religious studies and Christian history, his career was officially over.

The rain rapped hard against the window behind him as he sealed the brown U-Haul box with packing tape and stacked it on top of the four others sitting next to his desk, a fitting background rhapsody to his unceremonious end. He leaned back against the window and sighed, stretching his back before reaching for another box.

Two months ago, he was beginning another school year, excited to instill in another crop of America's finest a sense of faith and spiritual wonder through his classes on religious relics and Church history, helping them wrestle through life's haunting questions that inevitably arise at that phase of life. He himself had had a spiritual awakening as a young adult while serving as an Army Ranger in the wake of his father's death in the Pentagon on 9/11, launching him into his career of choice.

As a teenager, he had been interested enough with religion and deep spiritual questions. But it was more of a side hobby than his main hustle. Unlike his brother Sebastian, who had served as an altar boy in their family Catholic parish, his pursuit of girls and sports had highjacked his pursuit of the Blessed Virgin Mary and catechism. It wasn't until the carnage he had witnessed in Afghanistan, and then a roadside bomb took the life of his buddy Colton in Iraq that he got serious about religion and the big questions of life that began to needle his soul—about faith, life, and everything in between. And it wasn't until a tent meeting with a chaplain on a base in Iraq that he found some of the answers to those question. Which led to pursuing graduate studies in Church history, Christian theology, and religion with the intent of helping others discover what he himself had found. Not in a proselytizing way, mind you, as some sage on a stage. But instead as a guide on the side, enticing people to experience the heart of God through the memory of the faith.

Then Celeste Bourne showed up, and it all went to hell. Or heaven, depending on the perspective.

He eyed a set of bookshelves that wrapped the room crammed full of hundreds of books, journals, and monographs. He had been putting off wrestling this nine-hundred-pound beast to the ground, dreading the finality it would mean to pack away his research library. But it was time.

Might as well start with the As. But first things first.

He walked over to a stack of jazz records sitting next to his desk. He had waited to pack away his turntable until the very end. No sense walking to one's death unaccompanied by the smooth sounds of Miles David and John Coltrane! He chose a favorite: a 1980 concert in memory of Charlie Parker featuring Dizzy Gillespie, Milt Jackson, Raymond Brown, and others. He pulled out the transparent blue vinyl disc and set it on the player, then hit play. Within seconds his office was flooded with Nirvana.

Now we're ready to roll.

He pulled a chair over to the wall of shelves from a little table next to his door where he would meet with students to discuss test grades and assignment extensions and excessive absences.

Wouldn't miss that table, that's for sure! He put together a box and climbed up onto the chair, wondering how Celeste was getting on.

He had left her a few weeks ago recovering in a hospital after she had nearly died from a gunshot wound to her leg while the two of them were investigating the hidden location of the Ark of the Covenant. Last he knew, she was recuperating in a rehab facility in France, paid for by her employer, the Order of Thaddeus, an ecumenical religious order of the Church that sought to preserve, protect, and propagate the memory of the vintage Christian faith through any means necessary.

The Order was formed early in the life of the Church by Thaddeus, or Saint Jude as he is often known. He was acutely aware of the forces threatening the teachings of the faith, and he exhorted early Christians in a letter to "Contend for the faith that was once for all entrusted to God's holy people." Not only for the faith itself, but the shared, collective memory of the faith. He had worked toward institutionalizing this preservation effort with the ecclesiastical organization. A decade ago, the Order realized it needed to take more significant steps to contend for and preserve the memory of the faith. So they launched Project SEPIO, the full acronym being *Sepio, Erudio, Pugno, Inviglio, Observo*: Protect, Instruct, Fight For, Watch Over, Heed.

Rowan Radcliffe was the Order's Master, Celeste the operational director of SEPIO after having been recruited by Radcliffe while serving in MI6, Britain's military intelligence arm. They were a steady, sturdy guide for executing the Order's memory-preservation efforts, as well as a formidable opponent to Nous, an ancient cultic threat to the Church stretching back to the earliest days of Christianity. Through a series of events that threatened Silas's own life, he had been brought in as a sort of consultant earlier in the year. Which is when all of his troubles at Princeton started, leading to the growing pile of boxes stacked around his former office.

He finished cramming as many books as he could into the carton, then hopped down. He sealed it, then wiped his forehead.

An early mid-October cold snap had motivated maintenance to push the boiler to the max, flooding his office with stifling, humid heat. Not a good combination while one packed up their professional life. He assembled another box and climbed back up on the chair to continue working through the alphabet of his well-organized bookshelf.

Silas knew it wasn't exactly true that his Princeton problems started when SEPIO had recruited him for their ecclesiastical missions, taking him away from his teaching duties. If he were honest with himself, trouble had been brewing for the past few years. The dean of his department, Mathias McIntyre, had had it out for him from day one. Although Silas had certainly played his own part, giving the man plenty of ammo by bucking a system that had strict rules of hierarchy and protocol. Rules that got in the way of his goals and ambition.

He had been all set to realize one of those goals, the youngest professor to make tenure in Princeton's history after a series of successful archaeological and research finds, prestigious conference speaking slots, and peer-reviewed journal articles. Life was going just peachy.

That is, until a tenure panel was convened at the start of the school year and he was put on an administrative action plan that led to his ultimate dismissal after he had helped SEPIO uncover and ultimately foil three conspiracies meant to undermine, discredit, and destroy the Christian faith.

Didn't matter one bit to Princeton that he had managed to save the burial cloth of Jesus Christ and uncover the final resting place of the Ark of the Covenant. Now all he had was a room full of boxes and pocket full of worries. Who would take him now, a flunked-out college professor with degrees in religion and theology?

What about the Order? he wondered, reaching for a well-worn volume of Thomas Aquinas' *Summa Theologica*.

Radcliffe tried to recruit him earlier in the year after his first mission with SEPIO. The fight to stop Nous from destroying the

Christian faith marched onward, and there was plenty of room in the Order for people like Silas with his kind of military and academic experience. Surely the Order's efforts at preserving and protecting the memory of the vintage Christian faith was a worthy life-pursuit.

And yet, where was the prestige and glamor in that? Sure, he would get to flex his academic muscles through research and writing projects dedicated to his own personal interest in helping people re-discover and retrieve what Christians have always believed. But the Order was a below-the-radar operation, and SEPIO's work was even more shrouded in secret.

Which would mean no more speaking gigs or book and article contracts. Joining the Order would doom him to a life of obscurity.

Silas scolded himself as he climbed down off the chair with another box full of books. The Proverb was right: "Pride goes before destruction, and a haughty spirit before a fall."

Wasn't it that very spirit of pride the reason he was emptying his office in the first place?

"Silas, Silas, Silas..." he mumbled as he walked over to the Mr. Coffee sitting on a mini-fridge in the corner keeping hot a half-pot of brew from earlier in the morning. "What are we going to do?"

As he filled his mug, there was movement near his legs. "Hey there, Barnabas," he mumbled as his feline friend nuzzled against him.

He set the mug down, took a breath, and smiled. He scratched his faithful friend's ears, thankful for the interruption to his worrying. "There you go. That's a good boy."

Silas had picked up the beautiful slate-gray Persian while serving with the Rangers during the days of Operation Iraqi Freedom. The skin-and-bones cat had wandered into camp looking for a handout. He had always been a dog lover, but the pathetic sight tugged on his heart. He knew he was breaking protocol, but he was nearly done with his tour and it seemed like the right thing to do. And when things went south that fateful day on the road to Mosul,

Barnabas had lived up to his name: son of comfort. Now he was fat and happy, offering continued comfort when times got stressful.

Like today.

He walked over to his laptop to catch the latest news from CNN. Barnabas followed. He grabbed another box and put it together as the site buffered the live stream, then he walked it and his coffee back over to the shelves. No rest for the wearily unemployed.

After an advertisement for some hard-to-pronounce pharmaceutical, Wolf Blitzer came on with an election coverage update.

"If you're just joining us, there is a new poll out this morning giving fresh fodder to all three candidates running for the United States presidency. We can confirm that Robert Santos, the Democratic candidate has pulled ahead by five points to 37 percent, clearing the crucial margin of error that is sure to give his candidacy momentum in the weeks ahead. Amos Young, the Republican candidate, now has a slight edge over independent candidate Matthew Reed, standing at 32 percent and 31 percent respectively."

Silas shook his head as he climbed back onto the chair to clear another shelf of books. The bizarre election season filled with populist angst, conspiracies of Russian interference and hacking, and accusations of fake news culminated with Democrats nominating a Catholic Latino congressman from Texas, Republicans nominating a Mormon businessman-turned-philanthropist who scored big with a social media tech start-up, and a splinter group of religious and libertarian-minded conservatives putting forth a wealthy Evangelical governor from the Deep South as a third-party independent candidate.

The move had angered the conservative establishment and upended an election that was already making for a year-long made-for-Netflix spectacle. But some Evangelicals couldn't stomach the idea of a Mormon carrying the Republican torch to the election. Others believed it was the best chance in a decade for recapturing both the presidency and the Senate, and were not-so-quietly trying to discredit the third-party maneuver, given how it had split the

Republican Party. An unexpected side effect had been the siphoning off of votes from the Democratic candidate, but most commentators knew Santos would prevail. America was a two-party system, and inevitably a third-party candidate always crashed one of those two establishments. Publicly, Republicans were touting the core values of the democratic process and suggesting the times were ripe for an independent-minded candidate to transcend the binary choices offered to Americans for generations. Privately, they were furious—and they were circling the waters.

"Let me be clear," Blitzer continued, "Santos is far, far from out of the waters. Same for Young and Reed. All three candidates must win a majority of the Electoral College votes to win the presidency. If no presidential candidate obtains the necessary 270 votes, the decision is deferred to Congress. The House of Representatives selects the president, the Senate selects the vice president. With two weeks to go until Election Day, we're in for quite the ride."

Silas scoffed. "I'd say."

There was a soft knock at the door.

"Come in."

The door opened. Silas looked over as he continued packing. It was Miles, his teaching assistant. The man had served him well the past few years, helping him bear some of his professorial load. He was a few years younger than Silas, and the two had become good friends. He was going to miss him.

Miles folded his arms and leaned against the doorframe. "How are you getting along in here?"

Silas set a stack of books in the box, then took a swig of his coffee. "I'm getting there. Probably have the rest of the day yet to pack up. Then I'll be gone."

The man frowned. "I'm so sorry how all of this went down. Know that I advocated for you when Dean McIntyre interviewed me."

The sound of that name caused Silas's neck to burn red. He hadn't known the dean had gone all Stasi, interviewing anyone who had contact with him on par with the former German secret police. Did he question all of his fellow faculty colleagues? His students?

Whatever. That part of his life was over. Good riddance.

Silas grabbed another box, walked over to his desk, and started shoving items into it. "Miles, you're staring. You know how I hate that."

The man straightened himself, putting his hands at his side. "Sorry."

"What is it? I need to finish packing today before all my stuff is tossed to the curb."

Miles cleared his throat. "You...have a visitor, sir."

Silas set down a framed family picture of his childhood and looked up. "A visitor? Who?"

A familiar face framed by wet shaggy blond hair popped over Miles's shoulder.

His jaw dropped in stunned disbelief, then transformed into a wide grin.

"Grant?"

CHAPTER 2

"Dude!" the man in a long sleeve t-shirt, jeans, and pair of Vans said grinning, sounding and looking like he had just stepped off a California beach. He walked toward his old pal with arms wide open.

Silas smiled, and the two embraced in a bear hug. "What in the world are you doing here?"

Grant shrugged. "I was in town. Thought I'd stop by, check out the digs of my old college buddy, see how life as a professor is treating you." He paused and glanced around, then frowned. "Looks like life has seen better days."

Silas's face slumped. "Yeah, well...I've been let go."

"Bummer, dude. I'm guessing there's a far-out story on that one, so I won't ask."

He chuckled. "Thanks. There is, but...here—" Silas pulled over the chair he had been using in front of his desk, and motioned for his best friend from graduate school to sit.

He and Grant Chrysostom had studied together in separate doctoral programs at Harvard University's nonsectarian school of theology and religious studies. Silas under the direction of Henry Gregory, one of the foremost experts in Christian historical theology and comparative religion; Grant with Lucas Pryce, an expert in Semitic studies and a pioneering archaeologist whom Silas had taken down a month ago in a SEPIO operation. During their program, the two had been close friends but went very separate ways.

Silas's Christian convictions had drawn him into preserving the memory of the historic faith, and his Catholic background led him into relicology, researching mostly Church relics. Grant had been the spiritual-but-not-religious type, being drawn toward anthropology and the more adventurous field of archaeology. They had grown close on a dig at the fabled Tell-es Sultan with Pryce, the site of the biblical city of Jericho. Grant had even celebrated Silas's major win when he had discovered a series of scrolls verifying the Ark of the Covenant and became enraged when Pryce took credit for it. They had tried to keep in touch over the years, but between his heavy class load and Grant's work as a globetrotting religious-cultural anthropologist with a bit of archaeology on the side, it had been difficult.

"Gosh, it's good to see you," Silas said sitting behind his desk in his father's well-worn leather chair. "Just wish it had been under better circumstances."

"So you're leaving, been kicked to the curb?"

"Packing up for good."

"Bummer, dude. What's next? Another teaching gig?"

His gut began twisting with embarrassment, so he deflected. "Not sure. But I have a few prospects."

"Right on," Grant said nodding, his perfectly straight white teeth shining bright, a contrast to his bronzed skin.

"But you…" Silas continued, motioning to his friend and forcing a smile. "Goodness! Last I read you were hiding up in some monastery in Tibet studying the worship patterns of Buddhist monks. Is that right?"

"True that. The Dalai Lama has been good to me."

He almost choked on his coffee at the casual name drop. He set down his mug, and said, "As in *the* Dalai Lama, the figurehead of Tibetan Buddhism?"

Grant propped his feet on Silas's desk and stretched his hands behind his head. "His Holiness himself."

Envy wound its way up Silas's spine. He smiled weakly, trying not to show it. He wished he could tell him all that he had done the past year to save the Shroud of Turin and the Ark of the Covenant, and not to mention discrediting a fake gospel. But he knew the Order would pitch a fit.

He simply said, "Unbelievable."

An uncomfortable silence fell between the two. Then Grant cleared his throat, got up, and quietly closed the door.

Silas watched him, confused by the apparent shift of tension in the room. It appeared the nature of Grant's true reason for coming was about to be disclosed.

He turned around sharply, the casual demeanor gone, and fixed Silas with a look of determination. "Is this room secure?"

Silas laughed. "Is it secure? I mean, it's not like some NSA dark-room, if that's what you're after."

"But you can trust the fellow chilling in the next room, that he's not cupping his hands on the door or anything?"

He shifted in his chair. It wasn't like his friend to display flights of paranoia. "Grant, brother, you're making me nervous."

Grant quickly sat back down, glancing over his shoulder. Then he reached inside the collar of his shirt, fishing for something attached to a thin leather strap. He pulled out a disc and brought it out from around his neck and over his head. He set it on the desk in front of Silas with a thud, saying nothing.

What the...

It was a medallion. Hefty looking. About a quarter inch thick and the size of a piece of sliced grapefruit, made of what looked like bronze. It was clearly tarnished, with bluish-green patina caked on its surface from weathering and exposure to air or seawater over a period of time. Etched on the surface were logographic and syllabic values. If he were to guess, it looked to be an ancient Mesoamerican script. But then along the side...he tilted his head to take a closer look.

"What in the world?" Silas said.

Semitic script ringed the bronze disc.

He snatched the medallion and held it between his thumb and index finger like a pancake. He twisted it counterclockwise with his other hand to make out the etchings more closely.

Not only was it Semitic, it was biblical Hebrew.

What were Mesoamerican hieroglyphs doing alongside ancient Hebrew script on a tarnished bronze medallion around Grant Chrysostom's neck?

Silas set the heavy disc down on his desk with a thump then leaned back in his chair, eyeing his grad school buddy.

"In case you were wondering," he said, "now is the moment where you tell me some kick-ass story about how you came to be in possession of this relic."

Grant smiled slightly. "After we graduated and you got your cushy gig teaching here at Princeton."

"I'm not sure *cushy* is how I would describe it," Silas interrupted.

"Better than freelancing it as I've been for the past few years, hawking my intellectual wares to the highest bidder."

"Sounds about right," he grinned.

"Thanks. As you mentioned, I had been in Tibet with Buddhist monks on a religious-cultural mission with an outfit out of Harvard thanks to a wealthy benefactor. The goal was part anthropology, part archaeology. We were there to study the monks, but also some artifacts that had been unearthed in a recent mudslide. Anyway, that part isn't important."

He leaned forward, resting his forearms on Silas's desk. "A few months ago, after that project wound down, I was approached by an outfit out of Utah, called *The Society for New World Archaeology*."

"Never heard of them."

"I hadn't either, but they had been unearthing a number of ruins at a dig in Missouri. So, given my background in religious-cultural anthropology and archaeology, naturally they sought someone with my expertise."

"Naturally."

"So I get there, and this is a major operation with major money behind it. Top of the line equipment. Top of the line radio frequency technology. Even the tents and food were top of the line. We slept on freakin' Pima cotton 800-thread-count sheets!"

"That does sound like major money. So what did you find?"

"Lots of building foundations. Cooking utensils and stoneware. Even some bones from ritualistic graves." He paused and jabbed his finger into the medallion. "And this."

Silas's eyes widened. "You found this, at a dig in the middle of Missouri?"

His friend nodded. "What do you make of it?"

Silas picked up the disc again, running his fingers over its surface. "It's clearly old, the bronze having tarnished with age. Then there are these etchings. Hieroglyphs of some sort. Egyptian, maybe, given these other markings on the side, which are clearly Semitic." He shook his head and pointed to the thick side, exclaiming, "But you ain't digging up a medallion from anywhere with glyphs from any non-Afroasiatic cultures alongside these Semitic Hebrew alphabet characters here!"

Grant merely smiled. "What if I were to tell you early indication puts the etchings on the facade as pre-Colombian, early Mesoamerican glyphs?"

Silas sighed, growing impatient with his little game. "Alright, so they're pre-Colombian, early Mesoamerican glyphs. So what? Sort of remarkable there are these Semitic character markings on the side, but what do I know?"

"You don't understand the significance of this, do you?"

Silas scoffed. "No, I don't. And frankly, I'm a little preoccupied right now to care, given that I need to pack up my office after being fired."

Grant moved to the edge of his seat. "Let me spell this out for you, bro. Curiosity got the best of me, so I did some research while I was on that there dig. Apparently, the site was a former town founded by a one Joseph Smith, Junior."

Silas sat up straighter in his chair. "The founder of the Church of Jesus Christ of Latter-day Saints, of Mormonism? You found this medallion buried in a former Mormon town?"

He grinned. "Righto. And what some of my fellow archaeologists could gather, this here medallion was buried in what used to be a major temple of the upstart American religion. Now, I'm no expert on these things like you are, but from what I gathered there's some sort of cockamamie claim about a link between Israel and the Americas, something about Native Americans descending from a lost tribe or something or other. Which means the genuineness of what religious book largely depends upon said claim?"

The Book of Mormon.

Silas didn't voice what they both knew, but instead looked at the medallion again.

Grant continued, "I'm not aware of any professional non-Mormon anthropologist or archaeologist ever giving any merit to such a link between Mesoamerica and Israel—"

"Until now," Silas whispered.

"Bingo again. At least that was my gut reaction when I first saw that thing. It hasn't been fully tested and vetted yet. But that, right there, could be proof of a connection between pre-Columbian Native Americans and the Israelites."

"My God..." Silas leaned back in his chair and put his hands behind his head at the thought, all urgency to pack flying out the window.

Grant threw his arms up in the air. "This discovery has the potential to totally rewrite everything we know about Mesoamerican anthropology, ethnography, ethnology. Everything! This is likely the most significant find since those German miners pulled out that skull cap of Neanderthal man from the Feldhofer Grotto in the Neander valley."

Silas went to say something when a voice caught his attention outside his door. Actually two voices: the first one sounded deep and gravely and unknown; the other was his assistant Miles, sounding annoyed.

And alarmed.

He looked at his friend, furrowing his brow. "Does anyone else know you're here?"

Grant shrugged. "Don't know why—"

A sound caught both of their attentions, a thud. Then Miles's raised, muffled voice launched Silas out of his chair and toward the door.

When he reached it, there were sounds of a struggle, feet shuffling and papers being thrown and a chair scrapping across the floor before being overturned.

Then a muffled yell followed by a loud *thwack,* and the distinct sound of a body crumpling to the floor.

Miles!

Silas sucked in a lungful of air and flipped the lock to his office door.

He spun around toward Grant, jaw set and eyes narrowed.

"We've got company."

CHAPTER 3

"Get up!" Silas commanded Grant.

His friend stood and shuffled out of the way. Silas dragged his chair over to the door and wedged it securely underneath the copper knob burnished with decades of use.

He hustled over to his desk and flung open his middle drawer, fishing through the scraps of paper and pens and notebooks he had yet to pack. His fingers reached cold hard steel, and he withdrew his trusty Beretta M9.

"You still pack heat, prof?" Grant exclaimed.

"Old habits die hard," Silas said. "And it's a good thing, too, because I'm guessing they ain't here to play canasta."

"Who do you think they are? Why are they here?"

"Why do you think?" he said holding up the medallion by its leather strap.

Grant's face fell with worry.

"Just get over to the Mr. Coffee and stand back," Silas instructed.

The door knob turned. There was a thud against the door, but the lock and chair held. For now.

Grant nodded and grabbed his medallion. He slung it around

his neck, then hustled over to the small refrigerator sitting at the back of the room.

Silas followed and pivoted toward his office door, his back shielding Grant and arms outstretched for business. He whispered, "Who the heck did you piss of, Grant?"

Grant whispered back, "Why does it have to be me? Maybe someone's after that vintage vinyl collection of yours!"

"Because not more than an hour after you bring me some medallion, there's a pair of terrorists outside—"

He was interrupted by another thud, heavier and more demanding.

"Get down!" Silas commanded again, crouching down himself as the door lock exploded with fury.

Here we go...

The hostiles tried the door, but the chair held firm. They pushed against it again, and Silas could see it losing its hold. Then it slid away as the door was kicked in.

The door thudded angrily against the small table stacked with books, giving Silas a window to act.

He let loose a barrage of *one-two-three-four* bullets, each punching holes through the wood and sending the door riding on its hinges closed.

When it flung back open, thudding against the table again, he waited a beat. Like the old adage about not firing until you see the whites of their eyes, Silas waited for the black toe of a boot and barrel of a gun.

And there they were.

He sent four more rounds back into his poor door, receiving an angry callback of curses in a foreign language and instinctive gunfire that shattered his office window, making it clear he found his target.

The hostiles didn't even bother advancing with their piss-poor advantage and cover completely blown. It wouldn't be long before every available police officer in the tri-state area arrived, anyway.

Silas could hear shoes scuffling away, and then the outer office door open and slam shut.

He stood, weapon still at the ready. He inched forward, then glanced back at Grant who was still crouching next to the Mr. Coffee, eyes wide and chest heaving heavy breaths of clear fright.

He put his one hand out to stay his friend, then continued forward with his Beretta leading the way.

Sirens wailed in the distance through the shattered window as he reached the door. He came up to it, then eased his head around the wounded wood.

No sounds, no hostiles, no nothing. Except for Miles, who was crumpled on the floor and still.

He took a breath and eased himself around the door, Beretta outstretched and ready. He quickly padded forward into the outer office area to confirm it empty, then set his weapon on the desk and crouched next to his friend and colleague.

There was a bloody gash on the side of Miles's head and a trail of crimson leading to the floor. He was still, unmoving. Silas reached a trembling hand for his neck to check for a pulse, sending the good Lord a prayer for help.

"Is he...alive?" Grant asked softly coming up behind him.

Silas held his breath and glanced back to him as he felt the man's neck. He closed his eyes and sighed, then nodded.

He stood. "We've got to get him help, and fast. His pulse is weak and his breathing is shallow."

"Who the hell were those people?" Grant exclaimed.

Before he could respond, the door to the outer office area burst open.

"On the ground! On the ground!" someone ordered. "Now, now, now!"

Silas spun around to see three men in thick black padding and helmets with menacing black automatic weapons, red and blue pulsating light reflecting softly through the hallway.

They did as they were told, flattening themselves to the ground and raising their arms in surrender.

"Don't shoot! We've just been assaulted ourselves!" Silas cried out.

Within seconds those men in black were on them and roughly cuffing their hands.

Not the way Silas expected to end his last day as an almost-tenured Princeton professor. But par for the course with how his life had gone lately.

SILAS AND GRANT spent the next hour going over the events that had transpired with a slickly-styled man named Agent Gruff, which fit the not-at-all-sympathetic agent with the FBI's Joint Terrorism Task Force to a T. Within minutes of their apprehension, it was clear the two were victims as much as Miles, who had been rushed to Princeton Medical Center. But the authorities wanted answers.

Silas explained he was former military, serving tours with the Rangers, which explained his bullet-destroyed door and the Beretta that was sitting in a plastic evidence bag. Grant explained the two were friends from grad school, and he had dropped in on his buddy unannounced while passing through. Silas explained further that he had heard a scuffle in the outer room and feared for their lives after it was clear Miles had been taken out. Grant credited his buddy for saving their lives, putting a quick end to what could have been the death of them both. Neither of them shared the bronze medallion hanging around Grant's neck, a possible reason for the attack.

The agent pressed them both about why they might have been targeted. They said neither had a clue, though Silas offered his work with religious relics as a possible motive. Agent Gruff didn't seem to buy it, aiming a squinted, skeptical eye at them both. But he thanked them for their statement and said he may be in touch for some follow up questions.

By the time the two had raced to Princeton Medical, Miles was sitting comfortably in a hospital bed watching a surreal CNN report on the suspected terrorist attack against a Princeton professor he had just endured firsthand. When the two walked into his room, he nearly leaped off the bed with relief. Silas embraced his colleague, Miles was emotional from it all. Then they recounted the events.

"The two men demanded to speak with me?" Silas asked.

Miles nodded. "Obviously, you were meeting with Mr. Chrysostom, and they didn't have an appointment. You know how much of a stickler I am about that one."

Silas chuckled. "Don't I know it."

"But aside from that, they were shifty fellows who made me uncomfortable. I essentially told them to get lost, but they didn't like that. Started pushing through to see you. When I didn't relent, the one man clocked me!"

"Anything you can tell us about them?" Grant asked.

"Both wore black suits. The one fellow was short and stocky with dark hair. And the one who did all the talking was tall with close-cropped blond hair and a nasty scar running down his cheek. He's the one who hit me."

Silas shook his head, disbelieving the turn of events. Miles yawned and settled into his bed. Silas told him they would let him rest and would check in later.

They hugged again, then Silas and Grant left for Silas's car.

SILAS STARTED HIS AGING, sagging Jeep with a bit of a cough, then roared out of the parking lot onto Plainsboro Road. "You're not being straight with me," he said.

"What are you getting at?" Grant shot back.

"Like, for starters—" Continuing to drive, Silas reached for the leather strap around Grant's neck. "How the heck did you really come to possess this thing?"

"Hey!" Grant exclaimed, shoving Silas's hand away. "I found it, alright?"

"You found it? What, like sitting on a mess hall table?"

"No, I dug it up, along with a cache of other artifacts."

"But...it doesn't belong to you. The guy who paid for those 800-thread-count Pima cotton sheets does. Not to mention those muscle-heads who just stormed my office!"

Grant huffed and leaned back in his seat. "Sorry, alright? I had no idea they would come after me like that. And, what, are you going to turn me in to the Mormon medallion police or something?"

"No, it's not that," Silas said, picking up the pace as he drove. "I don't understand. Why bring it to me?"

"Look, I don't fully understand all the implications, but if this medallion checks out," Grant said, "if it is...whatever it is, some sort of actual archaeological proof that inscriptions using Old World forms of writing occurred in any part of the Americas before 1492. Then, bro, you may need to rewrite the book on your biblical and systematic theologies, as much as I might have to go back to square one on my own ethnology and anthropology. Because wouldn't that mean the Book of Mormon would have a legit claim on Christianity?"

Silas said nothing, his eyes narrowing and jaw clenching at the thought. He noticed his mouth had suddenly gone dry, and his pulse was quickening. He licked his lips and swallowed hard.

"Does anyone else know about this?" he finally asked.

"No, bro."

"No one else at the dig site? Your supervisor or the archaeological society funding the operation?"

"Not that I'm aware. I came straight to you when I realized what I had and what it might mean."

Silas propped his elbow on his door's armrest and glanced at his friend. "Why? You've never been interested in the Christian faith. Preferred freelance religion than its institutional variety, as I remember you saying after way too many shots of Jameson."

Grant chuckled. "Freelance religion. Nice. Yeah, that sounds like something I'd say. Especially after Jameson."

"So I don't get it. Did you have some sort of religious experience? See the Virgin Mary in a piece of toast or get some vision of Christ himself?"

He laughed again. "No, nothing like that."

"Seriously, kidding aside, what is your spiritual-but-not-religious self bringing me, a dyed-in-the-wool committed Christian and theologian, the most consequential religious relic, perhaps ever?"

Grant grew quiet, but continued smiling. "I've got my reasons. But mostly, I came for your help."

Silas decided to let the evasive answer go. He would press him later, after another late night of Jameson whiskey shots.

"What do you mean you came for my help? Doing what?"

"Figuring out what the hell this thing is, what it says. You know, since you're, like, some big-shot professor of religious history and relics and all."

"Ex-professor of religious history and relics and all," he corrected.

"Dude...you're not about to get all 'woe is me,' are you?"

Silas laughed. "No!"

"Need me to break out my violin and play you a sad song? Throw you a little pity party?"

Silas smiled and threw him a look. "I'm fine. Really."

"Good, because who needs establishmentarianism anyway? Besides, you know what I say. When you step in it, go get a new pair of shoes. Because it's all good, bro."

Silas said nothing. As he continued driving, he thought maybe it was time for a change. A new pair of his shoes, as his friend so eloquently put it.

"Speaking of a new pair of shoes." He took out his phone and searched for a name in his contacts.

Rowan Radcliffe.

"You want my help?" Silas asked.

Grant grinned. "Heck, yeah!"

"Well, here we go."

Silas selected the contact, held the phone with one hand and steering wheel with the other, and waited as the phone rang.

"Hello?" said a muffled raspy voice on the other line.

"Rowan? Is that you?"

"Silas? Is that you?"

He smiled. "The one and only. You don't sound too good."

"Caught a bit of the sniffles, but don't pay me any mind. I'm thrilled you called! I've been meaning to touch base after Addis Ababa and chat with you about my offer. Celeste says hello, by the way."

Grant raised both eyebrows, wrinkling his forehead. He whispered, "Celeste?"

Silas shook his head. "That's great. But, hey, I'm calling because I'm not sure if you've seen the news or not, but I've been...well, my friend and I have been assaulted."

"Assaulted?" the man exclaimed before sneezing loudly.

"God bless you," Grant said.

"Yeah, at my Princeton office. It's still unclear, but it may have something to do with a curious relic my friend from graduate school brought me right before the attack."

"Oh? Relic, you say? Do tell. But first, are you alright?"

"We're fine. My assistant, Miles, didn't fare as well, but he's recovering. About the relic, I'm not sure what to make of it. It's bronze, clearly tarnished with patina. But the weird thing is the glyph markings on the surface and around the side. Looks to be some sort of Mesoamerican logographic structure and..." he laughed. "You're going to think this is a joke, but along the edge it looks like Semitic markings, something in biblical Hebrew. And the guy discovered it at an archaeological dig in Missouri. Apparently, some sort of former Mormon settlement."

Radcliffe said nothing. The line went silent.

Silas looked at Grant, then furrowed his brow. "Hello? Radcliffe, you still there?"

"Silas...are we on speaker?"

He looked from the phone to Grant, then back to the phone again. He turned off the speaker option and brought the phone up to his ear. "You're good now. Is there something I should know about?"

"Mormon relic, you say? Are you certain?"

"Yeah, that's what my friend says, anyway."

"Get down to Washington as soon as possible. And bring the relic with you. Might as well bring your mate along, too. The chap could be useful."

"Why? What's going on?"

"I would much prefer that we speak in person, given the... circumstances. Do you remember where we first met?"

How could he forget. But given the secretive nature of the rendezvous point, he wasn't sure what Radcliffe was getting at.

"Go there. I'll find you," the man said.

Then the line went dead.

CHAPTER 4

WASHINGTON, DC.

The white Indiana limestone of the Cathedral Church of Saint Peter and Saint Paul stood starkly against the darkening blue backdrop of the Washington, DC, October sky, illuminated by the full harvest moon, its purity inviting the world inside to partake of the wonders of worship. Silas and Grant entered the sacred space through a pair of heavy oak doors along with an elderly couple who had come for the weekly Tuesday 6:00 p.m. Centering Prayer Service.

The grad school buddies had taken the Northeast Regional 93 Amtrak train from Trenton, New Jersey, to Union Station, arriving just as the heavy commuter traffic of Washington's elite was beginning the reverse trek in the other direction. An Uber brought them from Union Station to the Washington National Cathedral in order to make the evening prayer service, giving them coverage and ample opportunity to wander the cathedral and locate Radcliffe. Silas felt bad leaving Miles in the hospital. But after he explained the situation, his assistant told him to go settle the score. He seemed to be getting along well, anyway. And thankfully his executive assistant, Millie, had come to be by his side.

Silas held the door open for the older man, dressed in a black wool coat with matching fedora, and his better-dressed bride, a slight woman with gold earrings and a lipstick-red jacket, hair stuffed under a matching decorative hat.

"Why, thank you, young man," the gentleman said. "You get to be my age, and you don't mind a fella holding the door open for you."

Silas smiled as they slowly walked through the entrance. Grant followed behind as he led them into the nave. Lanterns hanging high above cast orange light down upon the sacred space below. Wooden chairs with small kneeling benches lined the nave, with several parishioners already seated near the front and readying themselves to open their entire being up to God's presence during the time of silent prayer, moving beyond thoughts, words, and emotions into a quiet communion with the Divine.

As an undergraduate student at Georgetown University, Silas had visited the cathedral several times for the evening prayer with a few classmates. Even though it wasn't a Catholic institution, the liturgy was familiar enough to help guide and ground his spiritually searching soul. The service started promptly at six with the deliberate strumming of a harpsichord just in front of the upper stem of the cruciform structure.

Silas walked farther into the nave, the siren song of the harpsichord beckoning him forward in worship. He grasped one of the wooden chairs from the back row, closed his eyes, and silently recited the prayer that his Lord taught the disciples to pray:

> *Our Father in heaven, hallowed be your name,*
> *your kingdom come, your will be done, on earth as it is in*
> *heaven.*
> *Give us today our daily bread.*
> *And forgive us our debts, as we also have forgiven our*
> *debtors.*
> *And lead us not into temptation, but deliver us from the*
> *evil one.*

*For yours is the kingdom and the power and the glory
forever.*

"Amen," he whispered, crossing himself instinctively.

Grant walked up beside him. "Alright, bro. You've gotten me into a church. Kudos to you. Now what?"

Silas softly chuckled and started walking back toward the narthex. "Told you I'd get you here, one way or another."

"Never expected it would be on some covert Jesus mission."

He grasped Grant's shoulder. "God works in mysterious ways, brother."

The two stood in the high-vaulted lobby of the national Episcopal parish glancing around the space for any sign of Radcliffe, the service continuing beyond them.

"Now what?" Grant asked.

Silas shook his head. "Not sure. This was where I was brou...err, met Rowan Radcliffe the last time."

He wasn't sure how he would explain to his college buddy how he had been whisked away in a dark-paneled van to the Order of Thaddeus's secret underground facility against his will the first time he had encountered the Order, even though they had saved his life.

"Who is this mysterious Radcliffe figure, anyway? And what of the...the Order of Thaddeus? Never heard of them, even in all my years of illustrious Catholic primary and secondary education."

"I told you. It's an ecumenical order dedicated to preserving the memory of the historic Christian faith, stretching all the way back to the early apostles. Let's wait for Radcliffe. He can explain it better than I can."

"Isn't this a pleasant sight for sore, old eyes," a raspy voice echoed behind them.

Silas turned around to see a tall, trim man with a slight Buddha belly and close-cropped gray hair walking toward them from the shadows.

He smiled. "Rowan."

The two embraced.

"Good to see you, Silas," Radcliffe said, grasping his shoulders. "And thanks for calling and coming down to me. Are you sure you've recovered from the incursion into your office? That had to have been quite the ordeal!"

Silas nodded as Radcliffe let go. "It was. But I think I've—" he stopped short and looked at Grant, "we both have recovered, given the circumstances. And we were happy to oblige."

"Well, you couldn't have come at a more providential time." Radcliffe's smile faded as he eyed Grant.

Silas gestured toward his friend. "This is Grant Chrysostom, the friend I told you about who brought me the medallion."

"Chrysostom? As in John Chrysostom, the Archbishop of Constantinople?"

Grant's face fell, and he glanced at Silas. Then he said nervously, "Uhh, no relation, sir."

Radcliffe breathed in deeply, narrowing his eyes and furrowing his brow. "Can we speak for a moment, Silas?"

The two walked away from Grant back toward the sound of the harpsichord.

"I'm not sure anymore about your having brought this Chrysostom mate here. Given what happened at your place of employ after the man showed up, I have to imagine trouble is still nipping at his heels. I don't know anything about him. Who he is, where he's from."

"What's to know? He's an old college buddy from Harvard and he's brought a significant religious relic to the Order's doorstep. At the risk of his own professional career, I might add. And, apparently, his life."

Radcliffe looked over at the man still sporting his cliché California attire. "You trust him?"

"Implicitly. One of the most honest, straightforward people I know."

He sighed and nodded. "Alright. Let's get on with it, shall we?"

Radcliffe walked away from the pair toward the southwest tower. Silas motioned toward his friend to follow. They quickly caught up to the old man as he unlocked a dark, walnut door leading into a stairwell. They descended halfway down the stairs when they were met with another small, short door. This one had a keypad. He typed in a series of six digits, then opened the door. It led into an elevator.

Once inside, Radcliffe pressed his palm against a hardcover book-sized piece of glass. It illuminated light blue, then turned green. Gears below immediately set into motion, taking the group far beneath America's house of worship.

He smiled. "Down we go."

Within half a minute they reached the bottom. Cool, dry air smelling of a summer storm flooded the carriage as the doors opened. The neo-Gothic interior of pale limestone above had been transformed into a world of white light, gray slate, and brushed metal several stories below.

"This way."

Radcliffe led them down a series of hallways lined with doors armed with the kinds of keypads from the elevator. Silas remembered walking down the same series of corridors after he had been brought here the first time.

As they rounded a bend, Grant whispered in Silas's ear, "Dude, where have you taken me?"

"Relax. It's the main operation center of the Order's special-operations unit."

"Special-ops unit? As in, like, Jihadis for Jesus?"

Silas laughed. "I wouldn't put it that way. But they are the more...kinetic aspect of the Order," he said, using Radcliffe's own language. "I'm sure Radcliffe will explain it all when we get to our destination."

"Which is where? A padded cell deep under some neo-Gothic cathedral?"

"Ahh, here we are," Radcliffe announced.

He pressed his hand against the same kind of glass that was at the elevator, lighting with the familiar blue light. After it turned green, the door unlocked and Radcliffe pushed it open.

Awaiting them was a well-appointed room far different from the rest of the facility. Instead of the sanitized gray, the room was entirely clad in dark wood. Floor to ceiling bookcases lined the walls containing biblical, systematic, and historical theological resources stretching back to the early Church. At one end was a large fireplace, the kind a person could walk into if they desired. A fire was crackling away, its hardwood smoke drifting out into the large space. A large wooden desk commanded the other end of the room, ornately designed with pillar legs and mahogany sides. A series of monitors stood behind it, all dark and hiding their purpose. At the center of the room was a sizable Persian-style rug. On top sat two leather couches facing each other flanked by two well-worn, overstuffed leather chairs. Rowan motioned for them to sit.

"Alright, Padre," Grant said. "Enough with the cloak and dagger routine. Who are you people? What is this place?"

Radcliffe looked at Silas, and he nodded his approval. "Go ahead. Tell him."

The man took a breath, eyeing the unknown quantity sitting in front of him. "Are you a religious man, Mr. Chrysostom?"

The man glanced at his friend. "Haven't been particularly so."

"Then you may not appreciate what we do here. You see, we believe that Jesus is who he said he was. The Image of the Invisible God, through whom and for whom all things in Heaven and on Earth, visible and invisible, have their being. The Son of God who came to live our life in order to identify with humanity. The Lamb of God who came to take away the sins of the world. The Life of God, who was raised by the Father to new life and sits at his right hand to make intercession for humanity, offering his new life to all."

Radcliffe paused, continuing to eye the suspicious man. "We are the Order of Thaddeus. And we've been actively fighting since the dawn of the Church to contend for and preserve that belief for future generations against vigorous attempts at assaulting that belief, both inside and outside the Church. And you have stumbled into one of our operation centers that those on the outside haven't a clue about. You can understand, then, how I might be a wee bit apprehensive for your being here."

Grant held up a hand. "Understood. Your secret's safe with me."

Radcliffe raised an eyebrow. "Is it? I don't mean to sound so rude, but you come out of nowhere and show up at our doorstep with quite the fanciful story of a Mormon relic. So you have to excuse my suspicions."

Grant looked at Silas, crossed his legs, then leaned back in his chair. "Look, I was raised Catholic. Went to Catholic grade school and high school and did all that. I may not buy into it all anymore, but I respect my friend. And when I found what I found, and thought about what it might mean to him and his religion, I wanted to help him out. Nothing more." He paused, looking toward the fire, seemingly lost in thought. Then he continued, "Besides, I've got a sister who's been caught up with that Mormon stuff."

Silas raised his eyebrows in surprise. He knew Mary pretty well from their time at Harvard. She was in the undergraduate program, Pre-Med if he remembered. He also remembered that she had been actively involved in an evangelical campus group. He couldn't believe she had jettisoned her faith like that.

Grant continued, "She's gotten all caught up with them and their group. To the point that she's totally cut off her family. Even tried to convince me to join in the fun. So you could say I've got my reasons for showing up on your doorstep with a fanciful story about a Mormon relic, as you put it. If you don't want it, I know people who would. Like my employer."

Silas hadn't recalled hearing his friend sound as bitter and full of revenge before. He understood why he brought him the medallion. It wasn't about religion, like it was for Silas. It was about family.

It was personal.

"I understand," Radcliffe said softly. "Forgive me. I will pray for your sister."

Grant said nothing.

Silas cleared his throat. "Before we ended our phone call you seemed to suggest the relic had arrived at the perfect time, given some circumstances. That there was something bigger going on."

"That's right," Radcliffe said.

Silas waited for him to say more. When he didn't, he asked, "Care to share more?"

Radcliffe paused, his eyes narrowed and fixed.

He said, "The Religious Right is about to endorse Amos Young for president."

CHAPTER 5

Did Silas hear him correctly? The Religious Right was endorsing a Mormon? For the presidential candidacy? Of the United States of America?

He said, "The Religious Right. Endorsing a Mormon for the highest office in the land. The one they believe with every fiber of their being is a Christian nation and must return to that Golden Age."

"That's what my sources tell me," Radcliffe replied.

"When pigs fly."

"Looks like winged pork is coming home to roost, bro," Grant offered.

"But that makes no sense," Silas said.

Radcliffe replied, "Well, not the entire Religious Right. Just one of their members."

Silas furrowed his brow and leaned forward. "Who?"

Radcliffe frowned. "Unfortunately, we're not sure."

"My money is on The Smiling Preacher," Grant offered, "I love listening to his Sunday morning pep talks. Makes me feel all warm and fuzzy inside."

"We don't think so. He's never exhibited a political bone in his body. Much too concerned with inebriating the masses on empty platitudes and mindfulness mumbo-jumbo. Politics would alienate people too much and limit the reach of his brand."

"If I were to guess, I'd say it's that Southern Baptist pastor out of Dallas," Silas sneered. "I recently saw he had this massive political rally disguised as a worship service, complete with the American flag and that damn song, touting America's greatness. Shoot, even a bald eagle was let loose in the auditorium!"

"What song?" Radcliffe asked.

"Sing it, Silas," Grant said. "I always loved the sound of your voice during all of those late-night study sessions."

Silas glared at his friend. Grant just smiled.

"You know," he began, "'Make America great again, make America great again, lift the torch of freedom all across the land,' goes one verse. 'Step into the future joining hand in hand, and make America great again.'"

"Holy shi—"

"Grant..."

"Seriously? That was sung at a Christian church?"

Silas said nothing, slumping back in his chair.

Radcliffe sighed. "Unfortunately, that doesn't surprise me. But he's small potatoes to being considered a major influencing factor in this election."

Silas asked, "But why would the Religious Right touch this election with a ten-foot pole? Much less a Republican candidate that isn't orthodox Christian, while distancing themselves from one in their own tribe?"

"You know that crowd. They are tied at the hips to the Republican Party. It doesn't matter who the other candidates are. It's Republican all the way, no matter the cost. They'll bind themselves even to RINOs!"

"RINO?" Grant asked.

"Republican In Name Only," Silas offered. "Someone who claims the Republican political label without the beliefs or the actions to back it up."

"Got it. But a Mormon? And with that filthy-mouthed reality star businessman from New York as his running mate?"

Radcliffe said, "Power does strange things to people. Even stranger things when you're used to having it and then lose it."

"They've got their candidate, though," Silas replied. "That Evangelical governor from Missouri or Louisiana or wherever the heck he's from."

"Alabama."

"There you go. Can't get more Republican than that."

"Or Christian," Grant said.

Radcliffe continued, "But he's an independent candidate, and apparently the worry amongst some of our brethren is that he's splitting the Republican vote and will tank the Religious Right's chances of securing power."

Silas replied, "So they hop in bed with a guy who's a member of a religion that claims to be just another Christian sect?"

"Apparently so."

Grant laughed. "A Mormon, an evangelical, and a Catholic walk into a brothel..."

The two stared at him with raised eyebrows.

"What? Sounds like the making of an interesting joke."

Silas smiled. Radcliffe did not.

"Well, I like the Catholic guy," Grant offered. "He seems pretty good, pretty Christian."

"Maybe so," Radcliffe said, "but if the Religious Right didn't rally around a Southern Baptist from Georgia, there's no way Evangelicals will support a Catholic congressman from Texas. Even if it means throwing their full weight behind a Mormon candidate."

Silas considered his words, then his face fell. "What about James Maxwell? Given the clout his father had and their Freedom University and Faithful Majority political action committee, what if it's him?"

"Doubt it. He and his cadre of Christian activists are too principled. I'd eat my left shoe if they came out of the closet in support of Amos Young."

The room fell silent, each person considering how the bonkers political year had been adding up.

"So what's the Order's interest in all of this?" Silas asked. "I thought you all were non-political, nonpartisan."

"We are," Radcliffe said shaking his finger. "Make no mistake about that. We have zero interest in...whoring ourselves, for lack of a better term, to either political party. Our primary, nay, our *only* interest is in preserving and promoting the historic Christian faith."

"But..." Grant said, one end of his mouth curling upward in expectation.

Radcliffe paused and looked at the ceiling, cupping his hands together as if carefully choosing his words. "But there is confusion about the reality of the Mormon religion. Internal polls suggest half of Americans believe Mormonism is a Christian sect. When asked to volunteer the one word that best describes Mormons, the most common response from those surveyed was 'Christian' or 'Christ-centered,' and still others volunteered 'Jesus.' 60 percent of voters who know of Young's Mormonism are comfortable with his religion, and another 21 percent say it doesn't matter. The Order, and frankly many of my colleagues around the Church, have a growing sense of dread that the confusion could worsen with someone like Amos Young leading the country. And..."

He trailed off, not finishing his thought.

"And what, Rowan?" Silas asked.

"And there has been growing chatter being reported by some of our operatives monitoring known Nous cells."

He sat up straighter. "Nous? What's their interest in an American election?"

"Probably the same interest the Order has. Nous cares about anything that undermines the historic Christian faith. And a Mormon president would sure do the trick, especially one endorsed by conservative evangelicalism."

"But they don't have the power to sway an election. It would take something pretty massive on their part to swing things their way. The will of the American people isn't easily swayed. At least we have that going for us."

"True, but there are unconfirmed reports of meetings between the Quorum of the Twelve and Nous operatives."

"Quorum of the Twelve?" Grant asked.

Radcliffe explained, "The highest office next to the Presidency within Mormon hierarchy. And not only that, but there has been a major push recently through clandestine means to verify the claims of Joseph Smith and the veracity of his writings from the supposed golden plates sitting at the heart of the alternative Christian faith."

Silas sank into his chair. That did sound odd. He looked over to his friend. He was beginning to see how the newly discovered relic was connected to the larger picture. A Mormon was running for the highest office of the land, one that had grown in power and reach in the years since 9/11 through two separate presidencies. People were already confused about whether the religion was just another Christian sect, like Catholicism or the Southern Baptist Convention. And given that Nous had been reported to have met with members of the Latter-day Saint hierarchy—none of it boded well.

What is going on here? What does it all mean?

The medallion.

Silas wondered, "Any chance this has anything to do with what Grant discovered?"

Radcliffe smacked his forehead. "Good Lord, that's right. The relic. Forgive me for the political sidetrack. We've been spinning behind the scenes here ever since the Republican convention in August. Let's get a look at this relic you found."

Grant glanced at his friend, apprehension flashing across his face. Silas nodded with reassurance. He reached underneath the collar of his shirt for the leather strap, then lifted the heavy metal disc over his neck.

He held it over the large wooden table in the middle, letting it spin and glint in the dim orange light. Then he set it down with a thud.

Radcliffe started for the medallion, but stopped. He looked at Grant for approval, his eyes greedy with expectation, yet also betraying a certain dread.

Grant nodded. Radcliffe snatched it up at once.

He held it in his palm, looking away from it and cocking his head toward it as if listening for a reply.

"Heavier than I expected," he offered.

"That's what I thought when I discovered it," Grant said.

"You discovered? Where?"

"At an archaeological dig in Missouri."

Radcliffe said nothing. He brought the bronze disc up to a lamp sitting to the right of his chair. He gently rubbed his fingers along its surface, stopping at each glyph and tracing them with his index finger.

"Fascinating...Certainly looks like Mesoamerican pictographs. By the way, I summoned Naomi Torres after I hung up with you earlier. Figured her background in pre-Columbian anthropology would be of use."

Grant blanched in surprise. "Did...Did you say Torres? Naomi Torres, from an excavation outfit out of Miami?"

"Well, not anymore. I hired her to join the Order," Radcliffe said proudly. "Why do you ask?"

He said nothing, turning away and smiling slightly.

"You know her?" Silas asked.

"You could say that."

Radcliffe looked up from examining the disc. Silas turned toward him, as well, waiting for a story.

"We sort of...dated a while ago."

"Figures," Silas said.

"What's that supposed to mean?"

He smiled. "Nothing. So, did it end on good terms or not so good terms?"

Grant shrugged. "Depends on who you ask."

"I guess we'll find out real soon, won't we?"

"Hold on here just a minute…" Radcliffe returned to the disc, beginning to examine the characters along the edge.

"Anything interesting?" Silas asked.

"It's all interesting. And these, I can tell these are definitely Semitic characters, as faint as they are." He used the nail of his thumb to scratch some dirt off the edge.

Grant explained, "Like I said when I showed this to you, Silas, I hadn't had the chance to translate any of the glyphs or characters, so I have no idea what they mean or what they are saying, or even how they are connected."

Radcliffe's forehead creased with concentration, his eyes squinting as he considered the characters. He spun the disk slowly counterclockwise and looked up from the disc out into the study from time to time, moving his lips as if he was translating the Hebrew from memory.

Silas moved to the edge of his seat. "What's it say? Can you make out any of the characters?"

Silence filled the space, except for the crackling and popping of the fire at the other end of the room.

At once Radcliffe breathed in suddenly, then set down the medallion, eyes wide with understanding.

He looked at Grant. He returned Silas's glance.

"Rowan…What is it?"

Radcliffe sat still, breathing deeply and quickly.

"This changes everything," he mumbled softly before getting out of his chair and walking toward the bookcases at the other end of the room.

CHAPTER 6

Radcliffe stood before the wall of books to the left of the massive fireplace, scanning them from left to right, his hand outstretched and index finger poised.

"Where is it?" he muttered as he continued fingering the tomes. His feet were planted as he pivoted from left to right, searching for the right book.

"What's changed?" Silas had followed him to the bookcase and was hovering over his shoulder. "The election? The Christian faith? Come on, Rowan. Throw us a bone, here."

Grant joined the interrogation. "Yeah, don't leave us in the dark, Padre. So not fair!"

"Ahh! There it is." He reached for a well-worn black cloth-overboard volume with tattered edges and stained pages. Clearly older than the room they were standing in.

He brought it with him to another bookcase and found another book, clearly knowing where to look for that one. He brought them over to a table stacked high with similarly aged books and set them next to each other.

The book on the right read "The Holy Bible: 1611 Edition, King James Version." The one on the left announced something entirely different.

The Book of Mormon.

"Look here in Isaiah 10:21." Radcliffe picked up the King James Bible, then read the passage: "The remnant shall return, even the remnant of Jacob, unto the mighty God."

He set it down then pointed to the Book of Mormon lying next to it. "You, there," he said pointing to Grant. "Look at 2 Nephi. Go on, read it."

Grant hesitated, then picked up the other book and read the passage: "The remnant shall return, yea, even the remnant of Jacob, unto the mighty God."

His eyes widened in disbelief. "They match!"

Radcliffe nodded. "Now look at this." He turned over one page in the Bible, to Isaiah 11:11. He handed it to Silas. He read it aloud.

And it shall come to pass in that day, that the Lord shall set his hand again the second time to recover the remnant of his people, which shall be left, from Assyria, and from Egypt, and from Pathros, and from Cush, and from Elam, and from Shinar, and from Hamath, and from the islands of the sea.

Radcliffe grabbed the Book of Mormon from Grant and turned the page to 2 Nephi 21:11, then read:

And it shall come to pass in that day that the Lord shall set his hand again the second time to recover the remnant of his people which shall be left, from Assyria, and from Egypt, and from Pathros, and from Cush, and from Elam, and from Shinar, and from Hamath, and from the islands of the sea.

"Another match!" Grant said bewildered.

Radcliffe held up the bronze medallion. "Here, look at the characters along the edge. This here Hebrew lettering translates, 'The remnant shall return...unto the mighty God. And it shall come to pass in that day, that the Lord shall...recover the remnant of his people.'"

"Whoa," Grant said. "Far out..."

Silas said nothing, not sure what to make of the discovery.

"These passages from Isaiah are thought to be prophetic texts of Yahweh's eventual vindication of his people, the Israelites. As you can see, these same verses appear in the Second Book of Nephi, which similarly serve as prophetic texts of the Jews' latter-day restoration when they believe in the Messiah."

"Whoa," Grant said again.

Silas asked, "So both the Hebrew Scriptures and the Book of Mormon reference the restoration of a remnant of Israel, an eschatological End Times gathering of the people of God?"

"Yes," Radcliffe answered.

"Then what do you make of these Semitic characters being paired with the seemingly Mesoamerican ones? Any clue what they might translate into?"

"Not a clue. But I'm sure Naomi will fill in the details when she arrives."

"But this has to be significant. That an ancient relic with Hebrew characters referencing both the Jewish and Mormon scriptures was discovered at a religious dig on American soil."

"Highly."

Silas turned to Grant. "Were you able to get this thing dated at all? You know, before you brought the archaeological contraband to my doorstep."

Grant grinned. "Not fully."

"We can let Zoe have at it once Naomi has a look," Radcliffe said. "Our resident techie has all kinds of gadgets and doodads that should analyze the relic."

Grant nodded, then said, "What little time my benefactors and I spent with the object before I...shall we say, borrowed it for a few days, did reveal a few things. The Mesoamerican glyphs told us it was for sure pre-Columbian, no doubt about that. And initial metallic alloy tests from the field indicated it was at least that old."

"Dear me..."

"I don't understand why any of this matters," he complained. "So some bronze medallion with some stick drawings and verses from the Old Testament was dug up in some pit in Missouri. So what?"

Radcliffe leaned forward. "It matters, because the Book of Mormon claims to reveal the early history of the Americas by chronicling the migration of the lost tribes of Israel from Palestine to the New World."

Grant coughed and threw a grin to Silas. Silas let slip his own laugh of disbelief, and said, "So we've heard. But nobody takes that seriously, right?"

Radcliffe smiled wryly. "I understand for historians such as yourselves this probably sounds utterly fantastical. But it is integral to the faith of Mormons, that the Native Americans of the Americas are actually long-lost Jews, originally descending from what we know of as Israel."

"So what is the history?" Grant asked.

Radcliffe motioned for the two to join him back at the center of the room for the story time. They sat down. He continued walking over to an alcove with several cabinets. He opened one cupboard and drew out a bottle of caramel-colored liquid.

"Anyone care for some Scotch?"

"Yes, please" both responded in unison.

After pouring three glasses, he grasped them together and shuffled over to the seating area and distributed them.

He took a long sip then launched into a Mormon history lesson.

"The original story, as tradition has it, was translated from a series of golden plates, known as the Golden Bible. They were supposedly buried in a hill in western New York, which a divine messenger named Moroni directed Joseph Smith to dig up and translate. The characters were said to be in some fanciful language scheme classified as Reformed Egyptian, making the process of deciphering the unintelligible lettering engraved on the golden plates an arduous one, taking him nearly a year plus a half. Fortunately for him, the man had the help of a trusted advisor, a one Oliver Cowdery. And, of course, with the help of divine guidance from above."

Silas scoffed. "So what does this...this Golden Bible say?"

Radcliffe settled in, taking another drink for the long haul.

"As Joseph Smith tells it in the Book of Mormon, the first migration had taken place soon after humanity's language had been confounded at the Tower of Babel. Apparently, God had commanded this group to travel over the great waters of the Atlantic until they reached what they called the promised land. That would be the Americas. Through the leadership of the prophet Jared and his brother, the so-called Jaredites produced a great civilization that lasted nearly two thousand years. Unfortunately, it was destroyed by internal conflict that ended in brutal and total war."

"Never heard of no Jaredites in Catholic school," Grant said after taking another swig from his glass.

"Well, Jared and his 'ites' are part of Mormon lore, rather than part of the Torah or Histories of the Hebrew Scriptures any Jew or Christian would teach. Anyway, generations later, after this first migrant wave, a second wave took place during the reign of Zedekiah, king of Judah. According to legend, at the command of God, the prophet Lehi and his friend Ishmael led their families out of Jerusalem and into the wilderness. Like the Jaredites before them, they crossed the vast ocean of the Atlantic and settled into the new lands of the Americas, which were said to be waiting for them to plant themselves deep into their soil. Soon they were joined by a final group migrating from Palestine, the Mulekites under the leadership of Mulek, a son of King Zedekiah."

"Again, Sister Hilda left that part out," Grant added, draining his Scotch.

Silas shot him a look. "Let him tell the story, would you?"

Radcliffe continued, "Despite God's supposed divine guidance of these Israelites, Moroni revealed to Joseph Smith that not all went well for these ancient migrants. A sharp division arose, creating two warring tribes: the Nephites, named after their mighty prophet Nephi; and the Lamanites, named after Nephi's brother, Laman. According to Smith's revelation, the Nephites were faithful members of the Church and believed in her revelations, seeking to keep the commandments of God. The Lamanites, however, were rebellious. Their minds were darkened by unbelief and were apostates from the Church."

"Then what happened?" Silas asked this time.

"Because of their rebellious ways, God pronounced a curse upon Laman and his seed, giving them a skin of blackness so that they might not be enticing to the white and exceedingly fair and delightsome Nephites, as the account says."

"Hold on right there," Grant interjected. "It actually says that? The Book of Mormon actually says that the dark skin of those who would become America's natives was a divine curse? And the ones who were blessed were white?"

Radcliffe nodded slowly.

Silas scoffed. "So blatant racism was weaved into Mormonism from the beginning?"

"Missed the PC train on that one, didn't they?" Grant said, then he shook his glass. "How about a refill?"

Radcliffe pointed toward the alcove. "Help yourself."

Grant did.

"Why don't you bring the bottle back with you," Silas interjected. "I'm gonna need it for the rest of this story."

"It gets worse," Radcliffe said. "As the account suggests, their appearance became repulsive, so that their blackness was loathsome to look upon. It was said that they became an idle people, full of mischief and subtlety. God had even warned the Nephites: 'Cursed that be the seed of him that mixeth with their seed: for they shall be cursed even with the same cursing.' Direct quote."

"Give me that." Silas took the bottle from Grant, uncorked it, poured himself three fingers worth, then sat back and took a long swig.

"It gets better: Smith suggests God was still merciful. He declared that if the Lamanites were to repent of their rebellious ways they could join the pure Nephites. In so doing, their curse would be taken from them, and their skin would become white just like the Nephites."

"Remarkable."

"But then this is where the story turns," Radcliffe continued. "For hundreds of years, these two lost tribes of Israel lived in enmity with one another. That is, until Jesus Christ appeared to all of them, offering his gift of salvation. Jesus of Nazareth, who had been crucified and resurrected in Palestine, is said to have appeared to explain these mysteries further to the inhabitants of the New World, as well as all of the things he had taught to those living in Galilee. All of these people eventually chose to follow Christ, which brought peace to the lands of the Americas and unity to all of its inhabitants. As the Book of Mormon says, 'There was no envyings, nor strifes. There were no robbers, nor no murderers, neither were there Lamanites, nor no manner of Ites; but they were in one, the children of Christ.'"

"I guess that's where the second testament of Jesus Christ comes in," Silas offered. "Because they believe he showed up in America with a special dose of revelation just for the Natives...err, the lost tribes of Israel."

"Exactly. However, soon afterward war again broke out among the Nephites and Lamanites. Millions were killed among these two nations, as the story goes, until all the remaining tribesmen gathered for one final battle near the Hill Cumorah, in the western region of New York. Incidentally, the same hill the famed golden plates had been buried. The wicked and rebellious Lamanites emerged victorious, allowing only a small handful of the Nephites to survive. Yet the fighting didn't end, for within a few years the Lamanites became so evil that they warred amongst themselves.

"When the great explorer and European Christopher Columbus arrived on the shores of the New World, Joseph Smith writes that these American Indians, as they had been known, were a filthy and loathsome people who had lost all memory of their Jewish origins, forgetting that their dark-skinned appearance was a curse upon them for their failure to obey God."

The two men sat in silence as Radcliffe ended retelling the basic contours of the story of the lost tribes of Israel found within the Book of Mormon, having each finished their second glass of Scotch.

Silas glanced at his watch just as Grant let out a yawn. It was getting late.

"Why don't you two boys head off to bed," Radcliffe offered. "Naomi won't be in until late in the night, and we can't move forward without her expertise anyway."

Grant stood and stretched. "Sounds good to me."

"Me too," Silas echoed. "I think I remember where the sleeping quarters are from the last time I was here. We'll see you in the morning."

The mystery of the medallion would have to wait.

CHAPTER 7

The emerging dawn of the new day came far too quickly for Silas after sleeping nary a wink. He had struggled to fall asleep at first, his mind filled with a torrent of questions racing with the implications of what his friend had uncovered and brought to him.

What if it was historical, archaeological proof that the claims the Book of Mormon made were genuine? That lost tribes of Israel had migrated to the Americas? That Jesus Christ had offered them a second revelation of himself after his resurrection? That Joseph Smith had indeed received this revelation from the divine messenger Moroni? And that the faith of this American religion, revealing this American god, lived or died by that history?

He woke up after finally settling in for sleep with the weight of the what-if implications still pressing their significance in against him, still needling him as he walked out of his room next door to where Grant was staying.

He knocked. Hearing nothing after waiting a beat, he pounded harder. From the other side a muffled "Hold your horses, I'm coming" came through.

Grant cracked the door, darkness shrouding his just-awakened face.

"Mornin' sunshine," Silas said.

"Dude," Grant moaned, his voice sounding like hungover gravel, "it's, like, eight in the morning."

He furrowed his brow. "Yeah...and that's what we call in the real world, 'sleeping in.'"

His friend scoffed and went to shut the door.

Silas wouldn't let him. "Come on, Radcliffe has breakfast waiting for us in his study."

Grant withdrew into the darkness. A few minutes later he emerged wearing his jeans and shirt from the day before.

"Hope he has a keg of strong black coffee ready."

"Actually, I think it's tea," Silas said as he left.

"Say it ain't so!"

They reached the heavy wooden double doors to the study and knocked, not being able to enter with the palm scanner standing guard. A few seconds later Radcliffe answered.

"Gentlemen," he said, opening the doors and bearing a large ceramic pot with four tea bags draped over the side.

Grant looked at the pot. "Damn Brit," he mumbled as he sauntered inside.

"This way." Radcliffe led them back toward the work desk from the previous evening, which had been cleared and set for breakfast. A basket of fresh muffins filled the area with the comforting smell of warm berries. As did scrambled eggs, bacon, ham, and a pot of coffee.

"Thank the gods above," Grant said with relief.

Silas poured a large mug of the black brew, then handed it to his friend.

"Muchas gracias."

"Looks like you need it more than me."

"Help yourselves," Radcliffe said as he sat down. "But this will be a working breakfast. Too much to do."

"Yeah?" Grant said after taking a large bite of a muffin. "Like what?"

"Like the medallion."

"What about it?"

"Now, you said you found it at a dig in Missouri?"

Grant spooned a large helping of eggs onto his plate and sprinkled some cheese on them. "That's right. What of it?"

"Missouri has been a highly significant parcel of land for Mormon lore."

"I thought it was Utah," Silas interjected.

"Utah is where they ended up, only years after they were driven from the lands of Missouri. You see, one of the major questions on the minds of Joseph Smith's followers was where God would build Zion, his New Jerusalem and when it would be built."

Radcliffe wiped his mouth with his napkin, then hustled over to a bookshelf and pulled down an aged volume. He sat down with it at his seat. "What's interesting is that Smith had given a revelation about its location in his *Doctrine and Covenant*." He opened the book and thumbed through it in search of a reference. Finding it, he said, "Here, listen to this: *'I say unto you that it is not revealed, and no man knoweth where the city Zion shall be built, but it shall be given hereafter. Behold, I say unto you that it shall be on the borders by the Lamanites.'*" He closed it and set it down on the table.

He continued, explaining, "Now, no one knew exactly where the borders of the Lamanites were. All the while Smith continued to release revelations about End Times horrors that whipped up the people into an apocalyptic frenzy. *'Prepare for the great day of the Lord,'* he would say. *'The day has come, when the cup of wrath of mine indignation is full,'* he said on one occasion. And *'The great Millennial reign which I have spoken by the mouth of my servants, shall come,'* he said on another."

Twirling a piece of bacon, Grant asked, "So, where was this city of Zion built then?"

"Well, on June 7, 1831, Smith gave another revelation about the New Jerusalem city, this *'land of peace, a city of refuge, a place of safety'* as he put it for the spiritually enlightened and worthy. After the church's General Conference he had this to say, again recorded in the *Doctrine and Covenant*."

He found his spot then read: "*'And thus, even as I have said, if ye are faithful ye shall assemble yourselves together to rejoice upon the land of Missouri, which is the land of your inheritance, which is now the land of your enemies.'*"

"So wait a minute," Silas said. "Grant finds an ancient medallion with Mesoamerican symbols and Semitic writings of prophetic texts in both the Old Testament and Book of Mormon in the very land Smith revealed would be the location of the New Jerusalem, which was along the borders of the long-lost Israelites?"

Radcliffe tilted his head, as if considering his point. "Appears to be the case, yes."

Grant asked, "Isn't the Show-Me State an odd place to envision a New Jerusalem?"

"Not really. Missouri was a pretty ideal place to build Zion, God's kingdom, given that the territory's large land parcels could easily accommodate thousands of Latter-day Saints. And it was remote, undeveloped, expansive, and supposedly close to the Lamanite territory. Which is to say, it was close to the lands of Native Americans, which was important since the Book of Mormon prophesied that mass conversions among the native population would precede Christ's second coming."

Silas picked up the medallion, considering its implications. He said contemplatively, "What does it all mean?"

"Good question. One that I'm leaving to Ms. Torres to help answer when she arrives. Hopefully she can fill in those details."

"Fill in what details?"

The three turned in unison as a Hispanic woman strolled through the double doors of Radcliffe's study. She had jet-black hair with smooth olive skin, wearing dark denim and a white button down shirt tied to the side.

She suddenly stopped midway into the large room, her face falling, betraying her surprise. She put her weight on her right leg and left arm on her hip.

"Grant Chrysostom..."

Grant swallowed hard and glanced to either side for some support from the brotherhood.

He found none.

He laughed nervously. "Hey there, Naomi. How's...How's it going?"

"Save your tired 'How's it going' line and all the other ones you've got stashed away in that pretty little head of yours. Haven't you forgotten—"

Radcliffe cleared his throat. "Ms. Torres, as much as I would love to witness the skewering of Silas's Harvard Divinity chum, I'm concerned about his eternal security and would rather you wait until after we've had a chance to sufficiently proselytize him."

"Yes, sir," she said quickly, righting herself and walking toward the group of men.

"I understand you met in another life, and bear some...baggage from that encounter. But the mission is afoot. Do you understand?"

"Understood. But what mission is that?"

Without saying a word, Radcliffe handed her the medallion.

Torres took it, turning it over in her hand and furrowing her brow as she inspected its surface. "What's this?"

"What do you make of it?"

She frowned, seeming to consider the disc as it settled in her hand. She said nothing, swapping it from hand to hand to see each side, spinning it around close to her face to get a better look at the characters along the side. Then she started tracing the glyphs on the face of the medallion. She took her time, bringing her face close to consider the etches on its surface, her expression seeming to reveal recognition.

Finally, she said, "Impressive Mesoamerican piece. Don't tell me you're the one who discovered it, Grant."

Grant went to offer a retort, but Radcliffe intervened. "It's definitely Mesoamerican, then? You're sure of it?"

She squinted one eye, as if suspicious of the question. She held the medallion in her palm and began to point out the various symbols.

"The glyphs are pretty straightforward. They depict a series of rivers, a mountain range or hills, an ocean or large body of water, and people or a village surrounded by trees. These three here look to be islands of some sort."

The three men stayed silent, nodding as she explained.

She flipped the relic over, squinting as she studied the backside. "This side is pretty beat up, but I think this one basically is the equivalent to the color 'white' and this one here…"

She trailed off, her face going slack and eyes widening with surprise. She let the medallion fall onto the table with a thud, looked at Radcliffe, then to Silas before settling on Grant, smiling slightly.

He furrowed his brow, cocking his head slightly with interest. "What have I discovered?"

She grinned, then took a breath. "A map."

"A map?"

"A map?" Radcliffe echoed. "To what?"

Torres looked at the facade of the medallion again lying on the table, considering the glyphs and making sure they were right. Then she flipped it over to check the two characters she could make out on the backside.

She nodded. "To the White City."

"The White City?" Grant said gliding upon a giddy laugh.

"Yes!" she squealed.

Silas and Radcliffe glanced at each other with looks of confused disinterest as the two celebrated.

Finally, Radcliffe interrupted. "Excuse me. I wish I could participate in your ballyhoo, but neither Silas nor I have a clue what you are getting at with this White City business."

Torres recovered, her face gleaming. "For centuries there has been this legend surrounding an abandoned civilization deep in Honduras, in a region called La Mosquitia. It's this vast unexplored jungle region with swamps and quicksand and deadly snakes and rivers and mountains. Early maps labeled the region Portal del Inferno."

"Gates of Hell," Silas said.

She nodded. "A fitting description for how unforgiving and impenetrable the region is. Which has frustrated explorers who have tried to uncover a mystery city that's at the heart of a tantalizing legend." She leaned against the table close to the relic. "The White City."

"The White City," Grant repeated.

Silas said, "And what is this...this White City?"

Now Grant leaned in closer to the table, as if wanting to be closer to the medallion as he told the story.

"Somewhere in that jungle it is said there's this lost city made of white stone. Some others refer to it as the Lost City of the Monkey God, saying it's an abandoned Maya city connected to monkey worship. I've never bought it, though."

"Then what is it?"

Grant picked up the prize he discovered, eyes shimmering with pride and greed as he stared at it. "An unknown, now vanished people group who built one of the largest cities in the Americas." He looked at Silas and Radcliffe. "And then suddenly abandoned it."

Torres picked the medallion back up. "In grad school, I remember our prof having us read Mayan texts that referenced major cities and temples not correlated with any known sites in the region. The references have stumped Mesoamerican anthropologists and archaeologists for decades. He referenced the legends surrounding the White City but dismissed them as myth. Then when I was..." she trailed off, the memory of her previous life as a researcher and treasure hunter haunting her. "When I was working for my uncle on an excavation of a sunken ship off the coast of Honduras once, the locals were pretty convinced there was something significant buried in the jungle of a region called Mosquitia."

"Why is that?" Silas asked.

"Everyone talked of a place of white with big ruins and sculptures. Ciudad Blanca they called it. I did a little digging into it all myself and discovered there were references among early European explorers, like Cortes, writing back to Charles V of rich provinces and a powerful people several miles inland from where they had embarked on the coast. One ethnologist from Luxembourg discovered some ruins built of white stone along a river butting up against the Mosquitia region. And an archaeologist with the Smithsonian's Bureau of American Ethnology established that the region had been inhabited by an ancient, unknown people who were definitely not Mayan."

"That's right," Grant offered, "I remember reading his research. He recognized the Maya built with stone, but the Mosquitia region had been settled by a separate, sophisticated civilization that had built great earthen mounds."

She set the medallion back on the table, shaking her head. "Ciudad Blanca. It's one of the last places on earth where a pre-Columbian city could be hidden and untouched. And here is a map that could take us straight to it."

Grant leaned back against the rim of the bookcase. Silas leaned forward toward Torres and retrieved the medallion from the table. He touched the facade with his index finger, tracing the glyphs, then flipped it over and eyed the back before turning it on its side to look at the Semitic characters.

"So now we have a medallion relic with Mesoamerican symbols and Hebrew writings of prophetic texts that are both Jewish and Mormon, found in Missouri, the territory Joseph Smith said would be home to the Kingdom of God. And it's a map to an apparent ancient lost city of a lost Mesoamerican civilization that vanished into the night. Sound about right?"

Torres nodded, along with Grant and Radcliffe. Silence filled the room as the quartet reflected on the revelation.

"What if..." Grant started, taking the medallion from Silas. "What if this medallion, found at the Mormon dig is a map to that lost tribe of Israel, the Lamanites—or whoever-the-hell they were?"

"Impossible," Radcliffe said resolutely.

"Why? You said it yourself, that the Book of Mormon chronicles the history of this people, from Palestine to the Americas where they set up shop, and then apparently met Jesus who granted humanity an enlightened path to salvation."

"But there has never been an ounce of historical or archaeological proof to verify the claim!"

"Until now," Silas offered.

Grant nodded. "Right, chief. What if this medallion is the proof Mormons have been searching for the past hundred years plus? A map to the location of the Lamanite civilization?"

A line on a phone next to Radcliffe started blinking, followed by a soft beeping ring.

Radcliffe picked it up. "Yes, what do you need?" His face was slack with impatience, then twisted into disbelief.

He dropped the phone and stood, then shuffled over to a television hanging above the fireplace. Grabbing a remote, he powered it on, then turned the channel to CNN. Along the bottom was scrolling *Live from Freedom University.*

Silas reached Radcliffe's side first, just as someone strode onto a stage.

He gasped. "Good Lord..."

CHAPTER 8

YORK, PENNSYLVANIA.

The Republican Party had finally caught an existential break.

They found a candidate who was young, charismatic, good-looking; he could string two sentences together, hadn't been caught on video making disparaging remarks toward women, was a Washington outsider in a climate of inside-the-beltway fatigue; he held firm conservative family-value convictions, yet also held the bonafides of a hip legend among Millennials, having launched successful start-ups that democratized information sharing and community, and engaged in Social Justice Warrior activism as a philanthropist.

Yes, things were looking up politically for the Republican Party. There was only one problem.

Their candidate was Mormon.

Perhaps not surprisingly, the broader American public couldn't care less, given its smorgasbord approach to religion and spirituality; whatever religious dish is right for you is A-OK with me. But among the Republican base—well, that was a different story.

Almost from the beginning, rank-and-file conservatives raised an eyebrow to the guy who talked like them, blowing all the conservative dog whistles and using similar Christian lingo. They liked him. Wanted their lives to mirror his, if they were honest. But, given the homegrown American religion wasn't considered a Christian sect, they were skeptical.

Compounding their angst was the inconvenient fact that one of their own was also a presidential candidate, albeit from a non-Republican party. And then a sweet former altar boy was speaking their language, yet from across the aisle as a Democrat.

So the 'Amos Young for President' campaign did what any campaign would do with those salted fields. They opened the doors to the mainstream media.

People named him America's Most Ineligible Bachelor, a swooning piece that highlighted the young, charismatic, good-looking Amos and his accomplishments. The article hit all the high notes of such entertainment-driven puff-pieces. There was the adorable picture of toddler Amos in the bathtub; a photo of him in a tuxedo before the homecoming dance, embracing his high school sweetheart, Miriam, donning a white dress in front of a red sports car; another of him on his mission in Honduras spreading the Mormon faith and building a medical clinic. Then it showcased the backstory of the successful philanthropist: his childhood roots in Utah to college at Brigham Young, his courtship and marriage of Miriam, and a string of successful social media startups that made the couple billionaires. And, of course, his favorite musical group (U2), all-time favorite movie (toss-up between *Braveheart* and *Gladiator*), and ice cream flavor (Ben & Jerry's Cherry Garcia).

The article ended with a touching photo of the family of eight, which began a year after the two married at twenty-three. Amos and Miriam sat in the middle, flanked by their five children: Ruben (17), Isaiah (15), Hanna (12), Jedediah (10), Rachel (7), and two-year-old Benjamin squirming in his dad's arms, an unplanned, but delightful addition to their family. The portrait was of a model American family, the kind you'd want as your neighbors or guiding the Parent-Teacher Association of your local school district.

Or as your First Family.

The same week, *Time* featured a policy-forward exposé more reminiscent of campaign-era coverage from past years. It covered the same highlights from his past, sans questions about his favorite ice cream flavor. It also gave equal focus to Miriam Young as the CEO of their nonprofit PayItForward, as much as it did the youngest presidential candidate to win a major party nomination at just over forty years.

Much of the piece explored the family's philanthropic ventures providing clean drinking water, malaria nets, and HIV/AIDS treatment to villages in Africa, a venture built off the back of their business success. The couple talked about their Mormon faith, and how it had activated them to live life inspired by the teachings of Jesus. They also gave the magazine an exclusive, which they were more than happy to announce: they were launching a new America-focused nonprofit under the umbrella of their existing one.

GiveBack would mobilize and empower Americans to give back to their communities through after-school programs to reduce teen drug use and delinquency; literacy and skills training, in order to help disadvantaged Americans get a leg up; financial education and assistance to help pull families out of poverty; and environmental awareness and protection, so that America's rivers and lands and air would survive for generations to come.

It was all a coordinated effort to tangibly, authentically live what candidate Amos Young had been campaigning on for months: America's moment, America's mandate. Coordinating with his political action committee, Restore America Now, the nonprofits catapulted the couple to instant stardom. America was equally smitten as in the old days of Camelot. In fact, news pundits from across the political spectrum were comparing the two to John and Jackie Kennedy.

In the *Time* article, Young parroted what he had expressed on the campaign trail: the second-classing of the American Dream to the globalist agenda, which had sacrificed our jobs; border security and national security; the destruction of traditional family values in the interest of the progressive social agenda; the transformation of Washington into a swamp of special interest elitists who had grown richer and more powerful, which he vowed to drain.

Young pledged to end the globalist, progressivist, elitist moment. It was now America's moment, and her forgotten fly-over-country Americans, fueled by an American mandate that put America first.

And America was eating it up.

Slowly but surely, the conservative base was opening up to the guy. Even Evangelicals were taking notice. Sure, the mainstream media polls had him neck-and-neck with the two other candidates. But the rallies said otherwise. The *Time* article ended with coverage of one of those spectacles, which had exceeded its capacity to the point that the fire marshal had to turn people away. It drilled down into the psyche of his supporters with uncensored quotations.

"He gets what's got us down," represented a common refrain. As did: "He understands me." His success also had driven his support: "He's the man to get the job done. After all, look at his success with all those start-ups! With that history of success, just think what he can do for America."

When asked about his Mormon faith, most of those interviewed were incredulous. "We're not electing a Pastor-in-Chief," one supporter said. "If his faith turns this country around, I don't care if he wears that damned secret underpants," referring to the traditional Mormon garment, a type of underwear worn by adherents of the Latter-day Saint movement after they have taken part in the endowment ceremony.

When someone who identified themselves as an Evangelical was asked if he had theological qualms with the candidate's Mormon faith, he replied: "Theological qualms? Once upon a time, many Protestants said the Roman Catholic Church was nothing less than the Mother of Harlots and Abomination of the Earth. Yet that Kennedy fellow did just fine."

"Perhaps it really was America's moment," the article ended, "and a Mormon with a mandate was going to lead us there."

The only problem was that blasted independent candidate. Had it not been for him, Amos Young would be sailing through the polls with nothing standing in his way to moving into 1600 Pennsylvania Avenue.

Perhaps his little campaign rally would rectify that.

"Alright, America. Time for another update."

Young smiled brightly into his smartphone camera with perfectly coifed blond hair, live-streaming another of his myriad of daily campaign updates onto his social media platforms. Miriam snuggled up to his shoulder, a staple of his daily updates.

"I have to say, I am super excited about what's going to happen in a few short minutes."

Miriam turned to him and playfully hit his shoulder. "Stop teasing them, Amos. So not fair!"

He playfully protected himself. "Hey, so not nice, Mir! Don't worry, they'll get in on the secret soon enough."

There was a knock at the door. When it opened a woman in a black pants suit appeared holding a clipboard.

"Sir, they'll be ready for you in one minute. Your whole family."

Young widened his eyes and smiled. "In fact, it's just about to be unveiled in T minus ten minutes. So stick around these sites for the live stream or turn into your popular news channel, because you're not going to want to miss this. This is Amos Young, pledging the next four years to be America's moment, America's mandate."

He flashed a bright smile and winked slightly into the camera, then turned it off. Amos and Miriam looked at each other and grinned. He clapped his hands together, and said, "Alright, kiddos, let's do this."

Miriam began to gather their children from around the Green Room and line them up by age. The crowds loved it when they presented themselves in this way, signaling their commitment to the family and to the values of conservative America.

Young kissed his wife before being led out into a hallway and down to an entrance off the main auditorium. The sound of a bass guitar and drums reverberated into the hall, muffling the sound of singing inside. He smiled slightly, knowing the sound of the popular evangelical song well.

"Shine, Jesus, shine," they sang.

He hummed along to himself as they continued through the chorus.

He knew it was almost time to make his debut to the crowd, a miracle in its own right. The song ended, and he could hear the voice of the man who had made it all happen begin to offer a prayer.

"Over here, sir." The woman led him through the door and to a marker on stage right. "After he offers some remarks about you, he'll say something to the effect of how honored he is to introduce you to the community. That's your cue to join him on the stage. Got it?"

Young looked at the woman, slightly annoyed at the hand-holding. But he offered the grin that had won over America. "Got it. And thanks so much for your care."

She smiled and blushed slightly, then left him as the stocky man with a sharp Southern drawl began his introduction after ending his prayer.

"And all God's people said..." James Maxwell offered.

The audience dutifully replied in unison: *"Amen!"*

"University family, this morning I have for you a real treat. I know there have been rumors flying around campus as to who might be making their appearance at our morning chapel." He paused, smiled, and leaned in closer to the microphone. "I think you're going to be pleased."

Murmurs of anticipation rumbled through the audience of students, faculty, and administrators.

"Decades ago, when my father established this university in one of America's most important historic cities, he was guided by one verse from God's Holy Word. Galatians 5:1, which you all should know by heart since it's plastered all over campus, so let's say it together."

"It is for freedom that Christ has set us free!" the crowd roared in unison.

"Yes. This verse was the driving motto of all that my father did. Not only with establishing this university to raise up young men and young women to proclaim the freedom that comes when one has been brought into a right relationship with God through Jesus Christ's life, death, and resurrection. But also his work to secure the freedoms of this country by helping elect God-fearing, God-honoring men and women who uphold the values of God's Word and principles of our Founding Fathers."

Several students cheered, others clapped. The stocky man gripped the wide, wooden podium like it was a Baptist pulpit. He continued his remarks like a Baptist preacher.

"That legacy is under assault in increasing measure from the left-wing, progressive policies of this administration. He was elected on the promise of hope and change. Hopeless change is what we got." Then his voice rose higher into a fevered pitch: "No, *Godless* change is what we got!"

The crowd loved that line, and everyone else on the other side of the camera newsfeed would, too.

"Gay marriage is now the law of the land. Abortionists have been unmasked under this administration as trading in baby parts for profit. Islam is winning across Europe and knocking on our own door. The globalists want open borders that traffic in ideas totally foreign and subversive to our Christian way of life. We need a mandate to stop the godlessness!"

He paused again. Like any preacher worth his salt, he knew when to ebb and flow the rhetoric to bring the audience to the edge of the homiletical climax. He was there, and so was his audience.

"And I know just the guy who has one."

A tidal wave of euphoric recognition swept through the auditorium. Some started shouting his name in rapid succession, hoping the man himself was waiting in the wings.

The stocky man smiled broadly and extended his hands outward, pushing them down to signal silence.

"Now...Now, I know some of you may have misgivings about this person. But there is more that unites us than divides us. We have much more in common than many might think when it comes to restoring America to its founding principles in the Christian faith, when it comes to ensuring freedom for all.

"It is my honor to introduce to you the next president of the United States of America. Amos Young!"

The Republican presidential candidate walked out onto the platform, the cheering crowd as intoxicating as ever. He breathed in deeply the fumes of their admiration and praise, returning their offerings with his trademark wide, white smile and both fists raised high into the air.

Young stood to the right of the podium where the stocky man was still standing, taking in the cheering crowd and giving the cameras some good B-roll. He turned toward the man and took his extended hand. He grasped his shoulder, dwarfing the Southerner by his height and athletic bulk, then whispered something insignificant into his ear, still displaying that bright grin.

Then he took over the lectern, and said, "Thank you, Dr. James Maxwell, for the invitation. And thank you, Freedom University, for your warm welcome!"

CHAPTER 9

Amos Young grasped the wide wooden lectern with his large hands, like a preacher gripping his pulpit before delivering a fire-and-brimstone sermon.

This was it. This was what his campaign needed.

An October surprise.

"I'm thrilled to be here at one of America's finest institutions of higher learning. When Dr. Maxwell invited me to come and address you all I thought we had entered a new Ice Age, that the fiery abyss down under really had frozen over!"

He smiled boyishly at his small funny, soaking in the obligatory laughter.

"Seriously, though, it is an honor to be speaking to you today and sharing with you my vision for this great nation."

He paused, still smiling, taking a breath before launching into his homily.

"Two-hundred-and-seventy-five years ago, this city was founded as Yorktown. It would go on to play a pivotal role in the life of this country, serving as the temporary capital of the Continental Congress. This city also witnessed a holy sight: the drafting of the Articles of Confederation and their adoption, which was the first legal document to refer to the colonies as the United States of

America. This sacred document was a precursor to the American Constitution.

"Now, I don't want to style myself as a prophet, although I've read many of your tweets claiming I'm as much." The crowd chuckled on cue. "But there is an urgency to my visit today. Because that sacred document, the Constitution of these United States, is hanging by a brittle thread. From enemies both inside and outside America, our cherished way of living, the principles by which we have built this great land and that have served us for generations are hanging in the balance."

He scanned the room, searching for something.

There it was, the red light of stardom indicating the position of the camera feed broadcasting his message to the masses. He looked directly into it and continued. "The citizens of America are now on the cusp of a great national effort to rebuild our country and to restore its promise for everyone. That's why I've called my campaign Restore America Now, because of the urgency with which we must come together to determine the course of America and the world for years to come.

"There is no doubt that we will face challenges and confront hardships. But I tell you what: We will get the job done."

He leaned in closer to the microphone. "It is America's mandate."

The auditorium erupted in applause and shouts of agreement, the adulation lasting for minutes.

Young gripped the lectern again. "In a few weeks, we will engage in one of our nation's most hallowed rituals. The election of the President of the United States of America. This ritual, which, when you think about it, is truly divine because of the manner in which our forebears imparted the tradition to us in the Constitution. This ritual is not merely a transfer of power from one Administration to another, or from one party to another. What we are about to engage in is a massive transfer of power from Washington Insiders back to the American People.

"For too long, Washington has flourished while the people have not shared in its wealth. Politicians have prospered while the jobs have left and the factories have closed. The establishment protected itself, but not its citizens. Their victories have not been your victories; their triumphs have not been your triumphs. While they have celebrated in our nation's capital, there has been little to celebrate all across our land as families and young adults and retirees have been left high and dry."

He paused, then fixed his gaze straight into the red light again staring at him from the black void. "That all changes. Right here, right now. Our moment, your moment has arrived. For today is America's moment driven by America's divine mandate."

The crowd went wild, instantly responding to the campaign slogan that had rooted Young's campaign from the beginning.

America's Moment, America's Mandate.

Adding *divine* was different, however. Perhaps it was merely a response to his venue. Know your audience was stop number one in the Public Speaking 101 tour.

He continued, "What truly matters is not which party controls our government, but whether our government is controlled by the people. And the first Tuesday of November is your chance to rise up, with one voice, and say—" he paused and looked away. "No, *demand*, who controls your destiny. I predict that it will be remembered as the day the people took back their country, becoming the rulers of this great God-blessed nation once again."

More cheers, more shouts of agreement reminiscent of a church service.

"The forgotten men and women of our country will be forgotten no longer. Tens of millions of you are becoming part of something historic the likes of which the world has never seen before.

"At the center of this movement is a fundamental conviction: that a nation exists to serve its citizens. America first is and will always be my priority!"

They were standing now, the fumes from the nationalistic speech intoxicating the crowd and compelling them to their feet.

"The American moment means better schools for our children, safe neighborhoods for our families, and good jobs for everyone who wants to work. It means rooting out the godlessness that has plagued our land. These are the just and reasonable demands of a righteous public, ones that sit at the heart of our American mandate.

"But the reality is, for too many of our citizens a different reality exists: poverty has trapped mothers and children in our inner cities; rusted-out factories are scattered like tombstones across the landscape of our great nation; our cash-flushed education system has abandoned our students, depriving them of the knowledge they need; and crime and gangs and drugs have stolen too many lives and robbed our country of so much unrealized potential."

He stepped back to take a breath, then leaned in for the killer line.

"This American carnage stops right here and stops right now, for today begins America's moment!"

The sound of agreement was deafening. It was easy to forget this was a chapel service of a major Evangelical university. For it transformed itself into part political rally, part religious revival.

"Every decision on trade, on taxes, on immigration, on foreign affairs, will be made to benefit American workers and American families. Nothing will escape the guidance of this American mandate. And I promise you this, on this 275th anniversary of our nation's First Capital, that I will fight for you with every breath in my body for our moment, for our mandate. I will never, ever let you down. America will start winning again!"

By now the crowd had seated itself, but the applause continued. So did the shouts of approval.

"We will win with jobs, bringing them back from the dead. We will win back our wealth, by bringing back our dreams. We will win on our roads and highways, our bridges and airports, our tunnels and railways across our wonderful nation by rebuilding them from the rubble. We will win at welfare by getting people back to work, rebuilding our tattered country with American hands and American labor. We will win in the world by reinforcing old alliances and forming new ones, uniting the civilized world against Radical Islamic Terrorism—"

He paused to take a breath, leaning into the microphone for rhetorical measure. "Which we will eradicate completely from the face of the earth!"

That last line arguably drew the loudest reaction from the Christian crowd. The cameras made note of it. As would commentators on the other side in later broadcasts.

"At the bedrock of our politics will be a total allegiance to the United States of America, and through our loyalty to our country, we will rediscover our loyalty to each other. After all, remember what the Holy Scriptures tells us: 'how good and pleasant it is when God's people live together in unity.'"

The audience seemed to like him quoting from the Bible. They gave him plenty of auditory recognition.

"To all Americans, from all across this great land, hear these words: You will never be ignored again!" His voice was crescendoing now. "Your voice, your hopes, and your dreams will define our American destiny. And your courage and goodness and love will forever guide us along the way."

The audience rose to an ovation in a fevered pitch. He wallowed in it, smiling broadly and offering the crowd two-thumbs-up approval. Then Young motioned for them to quiet and sit. It was time to close the deal.

"Folks, our Constitution is hanging on a thread. But there's hope. Because together we will make America strong again. Together, we will make America wealthy again. Together, we will make America proud again. Together we will make America safe again. And, together, we will make America great again.

"All because of four simple, but beautiful words..."

Before Young could voice them, the crowd finished his sentence. They shouted, *"America's moment, America's mandate!"*

He flashed the bright, wide-mouthed grin that had won over so many Americans, the one that was slowly winning over Christians, as well.

"Thank you. God bless you, and this fine institution. And God bless America!"

Young stepped to the side, waving as his family met him on stage. Red, white, and blue balloons fell across the auditorium while the orchestra played "The Battle Hymn of the Republic," a perfect ending to the full-court Christian nationalism.

Maxwell strode onto the stage again. He was beaming. He grasped Young's hand tightly and said something to him. They both laughed before the university president walked to the lectern.

The room continued to offer their approval of Young and his political platform. Maxwell allowed it, before asking them to take a seat.

"Wow, I must say, Amos, there's a bit of a Southern Baptist preacher tucked away in those Mormon bones."

The room erupted in agreeing laugher. Young threw his head back and guffawed, as well.

"Thank you for those inspiring words. The Constitution is hanging by a thread. Which is why I and the rest of the Faithful Majority would be proud to call you Mr. President."

He leaned in closer to land the plane. "This day, I am giving my unequivocal, full-throated endorsement of Amos Young for President of the United States of America. And I trust you will join me in seeing that he is elected."

It all happened so quickly that the four onlookers watching the CNN feed on the large television hanging above a fireplace in a dark-wooded study deep below the Washington National Cathedral hardly reacted.

Radcliffe was the first. "Lord Jesus Christ, Son of God, come quickly."

CHAPTER 10

WASHINGTON, DC.

J ames Maxwell. The evangelical Pope, himself.

"What on God's green earth have you done?" Silas mumbled. He folded his arms and sighed as a panel of CNN commentators convened to dissect the turn of events.

"Bloody hell," Radcliffe growled.

"Agreed. Knowing him and his father growing up, I would never in a million years have predicted what we just witnessed."

"Sounds like you know the guy," Grant said.

"My dad knew him. Served together in Vietnam and in the military in various ways, hopscotched around the globe together at the government's bidding. Our families were neighbors at a few postings. Played ball with his boys every summer. Eventually, they ended up in DC together but serving in different branches of the government. Dad at the Pentagon, Maxwell as a staffer in Congress."

"And now he's a Christian nationalist? Was he back then?"

Silas cocked his head, searching his memories. "I do remember my dad and him getting into it one time. Maxwell was pretty passionate about America, especially its supposed Christian founding. His religious zeal combined with his patriotism made Dad pretty uncomfortable. I remember one night during my senior year of high school them fighting over dinner about whether Maxwell's assumptions were history or revisionism. The relationship had soured after that."

He paused, then added, "After Dad died, Maxwell came to the funeral and expressed his deepest respect for him. He shared a few war stories, said he regretted how things had turned out. By then his star was rising."

Silas shook his head at the memory. If Maxwell was involved, he wanted no part of it.

"Sounds like a putz. And I'm assuming there's an old man floating around out there."

"There is," Radcliffe answered. "Or rather, there was. Passed away a few years ago. But back in the day, Maxwell's father had been one of the figureheads of the Religious Right, which crashed onto the political scene seemingly out of nowhere during the late '70s. His organization, the Faithful Majority, claimed victory when Ronald Reagan won the 1980 election, taking credit for his sweeping electoral college win. Their major platform was restoring the nation to its Golden-Years roots, a Protestant-based moral order where the Bible was read and kids prayed in school, its elected officials were Christian and sought God's guidance, and abortion was still an abomination. Their political action committee raised and spent hundreds of millions of dollars to elect political candidates who met their moral and policy requirements, and defeat those who didn't. A university was founded, Freedom University, to provide academic cover for the movement and nurture the next crop of Christian activists, growing to rival the size and influence of most Big 10 schools."

Grant asked, "What about his son? How does he come into play?"

Radcliffe continued, "His son was brought in early after a bout of alcoholism and drug abuse nearly tarnished the reputation of Dad and his squeaky-clean moral movement. After an intervention and literal come-to-Jesus moment, he brought James into the family business of Christian nationalism. His experience as a wartime hero gave him the political bonafides to lobby for American purity. His corn-fed good looks and boy-next-door demeanor made him the perfect face for the movement. And his entrepreneurial knack grew the Faithful Majority and Freedom University to the size and scope that it is today. He's become something of an influencer within evangelicalism on scale with the Pope himself, having garnered a degree of power within the Protestant movement. No Republican candidate can win without his and his organization's endorsement."

The Order Master sighed and turned off the television. "And it looks like the titular head of the Religious Right is trying to help Young's campaign win the White House."

Grant whistled. "An endorsement from the evangelical Pope of a Mormon presidential candidate. It's a new day in America, that's for sure."

"Maxwell is an opportunistic zealot," Silas growled. "His group insists this country was founded as a Christian nation and needs to get back to those Christian roots. How is strapping your cart to a Mormon president going to achieve that goal? It isn't even an orthodox, historic Christian sect."

"But that's what's so dastardly about the whole thing," Radcliffe said softly, as if beginning to understand the gravity of what had just transpired.

"How so?" Silas said.

Radcliffe startled, breathing in sharply. He looked to Silas then back at the television, as if remembering he had turned it off. He set the remote on the mantle and sauntered back to the seating area in the middle, along with the other three.

Radcliffe said, "This wicked and cruel copulation we've just witnessed on the stage of Freedom University. It all makes perfect sense."

"Whoa, Padre. Can we keep it PG?" Grant said.

Silas threw him a look, smiling slightly. Radcliffe ignored him. They all slumped in their chairs, defeated by the turn of events.

Except for Torres. "I'm sorry, but I don't see what the big problem is? Isn't the Order interested in seeing the Christian faith reign in America again? To provide a beacon of hope, to be that whole city on a hill—"

"No!" Radcliffe said cutting her off, his face warped with shock. "That is not the mission of the Order. Never has been the mission of the Order. Never will be the mission the Order. To see some sort of Christianized theocratic government at the helm of the United States, or any other government for that matter."

He sighed and took a breath, calming himself. "That metaphor, the city on a hill that politicians so often love to offer, particularly from the Elephant variety, originated not with early colonial preachers as is so often assumed."

"It was Jesus, wasn't it?"

The group collectively turned toward Grant, thrown off by his biblical contribution.

"What? I paid attention in Catholic school. What can I say?"

Radcliffe said, "Impressive, Mr. Chrysostom. And you're right. Jesus said in the Gospel of Matthew: *'Ye are the light of the world. A city that is set on a hill cannot be hidden.'* He wasn't speaking to Americans or Europeans or some long lost tribe of Israel. You. His disciples. Us. The Church. The Church is the city on a hill, not America. She is the hope of the world. Not America. And certainly not some popularly elected fool, in Congress or the White House, regardless of party affiliation."

He got up abruptly and sauntered over to the alcove again in search of another stiff drink.

"Radcliffe," Silas said loud enough for him to hear across the room. "You said you weren't surprised by the...copulation, as you put it. Why not? Why aren't you surprised an Evangelical and a Mormon got into bed together, so to speak."

He sat back down with his drink, then closed his eyes and took a long sip. "Let me explain a bit of Mormon eschatology."

"My catechism's a little rusty, Padre." Grant said. "Escha-what now?"

"A theology of the End Times," Silas explained.

"Like how the world will end?"

"More the end to which the world is heading," Radcliffe corrected. "Mormons believe they have a divine commission to prepare the world for Christ's millennial thousand-year reign in which they will serve as officers and administrators. The faithful Saint, such as Mr. Young, believes he is building the Kingdom of God, right here, right now. In this country."

"Boy, does that ever sound familiar," Silas said. "Maxwell and his crew have been preaching about America establishing God's Kingdom on earth for, how long? One of the less well-known preachers of the Faithful Majority who broadcasts his sermons each Sunday across the nation even subscribes to theonomy."

"Theo-what?" Grant said.

Silas slapped his leg. "Come on man. Get with the Christian lingo program."

He threw up both hands. "I am happily not religious, thank you very much."

Silas smirked. "Theonomy. The idea of using the Bible as a blueprint for America's laws and ways of doing government and constructing our society."

"Eek! That's, like, against the law of Separation of Church and State. Isn't it?"

Radcliffe said, "In a way, yes. But that hasn't stopped the Faithful Majority from dreaming about its reality, all in order to see the Kingdom of God established in America. Which brings us back to Amos Young."

He took another sip, catching an ice cube between his teeth. He crunched it to bits and swallowed, then continued.

"The likes of Young are especially beholden to such visions of nationalistic grandeur. It might surprise you to learn that members of the Mormon faith have always been part of the upper echelons of the U.S. government. The Ford, Reagan, and Bush administrations all placed Mormons in various staffer positions that were key to their administrations. And several high-ranking senators and congressmen have been of the Mormon faith. This idea of establishing the Kingdom of God in America is what motivates thirty-thousand full-time Mormon missionaries to preach the gospel. And this is what keeps these men working well into their eighties that would put younger people to shame."

Silas sank into his chair, crossing his legs to consider the apocalyptic vision of present-day America that Young had just outlined.

He said, "And Young thinks he is the one to bring about the Kingdom? From the White House?"

"Sounded like it to me," Radcliffe said. "And he basically repeated the prophetic mantra from Joseph Smith, that there will be a time when the Constitution will be hanging like a thread. He said it in that blasted speech that the day has arrived! Smith's prediction of constitutional destruction and revolution contains what has always been the Mormon American dream: the transformation of the U.S. Government into a Mormon-ruled theocratic government divinely ordained to not only direct the political affairs of the Mormon community, but eventually those of the United States, and ultimately the world."

Grant let a giggle slip, which elicited a not-so-subtle glare from Radcliffe.

"What? I'm sorry, but this sounds way too conspiratorial," Grant said. "Like X-Files level. Sell that yarn to Netflix. Maybe it'll be the next House of Cards."

"You laugh, but to officials of the Latter-day Saints, the U.S. Government is only a temporary convenience until the Church has established its millennial kingdom. To them, First Amendment freedoms were divinely provided as fertile soil to allow the seeds of Joseph Smith's revelations to take root and thrive. That was the early vision of Mormon leaders, and it is still commonly held today. And the prevailing Mormon conviction is that America will at some point crumble in the midst of severe political instability and internal strife. Waiting in the wings will be the Latter-day Saints, ready to use their vast financial wealth and political power to rebuild the government and restore economic prosperity."

Torres sighed. "But what would such a scenario really mean for America, a Mormon elected as president? Continued freedom? Greater liberty and prosperity? Maybe widespread pluralism and diversity?"

Radcliffe shook his head. "Doubtful. The history of Joseph Smith and his early movement is rife with atrocious deeds, corruption, vice, and intolerance. So far, the fruits of Joseph Smith's religious vision have included lust, greed, theft, fraud, violence, murder, religious fanaticism, bribery, and racism."

"Tell us what you really think," Grant scoffed.

He sighed. "I don't mean to sound like a bigot, here. Although, I understand among other company I jolly well probably do! At any rate, I'm not being discriminatory in my description. The history is there for all to see. Now, modern Mormonism has reformed somewhat since the early heyday. However, given Joseph Smith's own past, will Mormonism's future harvest be any different? That question remains to be answered in years to come."

"It may be answered more quickly than we'd like," Silas said.

Radcliffe set his drink down and leaned forward. "Which is why the Order needs you three to move out."

"Excuse me?"

"It cannot be a coincidence that your friend here found this map to some supposed lost tribe of Israel, proving the historical veracity of the claim made by the Book of Mormon during the election of a Mormon to the Office of the President, and days before the Faithful Majority announced its endorsement of him."

Silas had to give him that. It did sound suspicious.

"There is something afoot," Radcliffe continued. "Both with

Young the candidate and with Mormonism the religion. Something I fear will have great ramifications for the Christian faith." He sat up straight and breathed in deeply. "SEPIO needs to figure out what is going on."

Torres leaned forward. "Then what do you want us to do? You want us to move out. Where? Doing what?"

Radcliffe turned to her and glanced at Grant. "You and Mr. Chrysostom go search for the White City and find it. See if what this medallion suggests is true. Or not. I cannot imagine in a million lifetimes that this is a genuine archaeological artifact proving the Book of Mormon account correct. But...we need to know."

Grant held up a hand, and said, "Whoa there, Padre. I didn't sign up to no mission in the bush, whacking my way through some snake-infested, malaria-ridden, cannibal-populated—"

"It pays well."

"Oh, alright."

Torres sank into her chair, heat rising up her neck. She went to say something, then stopped.

Radcliffe turned to Torres. "Sounds like you two have something of a checkered past together, but I imagine he will be of tremendous use to us, given his experience with the dig that dredged up this medallion to the surface in the first place. And given your background in Mesoamerican anthropology and experience in excavation and recovery, I'm sure you'll get along well. Speaking of excavation, doesn't your uncle own an outfit out of Miami? What are the chances that he might aid our efforts?"

She blanched at the mention of her uncle, the wound of her not-too-distant past failures working with him still smarting.

"I mean, I could ask," she offered.

"Do that. Do whatever you need to do to convince him to supply the equipment and necessities for your operation."

She coughed. "Excuse me, *my* operation?"

"This one is yours, Naomi. You're the expert in Mesoamerican anthropology and pre-Colombian archaeology. I want to be clear: this is not a side project. This is our operation. Make it happen."

She stiffened proudly and smiled. Then she looked at Grant and sighed. "Looks like we're going to be working together again."

He smiled. "Looks that way."

"Now Silas, I want you to pay a visit to Maxwell. Figure out what the bloody hell he is up to! But play nice. Our best course of action to figuring out what is going on here is to get in with the Young camp. And I sense that will come through Maxwell. Which means you've got a delicate job ahead navigating this thread through this needle eye."

Silas nodded. "Delicate indeed. I'll leave this afternoon."

"You all will," Radcliffe instructed. "Time is of the essence. In a little over week or so is the election, and every fiber of my being is screaming to me that what you've uncovered, Grant, and the story you told, Naomi, and what we all just witnessed is somehow connected."

He paused, slumping into his chair, his face growing more serious.

"For decades now, alternative spiritualities have been on the rise. The fastest growing religious population in America is so-called Nones, the spiritual-but-not-religious who might be enticed by the spirituality of Mormonism. And given how they have branded themselves as an alternative sect to the historic Christian faith, and actually launched itself on the assumption that God had condemned that tradition as failed and flawed—let's just say not since the early challenges of Gnosticism and Arianism has the Order of Thaddeus been in this grave of a position to contend for the once-for-all faith entrusted to God's holy people."

Silas nodded and stood. Torres joined him, as did Grant.

"Let's roll then. For American Christianity," Silas said.

"No, for the *Church*," Radcliffe corrected. "Worldwide."

CHAPTER 11

YORK, PENNSYLVANIA.

"New poll numbers! Somebody get the candidate."

Waving an iPad over his head, the baby-faced, blond-haired-coifed senior campaign aide in desperate need of a shave named Jamie Richmond ran into the mobile operations center of the Amos Young for President campaign, a meeting room at the run-down Holiday Inn up the road from Freedom University. After Maxwell's endorsement, the candidate and his family and the Religious Right figurehead had spent the rest of the day together making the interview circuit in a makeshift studio at the hotel. Then the two had hopscotched from one campaign rally to the next in the surrounding region over the course of the night to create a resurgent wave of interest in and support for the Republican candidate.

Hopefully, the endorsement and the coverage had paid off.

Amos Young was fetched from his suite by his personal assistant Trevor Waxman, a junior political science major from Freedom who had taken the year off to play errand boy for the candidate. Young tried not to run down the stairs to the room, but he pushed his normal walking pace out of anticipation, tying his red tie on the way.

"Let me see them," he said when he reached his senior aide, the man who had put George Junior in the White House twice, though nobody knew it as he preferred the behind-the-scenes machinations of candidacies than the limelight.

Jamie handed him the iPad. Young snatched it then swiped it to life. "Has anyone opened the PDF?"

"Nope. Waited for you."

"And these numbers will reflect our announcement and activity from yesterday?"

"They should."

"Should?" Young threw him an annoyed look. "They damn well better. If the evangelical Pope's endorsement couldn't put Reed out of his misery, then nothing will."

He knew the arrangement had been one of convenience, rather than enthusiastic support. The Religious Right had been out of power for eight years, and their influence had been waning within the broader culture for more than that. Gay marriage had become the law of the land. Religious liberty had been under assault, with Christian hospitals and charities and universities being required to provide material support for things they were against, like abortion. Affiliation with Christianity had been waning. They saw the election of a Republican president as crucial to stopping the slouch toward Gomorrah, stemming the tide of cultural loss and sparking a resurgence.

Except their Republican guy wasn't their religious guy; he was a Mormon. And their religious guy wasn't their Republican guy; he was an independent.

The Religious Right was politically savvy enough to know that in America, an independent candidate has never worked and will never work, given our two-party system of governing. Once the fallout settled from the contentious Republican convention, with Amos Young being narrowly chosen as the candidate and the second-place Evangelical opting for an independent run, the Faithful Majority began quietly making overtures to the campaign to see how they might work together.

Initially, the perpetually politically paranoid Jamie thought it was a trick, some sort of ruse to gather intel for their Evangelical candidate and a way to embarrass them with false promises. To be honest, Young was flabbergasted they had approached him about the idea of not only an endorsement but a full-court partnership to win the White House. They had needed some reassurances, however. For starters, that President Amos Young wouldn't transform himself into Mormon Pastor Amos Young and use his office to further his religion. Which was ironic because that's precisely what they would have expected from Matthew Reed had the man performed better. But he had reassured them that his interest was in saving the Republic politically, not religiously.

Secondly, they had a short list of Supreme Court nominations they wanted him to draw from when he was sworn in and replaced the Catholic Justice who had died unexpectedly, ratcheting the stakes of the election into the stratosphere. That wasn't a problem, since he respected most of the names on the list anyhow, and their conservative policy issues aligned with his own. So he was able to forge a bond with the group over their shared political interest.

The final demand nearly broke the camel's back: dialing back his overt Mormonism and refusing to associate it with Christianity. This he declined. His life as a faithful Mormon congregant who had also served his church as a successful businessman, entrepreneur, and philanthropist was a staple of his campaign during the primary. To dial that back now would be entirely inauthentic and reek of opportunism, alienating what base he had in favor of a smaller Evangelical one.

He jokingly assured Maxwell and his clan that he wasn't in league with the Mormon hierarchy, but they made him swear by it. They really were fearful he was part of a Latter-day Saint cabal, and they would be party to their hostile takeover of the American government, leading to the persecution of the real Church. It took some doing, but he was able to assuage their fears.

Now the Religious Right was totally committed, having put all of their religious eggs in his political basket. The only question that remained was if their Evangelical base would follow them to his political font and taste and see that he was good.

Jamie brought the candidate a Diet Coke, his drink of choice. "Here. Drink." Amos took it and did. He continued, "With Maxwell's support at morning chapel and the campaign events yesterday on top of the day-long news coverage from the networks of the Religious Right ditching their candidate and hooking their wagon to you...You're right. If Maxwell's little October surprise didn't put a dent in the polls and shift this campaign, then this presidency will be decided by the House of Representatives."

Young took another swig before scrolling to the end of the digital document. He squinted in concentration as he read the bottom line. Then his face fell as he read the three numbers.

38. 20. 42.

"One blasted point?" he murmured in disbelief. He looked to Jamie for guidance.

"Let me see." He took the iPad and read what Young had read. The Republican candidate, him, had scored thirty-eight points with the American voters, followed by the Evangelical third-party candidate Matthew Reed with twenty. Leaving Robert Santos still in the lead, and one point outside the margin of error.

"Hmm," is all that Jamie could muster. "Well, look at it this way. The endorsement helped since Santos was up by five points yesterday morning and lost one as the day's events unfolded. And it has only been a day. When the Christian news outlets and alt-right sites begin filtering out the news that the Evangelical Pope endorsed Amos Young for president over one of their own, they'll come through. By the end of the week you'll be neck-and-neck with Santos, and whatever edge he might still retain will be comfortably within the margin of error."

Young stood sipping his Diet Coke, staring at the floor. "He better be."

There was a knock at the door, then it opened. It was Trevor.

"Sorry to bother you, but the man with the bow tie is here."

His mouth went dry and eyes widened slightly. He took another sip to recover and hide his reaction, then motioned with his hand.

"Send him in," he said to Jamie, "Leave us."

"Are you sure?"

"I'll be fine."

Jamie nodded, then left.

Young finished his Diet Coke, then sat down in a cloth chair and smoothed out his tie before his guest arrived. When he did, he remained seated.

"I didn't expect you for another few days," Young said as the man took a seat in the other cloth chair across from him.

"Good to see you, too, Amos," the man said wearing a forced grin and piercing bright blue eyes.

He smiled, then extended his hand. The man took it. "Always good to see a friendly face." He leaned back and smoothed his tie again. "Now what brings you here. Hopefully nothing I need to worry about."

"Have you seen the numbers?"

"Just saw them."

The man paused, crossing his legs. "Then you know we're still down."

"It's obvious the endorsement helped," Young said, channeling his senior aide, "since Santos was up by five yesterday morning and is now down by one. Besides, it's only been a day. Once the Evangelical community realizes their Pope has given me his imprimatur, I'll be neck-and-neck with Santos by the end of the week. And Reed will be toast."

The man straightened his bow tie. "We're not as convinced."

Young brought his hands together in front of him, cupping one fist in the other, resting each elbow on an armrest. He cracked his knuckles as he stared at the man across from him who had both blessed and cursed his life.

"So what the heck do you want me to do? The field is split, has been all summer. We're less than two weeks away from the election, and it isn't budging. And I don't see your people doing anything about it."

"We will. In due time." The man uncrossed his legs and switched, resting his arms on both armrests himself. "But we need you to do something for us."

The way the man with the bow tie said that last line was unsettling, with a don't-ask-questions-just-trust-me tone.

Young took a deep breath and rested both hands on the armrests again. "Alright, what?"

"We believe that a debate between you and Reed is just what the country needs to discover the differences between our two distinguished candidates."

His face twisted with confusion. "A debate? What, just him and me, no Santos?"

"Yes, arranged by the Faithful Majority. I've already spoken with Maxwell about the idea, and he loved it."

Young wanted to strangle the man with the perfectly tied noose hanging around his neck.

He went to Maxwell without my knowing about it?

"Does Jamie know about this? Did you consult with him? Why am I just now finding out about this?"

The man put one hand up. "Relax, Amos. You've got other things to worry about, like, you know, winning an election. We're here to support that effort. And getting you two on stage is exactly what is needed."

"Why would I agree to this? I'm winning by almost twenty points over Reed. Don't I have the most to lose?"

"Not by our calculation. If you convince a quarter of his supporters, then you're within striking distance of getting the 270 electoral delegates you need to win the presidency outright."

Young shook his head. "How do I even know Reed will agree to something like this? It's not like he needs to, even though he's clearly losing. He just needs to stop me from winning. That's his end game anyway."

The man smiled slightly. "He will because I've already reached out to Reed's campaign manager. They're open."

Now he was going to strangle the man.

Instead, Young rolled his eyes and sighed, contemplating how to move forward.

The man uncrossed his legs again and leaned forward, his eyes narrowing and forehead slouching.

"Amos. You will do this."

He said nothing.

"You will reach out to Reed personally and suggest the dual debate. The day after next you will get on a stage with him on Freedom Field, home to the Freedom University Crusaders. And you will do what you need to do."

A shiver of apprehension ran up Young's spine. Why did it seem like larger gears were turning into place that were outside his control?

"Great," he said. "I'll do whatever I need to do."

The man's demeanor quickly normalized, the same plastered expression of delight returning. He stood and reached out his hand. Young joined him and shook it. The man said he would check in later that day to see how the conversation went, reminding Amos of his leash. Then he left.

Young sat back down, breathing heavily. He had had misgivings from the start when the man in the bow tie showed up shortly after he announced his candidacy.

However, the others said the deal was necessary, for the good of the country—and their church. Said it was the price of power in a country ruled by a traditional, faithful Christian majority.

But he feared the deal he had made was with the Devil himself.

CHAPTER 12

MIAMI, FLORIDA.

The morning air was warm and humid, tinged with salt and the expectant hope of a thousand potential dreams realized in the Magic City of palm trees, fast cars, endless beaches, and even more endless parties stretching into the night.

Just how Naomi Torres left Miami a year ago.

Torres and Grant had arrived late the night before after having flown by a private jet belonging to the Order. They had checked into separate adjoining rooms in a modest motel a few blocks from Miami Beach, which Torres was walking along while Grant slept in.

The last time she was padding through the fine white sand was the evening her uncle fired her for getting caught by INTERPOL trafficking stolen historic artifacts. She had supplemented the income her uncle Juan Manuel Torres had provided her as lead researcher of his growing salvage and exploration company, San Jose New World Salvage and Exploration. It was part historical and cultural preservation effort and part money-making venture. He had hired her to lead the research team after she had finished dual graduate degrees in Mesoamerican and pre-Columbian studies at UCLA. Her work had earned her a reputation for historical and archaeological acumen, as well as the hard-nosed negotiating chops to deal with corrupt governments and even more corrupt treasure-seeking pirates operating out of the Caribbean.

It had started innocently enough. A few small pieces here and there from the collections she had discovered. Coins and figurines and pottery were worth hardly anything to anybody anyway. But then she had upgraded her thievery by swiping a few golden artifacts from a large salvage dig off the coast of Cuba. She tried selling them to the highest bidder, which happened to be an asset connected to INTERPOL. When she got caught, her uncle lost the contract with the Cuban government, sullying his and his company's reputation, which had a rippling effect across his other business relationships. Thankfully, he had been able to hold onto and maintain those contracts, but not before the damage had been done to his reputation.

Her uncle was devastated by the betrayal. It was especially acute given he had taken her in and raised her after her parents were killed by a drunk driver. And now she was tasked with convincing him to trust her again and help find the legendary lost Ciudad Blanca.

Torres sighed and reached for her belly with both arms, her stomach a twisted knot of apprehension, anxiety, regret, and embarrassment.

"There you are. I've been looking all over for you."

Grant came running up beside her, wearing the same t-shirt and jeans from the day before. He was holding two cups of coffee and a bag of donuts underneath one arm.

She stopped and turned toward him, furrowed her brow, then turned away and kept walking.

"You need a shower."

He frowned, then lifted his shirt toward his nose and smelled.

"No I don't," he mumbled, then hustled after her. "Slow down, would ya? I came bearing gifts."

She stopped and turned back toward him. He held out one of the coffees for her. She smiled slightly, her face softening at the man. She sighed and took it. He opened up the bag and handed her a chocolate-covered yeast donut with a thick dollop of white frosting in the middle. A bird's nest, they called it. Her favorite.

After all these years, he still remembered.

She wanted to hate the man after what he had done to her back in California while she was finishing her PhD. Leaving her as he did, engaged and planning a wedding, all because he had to "find himself."

But she couldn't. She still loved him.

They found a bench near a path at the head of the beachfront and sat down. He popped off the top to his coffee and blew across its surface, then took a sip. After biting into his glazed donut, he said, "So what do you make of this medallion and Ciudad Blanca? Any merit to the legend?"

She took a bite herself and shrugged. "I know plenty of people over the years have thought it does. There have been a few attempts over the decades. And this crackpot, Ron Blom, had pestered my uncle to lead an exploration deep into the jungle using the LiDAR technology we'd used on that salvage job in Cuba."

Grant leaned forward, taking a sip of his coffee. "I heard about that gig. And what happened afterward. Tough break."

He glanced at her. She looked at him briefly before averting her eyes and taking a sip of her own coffee.

She said, "Yeah, well, stuff happens. I've moved on."

"Clearly. But I didn't peg you as no Indiana Jane for Jesus." He chuckled at his joke before biting into his donut again.

"What would you know? It's not like you ever took an interest in my religion when we were together."

"At least they pay good, so that's a perk."

"That's not why I signed up with the Order," Torres said quickly.

Grant threw up his hands in surrender. "Alright, sweetheart. Don't get so defensive. I didn't mean to accuse."

"They're doing good work. Work I care about. Like finding out what's going on with this Mormon relic, and how it might affect Christianity."

He scoffed. "Who cares, anyway. They're all the same. Peddling an elixir of meaning and soda-pop happiness that comes at the expense of freedom and ends in nothing but heartache. When it comes to spirituality, I prefer to go it alone. I don't need nobody telling me how to behave and what to believe."

She bit into her donut then turned to him. "Then why the heck are you here? Clearly, it's not for the Church."

He looked away, across the beach and out into the ocean. "Remember Mary, my little sister?"

"Not so little anymore, but yeah."

"She got mixed up with a Mormon group back home. At first, it seemed alright, like it gave her a calling and meaning in life. She tried to talk us into joining, both me and my parents. I'm sure you can understand how that went with Mom and Dad."

She nodded, having known his devout Catholic parents well during the year-long engagement. "What was she thinking? That her parents were just going to abandon their Christian principles?"

"Right? Well, one night they had it out. They tried convincing her that Mormonism was a false religion. Dad brought out his Bible, of course, and started quoting chapter and verse. Then Mom started using some Mormon history on her. Sis wasn't having any of it."

Grant sighed and rubbed his face, as if the memory was draining him of energy. He stretched out on the bench and crossed his arms.

"Since then she's cut off all communication. Won't talk. Won't text. Last I heard she had been courting some Mormon dude and pretty much on her way to wearing those magical underpants. Now, I'm not discriminating against them or anything. I mean, look at me. To each his own and everything, including my sis. But if that medallion proves that...that Mormonism is true, then it's all over for my sister. She'll be vindicated. And we'll have lost her for good."

"I understand," Torres said softly.

He playfully hit her leg. "What about you? You go from treasure hunter to Jesus warrior overnight. What's that about?"

She smiled, feeling like she did a year ago when they were still together.

"Honestly, I needed a change. After I was...well, fired, and humiliated and my reputation tarnished, I got a call from my grandfather who knew this guy who had this religious organization that was all about promoting Christianity. They needed a researcher with a background in archaeology and the military. Figured my degrees and experience with the Israeli Defense Force fit the bill, so he passed my name along to Rowan Radcliffe."

"Old guy with the collar in the study?"

She smiled again. "Yeah, the old guy with the collar in the study. He and I met, and it seemed right. Plus, I thought it would be a decent opportunity to reconnect with my faith and do some good in the world."

"You never struck me as the overly religious type, Torres."

She continued staring toward the rising morning sun reflecting off the deep blue waves rolling onto the beach. She simply said, "I used to be."

Grant let the comment go, then pulled out the medallion.

"How about we take this thing and go on an adventure."

She liked the sound of that.

CHAPTER 13

YORK, PENNSYLVANIA.

York, Pennsylvania, was similar to Princeton, New Jersey, during the middle of October. The temperatures dropped into the mid-50s. The leaves turned a palette of muddy browns and sunburst reds and burnt oranges and brilliant yellows, dappled by the autumn sun or drenched by autumn rains. Chimneys sprang to life with crackling fires beneath. Cable knit sweaters were brought out, as well as mulling spices with cheap bottles of red wine for Silas's favorite fall evening treat.

So Silas felt right at home as he drove through the historic town of 59,000 people on his way to meet the good James Maxwell.

Also known as Yorktown in the early life of America, the city was founded in 1741 by settlers from the Philadelphia region and named for the English town of the same name back in the Old World. During the American Revolutionary War, York served as the temporary capital of the Continental Congress. The Articles of Confederation were drafted and adopted in York, though they were not ratified until March 1781. Making it the perfect spot for Maxwell's Freedom University to take root.

Freedom was founded in 1971 by Paul Maxwell out of the basement of Emmaus Road Baptist Church with 154 students. He had challenged his congregation to establish a Christian college whose students would "go out into all walks of life to impact this world for God, bearing the torch of Christ's freedom in the legacy of our Founding Fathers." Early students and faculty were inspired to influence the moral and ethical course of America, plunging into the deep end of America's culture wars that fomented during the '70s and gained steam through the '80s and '90s. With the passing of its founder in 2007, the family business passed to his son, who continued the legacy of training freedom-bearers for Christ, as their motto declared. In only four short decades, Freedom grew to become the largest private, nonprofit university in the nation, and the largest Christian university in the world, touching every sector of culture, business, professional institutions, and government with its sixteen schools and colleges, and more than 550 programs of study.

Silas drove through the main campus boulevard toward the historic Founder's Hall where he knew Maxwell kept his office. Brightly-colored poplar and maple trees that had turned with the season lined the road leading into the heart of campus. A large white dome peeked above the buildings that dominated the campus, forged in a Colonial Revival architecture that bespoke the founder's intent to serve as a beacon of hope for the country's Christian Golden Era.

He parked his car in a visitor's parking spot. A group of students walked past laughing, reminding Silas of what he was missing back at his former place of employ. A pang of regret twisted in his gut as he thought about his students and his classes on religious relics and historic Christianity. He wondered if anyone would take over teaching the classes he had carefully cultivated over the years. The administration probably canceled them, even though they were the most popular in the department, raking in thousands of tuition dollars.

He feared his life's work had been a complete waste. Saint Paul got it right: the days certainly are evil. Perhaps he could redeem the time with his little visit. For the sake of his vocation, the Church, the nation.

Sitting at the receptionist desk of the Office of the President was a short, cheery woman with a warm face, sophisticated gray hair spun up in a bun, and spectacles hanging down her nose. She looked up briefly from her keyboard when Silas came in through the door, then did a double-take. A broad smile replaced her concentration face.

"Silas Grey...as I live and breathe!"

"Mrs. Maxwell," Silas said smiling as he closed the door.

Georgina Maxwell, James Maxwell's wife, had served along-side her husband for years, handling his calendar of appointments and business meetings and acting as his gatekeeper. She had known Silas and his brother Sebastian and their father almost as well as James himself had, having joined him for family dinners and comforted the boys at the passing of their father.

She came around from her desk and stood on her toes to embrace Silas. He reached down to return the embrace.

"What on earth are you doing here, boy? Did you have an appointment I don't know about?"

He let go and stepped back. "Was in the area and thought I'd drop by to see Doctor Maxwell. Don't have an appointment, but... thought a certain Southern belle could swing something for me."

She giggled, then went back around her desk and sat down. "I'm sure we can swing something. James will be so thrilled to see you, just thrilled!" She opened Outlook to check her husband's calendar. "Now, let's see...You know, if you come back in an hour he has a good thirty-minute window between meetings where he comes back to check in."

Silas stepped forward toward her desk. "I don't want to intrude on his quiet time—"

"Nonsense," she interrupted waving him off. "Skipping one thirty-minute session of downtime won't mess up his beauty sleep.

Besides, he'd move heaven and earth to see one of Thomas Grey's boys."

He smiled and nodded at the mention of his father. "Thanks, Georgina. I'll come back in an hour."

He walked back down the stairs into the well-appointed lobby of marble columns, Neocolonial cloth loungers, and wood-paneled walls boasting of original memorabilia from the nation's founding. There were original newspaper clippings of *The Federalist Papers*, the article essays Alexander Hamilton, James Madison, and John Jay wrote to influence the vote for ratifying the Constitution. A first edition of Thomas Paine's *Common Sense* pamphlet that was so crucial in encouraging the common folk of the colonies to continue fighting in the face of overwhelming odds sat next to them. They even had one of two hundred copies of John Dunlap's Declaration of Independence, the first printing of the text.

After killing some time by eyeing the museum pieces, Silas walked back up the staircase to the second floor where Maxwell kept his office. He stopped abruptly during his ascent and looked back down into the hallowed space. He was struck by the lack of Christian relics. No Bibles or first editions of crucial Reformation tracts. No sermon copies from the First or Second Great Awakenings. Nothing that would set the space apart as obviously Christian.

The message seemed clear: we are celebrating the sacredness of our Christian nation, not our Christian religion.

Silas sighed and gritted his teeth, then continued back up the stairwell to the President's Office to ask Maxwell what the heck he was thinking.

"SIG!" Maxwell said, smiling and greeting Silas as Georgina ushered him into the sizable dark-paneled office. From a little boy, Maxwell had combined the first two letters of Silas's first name with the first of his last to form a nickname. It stuck ever since.

"Doctor Maxwell," Silas said, reaching his hand forward.

His grin widened and the man bypassed Silas's hand, embracing him instead.

"Now, what have I told you about calling me Doctor Maxwell? You make me feel old when you do that!"

Silas smiled. "James, then. Thanks for seeing me on such short notice."

"Nonsense! Always got time for Tom Grey's son. Come in, sit down!"

Silas took a seat in a leather chair in front of a commanding wooden desk reminiscent of the resolute desk he saw on a tour of the Oval Office a buddy had given him. Dim recessed lighting accentuated the richness of the space that was lined with old books and various pictures of Maxwell shaking the hands of famous Christian preachers and theologians, pop culture celebrities and sports figures, and American politicians. Including Amos Young.

"Would you like some coffee? Georgina makes a mean latte."

Silas smiled at his patriarchy. "No thanks."

Maxwell leaned back in his chair and put his hands behind his head. "How have things been? Last I heard, you were championing some crazy theory about the Shroud of Turin, wasn't it?"

Silas chuckled and raised his hands in surrender. "Caught me red-handed. The Shroud has been one of my pet research projects for several years now. But I wouldn't call it crazy. There is sound scientific and historical evidence for it being the authentic burial cloth of Christ."

"You know, I do remember reading something about that and your research. Fascinating stuff, the Shroud is. Can't say that I agree with your conclusions. But I appreciate your work fighting for the faith, nonetheless. And teaching at Princeton, too, right? Hopefully setting that God-forsaken liberal institution straight!"

Maxwell smiled when he said that last line. Silas tried to smile back, but the man's partisanship rubbed him the wrong way.

"I was, for a few years. I've since moved on to another opportunity."

"Really? May I ask where you've ended up?"

He wondered how much he should share, but figured the openness with his work contending for the faith would win him brownie points.

"It's an ecumenical organization that offers research-based information products highlighting and defending the historic Christian faith. You may have heard of it. The Order of Thaddeus."

He leaned forward with interest and frowned. "Isn't that Rowan Radcliffe's Vatican group?"

"It has roots in Catholicism, as it was a religious order formed in the earliest centuries of the Church, but it has since broadened to include a cross-section of the Church. Even Evangelicals are now part of our work. And, yes, Rowan Radcliffe is the Order Master."

"Rowan's a good man."

"You know him?"

He rose from his chair and walked over to a small alcove around the corner from a bookcase. "Somewhat. Appreciate his passion for defending the historic Christian faith, that's for sure. Are you sure you don't want a cup of coffee or anything? I've got a Keurig K-Cup with your name on it."

"Alright, sure. I could use a cup."

Maxwell continued the conversation from the alcove as the coffee brewed. "Georgina tells me you were in town and decided to stop by. What brings you to York?"

Silas hesitated, not wanting to lie but also wanting to be careful how he broached the subject.

"Actually, I'm here on Order business."

"Oh, and what business might that be?"

Careful, Silas.

"There are concerns about the election this year. Particularly the candidate some within the Church are rallying around."

Maxwell appeared with two mugs of black brew. He handed one to Silas, then he sat down and took a sip from his. He chuckled, and said, "You mean the candidate that I'm rallying around. You're talking about Amos Young."

Silas said nothing and took a sip himself.

"I understand that for some Evangelical purists my support for Young has raised eyebrows. And by most measures it would be considered unorthodox in most election cycles. But, Silas," he said leaning forward, "we've got a real chance at tipping the balance of power in the Church's favor!"

Silas furrowed his brow. "Since when has the Lord ever encouraged his people to pursue political power? 'Not by might, nor by power, but by my spirit, says the Lord of hosts.'"

Maxwell leaned back. "Zechariah 4:6. I see you've grown in your Bible knowledge."

Silas said nothing.

"But I've got one better: 'If my people who are called by my name humble themselves, pray, seek my face, and turn from their wicked ways, then I will hear from heaven, and will forgive their sin and heal their land.'"

Again, Silas said nothing, having no interest in the discussion devolving into a Scripture-quoting match.

Maxwell sat up straight. "Just look at the moral and religious state of our country. The Church is in decline. More people are claiming less faith than ever before. And more people are claiming pagan faiths than ever before. The Supreme Court is at a tipping point. Homosexuality has been completely normalized. Christians are being persecuted left and right. And now the gender identity of our kids is even being subjected to the social engineering of liberal activists! We need someone to champion the cause of Christ, take back our country for the faithful majority, usher in God's Kingdom, and bring America back to the vision of Christian faith our Founding Fathers envisioned when they founded this great nation!" He pounded the desk for good measure, then settled back in his chair with his coffee.

"And endorsing a Mormon is going to achieve those ends? He's going to build the Kingdom of God in America?"

"Why not? The Lord uses the unlikeliest of rulers to bring about his ends. Shoot, he used the pagan king Cyrus to undo the brutal policies Nebuchadnezzar brought against the people of God. He raised up Cyrus and called him his anointed for goodness sake! So why can't he be raising up a pious Mormon to bring this country back from the brink of eternal damnation by turning from their wicked ways and seeking his face once again?"

Silas considered this, then added, "Perhaps, but at what cost?"

"What do you mean, at what cost?"

"Aren't you at all concerned that the Christian Church is aligning so tightly with a leader of a religion that claims to be an alternative Christian sect? There's already so much confusion about what is authentically Christian. And now the Church has one of its major voices aligning with someone who simply isn't Christian. Not that there's anything wrong with that. I guess what I'm trying to say is, I fear your support and the Faithful Majority's support could give the impression that Mormonism is a valid, alternative Christian spirituality."

He grinned. "Is this Rowan speaking, or you?"

"Both!"

Maxwell shook his head. "I'm sorry, but I just don't see what's got you and the Order in a tizzy. It's not like the man is a fornicating, adulterous womanizer who's lived an unregenerate life of hedonism."

"Maybe not, but his running mate sure is."

"Can I finish?"

Silas sighed and nodded.

"As I have gotten to know Amos Young, I have looked within his soul and have seen a deeply pious man. Now, we may quibble over some of the orthodox distinctives of Christianity. But the man says he loves Jesus. Says he worships God. Says he's repented of his sins and seeks to live a moral life. So I'm not sure what more you or

Rowan or the Order or any other God-fearing American would want in a Presidential candidate."

Maxwell leaned forward, resting his arms on his desk. "Besides, we're not electing a Pastor-in-Chief anyway. But tell you what," he said cupping his hands on his desk. "Tomorrow we're hosting a debate right here at the university on Freedom Field between Reed and Young, sponsored by the Faithful Majority. Come and meet the candidate yourself. Stay for the debate. I'll get you an all-access pass, and you can see for yourself what kind of man Amos Young is like."

Silas paused, then nodded. "Alright, Doc...err, James." He grinned and stood up. "I'll take you up on your offer. And I thank you for your time, for listening to our concerns."

Maxwell stood and came around to the front of his desk. "Always a pleasure, Sig. And thanks for sharing your concerns. I think you'll see it my way once you get to know the man better."

The two embraced again, then Silas left. He said goodbye to Georgina and walked back down through the lobby of American patriotism and out to his car.

He sat in the driver's seat replaying the conversation. What annoyed him most was Maxwell's cavalier attitude about Young's faith and the implications of aligning the Church with it. All in the interest of power.

But he did consider his visit a significant win. Scoring that pass was just the forward momentum the Order needed as they tried to figure out what was going on.

CHAPTER 14

MIAMI, FLORIDA.

After lunch, Torres and Grant headed south to an industrial district on the outskirts of Miami. She drove them to a large warehouse near an inlet where a sizable expedition-style boat was docked.

Seeing it made her heart skip a beat. She missed the work she had done with her uncle out on that boat and in that warehouse, uncovering the mysteries of ancient cultures and salvaging those culture for the world to enjoy. Mostly, she just missed her uncle.

Torres pulled into a parking spot, then turned off the car. She sat still, unmoving, staring at the door to the facility she had walked through hundreds of times, an entrance full of promise and expectation and purpose.

Grant opened his passenger door, then slid one leg out. "Come on. You've got this."

She offered a weak smile, then opened her own door and got out. She opened the door to the entrance, finding no one around. Probably still at lunch. Then she heard laughter further inside the space where they conducted their research and cataloged their finds. One voice rose above the rest, its familiar timbre both comforting and painful.

She took a breath, lifted her chin, and strolled into the room that once belonged to her.

At once the small group turned toward her and her companion. Maggie, a hardscrabble woman with a long history in treasure hunting and her uncle Juan's partner, was the first to see her. She registered shocking delight. Then it hit Burt who she was, the captain of the docked fish and director of operations who seemed equally pleased to see her. And then her uncle, whose face was still shining with the punchline of the joke he had just told.

She smiled and offered a small wave. "Hola, mi tio."

A smile hung on his face, as if it had just launched from a trampoline and was waiting to return to Earth. It did, his face hardening, his eyes narrowing when it fell.

"What are you doing here?"

No one said a word.

She could read her uncle as if he were her own father. The pain and humiliation she caused him ran too deep for her to just waltz in and expect things to return to normal. So she kept it professional.

She wasn't there to cause trouble, she said, but had come on business. Without letting her uncle object, she quickly introduced Grant as a business partner, a fellow anthropologist who had been hired by a firm unearthing remains of an abandoned settlement in Missouri. They had brought him in as an expert on religious relics given its possible connection to Mormonism. During the dig, he had discovered an ancient Mesoamerican relic buried in Missouri, a bronze medallion that seemed to point toward the location of the fabled lost White City.

That got everybody's attention. Even her uncle's.

Torres spoke about the glyphs, how they were undoubtedly pre-Columbian and similar in pattern to Mayan characters but also distinct. As far as she could tell, they pointed to the location of a civilization deep in the mountains between two rivers, near a lake.

She explained how the backside had been worn down, but two characters still remained: white city.

"Ciudad Blanca?" Juan asked with a twinge of excitement.

Torres smiled. "Ciudad Blanca. You know the legends?"

"Sí, both the indigenous and European ones describing an advanced, wealthy civilization with complex trading networks deep in the mountains of Honduras, untouched for generations. Finding it would be the archaeological discovery of the century." Juan stepped toward his niece. "And this, this relic you speak of...Do you have it with you?"

Torres looked at Grant and nodded. He took it out from underneath his shirt and handed it to her. She walked it over to her uncle and offered it to him.

He took it, all animosity vanishing in the presence of a new archaeological mystery. He cradled the bronze disc carefully in both hands, then walked it over to the table between Maggie and Burt and set it down.

Torres and Grant joined them around the table. The group was silent before the ancient relic, studying it, considering it. She leaned over the object and pointed to the pictorial etchings.

"As you can see, these glyphs mirror Mayan pictorial representations, depicting a series of rivers, a mountain range, an ocean or large body of water, and people or a village surrounded by trees. These three here look to be islands of some sort."

Juan and his partners nodded in recognition. She continued.

"Now, even though these glyphs mirror Mayan ones, they differ in significant ways. The etchings are more primitive, less defined, but clearly based on the Maya. Perhaps there was a familiarity with the language as a neighboring dialect, I'm not sure. But I've spent some time going over the glyphs, and it seems like a map."

"A map?" her uncle said.

"See these connected lines with the triangles, like they are forming waves? These seem to represent three separate river networks. If I had to guess, they are the Patuca, the Guampu, and the Pau."

"Interesting," he whispered, arms folded, feet planted wide.

"And at the top of the Pau, we see these, well, houses with people. Representing a city or the epicenter of a civilization. These striations here are clearly a mountain range that surrounds the settlement. And these three small circles with peaks are meant to orient the entire map. They represent islands, the Bay Islands, if I had to offer a guess."

She stood back and looked at her uncle, whose face looked as though the gears were turning in consideration of what this might mean for him and his company.

"With these directions and with your equipment, tio, we can do what no one else has been able to do."

He turned toward her, smiling. "Unearth the legend of the White City."

She smiled. "So what do you think?"

His face held the smile, then fell. He looked to Maggie and Burt, then said, "I think we need to think this over. The opportunity is certainly appealing, but..." He trailed off and looked away, as if searching for the right words that would be honest without being hurtful. "But we need to assess it in light of present commitments and past experiences."

Torres grabbed the medallion and handed it back to Grant. "I understand. We'll leave you to your assessment. Good seeing you again, tio."

She left the room and Grant followed. They headed toward the exit when her uncle came up from behind.

"Naomi, wait."

She opened the door but stopped. She looked through the glass at the rental car parked outside, wanting to push through the exit and drive away rather than face her uncle again.

"You go," she said to Grant. "I'll only be a minute." He nodded and left for the car.

Turning around, she folded her arms and leaned against the door. She said nothing.

"It's good to see you, mi sobrina," he said gently. "Things haven't been the same around here since you left. And I've...I've missed you, too."

She lowered her arms, touched by her uncle's sentimentality. Tears spontaneously rose to the corners of her eyes; her throat began to grow thick with emotion.

She sniffed and wiped her eyes. "You know, I never properly apologized after everything went down. I don't know what I was thinking. I was so wrong. Not only to take what wasn't my right to take and steal from those cultures. But because of the damage I did to you and your reputation."

Her uncle stood silent, looking at the floor. Then he said, "Where have you been? Why haven't you reached out?"

"I didn't know I could," she said defensively. "You went...went ballistic when you found out about what I had done."

He looked up and exclaimed, "Can you blame me? You threatened everything I had worked so hard to create, my reputation and the reputation of this company. Not to mention the livelihoods of everyone who worked for me."

"I know. And I don't blame you. I was just so ashamed of what I had done."

Juan took a step toward her. She straightened up, pushing away from the door. He opened his arms up and motioned for her to come close. She did, and he embraced her.

"Perdóname, mi tio," she sobbed. "Perdóname."

"Shh, Naomi. All is forgiven. Especially after you brought me the archaeological find of the century!" he chuckled. "You work for this man who found the medallion?"

Torres let go of her uncle and laughed at the suggestion. "Not exactly. He discovered it working for some historical society and brought it to a new organization I work for. A Christian order, actually."

"A religious order? Su abuelo would be proud."

"He's the one who recommended me, actually. It's been a good change. A chance to do some good work after..." She trailed off and averted her eyes in embarrassment.

"Well, I think San Jose New World Salvage and Exploration would be honored to take up the assignment. But on one condition."

She looked up at her uncle.

Here it comes.

"You lead the expedition."

She registered obvious shock. "Me?"

"If you and your organization finance the operation, we'll provide the logistical support with equipment and manpower, as soon as tomorrow if you'd like. And, of course, we'd want most of the credit for whatever it is you find. But you're the best damn researcher I know, Naomi. So if you're not heading this operation, then we're not interested." He paused and smiled. "So, do we have a deal?"

Her eyes burst with tears, and she embraced her uncle once again, relieved to have reconciled with the only person in her life who mattered anymore.

CHAPTER 15

A fter Torres had emerged from her uncle's exploration and salvage yard and told Grant the good news that he was on board to help, the two celebrated an early dinner at a highly rated joint in South Beach, dining on fish tacos and Corona beer. Radcliffe was overjoyed at the news. Perhaps they would make headway soon on the mystery surrounding the medallion and its connection to Mormonism. He informed them he was sending Matt Gapinski to join them to assist with the operation. His muscle and experience with the Order's more kinetic activity through Project SEPIO would be useful.

Torres didn't object and agreed the man would be an asset to the operation, given her partnership with him in hunting down stolen relics from Christ's crucifixion in Rome a month ago. In fact, she owed the man her life, thanks to him having rescued her at the hands of the Nous thieves. They were set to pick him up from the airport the next morning, in time for them to leave for Honduras with her uncle's crew.

The two paid for the fish and beer, then headed back to the hotel. They had a long night of planning ahead of them before tomorrow morning.

Grant eased the car into a parking spot in front of their two rooms. The light from the car illuminated the facade of the motel in the waning evening, revealing the door to his room was cracked open.

"What the hell…" he said as he turned off the car.

A dark figure darted out of the left room, his room, running the length of the motel and past the main office.

Grant launched from his driver's seat and raced to the door, shoving it open and flipping on the light. Inside was a disaster: the mattress was overturned; drawers were pulled out; his overnight bag was open, its contents spilled all over the floor.

"Nous," she said coming up behind him in the doorway. "Gotta be."

He turned around sharply and shoved past her, then tore off after the black-clad figure.

"No, wait!" Torres called after him, but he had already committed himself. She followed him as he darted into an alleyway between the motel and a warehouse, tearing down the pavement toward a garage door at the end of the building.

She could see her partner up ahead. He was walking back and forth, having lost the man. She ran after him.

"Where'd he go?"

"I don't know," he said out of breath. "It's like he just disappeared. First Silas's office and now this!"

"What?"

He explained what had happened at Princeton shortly after he showed up at Silas's doorstep with the medallion. She withdrew a small gun from her boot and walked over to the garage door, which was closed but for a two-foot gap at the bottom.

"You were packing heat?" Grant asked.

"Standard issue for all SEPIO operatives."

"I have no idea what you just said, but it sounds mighty sexy."

She frowned and padded over to the opening, crouching lower and sweeping it with her gun. Grant came up behind her and lowered himself.

In hushed tones, he said, "You said a word at the door. Nous. What does that mean?"

"A terrorist organization out to destroy the Christian faith. Gapinski and I encountered them in Rome. They nearly killed me. Has to be them."

"Jeez." He ran his hand through his long blond hair. "Are you sure about this?"

"Not only did operatives follow you to Silas's office, now someone has raided your room. My guess is it's them, but we need to know who and why they're after you."

He rubbed the back of his neck. "I might have some idea."

She turned to him, her eyes searching for an answer.

"I sort of stole it."

"Stole it?"

"Yeah, swiped the medallion from the dig. I imagine my employer isn't too happy about that."

"I'd imagine not. But that guy wasn't no cultural foundation paper-pusher. He was a professional. Same as the ones who raided Princeton, I'd bet." She nodded toward the maw of blackness between the door and concrete ground. "Let's go."

He nodded, then followed her as she plunged into the darkness.

The two popped up quickly, readying themselves for a response.

They received none.

She glanced at him then padded forward, gun outstretched for action.

The vast open space was filled with boats large and small. Probably a storage facility for seasonal boaters. Two security lights showed dimly high above, casting angular shadows around the facility. A hum from somewhere undergirded the otherwise silent space, which smelled of stale ocean water and fuel.

Torres crept forward, weapon extended. Grant followed close behind. They eased along the backside of a large fishing boat, its aging hull caked with undersea remains. She rounded the vessel, aiming forward in the space between it and another boat.

It was empty, but for rigging dropped over the side and a few buckets and a mop left over from an attempt to clean the fishing boat's belly.

She glanced back at Grant. He was holding a pipe. He nodded at her, she nodded back.

A sound from the front of the boat caught their attention, sending the hairs on her neck springing at attention. Her adrenaline kicked her heart into fifth gear, motivating her legs to press forward toward the sound.

They quickly reached the rising wooden stern, both of them ready for a fight. A bucket lay overturned, a small amount of water spreading across the floor. She gripped the butt of her weapon tighter.

Someone was definitely there.

She moved out farther into the open warehouse between the row of boats and the outer wall, her ears straining and eyes scanning the space for signs of intrusion.

From behind the second boat shadow, a hulking figure suddenly emerged from the side. He came down hard on Grant's head, sending him to the ground, his pipe skittering across the cement with a clang.

Torres caught sight of the intruder just as he lurched forward, connecting with both hands solidly on her forearm. His grip was fierce and strong, a vice of sudden power wrenching against her weapon. She couldn't fight him off, and within seconds he had disarmed her and wrapped his forearm around her neck.

And her gun was now in his hands, pressed hard against her head.

"Where is it?" he growled in her ear.

She squirmed violently, trying to break free of his grip. But to no avail. She twisted her head to her right, continuing to fight the hold. Glancing down she saw a tattoo peeking out from underneath the black sleeve of his jacket, black lines against his white skin illuminated from the security light above. Two lines crossed themselves in the center, the ends of the middle line bending inward, the ends of the other line each bending downward.

She immediately recognized the symbol, the ancient phoenix rising to the surface, its wings sending it soaring in resurrection toward enlightenment. Only one organization was connected to that ancient symbol.

Nous.

Her instincts were right.

Grant growled, "Let her go you sonofa—"

"Now, now. Don't be hasty."

The man pressed the weapon harder against her temple, and squeezed her neck harder with the other arm, showing he meant business.

"The medallion," he growled.

Grant shook his head, still recovering from the attack. "What?"

"The disc of bronze hanging around your neck. Hand it over, tough guy."

So that is what this was about.

Torres, eyes wide with a mixture of anger and fear, nodded for him to hand it over. She had spent enough time with its characters that she felt confident in replicating them. She ran the glyphs through her mind, committing them to memory before they lost the map for good.

Grant narrowed his eyes, and said, "I recognize you, blondie."

"Oh yeah?" the man said. "How's that?"

He pointed to his cheek and motioned down from his ear to his jaw. "That wicked scar. You raided my pal's university office, didn't you?"

The man acknowledged nothing, except for a slight grin and short chuckle. He motioned toward Grant, and said, "Get to it."

Grant slipped his hand into his shirt to retrieve the object. He slid it up and around his neck and over his head, then tossed it at the man's feet with a clang.

"Pick it up," he commanded Torres, shoving her to the ground while training his gun at the back of her head.

She picked it up then slowly stood. The man grabbed it from her then shuffled backward, his gun trained forward on the two.

Grant stepped forward to Torres and helped her up. Then he glared at the assailant. "You and me ain't done, Paco."

The man smirked and continued backward, reaching the garage entrance. He crouched, keeping his gun extended and his back against the door as he eased himself out. Then he disappeared into the night.

Along with the only map to the lost city of the Lamanites.

CHAPTER 16

YORK, PENNSYLVANIA.

W hen Silas pulled his Honda rental into the campus library after dinner, he was still stewing over the conversation with Maxwell, about his and the Faithful Majority's support and endorsement of Amos Young.

He couldn't believe that the man had dismissed their concerns about aligning Christianity so blatantly with a non-Christian candidate. He'd never been all that political, or partisan for that matter. He had voted for both Republicans and Democrats and rarely spoke of politics with others. His service in the Army as a Ranger wasn't motivated by a conservative military impulse, but love for country, a sense of duty to protect, and a thirst for justice after his father's death on 9/11. So he was sure his angst wasn't politically motivated, but he was continuing to check his motives to make sure.

His mind drifted to his brother Sebastian, who had dotted on Maxwell when their families were close growing up. It was well before the man turned into a national political figure, but back then he had strong political views that he had closely aligned with his religious convictions. As a kid, Sebastian had been one of his early followers, even thought about a career in the culture wars. But after he had drifted from the Christian faith as a teenager and then further as a young adult in college, he had pursued a career in science instead. Now, he was totally alienated from the faith.

What was he making of all of this? How might this endorsement and support from the so-called Christian moral majority impact his own spirituality and confusion about faith?

If Maxwell wasn't going to take the faith of the Republican candidate seriously, then he would. Starting with the man's very own campus library.

Silas held the door for a pair of coeds leaving a late-night study session at the Paul Maxwell Library, a vast multi-level research facility dedicated to the late Maxwell. The sun had set hours ago, and the glow inside beckoned Silas to do what he did best when he was fighting a cause or trying to win an argument: research. He was embarrassed to admit that he had been woefully ignorant of the history of the Mormon religion, both its founder and its doctrine. So he carved out the evening before the debate on Freedom Field to bone up on the history of Mormonism and the founder itself.

As much as he was turned off by Maxwell and what his university and organization stood for, he had to admit it: they sure knew how to build a library! Boasting a million-book catalog, over two hundred searchable databases of every published journal, and a high-tech robotic book retrieval system, the place rivaled most major research institutions—even his former place of employment. It was also well-lit, tastefully decorated with an inviting palette of colors and couches, and even offered free coffee.

Silas was game for an evening brew, so he pumped himself a small cup from the carafe before heading for a computer terminal to search the catalog. Ten minutes later he had come up with a number of promising hits on Joseph Smith and his American-made religion. Before combing the library, he printed off a stack of journal articles and digitized historical sources from the era. Then he spent the next thirty minutes scouring the library to find the tomes, carrying a pile to a table in one of the reading rooms on the third floor overlooking Freedom pond in the center of campus.

The first book that caught his attention during his search was titled *Occultism, Folk Magic, and Early Mormon Spirituality.* Which sounded sufficiently inflammatory! He searched through his stack and found it, an aged book wrapped in fraying cloth from the late 1800s. He opened it and started reading.

The book explained that Joseph Smith, Senior, had a reputation as an occultist in his town and the surrounding region. Apparently, this long association with occultism actually helped draw spiritual seekers into the upstart religion, because his affinity with the paranormal engendered himself with other occultists. In fact, it rapidly became a haven for people like Junior Smith, who himself had been steeped in occult practices.

Flipping through the book, Silas found an interesting quote from historian D. Michael Quinn:

The first generation of Mormons included people with a magic world view that predated Mormonism...namely, witnesses to the Book of Mormon, nearly half of the Quorum of the Twelve Apostles, and some of the earliest converts from New York and New England.

Alright, but guilt by association makes not a case!

It was a maxim he drilled into his own students. He continued reading.

The book made further mention of the depths of the Smith family involvement in the occult, as illustrated by the various magical artifacts they kept in their household and used in conjunction with their beliefs. These included a magic dagger, three home-made magical parchments, a special pouch to hold the parchments, and a special "Jupiter" talisman, which Joseph Smith Jr. used for protection—apparently the very day he died, ironically. These artifacts, especially the parchments, were steeped in occult magic and had direct links to the kind of magic the Smith's used in finding buried treasure, an important aspect of the family business. The book outlined these magical artifacts in detail:

The Holiness to the Lord parchment: Used to procure visits from 'good angels.' The alleged date of creation was September 1923, the very same month Joseph said he received the visit and vision from Moroni. Symbols on the parchment included four pentagrams for invoking spirits and the initials I.H.S.—*In Hoc Signo*, meaning: "In this sign, you shalt conquer" the spiritist.

The Jehovah, Jehovah, Jehovah parchment: Included the magical symbols of the treasure-seeking angel Jubanladace, which was supposed to protect individuals from infectious diseases and sudden death, while enabling the bearer to locate buried treasure.

The 'Saint Peter Bind Them' parchment: Contained the symbol for Pah-li-Pah, the second of seven angels that were part of ceremonial magic. Properly invoked, the angel helped the bearer of the parchment find buried treasure. The reverse side contained an inscription for Nalgah, the third angel in ceremonial magic. It read: "Devoted to the protection of those who are assaulted by evil spirits or wishes, and those whose minds are sunk in fearful and melancholy apprehensions of the assaults of the Devil."

The book went on to explain that their artifacts had been inscribed with magic symbols and incantations, and also astrological markings. Which made sense because the Smith family and other early Mormons were entrenched in astrology. In fact, the day they organized the Mormon religion was April 6, 1830, considered the beneficial Day-Fatality in folk belief because it coincided with a special alignment of Jupiter and the Sun.

The Jupiter talisman was one of Joseph Junior's prized positions, for he was born under the astrological influence of the planet Jupiter. It contained Hebrew letters on one side, corresponding to numerical values adding to thirty-four in any direction across and a total of 136. According to Egyptologist E. A. Walls Budge, 136 was "the number for the spirit and Demon of the planet Jupiter." The opposite side contained various magic symbols, including the astrological sign for the planet Jupiter, a cross for the spirit of Jupiter, and a symbol for the orbital path of Jupiter.

Silas learned that these artifacts had been crucial to the family's treasure-hunting and money-digging endeavors. Joseph Smith probably gravitated toward the profession because his parents were heavily involved and themselves had been drawn toward occult ritual, white magic, superstition, paranormal phenomena, divination, and treasure hunting. One neighbor of the Smiths said the father was "a firm believer in witchcraft and other supernatural things, and had brought up his family in the same belief. He also believed that there was a vast amount of money buried somewhere in the country; that it would someday be found; that he himself had spent time and money searching for it with divining rods."

One of the other townsfolk associated with the Smith family had an interesting tidbit about Junior himself: Joseph gazed into a so-called peep stone or seer stone in order "to see chests of money buried in the earth. He was also a fortune-teller, and he claimed to know where stolen goods went."

Another neighbor, William Stafford, was reported to have stated that Joseph Smith Jr. used such a seer stone not only to "see all things within and under the earth but to discover the spirits in whose charge these treasures were clothed in ancient dress."

"My God," Silas whispered, setting down the book and looking out at the darkened evening below. He had no idea of the occultism that Mormonism and its founder had been steeped in. The deeper down the rabbit hole Silas went, the weirder the upstart American religion became in its dark, dank corners.

And there was Maxwell, jumping into bed with one of the most important figureheads of the faith by the sheer magnitude of the office he was seeking: President of the United States.

Silas shook his head and continued making his way through the book.

The author revealed more eyewitnesses who apparently testified that the Smiths engaged in elaborate rituals based on occult lore and folk magic. Even made animal sacrifices to appease whatever spirits might be guarding buried treasure.

"So they killed a dog," one neighbor testified, "and tried this method of obtaining the precious metal...Alas! How vivid was the expectation when the blood of poor Tray [the dog] was used to take off the charm, and after all to find their mistake...and now they were obliged to give up in despair."

A cousin of Junior Smith's wife, Emma, bore the same testimony, reporting that the sacrifice of white dogs, black cats, and other animals "was an indispensable part or appendage of the art which Smith, the embryo prophet, was then practicing."

"Sick!" Silas said.

But if that wasn't dark enough, the book exposed that sometimes the family relied solely on occult magic rituals and other ceremonies. A neighbor bore testimony to this fact, William Stafford:

Joseph Senior first made a circle, twelve or fourteen feet in diameter. This circle, said he, contains the treasure. He then stuck in the ground a row of witch hazel sticks, around the said circle to ward off the evil spirits. Within this circle, he made another, of about eight or ten feet in diameter. He walked around it three times on the periphery of this last circle, muttering to himself something which I could not understand. He next stuck a steel rod in the center of the circles, and then enjoined profound silence upon us, lest we should arouse the evil spirit who had the charge of these treasures. After we had dug a trench about five feet in depth around the rod...Joseph Senior went to the house to inquire of young Joseph the cause of our disappointment. He soon returned and said, that Joseph had remained all this time in the house, looking in his stone and watching the motions of the evil spirit—that he saw the spirit come up to the ring and as soon as it beheld the cone which we had formed around the rod, it caused the money to sink.

"This is clearly overt paganism!" Silas exclaimed. He continued reading. Perhaps the clearest picture of the Smiths' ties to occultism came from the autobiography of his mother, Lucy. In defending her family against charges of laziness, she wrote: "Let not my reader suppose that...we stopped our labor and went at trying to win the faculty of Abrac, drawing Magic circles, or soothsaying to the neglect of all kinds of business. We never during our lives suffered one important interest to swallow up every other obligation."

Did he read that right? Junior's mom said her family never neglected to attend to Abrac, drawing magic circles and soothsaying?

Soothsaying was another way of saying foretelling the future through divination tools, like tarot cards, omens, crystals, and peep stones. Drawing magic circles is an essential ritual used by occultists to gain power over evil spirits when they are involved in a particular purpose. In order to contact spirits, magic users often drew circles within circles, supposedly forming an impenetrable barrier for demons, which Joseph's father had done when treasure seeking, as described by William Stafford.

Then there was Lucy's reference to "the faculty of Abrac." Silas knew from his studies in early Church heresies that Abrac was a demon-god viewed by the heretical second-century Basilidians as the chief of the 365 genies ruling the days of the year. The magical word *Abracadabra* was rooted in Medieval folk magic from country peasants and others who practiced such rituals. They used the incantation as a protective power to guard against physical injury, danger, evil spirits, and diseases like the plague.

Silas set down the book and rubbed his eyes. His head was spinning with the significance of the history surrounding both Joseph Smith and his American-made religion. The occult roots seemed to change things for sure.

But how? In what way was this pagan past connected to what was happening now? With the discovery of the medallion? With the political campaign?

He yawned and stretched and wondered what time it was. Had to be getting late.

As if on cue, a young man approached him hesitantly and tapped his watch. "Sorry, sir, but the library is closing soon."

"Sure thing. I'll wrap up now."

After putting away his books, he gathered up the articles he had printed to read later at his hotel. He walked out into the crisp fall evening, the air smelling of dried leaves, burning wood, and rain. He breathed in deeply as he walked back to his car, satisfied with his progress and what he had uncovered.

"If at first you are confused," he had always insisted to his students, "research, research, and research some more!"

He went to put the key into his car door when he heard a noise behind him. In the window, he briefly saw the reflection of a silhouetted man.

Right before a black bag was slipped over his head and he was plunged into darkness.

CHAPTER 17

MIAMI, FLORIDA.

G rant was still cursing himself as they drove to the airport for not making a copy of the medallion.

"It's fine," Torres reassured him.

"It's not fine! What the hell was I thinking?"

"Well, nobody else thought to document it either. Including me. And I'm a professional at that sort of thing."

She took out a piece of paper from her back jean pocket. When they had returned to the hotel room the previous night, she immediately grabbed her Moleskine notebook and a pen and wrote down the glyphs she had committed to memory. It took her a few passes, but she was convinced she had gotten it right. Grant had confirmed from his own memory that their makeshift map looked to be true.

She scanned the characters again as they pulled up to the private terminal where chartered jets taxied in and out. She closed her eyes and ran the glyphs through her memory again, then looked at the piece of paper.

"I'm 98 percent sure this is right."

"Yeah, but it's that damn 2 percent that will kill ya," Grant grumbled.

She frowned at her new sidekick, then slugged him on his right shoulder.

"Ouch!" he exclaimed. "What was that for?"

"You doubting my intellectual superpowers?"

He threw up his hands in surrender. "Wouldn't think of it."

A burly man with a searching look and a camo knapsack appeared outside a sliding door to a security terminal for the private airport.

Torres smiled, surprised how happy she was to see her partner. "Pull over there. That's Matt Gapinski."

As Grant eased their car to the curb near the SEPIO operative, Torres rolled down her window. "Need a ride?"

The man turned toward the car, his furrowed brow rising in surprise as his face transformed into a broad grin.

"Torres!"

"Get in, Hoss."

"Hoss?" Grant whispered as Gapinski threw his bag in the trunk then hopped in the back.

She shrugged. "It's a term of endearment I picked up in our last mission."

Gapinski slammed the door and thrust his hand into the front of the car. "Matt Gapinski."

Grant smiled weakly and shook it. "Grant Chrysostom."

He cocked his head to the side. "Any relation to old Golden Mouth, the early Church father?"

"Your boss already tried that line. Sorry to disappoint."

"Well, your loss. Cool name nonetheless. Alright, where to?"

"My uncle's company. A salvage and exploration operation. The one I told you about. Anyway, we're loading up and heading out this afternoon. Tio has a private plane that will take us to Guanaja Bay Island. From there, we rent a Cessna to take LiDAR imaging of the jungle. Those topographical images combined with our map from the medallion will help us locate the lost civilization. Whatever it is."

"I have no idea what you just said, but it all sounds good to me. Just one question."

"Yeah," Grant said, "what's that?"

"Can we get some tacos or something? I haven't eaten since this morning."

Torres giggled. That was definitely the Gapinski she remembered.

Grant drove along U.S. 1 and found a food truck selling Mexican food and boasting of the best tamales this side of the Rio Grande. Gapinski was overjoyed. He bought four of the corn-husk goodness and a wet burrito. Figuring it might be a while until they ate again, Grant and Torres each bought two themselves before the crew headed back to San Jose New World Salvage and Exploration.

When they arrived, Burt was closing the rear roll-up door to a large U-Haul truck with their gear stowed inside.

"Burt, that's no fun," Torres said as she was climbing out of the car. "I was expecting to spend the next few hours breaking my back loading our gear. Like the good ol' days."

The brawny man chuckled as he wiped the sweat from his forehead with a red bandana. He stuffed it back in his pocket, and said, "Now, the difference, you see, is that last time you were the hired help while this time you're the paying client. Boss's orders."

She smiled weakly, embarrassed at the truth of the man's statement. The Order had paid her uncle well to lend SEPIO equipment and arrange help near the mainland.

"Make sure you leave me a crate or two to load next time. I miss breaking a sweat."

The man nodded and gave a thumbs up, then retreated to the front of the truck as her uncle came out of his office.

"Naomi!" he said, walking over with a lit cigar in one hand and a glass of clear liquid in the other.

She smiled as he walked over. "I see my check cleared."

He puffed on his cigar and smiled, then took a long swig of his drink.

"Indeed, it did. Thank you again for the business. But I have to ask." He puffed again, sending large tendrils of smoke into the hot, clear sky. "Why are you doing this? You mentioned some sort of possible Mormon connection to Ciudad Blanca. But I had heard a well-funded group of Mormon archaeologists had already tried to confirm those stories, scouring Mexico and Central America with numerous excavations. Provided some valuable, high-quality research. But in the end, their findings only clearly disproved the Mormon view. Some of the archaeologists ended up losing their faith. Some were even excommunicated, if I remember hearing correctly after they voiced their views. What are you hoping to find?"

She watched the smoke sail into the still air then expand and dissipate. She wondered herself what she was hoping to find. Adventure, getting back into the thrill of the archaeological hunt? Purpose for her life by re-engaging her life's pursuit? Reassurance for her own faith, even?

"Answers," was the word she settled on. "Something is clearly up, and it seems like there are some broader implications with this medallion and its claims about the Mormon faith. So, yes, answers are what I am hoping to find."

Her uncle took another swig of the clear liquid and puffed again on his cigar, eyeing her suspiciously. She hadn't told him about the assault and the theft of the medallion. Figured it might derail the operation if he knew she was in danger. She hoped he would leave it alone.

He walked over to her, handed her his glass, clenched his cigar between his teeth, and grasped both shoulders, looking her in the eyes. "Cuídate, mi sobrina." *Take care, my niece.*

She smiled and nodded, then turned toward Grant and Gapinski and took a swig of her uncle's alcohol.

"Looks like we're ready."

The three got back in their car and followed Burt for the private airstrip with their awaiting twin-engine plane.

Naomi smiled and waved to her uncle as they left, who was puffing on his cigar with a wide grin—clearly pleased that his niece was back at the helm of one of his company's missions.

WITHIN A HALF HOUR the convoy had reached the private plane, and in another hour the crew had unloaded the truck of equipment. Then they stuffed every last bit of radar frequency equipment; tents, backpacks, and other hiking gear; medical and food supplies; and weapons they could manage into the small twin-engine plane.

The ground crew had already finished the pre-flight check by the time the SEPIO operatives arrived and prepared the plane for take-off. A few mechanics were finishing their own preparations, checking levels of fluids and topping off the fuel. Gapinski was slated to fly the bird, so he debriefed with them while Burt, Grant, and Torres finished loading.

"So what's the plan, Torres?" Grant said as they loaded the last of the gear into the underside of the plane.

"Plan is to fly from Miami to the Guanaja Bay Island that sits just north of the Honduran mainland. Should be an easy three, maybe four-hour flight. It's about half the distance this bird can handle, so no worries."

"Man, your uncle spared no expense," Gapinski said coming around from the back of the Piper Malibu Mirage. He closed the door to the trunk compartment and tapped it for good luck.

"He bought this bird with his oil money and has held on to it ever since for special cases. And it didn't hurt the Order was paying top dollar for his help."

"Go, Radcliffe." He stood on his toes, stretching to see inside. "I bet it's pimped out with leather and fully reclining seats. Do we get champagne and little cartons of caviar, too?"

Torres shook her head. "Sorry, partner. I think you might find some tuna fish and a loaf of bread, but that's about it."

"Aww, man."

"But, hey, at least there's leather. From Guanaja we'll load the LiDAR equipment onto a smaller Cessna plane and coordinate a search grid with the medallion map in order to map the area and pinpoint the location of the lost civilization settlement. If all goes well, we'll set out on the ground for the White City in two days, max three. You ready?"

Gapinski grinned and rubbed his hands like a dog with a new chew toy. "Let's roll."

Torres followed him toward the stairs. Grant came around from the back after tapping the luggage compartment for good luck himself, when a mechanic slammed into his shoulder.

"Hey, buddy. Watch it!" he growled, nearly toppling over.

The man turned around and put his hands up, bowed his head and averted his eyes out of embarrassment as he backed up. "Apologies, sir." Then the man turned around and walked off.

Grant scowled and looked back at the man as he walked toward the plane's entrance.

"All aboard," Gapinski bellowed.

Torres climbed the stairs, Grant followed. After briefly eying the plane, Gapinski headed inside and brought the stairs up to a close. He eased himself into the tight cockpit and ran through his pre-flight check of the instrument panel before engaging the power. It hummed to life as the twin turbo engines spun to full resting speed.

He reached for the radio and engaged the in-flight option. It crackled to life.

"Ladies and gents," he said offering his best impression of a flight attendant, "welcome onboard Flight 2M3 with service from Miami to Guanaja Bay Island. We are currently next in line for take-off and are expected to be in the air in approximately seven minutes. At this time, please fasten that there seatbelt of yours and secure all baggage underneath your seat or in the overhead compartments. We also ask that your seats and table trays are in the upright position for take-off. Please turn off all personal electronic devices, including laptops and cell phones. Smoking is prohibited for the duration of the flight. Thank you for choosing Gapinski Airlines. Enjoy your flight."

Grant and Torres clapped slowly, mockingly.

He turned around and grinned. "Seriously, though. Buckle up. We're ready for takeoff."

He pushed the bird's throttle so that it slowly moved forward, turning the plane toward the private runway. After positioning it at the far end, he said a quick prayer and fully engaged the engines for takeoff. In under twenty seconds they were soaring toward the heavens and entering a cruising altitude of 20,000 feet, pushing it to just under 250 mph. Soon they were cruising past the shoreline of Florida and over the Caribbean. Forty minutes later they had entered Cuban airspace for a brief flyover. Soon they would be spending two hours over the Caribbean pressing toward their final destination.

Gapinski set the plane on autopilot and climbed out of the cockpit into the main cabin to stretch.

He said, "Soon we'll clear the Cuban mainland airspace and push out over the Caribbean again. T minus two hours and we should set down nicely on Guanaja."

"Dude," Grant said, "shouldn't you stay put?"

"Naw," he said, slapping the man on his shoulder as he walked past. "That's what autopilot is for. But don't worry, I've got my eye on it."

"How reassuring," Grant mumbled.

Gapinski sat down in a seat next to Torres and buckled himself in. "So what's the game plan when we arrive, chief?"

"First things first is getting that LiDAR imaging equipment in the air."

"And what is this lido-thingamabob you mentioned earlier?"

"LiDAR," Grant corrected.

Gapinski snapped his fingers. "That. What's that."

"Basically, its radar cuts through all the leaves and limbs of trees, plants on the ground, even the surface of the earth itself to reveal what's underneath. Think of it as a super x-ray. We'll use that data to coordinate with the medallion map, and then—"

The plane suddenly lurched, dipping and then rising back and shuddering with intensity.

"What the..." Grant said.

"Just turbulence," Gapinski reassured. "Nothing to worry about."

The plane evened out and then hit another speed bump. Minor in comparison to the first, but it still caused unease to flash across Grant's face.

Torres turned her seat and looked out the window. "Gapinski...I think we're, we're banking slightly."

"Huh?" he said looking out his own window.

A faint warning began to sound from the cockpit indicating trouble.

Grant pivoted to the open cockpit door. "Dude, there's some sort of warning sound coming from the front."

Gapinski was unbuckled and heading toward the cockpit. "I'm on it. The turbulence probably just disengaged the autopilot. Happens to these birds."

Grant glanced at Torres, then the two unbuckled their belts and headed toward the cockpit.

Gapinski was seated and staring at a series of dials and indicator lights on the large cockpit panel.

"Uhh, guys. We've got a problem."

He pointed to the gas gauge. Grant and Torres leaned in for a look, then turned toward one another in shock.

The red needle had dipped below the half-way point, well below where it should have been at that point in the flight plan. And it was falling rapidly.

They were running out of fuel. And fast.

"Always something," Gapinski cursed under his breath.

CHAPTER 18

YORK, PENNSYLVANIA.

What...Where am I?

After Silas had been bagged and the world went black, he tried like hell to fight his attacker. A stronger pair of arms had grabbed him from behind, while another one had inserted a needle into his neck.

That's when the world went officially dark.

He was starting to awaken from the effects of the drugs. He was stiff and groggy. He couldn't tell how long he had been out. Could have been ten minutes or ten hours.

Suddenly, the black bag was ripped from his head.

He was in a windowless passenger van in the back seat, hands bound behind him and strapped in with a seatbelt across his chest. Filtered light was shining through the front windshield, telling him it was the next day. Large boughs filled with colorful leaves came into focus. They were probably still in the Commonwealth of Pennsylvania, perhaps a park or an abandoned factory or parking lot deep in the countryside. But he had to have been out for hours.

A hand smacked Silas across his face. It came from a figure kneeling on the seat in front of him. A dark ski mask hid his face and dark clothing hid anything recognizable.

"You need to leave this alone, Mr. Grey," was all the man said.

138 | J. A. BOUMA

Silas looked to the side after movement caught his attention. A second figure was seated to his left, same outfit. The man reached with his left arm around his shoulder to reiterate the message.

"Leave this alone," the first man in front of him said again.

Silas could feel his chest pulsing with pressure. His head started feeling light from lack of oxygen and mile-high anxiety from the moment. His vision started blurring and ears started ringing. Panic was setting in.

Not the time to need his blue pills!

The same hand smacked him a second time, then a third.

Silas widened his eyes searching for a way to escape. He tried twisting his wrists out from his bindings. There was no use. Then he strained against the seatbelt. It didn't budge.

"No use, fella. You're stuck here until we have an agreement. Capiche?"

The voice was low and nasally. Definitely American, with a Midwestern lilt.

"Who are you?" Silas said through gritted teeth.

The man turned his head and sighed. "A friend of a friend who wants to warn you to back off."

Silas said nothing, the gears of his mind working overtime to piece together what was happening. And how he would get out of it.

"What friend? Who are you talking about?"

"Not important, partner. What is important, is that you walk away from pursuing anything to do with Amos Young."

Silas stopped straining and settled into his seat, staring into the blank eyes of his captor.

"What is it you think that I'm pursuing?"

"Young's Mormonism. His connection with the Faithful Majority. His partnership with James Maxwell. The medallion."

Partnership? Medallion? How telling. So there is a connection.

"I've never been one to follow orders...partner."

The man grinned underneath his mask, revealing a set of perfectly white teeth, the kind that takes money and time to create.

"Let me put it to you this way. If you don't stop your line of inquiry and go back home to your pathetic post-professorial life, a bag over your head and a van ride will be the least of your worries."

The arm around his shoulders gripped them tight, pulling Silas close to the left.

"Now, say the words," the man growled.

Silas was finding it hard to breathe. He wanted to put on a show of tough-as-nails defiance, but inside he was falling apart. He took a deep breath, then eased it out through his nose.

"Wha...What words?"

"I understand. I. Will. Back. Off."

Silas glanced at the man next to him who still had a firm grip on his shoulders, then back at the figure in front of him. He nodded quickly.

"No. Say the words."

"I understand," he quickly stammered. "I will back off. You have my word."

The man said nothing for what seemed like a full minute. He simply stared forward into Silas, through Silas.

He didn't avert his eyes, going toe-to-toe with the menace.

The carefully crafted teeth returned. "Good." Then the man flicked his head to the left before getting up and moving toward the front of the van. When he did, the mystery man loosened his grip on Silas and pulled his arm back, then suddenly got up off the seat. He flinched to the right and closed his eyes, before realizing the man had released his seat belt.

"Move," was all he said as he pointed toward the sliding door.

Silas obliged. He shuffled forward, hands still bound behind his back. His left foot caught something on the floor, sending him tumbling to the well of the sliding door.

The man came from behind him and reached over to the handle. Pulling it, he slid the door open. He shoved Silas out the door with his foot. He fell hard, face first onto rocky, broken pavement. His nose burst into a geyser of blood. It ran down his face as he turned over onto his back.

The man inside the van got out and lumbered over toward Silas as he writhed on the ground in pain. He heard another door open, and the masked figure who had been kneeling in front of Silas strolled over to him, as well, hovering over him for one final word.

Suddenly, the one man who had gripped Silas's shoulders dropped to the ground and grabbed his forehead, wrenching his head back as he laid on the ground.

"We have solemnly warned you," the other man who had been kneeling in front of him said, "and in the most determined manner, that if you do not cease this course of wanton abuse of one of our own, that vengeance will overtake you, and that when it does come it will be as furious as the mountain torrent, and as terrible as the beating tempest."

Silas fought the other man's grip even as his nose continued dripping blood down his face. As he did, he caught sight of something peeking out from the man's jacket sleeve on the underside of his arm.

What the...

A stick bird tattoo, rising toward the enlightened heavens.

Nous's calling card.

The man issuing the warning crouched low, getting in Silas's face one last time as his mind reeled from the revelation. "Do not despise our warnings, and pass them off with a sneer, or a grin, or a threat, and pursue your former course. Vengeance sleepeth not, Silas, neither does it slumber. Unless you heed our warnings and attend to our request, it will overtake you at an hour when you do not expect, and at a day when you do not look for it. For you, there shall be no escape. For there is but one decree for you: cease and desist, or a more fatal calamity shall befall you."

The man let go of his face and stood. He kicked Silas hard in his ribs, then again and stomped on his stomach. The other man walked behind him and grabbed his upper arms and began to drag him across the rough stone lot. Silas's eyes adjusted to the light, and he saw the van, a rust-colored monstrosity with a faded wrench and faucet and the name of a plumbing company that was missing the 'P' so that it read 'AAA lumbers.'

Behind him, he heard the hollow thud of the man's boots on wood steps before his back jammed against them.

The man laughed. "Sorry about that."

He heaved Silas up the short set of stairs that led to a front porch, then opened a door behind him and dragged him into a house of exposed beams and brick. It was musty, smelling of wet, rotting wood. It was dark, but for a faint amount of light filtering through the boarded up windows.

The man dragged him into what looked like a living room. He bound his feet tightly with the same corded rope as his hands, then walked out the front door, waving as he slammed it shut.

Silas heard the man crunch across the gravel. Then two doors opening and closing sounded before the van roared to life and faded into the distance.

He lay on the well-worn floorboards trying to catch his breath from the gut kick, his mouth filling with the taste of pennies. When he caught his breath, he spat blood out of his mouth and turned over to let it fall elsewhere.

He contemplated the man's warning, its language and tenor.

We have solemnly warned you, and in the most determined manner, that if you do not cease this course of wanton abuse of one of our own, that vengeance will overtake you, and that when it does come it will be as furious as the mountain torrent, and as terrible as the beating tempest.

It didn't seem right. It was so out of place. Like from another century. And yet, it was also familiar for some reason, and from a friend, no less. It felt like an important clue, so he repeated it again, then a few more times to commit it to memory.

He rolled on his back, the blood flow slowing. He breathed in deeply and exhaled slow, trying to catch his breath. He needed to get to Freedom University and to the debate, which was probably only a few hours away.

But where the heck was he? How was he going to get out of that damn house?

Then there was the fact he had been kidnapped by Nousati. Which was all the motivation he needed to get to the bottom of the conspiracy surrounding Amos Young and the Mormon medallion.

CHAPTER 19

Silas wanted to puke.

Saint Augustine had famously contrasted the earthly City of Man with the eternal City of God in his similarly titled book. The second-century early church thinker Tertullian had asked, "What has Athens to do with Jerusalem?"

According to what Silas was witnessing, apparently everything! At Freedom University, the cities of Man and of God were united in an arranged marriage. And by the looks of it, Maxwell was throwing the bachelor party.

After the van had driven off, leaving Silas alone in the abandoned two-story house, he had freed his hands by rubbing his bonds against the coarse red-brick of a fireplace until they broke. He had stopped the flow of blood to his nose, but he was still a mess and needed to get cleaned up before the rally. Surprisingly, his captors hadn't driven far outside of town, just a handful of miles from York to an abandoned farmhouse. Took him just under two hours, but he was able to walk back to the university and retrieve his car. Afterward, he had gone back to his hotel room to shower and change clothes. Then he raced for Freedom University, bringing his Beretta for back up. Just in case.

By the time he arrived at the open-air Freedom Stadium, the

sleepy college campus had been transformed into a carnival of political chaos rivaling the major parties' national conventions. The red, white, and blue colors of the field provided the appropriate backdrop to the political rally showcasing the two candidates, as well as the Christian nationalism on full display.

Campaign volunteers were passing out "Young for President" and "Vote for Reed" posters. Women in colonial-era costumes were waving American flags. There were even men on stilts dressed as Uncle Sam passing out campaign buttons from both rival campaigns.

Then there were the obligatory "God Bless America" bumper stickers, as if God had forgotten about 99 percent of the world. Crosses were draped with American flags around the cross beam where Jesus had bled out—as if his blood ran red, white, and blue, and only for Americans. Someone walked past in a military-green t-shirt with the words "God, Guns, and Guts. Made in America. Let's Keep All Three."

Silas wanted to puke.

After the word had gone out to the media that Freedom was to play host to the campaign debate between the two rival conservative campaigns, the political machines supporting each of the candidates launched into full-throttle engagement. Supporters for both the 'Amos Young for President' and 'Matthew Reed for President' campaigns were bussed in from the surrounding states to offer a show of force in support of their candidates, bringing with them the political and religious paraphernalia.

There were some questions as to why the Democrat candidate, Robert Santos, wasn't invited. The Faithful Majority brushed aside those complaints, insisting the rally was meant to help Christian Republicans make sense of the presidential election. The Catholic Democrat simply didn't have a role in such a decision. The Democratic National Committee cried foul, claiming federal election law required equal airtime this close to Election Day. But since the event was being billed as a political rally, rather than a political debate, and it was broadcast live by the nonprofit Christian Broadcast Network, which wasn't subject to federal oversight, and merely reported on by the major networks, the university was able to get away with their little political coup.

Silas walked through a metal detector and flashed his all-access pass to the gate attendant at Freedom Stadium where the political debate would soon be taking place between Amos Young and Matthew Reed. The young man stiffened at the sight, probably wondering who the dignitary was. He waved him in and told him to have a blessed day.

An ache grew in the pit of his stomach as he waded through the brothel of Christian nationalism, the "Battle Hymn of the Republic" now providing the soundtrack to the frenzy.

He had no qualms with the Church being actively involved in the public square. Christians should vote, vocalize arguments for the good of society, even lobby for policies that aligned with God's intent for human flourishing. He also had no problem with them working in government for the sake of the common good.

But this political spectacle conjoined to obvious Christianity?

Silas wanted to puke.

He hung back near the main entrance at the fifty-yard-line, taking in the circus. At one end sat the field house, and in front of it sat a stage with two podiums. Below was a thirty-foot security buffer guarded by Secret Service agents. The field itself was packed with a standing-room-only crowd. On either side, the bleachers were similarly filled with committed evangelical Christians eager to hear the two candidates representing their political views convince them that they had their religious ones in mind as well.

And Young was the one who had all the heavy lifting to do with this crowd.

Suddenly, there arose a great cheering from the front of the mass of bodies near the stage. Silas looked toward the front to see the man himself, James Maxwell, taking the stage. He strode to the podium waving to the crowd and working it with thumbs up and a wide grin. Now the entire stadium was engaged in rapturous applause and cheering.

Maxwell was their man. And in their heart of hearts, they wished he was the one running for president.

In his own heart of hearts, Maxwell probably wished he was, too.

He motioned for the crowd to quiet itself. It took a minute, but it finally wound down so that he could commence the morning festivities.

"Welcome, welcome. It is so good to see so many fine, upstanding, modern-day Christian patriots assembling to help this great land heal from the past eight years of spiritual misery and darkness and chaos!"

The crowd cheered in agreement. Silas shifted uncomfortably at the tenor and tone Maxwell was already bringing to such a spiritually taut environment.

It didn't bode well for the rest of the hour.

The man turned around. As he did, a massive American flag unfurled behind him, along with the Christian flag of white with a red cross embedded in a blue corner square.

The crowd went wild with appreciation.

Silas wanted to puke.

"You know, growing up in public school in the mid-'50s, that flag and the pledge that accompanies it was a hallmark of our education. You couldn't get two minutes past the sound of the bell announcing the start of class without standing at attention, raising your hand to your heart, and voicing those beautiful words. Now, such a pledge and even the very flag itself is considered a trigger of oppression! How dastardly. So I think it appropriate that we resurrect that sacred tradition this morning by pledging our allegiance as God-fearing Americans to the flag of the United States."

More shouts, more cheering as Maxwell led his congregation in the political-religious anthem.

Silas could have sworn he heard the apostles and early Church fathers turning over in their collective graves at the sight and sound. The crowd might as well have been declaring "Caesar is lord!" right then and there, the political rallying cry thousands of early believers gave their lives to deny through bloody persecution and martyrdom.

When they were finished, Maxwell said, "Before I introduce the candidates, let us bow in prayer for America, that God would use these men to heal our land. Let us pray."

"Almighty God," he began. "In the history of the world, there has never been a nation like America. Founded by men and women seeking religious freedom and rooted in the Word of God, you sovereignly directed them to establish a beacon of hope upon the shores of this vast Promised Land, dedicated to the divine proposition that every single person on the planet is created equal in your eyes and endowed by their Creator with certain unalienable rights.

"We are indeed one nation under God!" He boomed, eliciting *Amens* from the crowd.

"By your care, you have delivered us from strife and war, both at home and abroad. By your blessing, we have prospered. And by your guiding hand generations of men and women have been raised up who have devoted themselves to preserving life, liberty, and the pursuit of happiness, here and around the world.

"We have been a city on a hill, a light for all the world that cannot and will not be hidden! From our shores, we have sent forth the hope of liberty and freedom through the greatest force of Christian warriors in history."

Maxwell fell silent. Then he continued, more solemn.

"But now, Lord, America has become like Gomorrah, falling into darkness and disobedience, iniquity and indifference.

"We have sinned against you in thought, word, and deed—by what we have done and by what we have left undone. We have not loved you with our whole heart, we have not obeyed your laws. In fact, we are trampling them underfoot! We, your people, come humbling ourselves before your throne to pray and seek Your face.

"Forgive our sins and heal our land!" he boomed again, eliciting more fervent *Amens*.

"Raise up leaders who understand the times, how the Constitution hangs in the balance, on a fast-fraying thread."

Are you kidding me? He just invoked the prophetic words of Joseph Smith!

"Give us leaders who know where we should turn, how we should go, and what we should do to return back to you and your commands. May Liberty's torch burn bright and strong, inflamed by the righteousness of your people.

"Lord, you tell us in your Holy Word that if my people, which are called by my name, shall humble themselves, and pray, and seek my face, and turn from their wicked ways; then will I hear from heaven, and will forgive their sin, and will heal their land.

"We pray you would strengthen both of these men for the task ahead, and that you would raise up similarly gifted and equipped pious men of God who would make America great again by helping us turn from our wicked ways and back to you.

"God bless Amos Young and Matthew Reed. And God bless America!"

Then he closed: "In Jesus' name...and all God's people said?"

"Amen," the crowd dutifully shouted, cheering and waving their banners of red, white, and blue.

"Amen!" he shouted back.

The crowd was electrified by Maxwell's spiritual rallying cry, priming them like ravenous beasts to partake from the nationalistic table spread before them.

"It is my honor, as President of Freedom University and Chair of Faithful Majority to introduce to you two fine, God-fearing Americans who are running to preside over this great nation. Please welcome Amos Young and Matthew Reed."

As the candidates appeared before the clapping, cheering crowd Silas found it interesting that neither Young's Mormonism nor Reed's Evangelicalism were mentioned. Perhaps an intentional avoidance on the part of the Faithful Majority?

The crowd quieted down as the candidates took their positions behind their respective podiums: Reed on the right, who was sporting a baggy, frumpy-looking double-breasted blue suit and was dwarfed by his opponent's size and age; Young on the left, who was looking trim and vigorous and appealing in a fitted black suit. The contrast was stark.

Maxwell took a seat at a table a few feet in front of the candidates, playing the role of moderator.

"Alright, gentleman, let's begin. We've got a lot of ground to cover to give Christian America a more thorough understanding of your candidacies in order to help them vote for God's man in the coming week. The first question is to both of you. Would you please give a brief testimony of your relationship with God and to the Christian faith? We'll start with you, Mr. Reed."

This should be interesting.

"Thank you, Doctor Maxwell," Reed began, "for your work in trying to unify Christians from around the country in the interest of healing this great land."

He paused to gather his thoughts, then smiled. "What can I say but repeat what has already been said: Amazing grace, how sweet the sound that saved a wretch like me! I once was lost, but now am found; was blind, but now I see. Before I found Christ...or, rather, before Christ found me, my life was a mess. I didn't grow up in a Christian home. My daddy was an alcoholic, who beat Mom at night for sport. I fell in with the wrong crowd as a teenager searching for meaning and purpose. And it wasn't until a sweet African-American woman on a bus from Saint Louis to LA shared about how much God loves me, so much so that he sent his Son, Jesus Christ, to die for me—it wasn't until I heard that glorious news that I finally found what I had been looking for all my life.

"I stand before you today a sinner saved by God's grace. That's my testimony. I once was a very lost young person who was carrying around a pocketful of burdens. It's only because of the crazy, furious love of God who died on the cross in my place to free me from my sins and my shame and my guilt that I am who I am. And also because of a black woman on a Greyhound bus who decided to share that love with a lily-white guy from the Deep South. Thank you."

It was clear the crowd loved the Evangelical's testimony of faith given how loud it got. Now for the million dollar question:

How would they respond to Young's testimony?

And what would he even say?

The cheering and applause died down, and Young stepped closer to his podium.

"Thank you, Matthew, for your heartfelt testimony," Young offered, smiling broadly and nodding to his opponent. "And thank you, James, for offering this arena for the two of us to explain our differences, but more importantly to rally the Christian community to fight for the soul of this great land."

Young cleared his throat, then smiled awkwardly before offering his answer.

"I know that the Christian faith is the true faith of God. I have a testimony that God answers our prayers, that he loves us, and that he sent his Son to die for us. I bear testimony that our Savior is our perfect example, that he did perform the atonement for us, and that through him we all may be able to return to live with our Father in heaven again. I have felt an intense burning in my bosom many times in my life, which I carry with me each and every day of my life as a sign of the work of Christ in my life.

"Throughout my life, I have diligently sought God regarding my path in life. I am so grateful for the scriptures so that I can find that direction by continually feasting upon the Word of God. I know that the Bible is true and gives us direction in our lives each and every day. I have read the Bible and prayed regularly for some forty years since my childhood. I am so grateful that I have been able to grow in this knowledge through the guidance and assurance of the

Holy Spirit. What a wonderful blessing it is to be a member of the church. My hope and prayer is that all might have the opportunity to gain this knowledge for themselves. Thank you."

Silas looked around the crowd, which was nodding and smiling in response, seeming to buy that what Young experienced as a committed Mormon was what Reed experienced in Christ as a committed Evangelical.

Remarkable.

"Thank you, gentlemen, for testifying to your faith in Jesus Christ." Maxwell swiveled in his chair toward the crowd. "Why don't you show your appreciation for both of these men fearlessly, publicly bearing witness to Christ this morning."

The crowd responded with rapturous applause and shouts of affirmation, as if Saint Paul and Saint Peter themselves were standing up on the stage before the crowd and cameras.

Then a sound split through the afternoon air just above the din of the cheering crowd. A crack reminiscent of the distant sounds of conflict Silas had heard countless days while on tour in Iraq.

Was that a gunshot?

In an instant, Matthew Reed's head snapped back to the right in a spray of blood and gore, his body crumpling to the floor in a lifeless heap.

Another shot rang out.

The left side of the podium in front of Young exploded, shards of wood flying up and out and away from the explosion toward the right. The candidate fell backward, whether from being shot or out of sheer shock, it wasn't yet clear.

Either way, this much was clear:

The Evangelical third-party candidate for President of the United States had just been shot.

Assassinated.

The Mormon Republican candidate was still standing, leaving him to sweep the political field.

This changed everything.

CHAPTER 20

MIAMI, FLORIDA.

"You two strap in. It's about to get crazy."

Torres and Grant scurried back to the main cabin and buckled themselves securely.

Gapinski tightened his belt buckle and firmly grabbed ahold of the control wheel, regaining control of the plane and leveling it out after the autopilot shut off.

They had just cleared the Cuban mainland and were now over the Gulf of Batabano. He had steered the plane toward Isla de la Juventud in the hopes they could land on dry ground instead of in the water. There was a small airport just south of the small city of Nueva Gerona. The Southern Baptist in him started praying like there was no tomorrow that they would make it to the island and to the airport before their fuel ran out.

Because there literally could be no tomorrow.

It was going to be close. Real close.

"Mayday. Mayday. Flight 2M3 is losing fuel, and fast. We request emergency clearance to land at Aeropuerto Rafael Pérez. Does anybody copy?"

All he received was static.

"Spared no expense huh, Torres?" Grant complained from the back to his companion.

Suddenly, the plane dropped and shuddered. She screamed. So did Grant.

"Gapinski...what's going on?" Torres yelled.

It leveled back up and reached smoother air.

"Sorry about that. Another patch of turbulence. Good news is I can see the island. Bad news is we're in the red and almost out of fuel."

Then the plane fell silent, the hum of both engines ceasing.

"Strike that. We are out of fuel." He flicked at the fuel gauge with his middle finger. Seemed appropriate. It showed three more notches until empty. "And apparently our fuel gauge stopped working."

"What the hell are we going to do?" Grant shouted from the back. "C...c...can you land this thing? Will we reach the shore or any sort of airport or landing area? Please tell me you've done this before!"

"Relax, buddy. We're not going to—"

Turbulence interrupted him, dipping the plane again and causing it to shudder before it popped back up.

"Die..."

GRANT TURNED TO TORRES, taking her hand across the aisle, his face a twisted mess of fright and regret. "I'm so sorry I abandoned you all those months ago."

The plane vibrated over another pocket of air as it started falling toward the ground, causing Grant to shudder.

He paused and swallowed, then blurted out: "I love you! Still. Since the day we met and the day I left. I know it was my fault. All my neuroticism and selfishness and arrogance and—"

"Grant..." she said interrupting.

"No, hear me out! We may never get another chance." He turned and looked out the window. They were firmly over land now, and the plane had dipped below the cloud line. He could make out squares of farms and a town was coming into focus in the distance.

He turned away and closed his eyes and gripped his seat. "Dear God!"

"Grant, it'll be alright—"

"Alright? How can you say that? We're plummeting toward the earth in a solid aluminum tube at hundreds of miles per hour. It ain't alright!"

The overhead speaker crackled to life. "Hey, guys, Gapinski here. Of course, you already knew that. Anyway, I see the airport. I think we'll make it, but it's going to be close not having our engines. And with all these buildings and trees...Anyway, should be landing here in under fifteen."

"Dear God!" Grant exclaimed again, gripping his armrests tighter.

GAPINSKI PICKED up the radio again, hoping that the third time really was the charm.

"Mayday. Mayday. Flight 2M3 has lost all fuel. We're coming in fast and furious like Vin Diesel, but without engines. We request emergency clearance to land at Aeropuerto Rafael Pérez. Does anybody copy?"

Again, a stream of static was his only reply.

But then a voice broke through, speaking a string of Spanish that Gapinski couldn't understand.

"Torres, no hablo español! Can you help a brother out?"

"Coming!"

"No! Don't leave me," Gapinski heard Grant say. He chuckled and shook his head.

Torres rushed into the cockpit and settled into the empty copilot chair. Gapinski handed her a radio headset. "Buckle in and start talking. Tell them we've lost fuel and have no engines, and...

well, basically we need them not to shoot us out of the sky, and we're going to crash land, so we need help."

She said she understood then started speaking rapid Spanish into the headset as the features of the land below became more pronounced.

The plane started shuddering again as it approached the airport, the control wheel vibrating in Gapinski's grip. Torres glanced at him with wide eyes as she stopped talking and waited for a response.

Within a few seconds, another stream of Spanish filled both of their headsets. The airport had made visual with them and would make sure their two runways were clear and all planes stayed away. Emergency crews would be on standby.

"Gracias!" Torres tore off her headset and relayed her conversation with the airport.

"Good work. Now comes the fun part."

They were now over the town, bright houses of sea blue and salmon pink and lime green rushing underneath them as they approached the south end of town. The houses transitioned into a charred mess of trees and grass and bone-dry dirt, clearly having not seen the sight of a rain cloud in months.

"There it is!" Torres exclaimed, lifting out of her seat in excitement at the sight of the airport. "We're going to make it, right?"

She turned toward Gapinski, her face panic-stricken.

He smiled slightly and nodded. Then engaged the landing gear to prepare for their landing.

There was a loud grinding sound, followed by a screech and then a loud clicking noise.

His smile quickly turned into a grimace. "Always something!"

"What happened?"

"What was that noise," Grant shouted from the back.

"Landing gear. Totally jacked up. Crapola!"

Torres huffed and ran her hand through her thick black hair. "What are we going to do?"

"Land this bird without engines and without legs. That's what I'm going to do."

The runway was now in sight. The only thing standing between them and it was a chain-link fence and a patch of dry earth. Two super-bad scenarios Gapinski did not want to think about.

If they hit the fence, it could seriously mess up their approach and send them into several gymnastic maneuvers not meant for a plane. If they hit the patchy, uneven ground with a naked belly... well, Gapinski didn't want to think about that either.

They had to make it to the runway.

Within a few seconds, they'd know their outcome.

"Hold on!" Gapinski bellowed.

The plane entered the airport airspace with surprising speed considering it had been flying without engines. It barely missed the top of the fence as it barreled toward the runway. Super-bad scenario number one averted.

Now on to super-bad scenario number two.

Gapinski strained against the control wheel, pulling it with all he had to keep the plane's nose as high as possible in order to pass over the uneven dry ground below.

A few feet and they would hit the flat, smooth surface of the runway. All bets were off if they fell short.

It was going to be close.

Very close.

"Just a few more feet..."

The nose tipped down just as the bird came within a yard of the black pavement, clipping the dry earth on its approach.

It bounced high off its surface like a young child falling from a swing, Newton's third law of motion kicking in. The energy of the fall immediately compelled an opposite reaction, sending the nose high and the belly back to the earth, slamming hard against the blacktop. The force of the impact tilted the plane slightly to the right, cracking the wing in the middle.

"There goes the wing." Gapinski was sweating profusely trying to keep the plane stable. It bounced again, then slammed back down but remained fixed to the earth this time, skidding along the surface, the screech deafening. Sparks were cascading along both sides of the plane. The acrid smell of burning metal began to fill the cabin.

The end of the runway was quickly approaching, the plane leaning to the right as it continued skidding with seemingly endless amounts of energy. After that was the charred landscape of the Cuban island, some uncertain topography, and then another chain-link fence. At which point all bets were off.

Torres closed her eyes and crossed herself and started mumbling a prayer. Gapinski joined with his own appeal to the Almighty, but kept his eyes opened and firmly gripped the control wheel, keeping it as steady as he could.

Another hundred feet and they would be wishing for that turbulence again.

The bird started slowing as they approached the end. But would it be enough?

"Brace yourselves," Gapinski yelled.

The momentum suddenly shifted in their favor. The plane slowed even more, friction finally doing its job. Within a few seconds, they had stopped to a halt a few feet from the edge of the runway, the sound of sirens replacing the ring of panic in their ears.

Gapinski ripped the headset off, sighed, and slumped in his seat.

"Now that's what I call an entrance."

CHAPTER 21

YORK, PENNSYLVANIA.

W ithin seconds the cheering crowd had transformed into screams of panic and pandemonium.

Women were screaming. Parents were crying out their kids' names. Men were shouting for people to take cover and pointing in every direction looking for the source of terror. People were flooding in every direction, unsure where to find safety.

Secret Service agents flooded the stage. One group had surrounded Amos Young and bulldozed him off the platform behind black curtains. Another group had surrounded the fallen body of Reed, guns outstretched, while a smaller group prepared to extract him. A few seconds later, three agents carried him off the stage behind the protective curtains, ringed by five or six agents.

Silas whipped around to search for the origin of the shots. Having received training in the basics of sharpshooting as a Ranger, he could ballpark where the shots came from.

Given the trajectory of the shots, they had to have come from the left side of the stadium. The seating was more like a major league football field than a college campus, complete with two sections of bleachers and three levels of suites.

The perfect perch for anyone interested in orchestrating an assassination with clear shots of the stage and candidates.

He saw two figures silhouetted by the high sun running across the roof of the building. Barely noticeable, but there they were.

The shooters.

He looked back at the front platform, which by now had been cleared. He looked back toward the rooftop where the assassins had been staged, then at the sky and around the area.

He noticed there was no wind, and the sun was still at their backs.

If the assailants had meant to kill both candidates, they could have. Presumably, both were highly trained marksmen who had positioned themselves at the best possible location with perfect weather conditions within a more-than-comfortable kill zone.

One made his mark, the perfect kill-shot. The other one missed, by a wide margin.

Why?

Unless...

That was the point.

One was meant to make his mark, while the other one was meant to miss.

Which meant the Evangelical candidate, Matthew Reed, was supposed to die.

And the Mormon presidential candidate, Amos Young, wasn't. It was staged to look like he was, as if the terrorist assault was a broader attack on America's electoral system. Rather than just a surgical strike on a single candidate.

He had to get to the assailants. Stop them from escaping, identify them for the purpose of his own investigation.

But the crowds were surging now toward the main entrance to the field, in the opposite direction where the assassins had fled. And he was caught in the deluge, debris in the river of panicked bodies rushing away from the danger zone.

Then there was the fact he had to leave his weapon in his vehicle because of the tightened security. So even if he did catch up to them, he couldn't fend for himself anyway.

Time to make a decision.

He turned toward the main entrance and lurched forward with the crowd, pushing his way through until he had squeezed through the entrance and out into the wide-open campus. Sirens were screaming toward the heart of the university as Silas ran the length of the school to the library parking lot where his car was parked. Which was providential, since most everyone else was parked at the other end of campus and near another thoroughfare leading out of the school. He knew it would take several minutes for the perpetrators to get down from the three-story roof of that suite overhanging the north bleachers. Enough time for him to get back to his car and hopefully intercept them.

That was the plan, anyway. The hope.

Silas slid out of his parking spot and turned onto another road taking him around the backside of the campus toward the dormitories and the main center of campus of academic and student life buildings, including the stadium. He knew it was the only other road available to the hostiles. With any luck, he would intercept them.

As he raced toward the other side of campus, he came to a stop sign. He went to turn left when a vehicle rushed through a four-way stop from the same direction. Silas jammed on his brakes and his horn as the van passed, nearly toppling as it pivoted left.

A rust-colored monstrosity with a faded wrench and faucet.

And with the name of a plumbing company that was missing the 'P.'

Score.

He offered a prayer of thanksgiving for God's providence as he reached into his glove compartment to retrieve his weapon, his trusted Beretta M6. He chambered a round, then he swung his Honda around the four-way and floored it.

He kept at a distance from the vehicle ahead, which was snaking its way through the campus toward the main entrance. It turned sharply onto the main road of York, driving west away from the city.

A group of people fleeing from the stadium crossed the road. Silas had to slam on his brakes to keep from hitting them. A few turned toward him with their hands up, as if he were the gunman himself. He waved them along. They scurried across the road to safety.

He sped past the last of them then turned out of the main university entrance toward the assassins. He could see the van a quarter-mile ahead speeding past oncoming emergency and police vehicles. They had no idea they were heading in the wrong direction, that their object of desire was staring them in the face.

Silas pushed his Honda forward, but not too much. He hung back from the van to keep from arousing their suspicion. They had also slowed, probably with a similar idea. No use drawing attention to yourself when a stream of vehicles flashing the reds and blues were coming your way.

The road took them away from the university and police and media presence and out into the Pennsylvania countryside. As he drove, he dialed Radcliffe. Probably best to check in with the chief.

"Silas, are you alright? I've been watching CNN, saw the whole bloody spectacle! Were you there? Did you—"

"Yes, I was there. Saw the whole thing. As well as the two assailants."

"And?"

"It was Nous."

"You're certain?"

"Certain."

"But why? This makes no—"

"Late last night, I'm pretty sure the same hostiles kidnapped and then threatened me if I kept pursuing my investigation."

"What?"

"Slipped a black bag over my head and injected me with some paralytic liquid that made me go limp and black out."

"Why am I just now hearing about this? Are you alright?"

"I'll take your beating about protocol later. Anyway, one of them had a bird tattoo that matched ones I've seen before on other known Nous operatives. And the van they drove me in just barreled out of campus."

"Good Lord...Nous involved in assassinating an American presidential candidate? Seems so unlike them to get involved in something so overt that would draw attention to themselves."

Silas shook his head. "I don't get it either, but I'm tracking them now."

Suddenly, the van stopped short before a covered bridge, then took a sharp right down a dirt road. He knew exactly where they were heading.

The abandoned red-brick farmhouse.

It must have been a staging ground for the pair, which was why they had brought Silas there after they had kidnapped him from the library. He eased his Honda to the right down the dirt road, but let the van continue without following.

"Radcliffe, I've got to go. Their van just pulled off back to the abandoned house they left me in earlier this morning. I think I'm about to find our answers."

"Don't do anything rash, my boy. Perhaps you should wait for SEPIO back—"

"No time. It's now or never."

Radcliffe told him to be careful and call the minute he finished whatever incursion he was launching. Silas promised him he would and ended the call.

Made perfect sense for them to return to the house, as the authorities would never have figured the assassins would stay local. The police would probably broaden their search south toward Baltimore, east toward Philly, and north toward Harrisonburg and beyond. The pair would probably remain holed up inside until the heat passed before being extracted.

Which gave Silas the perfect opportunity to pounce.

He parked a half mile down the road from the house underneath a large weeping willow tree beside a quiet stream. He remembered seeing the other end of it cut through the property when he left the house. So he followed it back to the lair.

He ran along its short banks, recalling childhoods past when he and his brother Sebastian spent hours as pirates and marines and native warriors in the woods near their military base. Those were simpler times when all he had to worry about was staying quiet enough to surprise his brother during a raid on their tree fort or come home for dinner on time to avoid their father's paddle.

He wondered how Sebastian was doing as he snaked along the backwoods. Except for a brief phone call while he was in Chartres, France, while on mission a month ago, it had been months again since they had talked. He had meant to change that, but their relationship seemed unsalvageable at that point. Especially after the summer betrayal.

The sight of a rusty van peeking through the woods snapped his mind back to the moment.

Focus, Grey.

A breeze struck through the forest, and he breathed it in deeply and began counting backward from 1000 as he approached the property, part of a pre-game ritual he had developed during his tours in Iraq and Afghanistan to get his head in the action.

990. 989. 988.

He came up quickly to a massive oak tree roosting near the stream, crouching low and flexing his hand around his weapon. The smell of cooking meat caught his attention. His stomach rumbled in protest.

957. 956. 955. 95—

The front door opened and out walked two men.

One tall and slender, with a buzzed golden head. The other below average height, solid build, and bushy brown hair.

The men from the van. Couldn't be sure as they had been

masked, but they looked about right. The van certainly fit, and no one else seemed to be around.

The man with the buzz cut lit a cigarette. They started talking. He strained to hear the conversation, the whisper of the trees with the late-October breeze making it difficult.

"What now," the stocky man said to his partner.

The blond drew in deeply from a cigarette. "We wait."

"Wait? How long?"

"Weeks. A month or more."

"A month?" the stocky man said throwing his arms in the air.

"Yeah. A month. Orders from the man in the bow tie himself." The man blew out the blue smoke high into the air.

Man in the bow tie? Neither Silas nor SEPIO had known of another entity involved. He would have to circle back with Radcliffe about a possible identification of this mystery man. Could be an essential link in the conspiracy surrounding Young.

"Besides, the authorities will be wetting themselves searching the airports and train stations and buzzing up and down the highways stretching for miles from here. No way would they suspect the greatest political assassins since Lee Harvey Oswald are sitting and having a smoke a few miles up the road."

The other man started pacing head down, saying something Silas couldn't make out.

"Relax." The man took another drag on his cigarette. "We weren't supposed to prevent his escape anyway. Orders were to apprehend and intimidate, nothing more. We knew he'd escape. Any Ranger worth his salt would."

They knew he was a Ranger. Unsettling.

"What if he identifies us, turns us into the police?"

"What is he going to say? I was kidnapped by a tall skinny guy and a short stocky guy, both wearing masks and dressed in black? Big whoop."

"But—"

"Relax, Ruben." The man finished his cigarette and threw it to the ground. He walked over to his partner and slapped him on the back. "We did it. We made history. Now let's celebrate, shall we? A few more minutes and the steaks will be ready."

The blond turned around and opened the door. He walked through, the stocky man followed.

Silas flexed his fingers around the butt of his Beretta.

Time to move.

He padded across the open lot, weapon at the ready on taut arms outstretched in front. The soft carpet of ankle high grass muffled his steps, providing the perfect approach. He angled across the property from one oak to another. A few more steps and—

The porch door opened. He froze.

"Forgot the beer from—"

The stocky man froze, his expression one of shock. Then panic. A second later, he yelled behind him: "Ephraim, the rat is ba—"

In an instant, he fell backward from three shots to the chest. The shots clanged like clattering pots and pans throughout the property.

Since leaving the Rangers, Silas had vowed never to kill again. But it was either him or Ruben. And Silas preferred to live another day. Seemed like the new normal since joining with SEPIO.

He bypassed the porch and ran back along the stream, hugging the edge of the house and crouching under windows. There was a slim chance the cigarette man would rush to the porch, and he wanted to be far from it if he did.

He came to a corner and pressed his back against the outer wall. He waited for a beat, then quickly pivoted around the wall, weapon outstretched and ready for any danger.

There was none. Only a smoking grill full of sizzling steaks.

He was at the back of the house, near the kitchen where a screen door opened to a short set of stairs that led to the small back patio. Silas padded forward, crouching underneath a square window and settling next to the door, pressing his side against the building.

A long tear in its screen flapped in the breeze. From the other side he heard not a sound.

His breath caught in his throat at the uneasy silence. Adrenaline pinged his gut, causing him to look behind him.

Not there. So where was he?

Silas gripped his Beretta with his right hand, then slowly opened the screen door with his left. He positioned his foot just inside the doorway, letting the door rest against it. In one motion, he slid his leg inside, then quickly pulled his body forward inside the door frame and to the right inside a kitchen.

Empty, but for a colander of green beans in the sink and corn on the cob boiling on the stove. The lid made a rattling sound that he almost mistook for footsteps.

He stepped forward. The floor creaked. Badly. He held his breath, straining his eyes and weapon ahead. He waited for a second. Then he stepped to the left, hugging the countertop and passing by the square window. He saw nothing and no one.

The square window shattered behind him as three shots exploded through the glass.

Silas crouched low behind a counter bar that opened up into the main house. Without looking, he reached overtop and sent three of his own rounds into the black void, not knowing and not caring where they went.

He was a sitting duck. Not good.

He stole a quick glance above the countertop and saw the blond cigarette man crouching up a set of stairs near the front door. He had a height advantage, but he was exposed.

Four more rounds sent the man crouching for cover.

He couldn't do this all day. Eventually one of them would run out of rounds.

And Silas guessed the other guy was packing way more heat than he brought.

He popped up again quickly, saw the man and aimed.

A round exploded behind him, then another into the kitchen

door frame before he was able to pinch off four rounds himself.

The first one went high and wide behind the man.

The second one shattered the main stairway post to the man's left.

The third one splintered the railing, causing the man to stumble backward.

And the fourth round entered through the soft tissue of the man's upper right thigh, shattering his femur then tearing the femoral artery, and sending a geyser of blood shooting in the air.

Silas crouched low again as the man screamed and writhed in pain. Then he heard a thudding echo, several in rapid succession.

The man was scurrying up the stairs.

He cautiously stood, his legs taut like springs. He outstretched his Beretta, ready to fire at any sign of movement. He padded slowly through the dark space, tendrils of light filtering into the living room through the boarded windows and casting long shadows.

Holding his weapon firmly in front of him, Silas crept forward toward the stairwell. He twisted left and aimed up the wooden stairs to the second floor.

All was silent. The thudding echoes had stopped.

Streaming from the top was a rectangle cloud of light from the left, brought about by the illumination of dust from the only window on the second floor not boarded.

He stepped on the first step. It creaked loudly. Silas cringed and held his position, weapon trained upward.

Might as well just go for it.

He did, padding deliberately up the stairs following a trail of blood until he could make out the floor above.

He stopped and waited.

Nothing.

He saw more blood, crimson and smeared and angling toward the left.

Gotcha.

He inched upward, twisting his body right and ready for—

A barrage of rounds sprayed through a doorway, splintering the frame and exploding into the stairwell walls, catching Silas off guard.

He jumped left and tripped over his feet, sending him down the stairwell. He fell halfway before he was able to grab the railing with his free hand and stop his fall.

The gunfire stopped as suddenly as it began, followed by the familiar *click-click-click* echo of a weapon running on empty.

Silas brought himself upright but winced. He had twisted his ankle in the fall.

He pushed through the pain and quickly ascended the stairs, pivoting sharply to the left and inside the room and to the right.

Leaning against the far side underneath a window was the cigarette man, legs outstretched and arms to his side. His breathing was labored, but his eyes were staring forward still full of life.

"It's over, tough guy," Silas said, moving closer with weapon outstretched. That's when he saw the scar—wicked and jagged, running from ear to jaw. Just as Miles had described the hostile.

He narrowed his eyes. "You..."

Before he knew what happened, the man stuffed something into his mouth, bared those perfectly white teeth, and crunched down, grinding something between them before he swallowed hard.

"No!"

Silas moved quickly to the man's side and bent down, then grabbed his jaw and tried forcing it open.

But it was too late. The man's eyes rolled back, and his mouth started foaming.

The only link between the assassination of the Evangelical candidate and the wider Nous conspiracy had just ingested a suicide pill.

He thought that only happened in the movies.

Apparently not.

"Just great."

CHAPTER 22

NUEVA GERONA, CUBA.

W*hat a mess.*
Her first mission for SEPIO and they nearly crash-landed in the Caribbean. And they were no closer to discovering the location of the medallion or whether the lost civilization in the Honduran jungle was somehow connected with the Mormon account of early Mesoamerican history.

Then there was her uncle. He had entrusted this lucrative operation to her, lent her the equipment and the airplane. And what did she have to show for it?

Torres and Grant walked over to Gapinski as he finished debriefing with a tall man in military fatigues looking as if he was in charge.

"How goes it?" she said.

"Well, considering we just dropped 20,000 feet to God's green earth and lived to tell about it, I'd say pretty good."

"Did you get a look at the plane, our cargo?"

"Plane is toast, obviously. But miraculously nothing seemed damaged in the underbelly. The way we came in and slid down the runway probably prevented any damage. And that's one tough underside. Only problem is, we're stuck here until we can secure another plane."

"Already working on that. I called my uncle and told him the...news."

"How'd he take it?"

She shrugged. "Thankful I was alright. We all were alright. But understandably irate that his plane had crashed into pieces, vowing to get to the bottom of whatever happened. He's sending us another one of his planes to press onward, as well as a few of his own security detail."

"Can't be too careful I guess."

Another man in fatigues approached them. He was wiping grease off his hands with an old mechanic's rag.

"Hola," he said.

The three responded in kind.

"Se hablo español?"

Torres said she spoke Spanish, and the two began speaking together. The man was the chief mechanic for the airport, and he launched into a detailed explanation of their preliminary investigation into the cause of the crash.

"What's he saying?" Grant asked.

She held up a hand as the man continued speaking, wanting to get every detail. Her eyes narrowed at times, then her forehead creased in surprise.

Gapinski and Grant looked on as they spoke.

"Gracias, Mateo," she finally said.

The man smiled and nodded, then walked away.

"What's the word?" Gapinski asked.

Torres breathed in deeply. "Mateo, Matthew, the head mechanic for the airport, says the preliminary report blames the crash on a loss of fuel."

"No crap," Grant said.

"But here's the thing. The reason why we lost fuel is because the fuel line was cut."

He shook his head. "Wait, what? The line was cut?"

"Well, 'breached' is the word he used. It was severed in a way that delayed the flow of the fuel. His guess is we were meant to fall out of the sky farther out at sea, but the turbulence we experienced jostled the line, causing more fuel to leak and flow than intended."

"So foul play?" Gapinski said.

She nodded. "He said there's no other way to put it. We've been sabotaged."

Grant put a hand on his forehead. "What the..."

"There's only one party that would want to take us out and stop us from reaching those ruins."

Gapinski nodded. "Nous."

"Has to be. There must be something to this medallion and this lost city. The fact they went to such lengths as to cut our fuel line in the hopes we'd crash and burn, or crash and drown is nutso to the max."

Grant's eyes widened. He looked away, recognition flashing across his face.

"What is it?" Torres asked.

He looked at her and shook his head. "It's nothing...I'm sure."

Gapinski stepped forward. "Buddy, in our line of work there's no such thing as 'it's nothing, I'm sure.' Do you know something? Did you see something?"

Grant looked at the ground. "Well, there was this guy. A mechanic. He bumped into me after coming out from underneath the plane."

"OK..."

"It's stupid, but I saw something when he lifted his hands in apology. A tattoo of some sort."

"Like a bird? A phoenix?"

"Not that. It looked like the tail of a...of a snake."

Gapinski looked at Torres then whipped out his phone and dialed a number.

"As I said, it's probably nothing."

Gapinski looked at him while his phone dialed, and said, "What did I say about—"

"Gapinski," Torres said cutting him off. "What is it?"

He frowned. "The tattoo."

"What about it? It's not Nous."

"Yeah, I know. It's far worse."

She furrowed her brow in confusion. "What could be worse?"

"Radcliffe, it's Gapinski. Yeah, we've had a slight development. First off, we nearly crashed to our death."

"Put it on speaker," she said.

He did. "Radcliffe, you're on speaker now. Come again."

"I asked, you what?"

Torres said, "Our fuel line was messed with in Miami before we took off, which caused fuel to leak. We almost crashed halfway."

Gapinski continued, "But don't worry, I managed to land us safely on a small island south of Cuba. Well, safe is relative. All that matters is that we're alive."

"Praise the Lord for that!" Radcliffe said.

"But we've got a bigger issue." He looked to Torres. "Like Torres said, our fuel line was messed with. Or, rather, someone messed with our fuel line. Head mechanic on site at the airport says we've been sabotaged."

"Good Lord! How did this happen?"

"Grant remembers some shifty-looking dude coming out from underneath the plane before we boarded. And get this: he thought he saw a snake's tail poking out from underneath his mechanic uniform."

Radcliffe went silent for a moment. He continued in a low voice, "Are you sure? A tattoo of a snake?"

Gapinski looked to Grant for confirmation. The man nodded. "That's right. Grant here. I'm pretty sure it was a snake."

"Well that ups the ante, that's for sure," Radcliffe said.

"Clearly, I'm in the dark," Torres said. "What's the deal with the snake tattoo?"

"Danites," Gapinski said.

"Who?"

Radcliffe explained, "The Danites were a fraternal organization founded by the Mormons in 1838. They operated as a vigilante group and took a central role in the events of the 1838 Mormon War."

Gapinski snorted. "Vigilante group is putting it mildly. Think the Swiss guards of the Vatican."

"So, what, they're like the secret police of the Latter-day Saints, or something?" Torres asked.

He nodded. "And their symbol is the snake. Their methods have been rumored to involve policing, paramilitary and militia duties for the religion, covert operations like guerrilla warfare, even assassinations."

Grant asked, "And these are the fellas that severed our fuel line?"

"Appears that way. If you saw a snake tattoo on a guy walking away from our plane after having just serviced it mechanically, then we just got screwed over by the Mormon mafia."

"But I thought that Nous organization, or whatever the hell it's called is what's been dogging us. They stole the medallion. Torres confirmed the tattoo symbol."

Gapinski shrugged. "Looks like there's another sheriff in town."

"Or," Radcliffe added, "we know for certain now that Nous and the Mormons are working together."

"Nous and the Mormons in cahoots? But why? What could the Latter-day Saints possibly have in common with an avid enemy of the Church? Doesn't make sense."

Torres said, "It does if you're seeking to find archaeological and historical evidence to validate a religious text that undermines the historic Christian faith."

Radcliffe added, "And just as a Mormon has become the Republican candidate for president."

She smiled skeptically. "You think there's still a connection between the two?"

"I do." He paused, then whispered: "Now more than ever."

"How certain? Have there been any developments with Silas?" Radcliffe said nothing.

Gapinski looked at Torres. "Radcliffe, you there?"

He paused again, then continued, "There's been a shooting."

Torres's eyes widened. "A shooting? Where? Is Silas alright?"

"Silas is fine. It's the other guy. Matthew Reed."

Gapinski said, "The spoilsport Evangelical?"

"Yes. He's dead. Assassinated at a political rally organized by the Faithful Majority. He and Amos Young were set to debate Lincoln-Douglas style when two sharpshooters took out Reed and nearly took out Young. But it seems likely that the attempt on Young's life was merely a ruse."

"Well ain't that a fine kettle of fish," Grant said.

"Always something," Gapinski said.

Radcliffe continued, "Silas was at the rally and saw the gunmen, then he took off after them after the shots rang out and Reed fell."

"That's my boy!" Grant said.

Torres said, "Did he catch up with them? Find out any leads?"

"We're waiting to hear back from him. But there is an added layer to it all. The night before, Silas had been conducting research at the university's library when he was kidnapped."

"Kidnapped?" Grant and Torres both exclaimed.

"By whom?" asked Gapinski.

"Is he alright?" asked Torres.

"He's fine. Got knocked around a bit, and they tried to scare him off from pursuing his investigation into Young. Of course, Silas declined their invitation and went to the debate anyway."

"That's my boy," Grant said again.

"But he did catch sight of the telltale signs of Nous. The infamous stick-bird tattoo we've all come to know and love. And, apparently, they were the same fellows who just felled Reed."

Torres interrupted. "Wait a minute. You're telling us that Nous just took out the independent Evangelical candidate?"

"It appears so. And I have to imagine that your own attempted takedown and the assassination of the independent candidate are linked. In this case to tamper with the election—"

"And elect Amos Young President of the United States," Gapinski said. "The first Mormon candidate for president."

"Exactly."

Gapinski put a hand on his hip. "So let me get this straight. A few days before we leave for Honduras a Nous operative hijacks our medallion with a map to a lost civilization settlement that's found at a Mormon archaeological dig, which presumably points to lost tribes of Israel described in the Book of Mormon. Then when we set sail to go find said civilization to validate the Book of Mormon account, a Danite messes with our fuel line and probably our landing gear, nearly sending us to Davey Jones's Locker. And along the way another Nous operative takes out an independent presidential candidate after kidnapping Silas and warning him to back off, basically handing the election to a Mormon. That about sum up our current situation?"

Radcliffe paused. "That sounds like the long and short of it, yes. Do you have a plan to move forward and get to those lost ruins?"

Torres spoke. "I've already spoken to my uncle and have a second plane arranged. He's sending some trusted guys to help out. Give us another day, and we'll be scoping out the region of that medallion map in no time."

"Excellent. I don't think I have to spell out what we are facing, here, and why your mission is even more vital than ever. And I also don't think it's too much hyperbole to suggest that the Christian faith even depends upon it. The separation of Church and State, and integrity of the authentic Christian faith are hanging in the balance. So get to work."

CHAPTER 23

"What the hell just happened?" Young roared at the man in the bow tie sitting across from him at a secure location outside the city.

He was still having a hard time catching his breath and moderating his pulse three hours after an assassin took out his political opponent and nearly sent him to early retirement, as well.

The sound of the exploding podium still echoed in his head. The sound of his opponent's exploding head was even more etched into his memory, a juicy watermelon being sliced in two replaying itself on an endless loop. The last thing he remembered from the morning was seeing the body of Matthew Reed slump to the floor like a rumpled bathrobe. That image, too, was on repeat.

A large splinter of the shattered wooden podium had been embedded in Young's right arm, which had to be pulled out by a Secret Service doctor. He would be fine, but the bandage was a constant memory chaser of the morning's event. He swore he was still finding pieces of wood embedded in his clothing even after changing.

Within seconds of shots being fired, Secret Service agents had surrounded him and shoved him off stage and behind the protective black curtain, and then into an awaiting van on the other side of the field house, which brought him to the secure location even he didn't know where. Twenty minutes later, his family was brought to him, and then shortly after that his senior staff. Everyone was understandably shaken. Young had to put on a brave face to comfort his hysterical wife and sobbing kids and frightened staff. It was only now, alone with the man he had grown to loathe, that he could let loose.

"Relax, Amos. Pull yourself together."

"Relax?" Young roared again. He looked around the empty room, then closed his eyes and took a breath. No need to draw any unneeded attention to the man no one was supposed to know about.

He continued in a more hushed tone. "What do you mean, relax? I was nearly taken out by terrorists!"

"Don't be silly. You weren't."

Young leaned forward. "What do you mean?"

The man breathed in, sat back, and crossed his legs. "Everything went positively according to plan."

"What do you mean, according to plan?" he hissed. "This was you?"

"The less you know, the better."

Dear God, what have they done?

The man continued, "All that matters is that the man standing between you and the presidency has been...removed. Word on the terrorist attack, as you put it, has already filtered out into the wider American public through Facebook and Twitter. Any wavering Republicans and evangelical Republicans who had been siding with Reed will come flocking to your side. Not only because you're a survivor and sympathy tends to draw people like flies to a porch light. But also because they can't stomach voting for a Catholic Democrat no matter how skeptical they might be of a Mormon Republican."

Young said nothing. He looked away from the man and out the

window of their top-story room, his brain a fog of jumbled thoughts.

This can't be real.

"Tonight you'll be polling comfortably ahead of Santos and outside the margin of error with ten days to go until the election—Mr. President."

His head snapped back to the man. Mr. President. He liked the sound of that. A weak smile escaped. He quickly drew it back in and stood and walked to the window.

"I need you to be honest with me," Young said staring at the emergency vehicles below. "Did the Quorum know about this? Were they aware?"

The man sat still, unmoving and unspeaking.

Young didn't turn around, the red and blue lights below having a calming effect on his mood. He was going to wait for his response.

Finally, the man said, "They were more than aware. They gave the go-ahead."

He let a sigh slip. It wasn't the course of action he would have chosen. He wanted to win, yes. But this? Yet, he had to admit, it had gotten the job done.

"Why didn't they tell me?"

"Would it have mattered if they had?"

Probably. Which was the point. Their goals were the same. He just wanted to take the moral high road to get there. This was a different path on an entirely different planet, one a shadowy organization had been inhabiting for millennia.

When he had been approached early in his campaign by a one Rudolf Borg, a tall man with a menacing grin and darkness in his eyes, he was skeptical. The Mormon President, Russell Nelson himself, had made the introduction, bringing him before the Quorum. He had never heard of the man's religious order, Nous, but the current President of the Church of Jesus Christ of Latter-day Saints vouched for him. Apparently, the two of them had a history. He had explained to Young how his organization and the

Church had similar interests, and that their work behind the scenes could ensure victory.

The man made an impassioned plea for how aligning into a partnership would be mutually beneficial for their shared ideals and principles. Ones of purity and enlightenment; of self-discipline and self-salvation through the impartation of secret knowledge; of the Republic of Heaven, established through the hands of able-bodied, enlightened men; of attaining the celestial realm and the godhood.

Of a political restoration movement within America.

President Nelson had gone further in his revelation, explaining how Nous had influenced the course of various spiritual movements through history and had, in fact, been closely aligned with his own religion founded by Joseph Smith. Young remembered being shocked by this revelation. The others had not been. He knew running for office and joining the upper echelons of his religion would afford him certain privileged information. He just hadn't been prepared for this type of revelation.

In the end, the Quorum voted to align with Nous and granted them wide latitude for unfolding their mutually shared vision for America, solidifying a partnership that had begun nearly 200 years prior.

Young shoved aside the memory of those initial events of his campaign. He turned around and put his hands in his pockets. "What now?"

"Now, go gather with your family and get in front of the cameras. ASAP. The country needs to see you alive and healthy. And also resolute. Take a pill, take ten if you need to. But there can be no emotion other than steely resolve to fight for the American people and fight against the terrorism that killed a fine American patriot—blah, blah, blah."

He leaned against the window and nodded. "What about the other thing? Are we any closer?"

"You worry about this thing. Let us worry about the other thing. Within days we'll have what we need."

He sighed and nodded again, then nodded toward the door. The man stood up silently and went to walk out, but then stopped. "I almost forgot."

The man turned to face Young. "The Quorum is meeting the day after next and requires your presence."

Amos caught his breath, then recovered. He nodded and told him he would be there. Then the man walked out.

He turned back around and looked out of the window. A swarm of media trucks had assembled outside. Apparently, it wasn't as secure of a location as the Secret Service had thought.

Several minutes ticked by as he continued staring, letting his mind rest from the madness of the day and what was unfolding. What he himself was unfolding in due time.

Matthew Reed was dead.

He let that sink in, and all of the implications that meant—not least of which was for his campaign.

His goal was within reach. He could see it, taste it, feel it. Just another week and it would be his.

Then a few more months and all would be won, all would be theirs.

Until then, it was show time.

CHAPTER 24

Silas sat next to the lifeless body in the second-floor room running the series of events that had unfolded that day through his mind.

After the blond man had convulsed to his death, Silas had walked downstairs to the assailant he had killed on the front porch. He had retrieved his weapon and checked the man over. There was no ID, but there was that tattoo he had seen earlier.

He had dragged the body inside the red house and secured the door, hoping no random motorist had driven down the country road and spotted it. Then he had returned upstairs where he checked the pulse of the man lying a few feet from his side to confirm he was dead. He was.

He sat next to the man and contemplated the gravity of what had transpired over the past fourteen hours and the implications of it all.

Nous had kidnapped him, and then warned him to back off pursuing anything about Young's Mormonism, his connection with the Faithful Majority and partnership with James Maxwell, and the medallion. Nous had taken out one of the U. S. presidential candidates and had almost taken out another, though he was sure that second attempt was a ruse. And the two assassins were lying dead with him inside an old abandoned farmhouse a few miles away.

He sighed and rubbed his face. What a day. And what did he have to show for it? Sure, confirmation Nous was definitely involved in the assignations and the warning against pursuing Young and the medallion, which also definitely suggested their involvement directly with the Young campaign as well as the medallion itself.

But beyond that, nothing hard, nothing substantial to break open the conspiracy and bring clarity to both confusing scenarios.

He sat staring at the ceiling and gently banged his head against the wall. He thought back to that cryptic warning. He could have sworn he had heard it before or read it somewhere. He closed his eyes to recall the exact wording again.

We have solemnly warned you, and in the most determined manner, that if you do not cease this course of wanton abuse of one of our own, that vengeance will overtake you, and that when it does come it will be as furious as the mountain torrent, and as terrible as the beating tempest.

He opened his eyes. He had an idea. He took out his mobile and brought up its browser. Then he went to Google and typed in the exact phrase he had memorized, all of it, and hit Search.

He clicked the first page that appeared, one from Wikipedia. The first sentence told him all he needed to know.

"Are you kidding me?"

He brought up his contacts and dialed Radcliffe. His mind was racing as he waited for him to pick up.

This couldn't be true. But if it was, this changed everything.

"Silas, my boy, I've been worrying my head off over here waiting for—"

"Radcliffe," he interrupted, "this whole thing just took a turn toward the crazy!"

"Oh? Can I assume, then, that you found something of import in your raid on that Nous lair?"

"You could say that. Before the Nousati dumped me off at that abandoned house, one of the guys warned me to drop investigating Young and his campaign. And he used this odd phrase, saying they had solemnly warned me in the most determined manner that if I didn't cease my course of wanton abuse that vengeance would overtake me as furious as the mountain torrent, and as terrible as the beating tempest."

"That's what he said?"

"Almost word for word. I could have sworn that I had heard or read the warning before. The words sounded so familiar, but I couldn't place them. So I just googled what I remembered before I called you and discovered where it came from and why it had been so familiar."

He took a breath, then said, "It's the Latter-day Saints, Radcliffe. A warning from some vigilante group within the Mormon Church called—"

"The Danites..."

"How'd you know?"

"Let me ask you this: did one of the assailants bear a tattoo resembling a snake of some sort?"

"Not sure. Let me check."

He lifted the dead man's sleeve, expecting the infamous stick-figure bird. Instead, there was something else poking out from underneath his jacket sleeve. A snake, black and coiled and ready to strike.

"Yes, actually. The lead guy has it on his forearm. And get this: its the same guy who raided my Princeton office looking for Grant's Mormon medallion."

"Are you sure?"

"Pretty sure. He's got a wicked scar running down his face like Miles described.

"Bloody hell. Well, the plane carrying your mate and Gapinski and Torres was sabotaged by a man bearing the same markings. Nearly sent them to the bottom of the ocean."

"Goodness! Are they alright?"

"They made it, by the providential hand of God, no doubt. I am certain the Danites were responsible, just as they were apparently involved in the raid on your office trying to get their hands on that medallion. Our organization has faced this menace on and off since the nineteenth century. Over the years, they have varied their role within the religion to internal enforces of their laws to external threats and activities, even political. In recent years, they have become something of a theological propaganda machine, trying to make the Mormon faith respectable and an alternative sect of Christianity. Chaos and confusion are their tactics. And they play them in spades."

"Looks like their chaos weapon of choice was just masterfully played." Then he whispered, "But what about Young..."

"What's that you say?"

Silas shook his head. "I just said, what about Young? What's his involvement? He has never shown himself to be anything but a family man and faithful Mormon, like any run-of-the-mill church-goer. No different from Reed, in fact. God rest his soul."

"What are you getting at?"

"What I'm getting at is, at this point we know that, along with Nous, some fringe vigilante sect within the Mormon Church is involved with what just went down at Freedom University! Makes sense they'd want their man in the highest office in the land—but this is just crazy. And is it a bigger conspiracy? Who else does it involve? Young himself, even Maxwell?"

Radcliffe coughed, nearly choking. "I cannot imagine James Maxwell was just involved in assassinating a presidential candidate!"

"Alright, probably not that. But..."

"But what?"

Silas shook his head again. "We're flying blind here, Radcliffe. The election is nearly a week away and has just been overturned by two October surprises. The Faithful Majority has endorsed a Mormon Republican candidate. Which is already creating confusion about what is authentically Christian. We've got a dead independent Evangelical candidate on our hands now who, by all accounts, was assassinated by Nousati with connections to a vigilante group in the Mormon Church. Then there's the fact some Mormon relic was unearthed that may or may not corroborate the historicity of the Book of Mormon, which will lead to a whole other set of issues with the historicity of the Christian faith. There are just too many unknowns and missing pieces."

"I agree. The good news is that Gapinski and Torres and your mate should be heading to Honduras soon. So we should have clarity on that puzzle piece in short order."

"Finally, some good news!"

"But I do agree. At the other end, there are a whole lot of unknown variables."

Silence fell between them as they both contemplated the gravity and confusion surrounding the turn of events. Silas looked at the body of the dead Nous operative, who apparently was also part of a paramilitary group in the Mormon church.

While cradling the phone, he slipped a hand inside a front pocket but found nothing. He repeated the search in the other one. He scored something. He pulled it out. It was a business card of some sort.

The Society for New World Archaeology. Asher Avard, President.

He remembered that was the very organization that had sponsored Grant's archaeological dig in Missouri. *Interesting.*

"Radcliffe, hold up. I found something."

"What's that?"

"A business card with some name on it. *The Society for New World Archaeology.* The same outfit that had been running Grant's dig."

"Goodness."

"Hold on a second."

He cradled the phone again, then took hold of a zipper on the man's black jacket and pulled down on it, then pulled it back to reveal the insides.

Something slipped out of a side pocket, falling out to the floor. He picked it up.

"I found something else."

"What's that?"

"Looks like some sort of an ID badge, for an Asher Avard. The same owner of the business card from that Society."

"Where to?"

He shook his head. "Not sure. Doesn't say. It's got the picture of the guy lying in front of me, who I assume is this Asher Avard character. It's also got some sort of microchip embedded underneath." He flipped it over, and that's when the light caught something.

"Wait a minute...there's some sort of holographic image on the back." He moved his hand right and left, up and down to let the light reveal the image again.

Silas furrowed his brow. He saw what looked like the profile of a man holding a long stem up to his mouth, the end in the shape of a funnel.

He recognized it immediately.

"Major score" was all he could say.

"What is that?" Radcliffe asked.

Silas's mouth went dry, and his hand went limp with the significance of what he was holding. "I think it's an ID card to the Salt Lake Temple."

"What?" Radcliffe exclaimed.

"The, the card. The ID card or entrance keycard or whatever it is. On the back is a holographic image of Moroni, the golden Angel Moroni that stands on top of the capstone of the temple. I read in my research how it symbolizes the angel mentioned in Revelation 14:6 that will come to welcome in the Second Coming of Christ. It's on this card! This Asher guy must have worked there. Or at least had access privileges there. We can use this to get inside and get to the bottom of this conspiracy!"

"Come home, Silas. Immediately get in your car and drive back to DC. You could be in danger, and we need to prep you for phase two of your mission. Salt Lake City, Utah."

Silas stood, ready to leave. "Agreed."

"And, Silas, do you have a knife on you?"

He furrowed his brow. He always carried a knife on him, but what did it matter? The assassins were dead.

"Yes, why?"

"Because we're going to need his hand. Both of them."

"Excuse me?" he exclaimed.

"There might be a microchip embedded in one of them that gives high-ranking Mormon officials access to the building. We can't be sure the card is all you'll need. Which is why we need..." He trailed off.

Silas said nothing. He stood at the room door staring at the dead blond man, contemplating what he was being asked to do.

"Radcliffe...Are you sure about this? Cutting off a man's hands—"

"Just get them," Radcliffe interrupted. "And meet back at SEPIO headquarters, pronto. You're going to need lots of preparation for this mission." Radcliffe ended the call.

Silas slid the phone back in his pants pocket, then reached down inside his boot and retrieved the serrated knife he'd had since his time as a Ranger. Never left home without it.

Never thought he would use it for what he was being asked to do, either.

He stepped over to the man whose arms were outstretched and resting before him, as if he were offering them as a gift.

Silas crossed himself before crouching down.

Sorry, man.

CHAPTER 25

LA MOSQUITIA, HONDURAS.

"Are we there yet?" Torres shouted over the din of the twin-prop Cessna engines as the plane floated over the lush canopy below.

"You're as bad as my nephew," Gapinski shouted back. "We'll get there when we get there!"

She huffed and folded her arms. The anticipation was killing her. She was on the verge of uncovering one of the greatest remaining anthropological and archaeological mysteries of the century. And waiting had never been her strong suit.

Green hills flowed beneath her like an emerald ocean under a glass-bottom boat. All shades of green—mint, asparagus, lime, teal, aquamarine, you name it—were unrolling before them in giant puff-balls of opulent beauty. The River Pao, a lazy flow of chocolate, snaked through the jungle canopy. A flock of large winged birds floated out of the trees away from the plane. She smiled, wondering what their world below looked like, and what it had been hiding for millennia.

It was great being back in the saddle of her own exploration again. After they had been marooned on the small island south of Cuba, the trio had booked hotel rooms for the night while waiting for her uncle to send help. The next afternoon another plane arrived with three others, ex-military contractors with Blackwater. She thought they were overkill, but her uncle wasn't having any of it. He had phoned in a favor, got the extra manpower, and sent them her way overnight. A day later they were finally in Honduras flying a rented Cessna toward a point nestled in the mountains with thick tree coverage at the head of a river that the Mormon medallion seemed to indicate was the location of a civilization.

Probably Ciudad Blanca, possibly the purported lost tribes of Israel.

But that was to be determined.

Grant leaned close over her shoulder to join her view, his body pressing close against her. He smelled of cheap hotel soap and weeks-old clothes and the coffee from that morning, a heavenly combination that made her heart beat faster.

"Killer view," he said grinning. "Can't wait to slog through the underworld and dig up what's been hiding underneath for the past 1400 years."

"What my uncle wouldn't give right now to be up here with me. He used to tell me stories about the ancient lost civilization as a girl. It's been one of his dreams to discover the hidden city and return it back to his people."

He snuggled his face in closer to her shoulder. "I'm sure he's thrilled his favorite niece is the one up here leading the charge."

She smiled, and simply said, "Yeah."

"Alright, Ms. Impatient Pants," Gapinski said up front. "We're nearing the coordinates you gave me."

She startled and turned around to face a sizable green box positioned in the center of the plane. She flipped the switch on the unit. It hummed to life and ran through its start-up cycle.

"What is that contraption anyway?" Gapinski said from the front.

"A LiDAR imaging scanner," she said casually as she fiddled with the unit.

"Oh," he replied. "And...what is that?"

"Light radar. Short for Light Imaging, Detection, And Ranging. It's a surveying method that measures the distance to a target by illuminating it with a pulse of laser light. Then it measures the reflected pulses with a sensor. The technology was developed soon after the discovery of lasers in the early '60s. Basically, it works like a radar by bouncing lasers off of objects, capturing what's reflected back and measuring the time it takes to go there and back, giving someone the distance.

"NASA used it to map the moon's surface and do large-scale terrestrial charting, but it's only been in the last few decades that the resolution needed for archaeological explorations has been fine-tuned enough. They began testing the advanced radar system over various jungle areas in the mid-'90s to determine if the radar could penetrate the dense foliage to reveal what was below."

"And?"

"One team found ruins of a previously unknown, twelfth-century temple hidden underneath the tree canopy in Cambodia. Another uncovered old trade routes across the Arabian Desert, tracked the old Silk Road, mapped Civil War sites."

"Wow! That's crazy amazing."

She chuckled. "Sure is. By combining digitized images in different wavelengths of infrared light and radar and running it through computer algorithms, we're now able to see fifteen feet below the desert and basically peel back the treetops to see what lies beneath. It has totally revolutionized archaeology. Really, the greatest archaeological advance since carbon-14 dating."

Grant scoffed.

She folded her arms. "What?"

A playful grin splayed across his face. "LiDAR produces images of landscapes faster than people walking the same area, and with more detail, sure. I'll give you that. But the greatest archaeological advance since carbon-14 dating? Come on! High-resolution images are not good archaeology. All it offers is discovery, not knowledge. LiDAR may be good science, but it ain't good archeology."

She slugged him in the arm.

"Ouch! What'd ya do that for?"

"You self-righteous little purest snob! I may not have been on fancy digs paid for by deep-pocketed sugar daddies, but I've done good work with LiDAR. Made some important discoveries, so don't knock it 'til you try it, buddy."

Grant held up his hands in surrender. "Alright, alright! Let's see how this contraption...err, this magnificent piece of archaeological hardware of yours works."

She smiled slightly then set to work at the LiDAR computer station.

"So, will this doohickey of yours actually see through the trees to the world below?" Gapinski asked.

Torres glanced at Grant who was suppressing a grin.

"Not exactly. The LiDAR beam doesn't actually penetrate through the trees."

"In fact, it bounces off every leaf and twig," Grant said.

"But it does pulse through the tiny holes and gaps in the canopy to the ground below and reflect back to the plane. If you've ever laid down in a forest or a jungle, you can see through to the sky through all of those flecks. That's what LiDAR exploits to see the world below, creating what scientists call a 'point cloud,' billions of points showing the location of everything those laser beams touch. The software on this computer here eliminates all of the leaf and twig readings to piece together only the relevant terrain features for our archaeological purposes. Including roads and buildings and temples and monuments and whatever else was left behind from Ciudad Blanca.

"Once the equipment is primed and ready, we can position the plane and start our passes. We've got to map four quadrants covering a hundred square miles. So get comfortable. There's a long day ahead of us."

Fifteen minutes later Torres directed Gapinski toward the first quadrant, T1, and instructed him to level off the plane to an altitude of 2,500 feet above the ground. Once in place, she started the imaging collection of the green-box computer terminal. For the next few hours, the Cessna flew back and forth in a lawnmower pattern over the jungle, bombarding its canopy below with 125,000 infrared laser pulses per second and recording the reflections on a large disc attached to the underside of the plane. As the beams bounced back, the elapsed time would give the exact distance from the plane to the reflection point, offering the explorers a map of the world below.

At several points the plane was buffeted by thermals, knocking it back and forth, up and down. Torres thought she was on the verge of retching at one point, but the feeling passed. She was drenched with sweat, both from the experience but also from the cramped space.

By late mid-afternoon, everyone was getting restless. They had enough fuel for another two hours, but the soaring temperatures and the constant jostling and monotony were threatening to ground their mission.

"How much longer?" Gapinski asked over the din of the engine. "My stomach is eating itself, and I have to pee like a racehorse!"

"We've just finished quadrant T3. Another hour or so and we should have all four quadrants mapped."

"Another hour?" He exclaimed, turning over his right shoulder and taking the plane with him.

"Hey, watch it!" She checked the LiDAR imaging as the plane veered off course momentarily.

He righted the bird back on course. "Sorry! But seriously, I don't know how much more of this I can take."

"Just keep the plane on course, you big baby. We'll be finished soon enough."

He mumbled something under his breath and saluted her, then kept flying the course she had laid out for him.

Over an hour later, Torres announced good news to all: "That does it! Let's head back to Guanaja."

"For real?" Gapinski said, turning around again. And tilting the plane.

"Dude," Grant said, "You've gotta stop doing that!"

He banked the plane even more for good measure. "How's that? You like that?"

"I think I'm gonna be sick, dude. Stop it!"

Gapinski laughed and righted the plane then set a course due east. Soon he had landed the plane and taxied it to a private hangar her uncle reserved. The ex-military crew sent over by her uncle helped them unload the bulky LiDAR equipment, and Torres quickly went to work crunching the data to produce images that would, hopefully, give them a glimpse of the world below the tree line. Meanwhile, the boys wandered off to rustle up some food.

"We come bearing gifts," Gapinski said twenty minutes later, grinning and holding large brown-paper bags.

"Great timing," Torres replied. "The software is nearly finished crunching the data. The raw images should start to resolve shortly."

Grant rushed over. Gapinski crunched into a taco.

It was the moment of truth. Either there would be indications of a civilization in the valley, or not. Which meant either the medallion had a map to such a lost civilization etched on its surface, or not. And the Book of Mormon correctly recorded the history of the lost tribes of Israel.

Or not.

Grant bent over an LCD screen next to Torres. There was his scent again. Heaven. She swore she could feel heat radiating from his body. She inched closer, drawn to her former lover in the thrill of the archaeological chase. If Gapinski hadn't been crunching away over her shoulder, she would have taken his hand.

"Here they are!" Grant exclaimed, shaking her from her trance.

She breathed in sharply, making a squeaking sound like a balloon.

"Would you look at that..." was all Grant could muster.

"Whoa," Gapinski said as he crunched the last of his tacos.

The images were in grayscale, but they were unmistakable. In the T1 quadrant north of the streams, there were two rectangular features and several long, pyramid-like mounds arranged in blocks covering an area of a hundred acres or so, as well as two objects that looked like square pillars.

While Gapinski wouldn't have known what they were looking at, the two historians were stunned. There they were: a large set of ruins that seemed to be from a vast city and were part of a lost civilization.

They had found Ciudad Blanca.

"These ruins definitely are not Mayan," Grant said first. "These belong to an ancient culture all their own. They must have dominated the region centuries ago."

Torres pointed at the screen. "Look at the ceremonial architecture, here, and the giant earthworks and all of the plazas scattered about in quadrants T1 and T3."

"So it's a city, then?" Gapinski asked.

"Telltale archaeological signs of cities, no doubt," Torres answered. "Not how an average person would define one, mind you. But for us anthropologists, a city is a complex social organization that has multiple functions, with stratified populations and clearly defined divisions of space connected to the surrounding villages spread out in all directions in the region. Cities had specific functions in these kinds of civilizations, which were mostly and especially ceremonial. They were heavily invested in agriculture, so you had granaries and markets to store and sell the goods. And then they housed the civilization's major monuments."

"Is it a big one?" he asked.

She smiled. "Oh, yeah."

"Massive," Grant added. "I've seen the major Mayan city of Copán in western Honduras. And this one is definitely comparable. Over two square miles, I'd reckon. And look at these settlements stretching outward in T1. I count eleven of these along the river. Maybe more. Probably part of a chiefdom ruling the river valley.

Definitely larger than anything I've ever heard being found in the Mosquitia region. There has to be farming hamlets, here, and monumental architecture, canals, and roads, even signs of terraced hills."

"Reminds me of some of the other major settlements in the region," Torres added. "Like Las Crucitas de Aner."

"But this has got to be three, four, maybe five times as big!"

She turned to Grant. "You know what this means?"

He smiled and nodded.

"This unknown civilization had been widespread, spreading out from this central polis. Like LA or New York. Possibly just as or even more powerful and successful than the Mayans! We've found it. We've discovered Ciudad Blanca!"

Instinctively, she threw her arms around Grant, then drew back in surprise.

"Sorry..." she said, reddening and pushing her hair behind her ears.

He smiled. "Oh, come on. For old time's sake."

She smiled back, then embraced him. He wrapped his arms around her, then tightened his grip slightly. She let him.

Finally, some good news.

"But guys," Gapinski said turning around toward them. "Doesn't that also mean the medallion is right?"

Torres let go of Grant, so did he. She shook her head and frowned. "What do you mean?"

"Hello? Aren't you forgetting the map that led us to this place was found at some Mormon hole in the ground?"

Torres and Grant looked at each other.

He continued, "For decades, historians have totally doubted the account of the Book of Mormons, saying it's junk history. That the entire book, not to mention the religion itself, hinges on whether this account is true, if it's factual. If it's *historical*."

The two said nothing.

Gapinski threw his hands in the air. "Well, doesn't this prove them wrong? That the lost tribes of Israel really did settle in the Americas? That the account of the Lamanites is true. That the Book of Mormon is true." He stopped to let that sink in, then said, "That Mormonism itself is true?"

Did it?

As if reading her mind Grant turned to her. "Only one way to find out. After all, you know what they say."

"What's that?" Gapinski asked.

Torres answered for Grant: "A site isn't really 'found' until it's ground-truthed, verified with boots on the ground."

Next stop: Ciudad Blanca.

CHAPTER 26

WASHINGTON, DC.

Silas was awakened by the smell of brewing coffee and frying bacon. Nothing like them in all the world. For a moment he had forgotten where he was. A dull throbbing in his hand reminded him.

He had driven the two hours south from York to SEPIO headquarters at the Washington National Cathedral after he completed the gruesome task of severing both of the blond man's hands. He understood why it was necessary; there very well could be a subcutaneous microchip embedded in either of his hands. But he gained no pleasure from doing it. He had carefully wrapped them in the man's jacket and set them in the trunk, hoping the smell of severed flesh wouldn't reach the main cabin. Thankfully it hadn't.

It was a good thing he followed through on Radcliffe's request because Zoe had indeed found a rice-sized microchip on the underside of his right palm. An on-site doctor had cleaned and sterilized the chip and inserted it underneath Silas's own skin. He didn't like the idea of being tagged. Reminded him of the Military Industrial Complex he had fought to escape. But for the sake of the mission, he relented.

Afterward, he was told to get good rest, because the next day he was being sent to Salt Lake City, Utah, to infiltrate the Temple and get to the bottom of the conspiracy surrounding Amos Young, Nous, and the medallion—and whatever connections and implications all three might have with the Mormon Church.

He massaged his hand as he walked down the hall to Radcliffe's study, his stomach protesting at the smell of breakfast. Radcliffe greeted him at the door.

"Ahh, Master Grey, come in. Hope you got good rest."

"I feel like I could sleep another day away." Waiting for him inside was a spread similar to what he and Grant enjoyed a week ago. He took a seat at the table ready to eat and prep for the next leg of his mission.

"Sorry, but no rest for the weary. Time is of the essence!"

He picked up a phone on the table as Silas piled his plate with eggs and bacon. "Zoe, Silas is awake. Please join us in the study. And hope you've brought your appetite."

Radcliffe reached for a muffin with one hand as he poured Silas some coffee. "How are you feeling?"

"A bit dazed, if I'm honest."

"I understand it's been an unnerving few days, in more ways than one. I'm afraid it's not about to let up. We're nearing the election, and we're also getting closer to understanding what your friend's medallion is all about."

Silas took a swig of his coffee. "Any word from Torres and Gapinski?"

He nodded. "They reported in last evening. They've found...something."

"Something?"

"Ruins of some sort."

"Really?" Silas said with interest. "So the medallion is true? It's a map pointing to a city?" He hesitated before adding: "The lost tribes of Israel?"

"I wouldn't go that far. It's *something*. That's all we know. We'll know more in the next few days. The team is set to start traipsing through the jungle. Shortly, actually."

Silas nodded as he shoved a forkful of eggs into his mouth. The door opened, and Zoe walked in carrying a laptop under her arm.

"Hey, Silas. How are you feeling?"

He wiped his mouth. "Radcliffe just asked me the same question. Ready. So what do you got for me?"

She sat in a chair between the two men and opened her laptop. In many ways, the petite Italian behind thick blue-framed glasses was the brains to SEPIO, providing research and logistical support for the brawns who were out in the field executing the mission. On more than one occasion she had saved their hide.

"I must say, Silas, you've outdone yourself this time."

He laughed. "What do you mean?"

"I mean, the man you found, Asher Avard. I did a little digging around and found a small paper trail on the guy. He is indeed the president of *The Society for New World Archaeology*. Or, at least, he was. Dug a little further—well, a lot further, and discovered the Society is a front organization for the Church of Jesus Christ of Latter-day Saints."

"Really?" Radcliffe said. "Do tell."

"Apparently, it was founded decades ago by a wealthy businessman with ties to the Quorum of the Twelve."

"The what?" Silas asked.

"The main governing body of the Mormon Church," Radcliffe said.

Zoe nodded. "Right, and with the purpose of discovering archaeological evidence for the Book of Mormon."

Silas crunched into a piece of bacon. "And this guy, Avard, was its president?"

"Not only that, but I've searched the archive of intel that SEPIO agents in the field have collected over the years and came across an entry on Avard from the '80s." She waited for a beat, smiling at her success. "He's a Danite."

"But we already knew that."

"But not just any Danite. A great-grandson of Sampson Avard, one of the founders and leaders of the Mormon vigilantes."

"So the man followed in his grandpappy's footsteps..." Silas said.

She nodded and smiled proudly.

Radcliffe said, "So you're telling us the man who kidnapped Silas and then assassinated the American independent presidential candidate was the head of the Mormon secret police?"

She nodded. "And apparently moonlights as the head of their archaeological propaganda arm, as well."

Silas took the ID card out of his pocket and stared at it. "The two strands we've been tracking to make sense of this conspiracy, Young and the medallion, converge in this man."

"So far, yes."

"Anything else, Zoe?" Radcliffe asked.

"No more 'ah-ha moments,' sorry."

"What about the mystery man I mentioned to Radcliffe? The guy I heard about at the farmhouse. The man in the bow tie?"

She shook her head. "Sorry. I haven't found any references in our existing intel on the LDS Church, and nothing has surfaced from the spider bots crawling through the internet. I'll keep looking, though. Seems like it could be an important clue. But I did put together what we have on the Salt Lake Temple. Unfortunately, the intel on that building is on the slim side since no non-Mormons are allowed inside. It's like the Vatican: totally impenetrable, locked down, mysterious."

"Then where does that leave me?"

She shrugged. "I've sent what intel we have to your smartphone, including a layout of the Temple itself."

"Can you tell me anything about the building?"

"Not really, I'm afraid. It's been over a decade since we've had anyone from SEPIO embedded within the LDS administration. The schematic I'm sending you pre-dates even that intel, so I'm not sure how reliable it is anymore, given it's a few decades old. But it should be a good starting place for your mission. Then you've got Avard's ID card and, of course, his chip in your hand. We're going to have to doctor you up a bit, even though you bear a striking resemblance to the man. A little on the shorter, slimmer side, but it'll do."

"Excuse me?" Silas interrupted, looking with confusion from Zoe to Radcliffe.

"No need to worry, my boy," he answered. "It's all standard cloak and dagger routine."

"We'll fit you with a blond wig and blue contacts," Zoe explained, "and give you a pair of bright white teeth to match Avard."

Silas licked his teeth with his tongue, wondering what was wrong with the set he had.

"You'll be a regular Double O Seven!"

"Great. I just hope they haven't discovered the man is missing, even dead. Because that will bring this whole operation to a quick and painful end."

Radcliffe said, "You're right, which is why time is of the essence."

"But what exactly am I looking for?"

"That's to be determined. But anything that would reveal the main motivations behind Young's candidacy and the interest the Mormon Church may have with him being president. With any luck, and a strong dose of God's providential intervention, you'll discover the key to solving this whole riddle."

Silas hoped he was right.

And hopefully before the election.

CHAPTER 27

LA MOSQUITIA, HONDURAS.

The helicopter came in fast and halted hard a few feet above a small clearing a little over a mile from ground zero.

Torres had spotted the landing zone on their return trip from mapping the region with the LiDAR equipment the previous day and recorded the coordinates to pass along to their chauffeur, one of her uncle's ex-military contractors who had been assigned to drop off her, Grant, Gapinski, and two other grunt recruits with thick necks and even thicker arms. Nick and Todd, twin brothers from Texas, who both had previous experience in Central America. She made it clear to them she was in charge, which they seemed to accept without issue.

They had lifted off in a rented military chopper from the airport on Guanaja at the first sign of dawn to maximize the daylight. Once they reached the landing zone, the plan was to establish headquarters then hike through the dense jungle to the site of the lost settlement in sectors T1 and T3 of the LiDAR map. Depending on how long it took them, they would survey the site, catalogue their finds, and carefully assess the ruins. If all went smoothly, they should only need to spend a night, two max out in the unforgiving, untouched lost world.

Gapinski was first to be boots on the ground. Because of the drop from the chopper, he helped Torres, Grant, and the two contractors land safely on the LZ. Each person bore their own backpack with gear. They were also given a handgun and hunting knife. Since they didn't know what to expect from Mother Nature, Gapinski and the two recruits each carried an automatic rifle. They would also come in handy in any other unforeseen circumstances.

As in, if Nous or the Danites showed their faces.

After disembarking, the five quickly grabbed their gear and cleared the LZ, keeping their heads down as the chopper lifted back into the clear blue sky, leaving them in silence. Soon the void was filled with a strange, loud guttural hooting from deep within the jungle. It started in a whimper but quickly crescendoed in intensity.

"What in the world is that?" Gapinski asked, raising his rifle slightly.

"Howler monkeys," Nick said, one of the contractors. "Responding to the noise of the helicopter."

"Nobody told me nothing about no howler monkeys..."

Torres slapped him on the back, causing him to jump. "What, you scared of a wittle bitty monkey, Hoss?"

"Had a bad run-in with a howler once," he said eyeing the jungle. "Let's leave it at that."

Nick said, "You picked the wrong mission then, brother. The jungle is filled with 'em."

"Always something," he complained.

Torres turned around to face the group. "Alright, grab your gear, get a machete, and let's go set up camp." She nodded toward the wall of foliage, an impenetrable mass of green vegetation and bright flowers that looked more like the side of a cave than the start of a jungle. "Ciudad Blanca awaits."

She led the group forward, followed by Nick who had his machete ready. He started hacking at the wall, Torres and Gapinski joined him. Soon they had cut a cave-like hole heading into the dark world beyond.

They emerged into an Oz-like world of wonder, their previous black-and-white existence quickly transforming into full-on high-definition color. It was as if they had found Eden itself.

Thick trees, trunks two or three feet in diameter, stretched toward the heavens like columns of a cathedral, their boughs full of leaves the size of Gapinski's hands forming a barely-penetrable canopy. The humid air was heavy with the dizzying scent of spicy earth and flowers and rot. Flecks of golden rays found their way into the sanctuary below. Birds sang from the rafters of their cathedral. Howler monkeys continued their roar, an offering of worship or an auditory assault, depending on whether you were Gapinski or not. The area was relatively flat and forgiving and open. Not the Four Seasons in Cancun, but it would do.

"So, what now?" Grant asked.

"Time to build the camp," Todd said, a linebacker-of-a-man with a bald head and covered in tattoos. "Create a clearing with your machete for your own personal bungalow. String up your hammock between two trees ten feet apart. Make sure your rainfly and mosquito netting will drape around. Nothing worse than being wet and eaten alive."

The five set off in different directions to find a private place to roost for the night. An hour later, they began making their way back toward the center where Nick had already been digging a pit for a fire. Todd had felled some thick trees to use as benches. The monkey choir had died down, having become more comfortable with their visitors. Gapinski seemed visibly relieved.

"Gentlemen," Torres said to the men, "shall we?"

After checking their packs for emergency supplies, the group set off into the jungle. They came to a stream at the edge of a wall of trees standing between them and the lost civilization beyond. It was about three feet deep and fifteen feet wide, with crystal-clear water limping lazily along. The five made it across with ease.

On the other side, a thicket of heliconia formed a virtual wall. They hacked through it together, easily felling the fleshy vegetation. Beyond, they slogged through two muddy channels. Gapinski nearly lost a boot as they struggled through the morass of thick mud, sinking up to their thighs in spots. The embankment beyond the floodplain rose at a steep forty-degree incline, covered tier after tier with a barricade of green and brown foliage dotted with bright orange and pink and yellow flowers. They struggled hand and foot, climbing upward and grasping at anything that would give them purchase: vines, roots, branches, each other. The struggle, however, was worth it. For at the top, the embankment flattened out immediately, and they were facing a long ditch and mound that appeared man-made.

"The edge of the city," Torres said breathlessly. Grinning, she shouted, "We made it!"

Grant matched her grin, then high-fived her.

The howler monkey choir struck up again. Whether they were celebrating or complaining wasn't clear.

"Would you shut up already!" Gapinski bellowed around the jungle. The howling died down slightly. "Thank you!"

"Check this out," Grant said walking toward the base of an unnatural-looking slope. He crouched down. Torres came up to his side and knelt with him.

"Looks to be some sort of earthen pyramid," she said.

"Looks like a pile of dirt and leaves to me," Gapinski said coming up beside them.

Torres ignored him. "Let's keep going." She labored up the side of the pyramid and reached the top. The other four followed. They paused for a few minutes at the highest point of the lost city, then descended down into what looked like a plaza. They spread out in the large open clearing, the trees parting to let in some of the sunlight from the clear sky above down into the settlement.

"Over here," someone shouted.

It was Nick. He was cutting away vines and peeling dirt and

moss off of a large stone. The others quickly joined him. "I found this. It has a shape to its surface. Looks like there are several more." He pointed as he kept pulling back and cutting away the vegetation.

Grant smiled at Torres, and the two set off to join Nick in the fun. A few minutes later they had uncovered flat stones sitting on round, white-quartz boulders.

Torres said, "These have to be cultic altars or some other type of cultic ceremonial platforms."

"Which proves they did use cut stone for building," Grant said beaming. "This had to have been an important site. It's similar to what I encountered at Copán. We'll want to clear away the dirt later to see if any of them have carvings."

They kept walking, spreading out more in the settlement. There were several mounds and berms and raised earth platforms. Grant thought one of the areas could be a Mesoamerican ball court, given its similar geometry and size to others he had excavated elsewhere, but it was too soon to determine.

They hacked their way through more jungle. On the far end, there was a large mound that looked to be eight feet high by something like twenty feet long. It was perplexing, to be sure, with a sharply defined base and steep walls. Gapinski thought it looked like a bus. He wasn't too far off.

Torres was mesmerized by their surroundings—by the misty, humid air and silent mounds and raised earthworks that bespoke of an ancient people who had settled here and given birth to generations who had played games and made war, who had died and fled. There was a spiritual quality about the place that enchanted her, as if the past had suddenly dissolved into the present. It all reminded her of why she had gone to graduate school in the first place: to rediscover and uncover her own pre-Columbian roots. It also made her depressed, thinking about the life she could have had. Perhaps she could do some good here for her people, discovering this lost civilization.

"Hey, look over here!" Gapinski shouted. "Some weird stones. Looks like a head!"

Torres and Grant ran over to where he was pointing. Sure enough, poking up out of the ground were the tops of dozens of carved stone sculptures, floating like icebergs on a sea of leaves and moss and dirt and rot.

"Is that a jaguar?" Gapinski asked.

"Looks that way," Torres said. "And look over here. The rim of a vessel of some sort." It was decorated with a vulture's head.

"More stone jars over here," Grant said several feet away. "Looks like snakes carved around the neck."

"I've got a throne or a table over here," Nick said farther up from the group.

"Another one over here," Torres said, "and this one has glyphs!"

"What?" Grant exclaimed shuffling over to her location. Gapinski joined, as did Nick and Todd.

"Who has the trowel?" she shouted.

"I do," Nick said. He handed it to her.

She started carefully digging, peeling back layers of earth to reveal more of the artifact. Grant gasped, covering his mouth. She smiled and dug faster.

It was a large sculpture at the base of what looked to be another pyramid. It was lying on its side, in the shape of a large 'U,' with its left side higher than its right. On the higher side at the base were what looked to be two feet. Rising above it was a head-like shape that swooped down into a point. If she were to describe it, it seemed like a beak.

"It's a vulture statue," Grant said mesmerized.

"A what?" Gapinski said, face twisted with a mixture of confusion and revulsion.

Torres said, "A vulture statue. In Mesoamerican cultures, the statue depicts a shaman in a spiritually transcendent state, as a vulture."

"And look," Grant said sweeping his hand around the area. "It seems to be placed in the center of a cache of them at the base of this pyramid."

"Maybe some sort of ritual collection," she said looking around. "Have you seen this in other Mayan cultures? I haven't."

"Which means it could be some sort of key to what distinguished the people of Mosquitia in this settlement from its neighbors."

"Maybe," she said.

Todd was walking over. He had something in his hand.

Torres stood and wiped her hands. "What's that?"

He was smiling. "A were-jaguar."

"Dude, what the hell are you doing?" Grant exclaimed.

The man's face fell and he looked down at the stone figure. "What do you mean?"

"Why are you carrying it?" He asked with an edge to his voice.

"I dug it up over there." He nodded toward the base of the pyramid. "Thought you'd want to see it."

Grant sighed and turned around. "You should have left it."

"He's right," Torres said, "you should have left it alone. But let's have a look."

Todd set it down carefully on the dirt floor.

Grant said, "Yup, definitely a were-jaguar."

"I agree," she said.

"Sounds like a superhero," Gapinski added. "What is it, anyway?"

"Supernatural entity, even a deity. Throughout the Americas, traditional shamans and priests claimed special relationships with certain animals. The were-jaguar head is a classic example of Mesoamerican depictions of half-human, half-animal beings where the shaman both drew his power from the jaguar animal and transformed himself into one. They were considered masters of jaguars who could influence them and channel their spiritual energies. Same thing for the vulture statue."

"Which has typically been an Olmec supernatural deity motif," Grant added, "So to see it out here…"

"What do you suppose that means?" Gapinski asked.

Torres stooped back down to the statue. "Well, between this statue and the vulture one and other animal depictions, this definitely places this civilization firmly in the Mesoamerican camp."

Grant added, "I agree. A remarkable find. Truly a lost civilization. But a pre-Columbian, Mesoamerican civilization."

"So not Jewish," Gapinski continued.

Torres and Grant both giggled.

"Definitely not," she said.

Grant added, "No sign of Semitic characters or supernatural motifs or other glyphs."

"I don't get it," Gapinski said. "I thought the Mormon relic was all Johnny-marks-the-spot on this plot of dirt."

"It did," Grant said. "And it was. Spot on, in fact."

"Just not a Jewish tribe lost from some canoeing trip across the Atlantic?"

"No way," Torres offered. "It's a lost civilization. No doubt about that. But not the lost tribes of Israel. Not the so-called Lamanites. These are definitely Mesoamerican ruins with no indication of any direct or indirect Semitic connection or—"

"Hold a minute," Grant interrupted, putting up his hand.

She walked up next to him furrowing her brow. "What is it?"

He was searching the trees and glancing into the sky. "I thought I heard something."

Gapinski turned toward him and chuckled. "What's that? Thought you saw the lost monkey god?"

"Hush. I hear it, too," Torres said.

The three of them stood still, the sound of the jungle filling in the void.

Torres stepped forward and looked into the sky. She could hear it in the distance. The sound of rumbling thunder, perhaps? Except the sky above the emerald canopy was clear and bright. Not a cloud to be found. Or maybe it was just the wind through the trees.

"Is that thunder?" Gapinski asked.

Torres put out her hand to silence him.

"It's getting closer," Grant said softly as he joined Torres at her side.

She recoiled backward, eyes widening and mouth going dry. "That's not thunder."

Grant turned toward her, face flat. He nodded. He recognized it, too. He looked at Gapinski, and said, "Helicopter. We've got company."

"Let's get out of here," she said as the large mechanical thwapping bird closed in.

"Always something," he mumbled under his breath as he chased after Torres.

CHAPTER 28

SALT LAKE CITY, UTAH.

T he four-hour flight was uneventful. Silas mostly crashed to cope with the air travel; he hated flying. But his ankle had been bothering him from the fall he took the day before, making rest hard to come by. It was late afternoon when they landed in Salt Lake City, Utah, the religious epicenter of the Church of Jesus Christ of Latter-day Saints. A fifteen-minute Uber ride later and he was standing in Temple Square, a ten-acre garden plaza owned by the LDS Church.

In 1847, when Mormon pioneers arrived in the Salt Lake Valley, Brigham Young himself had selected and claimed the plot of desert ground as the spot for the Temple, proclaiming, "Here we will build a temple to our God." The square now consisted of a conference center; tabernacle, housing the famed Mormon Tabernacle Choir; museums and libraries dedicated to the church's history, as well as to archiving family genealogies; various administrative office buildings; and even a hotel in honor of their founder, Joseph Smith. Then, of course, there was the massive Salt Lake Temple gleaming white with six towers, the center of which was crowned with the golden angel Moroni, the divine messenger who Mormons believe visited Joseph Smith.

Measuring 210 feet at its highest pinnacle, groundbreaking ceremonies were presided over by Brigham Young, who laid the cornerstone on April 6, 1853, twenty-three years after the religion was founded. The temple intentionally includes some elements thought to evoke Solomon's Temple at Jerusalem, like a baptismal font mounted on the backs of twelve oxen, just like the Molten Sea in the original Solomon's Temple. The six spires themselves represented the power of the priesthood, representing the LDS Church hierarchy as patterned after Israel's: the Melchizedek, or "higher priesthood," and the Aaronic, or "preparatory priesthood." Several carved stones on the temple face depicted the sun, moon, and stars, corresponding to the celestial, terrestrial, and telestial kingdoms of glory in the Mormon afterlife and drawn from the Freemasonry practiced by many early church leaders.

Silas stood before the building mesmerized by its white Gothic grandeur, similar feelings rising to the surface that he had felt in Saint Peter's Square in Vatican City before the basilica. It unsettled him that the building had the power to evoke the adulation and devotion of Mormons, just as Saint Peter's Basilica had for him and the crowds of pilgrims that had joined him for Mass. Yet why should he be? He imagined the same was true of Muslims at Mecca or Jews in the Holy City or even the Neolithic ancestors at Stonehenge. Spiritual locations and monuments and relics had anchored the human experience from the beginning of our existence.

In many ways it made sense. After all, we're all hardwired for needing such connections to the divine, for grasping after tangible experiences rooted in stone and wood, gold and marble to make sense of this world and its complexities and meanings, its beginning and direction and end. The quest for any sort of spiritual or religious fulfillment is what makes us human to begin with, separating us from the rest of our fellow mammals. As the French philosopher Blaise Pascal said: "There is a God-shaped vacuum in the heart of every man." This temple and its religion offered to fill the void.

And yet, Silas knew it was a square-peg offering for the round-hole of the human heart. Because Pascal's wisdom continues: "which cannot be filled by any created thing, but only by God the Creator, made known through Jesus Christ." And it wasn't the Jesus Christ offered by Mormonism, but the one at the center of the good news preached by the apostles and at the center of historic Christianity.

A shiver rippled up his spine as he contemplated the spiritual power the building and the religion it symbolized had over countless human hearts. A power that could grow in might and reach if Amos Young was elected President of the United States of America.

He had to get to the bottom of what Nous and the LDS Church were up to.

Here we go...

He approached the gold doors of a side entrance to the temple he had observed various personnel entering and exiting for the past hour. They didn't look like your run-of-the-mill Mormon pilgrim, but rather official religious administrators. Many of them had walked over to the entrance from the nearby church offices. He was certain it was a separate entrance for LDS officials.

One Asher Avard surely would have used.

The traffic had slowed in the last twenty minutes. He hoped he wasn't too late. He pushed through the doors and approached what looked to be a security checkpoint.

A man put up his hand and rushed toward him. "Sir, the Temple is now closed. You'll need to leave."

Just look like you belong, and you can fake almost anything.

Silas repeated the mantra as he continued forward. He smiled and reached inside his jacket.

The man flinched, his hand reflexively moving toward his sidearm.

He quickly put his other hand up. "Hold on there, son. I'm reaching for my ID." Silas retrieved the white plastic card and flashed it at the man.

His eyes widened briefly in recognition. He cleared his throat. "Sorry, sir. I'm new here and hadn't recognized you immediately."

Thank the Lord for that.

The man motioned for Silas to step over to a turnstile with a slot and a palm reader. He rubbed the spot on his left hand with his right thumb where the rice-size chip was inserted underneath. He wasn't exactly sure what the security protocol was, but he placed his hand on the flat glass surface anyway.

Lord Jesus Christ, Son of God, please come through for me!

Nothing happened.

He looked up at the man, brow furrowed in feigned confusion.

The man waited for a beat then glanced at the slot. "Your card, sir."

Silas flashed an irritated look at the man, then slid his card into the slot. A chirp was emitted and the glass beneath pulsed blue. One, two, three waves.

Then solid yellow and a sound indicating trouble.

"What the heck is going on?" Silas inquired.

The man looked up at him. "Try it again."

He took in a controlled breath then breathed it out nonchalantly. He glanced at the man and back to the palm reader, then complied.

First blue pulse. Second blue pulse. Third blue pulse.

Yellow. Failure sound.

His heart started galloping forward more quickly. It wasn't going to work. They must have disrupted or broken the microchip on extraction or insertion. Or maybe they had missed another piece of the security measure on Avard, causing the failure.

Not good.

The man huffed and looked over at his partner, who had stepped closer. "I thought we'd gotten this thing fixed?" he mumbled. "Sorry, sir. As you know the upgrade hasn't gone so well. Some people are being incorrectly flagged as false failures."

Silas channeled his inner Avard and laid into the man. "Yes...

well, I thought I made myself clear that this was to be rectified immediately. We can't have the security of our Temple compromised. Where is your superior?"

The man looked down and rubbed the back of his neck and glanced over at his partner. "He's left for the evening. It's just us. But some people have had better luck by pressing down more firmly. For some reason, the microchip reader signal isn't as strong as the last version. So, if you wouldn't mind giving your hand another try. And press down more firmly this time."

Silas looked at the man and then at his partner, making a display of anger and insult at the security failure.

He slammed his hand down on the piece of glass and pressed into it hard.

Again: one, two, three blue pulses.

Then bright green.

The two steel bars retracted, and both security guards let out a sigh that signaled relief that the high-ranking LDS official standing in front of them had finally been cleared.

Silas nodded to the man, who smiled briefly and nodded back. As he walked through the gate, he breathed in and out in relief.

He had done it, he had infiltrated the Salt Lake Temple.

Now to figure out what the heck is going on inside these white walls.

CHAPTER 29

The hour was getting late as the sun began retreating for the day. The chance to putting all of the pieces of this religious-political conspiracy together growing slim.

Silas moved with casual deliberateness through a long white hallway adorned with blue carpet and crystal chandeliers. Gold-gilded crown molding bordered the doors and ringed the ceiling, with a winding staircase leading upward at the end. He was struck by the whiteness of the sacred structure: the exterior gleamed white from the quartz monzonite, lighted by bright white lights at night; the interior was equally as white, its walls gleaming divine purity and celestial enlightenment.

Perhaps there was something to the White City legend in Central America. Then again, if there was, that would mean a whole new set of problems for the Christian faith. He hoped his fellow SEPIO operatives were having as much luck as he was and were getting to the bottom of their own mystery.

He began climbing the stairs, taking them by two, when he noticed a small door just behind the stairwell. Next to it on the wall was the same flat black-glass panel and keycard slot that greeted him at the security checkpoint. He ignored it and continued ascending.

Let's see where this goes.

Above him he heard two voices, probably security guards, chatting about yesterday's Utah Jazz and Boston Celtics game, sending him quickly back down the stairs to the door. He inserted his keycard into the slot and slammed his hand against the panel, hoping the microchip wouldn't act up again. Within seconds the pulsing blue light turned to green, and the door unlocked. The voices were growing, so he opened the door and hustled inside.

The keycard!

The door slammed against his arm as he reached out and around for the plastic card. He fished for it with his fingers, then snatched it and secured it in his pocket as four legs in dark dress pants reached the bottom of the stairs. He shut the door carefully so as not to draw attention at the late hour.

The corridor, he discovered, was long and seemingly ran most of the length of the temple. It was also different from the rest of the inside. The light was dim and walls gray. He opened his phone to the schematics Zoe had given him and searched the floor plans of the first floor. There was no sign of it. Clearly, it was meant to be shielded from the eyes of most people walking through the sacred building. But where was he?

Several doors lined the hallway, all facing him with blackened glass. It looked like an office suite, as nameplates were positioned over keycard entry boxes to the right of the door handle

Wait. What was this?

He stopped at one door midway that seemed to take up a larger section of the hidden corridor.

A smile flashed across his mouth.

Asher Avard.

Score.

He put his keycard into the slot, then turned the handle and walked inside.

That was a mistake.

Inside were two men in black suits sitting around a table in the center of a long rectangular room flanked by computer terminals and security monitors lining the walls. One man was sitting with his back toward the door, the other was facing him. That man stopped mid-sentence when Silas walked through the door, eyes widening then transforming into a scowl.

"Who are you and how did you get in here?" the man growled with authority as he began to stand.

The other man turned around and offered the same face of discontent.

Just great...

He had no time to think, only react. So he rushed the man still sitting down, throwing his arms around his neck. The other man shuffled around the table to his aid, while the seated man reached for Silas's head, grabbing at anything he could get his hands on.

Silas dragged the man using his wheeled chair and spun him to the left. As the other man came around the table, he leaned and kicked him square in the stomach. The man doubled over in pain and stumbled backward.

The seated man used the distraction to grab hold of Silas's face, tearing at his nose and ears. The man held on for dear life as Silas continued squeezing his neck. His face burned, but just a few more seconds and the man would be unconscious.

Silas pivoted to the right and dragged the chair back as the other man recovered.

"Who are you?" the man said winded. "You're certainly not Avard, though you're playing like him."

"Just a man on a mission, friend."

The man narrowed his eyes and glanced to his left.

The hands of the other man in the chair started to give way. Silas pulled out of the man's grip as his arms flopped to his side and head drooped down toward his chest. He followed the other man's gaze and saw what he was after.

A pistol, lying next to a computer monitor.

Silas shoved the chair toward him as his partner's world went black and lunged for the weapon. The man fell forward and grabbed Silas's leg, jamming his fist in his left kidney.

Silas missed the table and fell to the floor. The man scrambled over him to reach the weapon. He turned on his back and sat upright in one quick motion, head-butting the man in his solar plexus.

The man cried out and sat up holding the weapon, then pointed it at Silas. Without letting up his attack, he reached for the weapon, seizing it with both hands and causing it to discharge.

Silas used the event to jam his right hand into the man's bottom jaw, then again. The man's teeth made a sickening crunching sound as his neck snapped back once, then twice. The man stumbled backward. He lost the gun. It skittered across the floor.

Climbing onto the man, Silas sent his fist into his head—once then twice. It was the third blow that finally rendered him unconscious.

Silas slid off the man and onto the cold tiled floor. He reached for the weapon, grabbing it and stuffing it in his waistband. He was breathing hard and aching from the fight. Not what he had expected, that's for sure. He hoped against hope that no one heard the gun blast.

No time to worry about that now. Move it, Grey!

At the far end of the room was a separate enclosed space. Probably Avard's personal office. He ran toward it and pushed through the unlocked door.

His desk was a mess. Documents and photos were strewn about. One folder was marked 'Matthew Reed.' He opened it. Inside were detailed notes on the man: his past associations and financial records, a list of campaign events, detailed outlines of his campaign platform policies.

He set it down then picked up another folder, marked 'Faithful Majority.' It was thick and well-worn. Inside, there was a sheet of paper with a list of names sitting on top. It listed in neat rows each of the members of the Religious Right organization, various pastors and political activists. Next to several of the names were large dollar amounts. The largest of which was next to the Faithful Majority: $6.5 million.

Silas shook his head. He couldn't believe what he was seeing.

Did the Mormons buy off the Religious Right?

It seemed inconceivable. Then again, it seemed inconceivable earlier in the year that they would have endorsed a Mormon over an Evangelical to begin with. Why not for money?

He closed the folder and threw it on another pile of folders and shuffled through the rest of the contents on the desk. Underneath he found a large map of the State of Missouri folded in half. When he opened it a browned piece of parchment with faded cursive writing fell out. It was a letter, and at least a century old by the looks of it. He flipped it over.

What the...

He began reading the contents, wondering what secrets it held.

CHAPTER 30

F rom your brother-in-the-faith and an apostle of Jesus Christ by the will of God, to the Latter-day Saints which are at Missouri, to the faithful in the Faith: Grace be to you, and peace, from God our Father, and from the Lord Jesus Christ.

I write to you this account, having heard of your recent trials and tribulations at the hand of the United States government, trusting that the truth of the account will act as a balm of Gilead for your troubles and a bulwark against doubt's hint.

At a particular hill in the town of Manchester, in Ontario County, there was deposited a Golden Bible. Contained within this sacred text was the ancient record of a divine origin of the peoples of the Americas, as well as the destiny of this Great Nation.

After a goodly dose of religious fervor swept through my county, I had begun to ponder my spiritual course. Seeking direction for my journey, I turned to my family's Bible, happening upon a startling passage that spoke directly to my situation, from the Book of James, the first chapter, verse five: "If any of you lack wisdom, let him ask of God, that giveth to all men liberally, and upbraideth not; and it shall be given him."

It was like an impartation of revelation bolted down out from heaven itself and struck me square between the eyes. I thought to myself: "I must either remain in darkness and confusion or else I must do as James directs, that is, ask of God."

The next morning, on a clear, cloudless spring day, where the sun shone bright and strong, and the world sang of hope and expectation, I ventured into a secluded forest on the outskirts of town to make good on the revelation from the Good Lord. I got down on my knees and prayed, and what happened next was nothing less than astonishing!

I saw a pillar of light exactly over my head above, the brightness of the sun itself, which gradually descended until it fell upon me....When the light rested upon me, I saw two personages, whose brightness and glory defy all description, standing above me in the air. One of them spake unto me, calling me by name, and said—pointing to the other—"This is my Beloved Son, hear Him."...I asked the personage who stood above me in the light, which of all the sects was right—and which I should join. I was answered that I must join none of them; he forbade me from joining any of the churches, for they were all wrong, and the personage who addressed me said that all their creeds were an abomination in His sight: that "they draw near to me with their lips, but their hearts are far from me; they teach the doctrines and the commandments of men: having a form of godliness, but they deny the power thereof." He again forbade me to do with any of them: and many other things did he say unto me, which I cannot write at this time.

Immediately, after the impartation and vision receded into the warming day, I sought the religious leaders and other townsfolk to relay the revelation imparted to me. To my disappointment, every last one of them believed me not. I tried in vain to tell them of my experience, but they subjected me to harsh persecution.

It was said, how very strange it was that an obscure boy, of a little over fourteen years of age, and one, too, who was doomed to the necessity of obtaining scanty maintenance by his daily labor, should be thought a character of sufficient importance to attract the attention of the great ones of the most popular sects of the day and in all manner to create in them a spirit of the most bitter persecution and reviling. But strange or not, so it was, and it was often the cause of great sorrow to myself.

For three years, I toiled under the weight of the peculiar experience and confused by what it meant for me and for the people of my land. It wasn't until September 21, 1823, that I received an answer to my pleas. I was praying near my bedside in the dark, as I often do in beseeching the council of Elohim, when a light filled the room and continued to increase until the room was lighter than at noonday.

Suddenly, a heavenly personage wearing a white robe appeared. His whole person was glorious beyond description, and his countenance was truly like lightning.

"I am Moroni," this messenger declared himself, "a resurrected and glorified servant of the Lord."

He announced that God had a mission for me, one involving a book of golden plates that chronicled the history of America's former inhabitants and contained the fullness of the Gospel as delivered by the Savior to the ancient inhabitants. These golden plates contained the engraving of the pure doctrines of Christianity, as opposed to the dogmas taught by the denominational churches of the day. This precious treasure had been deposited in the earth centuries earlier.

It wasn't until the fullness of time that Moroni allowed me to retrieve the plates imprinted with the long-lost history of the ancient inhabitants of the Americas, composing the legacy in a new testament of Jesus Christ. Now I had everything I needed to bring forth the sacred text that would serve as the basis for the newly revealed religion of the Most High.

I commenced copying the characters of the plates through the aid of my principal scribe, Oliver Cowerdy, I copied a considerable number of them, and by means of the Urim and Thummim, I translated them. As the fruits of my labor through my partnership with Cowdery began to unveil themselves, it was clear that the plates continued a chronicle of God's dealings with the early inhabitants of the Americas, from approximated 2,200 years before the birth of Jesus Christ to 421 years after his death. The divine revelation explained how these inhabitants arrived in the New World by way of three migrations from the Eastern hemisphere.

Had it not been for the faithful prophet-historian Mormon, who wrote down on golden plates the history chronicling the inhabitants of the Americas, it would have been lost. He delivered these plates to his son, Moroni, who added a few words of his own and then buried them in the Hill Cumorah, where these laid for centuries until I found them and translated them in fulfillment of the prophecies.

I have told you the accurate account of how the Book from the golden plates deposited deep within the earth and entrusted to me, by the Father's servant, Moroni, came to be revealed to mankind.

All of the doctrines of the gospel are taught in their entirety and completeness in the Golden Bible with much greater clarity and perfection than those of the same doctrines revealed in Christ's original Testament. Let anyone place in parallel the teachings of these two great books, and you will find conclusive proof of the superiority of the lessons and instructions offered by the golden plates, reciting the providences of God in the necessary and vastly important matter of redemption, as well as the laws of nature and of Nature's God. It predicts the regathering, restoration, and other manifold blessings of Israel as another witness to the truth of Jesus and the establishment of his kingdom.

Jesus Christ, referring to the time when he would manifest himself in the latter days, declared that whereas he manifested himself to his own people in the meridian of time and they rejected him in the latter days he would come first to the Gentiles, and then to the house of Israel. He says: "And behold, these people (the Nephites) will establish in the land, (America) and it shall be a new Jerusalem."

Behold, I have opened my mouth and have begun to preach to you who read my testimony, the words that the divine Messenger Moroni had first imparted to me in the vision, that all the Churches and Denominations on the earth had become corrupt, and no Church of God on the Earth but that which Elohim would shortly rise up, which would never be confounded nor brought down and be like unto the Apostolic Church.

Many other things did he, the angel of Light, say unto me which I cannot write at this time. But this one thing I leave with you, a final impartation given to me. The enclosed medallion, an ancient object of bronze and divine insight, should provide sufficient proof of these ancient *mysteries to assuage your worries and offer encouragement to keep fighting the good fight. I will explain more when I arrive in short order.*

Brothers and sisters, I have seen that a time is coming when the Constitution of these American lands, forged in the soil first trodden by God's chosen ones, will be torn and hang as it were by a thread, nearly destroyed. A terrible revolution will take place in the land of America, left without a Supreme Government. At a crucial time, the righteous of our country, the Latter-day Saints will be rallied with gathered strength, sending out Elders to gather the honest in heart to stand by the Constitution of the United States, stepping forth to rescue it from utter destruction above all other people of the world.

We alone know, by an impartation of revelation, how the Constitution came into being; we alone know the destiny of this great nation. In these last days, God will set up a Kingdom, never to be thrown down. The whole of America will be made Zion of God, ruled by the exalted saints of all ages who have attained the godhood itself. It is our destiny.

See how large a letter I have written unto you with mine own hand. Brethren, the grace of our Lord Jesus Christ be with your spirit. Amen.

———

IT WAS SIGNED, *Joseph Smith*. And it referenced the medallion!

So it was real?

He turned to the map. A square was drawn around a site and labeled Far West, MO, in red marker. He recalled this town from his research. It was founded by Missouri Mormon leaders, W. W. Phelps and John Whitmer. The design of the town resembled Smith's plan for the City of Zion and had become the headquarters for the Latter-day Saint movement in early 1838. Weirdly, Smith taught that the Garden of Eden had been in Jackson County, Missouri, and when Adam and Eve were expelled they moved to the area of Caldwell and Daviess Counties, Missouri, where Far West was located. Smith must have sent this letter to them along with the medallion.

Silas held the letter and the map, staring at the wall. His breathing began to pick up, apprehension and anxiety started to twist in his belly. He worried what this little piece of history meant for the Mormon religion. As well as for the historic Christian faith.

He went to set down the map and letter when he noticed another map. He set them aside and picked it up. It was Honduras. Paper-clipped to it was a color photo of the medallion Grant had discovered. A red 'X' marked a location at the end of a river network in a mountain valley of dense forest.

The Danites knew the location of Ciudad Blanca. Which meant Nous did, too!

Torres and Gapinski and Grant were in trouble.

He pulled out his cell phone to text Radcliffe. There were zero bars available.

He huffed in frustration, but before shoving the phone in his pocket, he took pictures of the maps and letter. Then he left Avard's office and walked back into the dimly-lit hallway. He closed the door and looked back toward the small door he came through earlier, then went down the rest of the corridor. At the end, he noticed a single entrance with two small metal doors. An elevator.

He ran over to it and pressed a small button with an up arrow. Immediately the door opened, he stepped inside. Another flat black glass panel and keycard slot greeted him. He slid the card into the slot and pressed his hand hard against the panel, then held his breath. As it read his palm and microchip, he noticed there were no buttons like a typical elevator, nothing that would allow him to select a floor.

Odd.

The glass beneath his hand flashed green. The doors closed, then the carriage suddenly jolted to life and lifted upward, gaining momentum through the Temple toward a predetermined destination.

Where it was heading, he had no idea. In a few seconds he would find out.

CHAPTER 31

LA MOSQUITIA, HONDURAS.

Within minutes Torres, Grant, Gapinski, and the twins had returned to the camp and set to work cleaning up any trace of their existence as evening approached.

Nick filled in the fire pit, Todd shoved the logs he had cut as benches far into the jungle. The rest made quick work of dismantling their hammock bungalows, sweeping the floor for any sign of human presence.

"What the hell is that?" Grant exclaimed.

Todd had walked over cradling something in his hands. He looked down and said, "The were-jaguar."

His eyes widened. "You took it with you?"

"Well, I sure wasn't going to leave it for those hostiles to find! Which would have been a dead giveaway that others had just been there."

"It's not like we didn't dig all over the place anyhow, Brainiac!"

"Boys!" Torres exclaimed, stepping between the men. "Put away the swords. We've got bigger things to worry about."

"Yeah," Gapinski said, "like who on earth just swooped in all Black Hawk Down like."

"Who did just swoop in on us?" Grant asked Torres.

She shrugged. "Could be military, though I can't see why since they hadn't known of our little expedition. If I had to guess, it's the Danites or Nous."

"Or both," Gapinski added.

She looked at him and nodded.

He picked up his automatic rifle and shoved in a magazine. "Glad we came prepared, then."

The twins retrieved their own weapons and slung them around their shoulders. They nodded, looking for a fight.

Torres put out her arms, and said, "Hold on. Before we go all Rambo on whoever-it-is that just swooped in from the heavens, we need information."

"What do you mean?" Grant asked.

"Who, what, why."

He looked confused.

"Who are they? What do they want? And why are they here? Guns aren't going to do the trick. We need to get back up to that site and watch and listen. That's it."

He nodded. So did Gapinski. Took the twins longer, but they grudgingly agreed to more clandestine means than what trigger-happy Texans were used to. But they all agreed on one thing: they would return to the dig locked and loaded.

After hiding their backpacks and gear, they set out back toward Ciudad Blanca. They waded the river, crossed back across the muddy floodplain, and climbed the river bank to the raised mounds indicating the edge of the city. But instead of moving forward they cut right, hacking a hole into the vegetation wall and circling around along the back toward the center of the ancient city.

The howler monkeys were full of sound and fury when they arrived, setting Gapinski on edge. His only consolation was that this time it wasn't directed at them.

Their progress was slow going, but they managed to cut a wide arc around the main city area. Slice by slash, they drew closer to where they had spent the afternoon and where they had heard the sound of the incoming chopper.

"What's that sound?" he whispered to Torres as she hacked at the foliage in front of her.

She stopped and listened, not having noticed anything while concentrating on the task at hand. "Something mechanical, sounds electric."

"Generator," Grant said continuing his work.

"What would they need that kind of power for out here?" Gapinski wondered.

"Whatever it is," he replied slicing through a thicket of flowers, sending bright orange petals to the ground, "It ain't good."

"Hey," she said turning around and looking behind the group. "Where are the twins?"

"Said they were going to hack their way around to the other side. Something about getting a different angle."

She shook her head and went back to attacking the thick growth. "Whatever. They just better not get themselves killed, because I ain't dragging their butts back to the landing zone."

The trio spent the next half hour slowly making their way through the jungle. They finally came to a clearing that brought them up to a ridge overlooking the site. The light was fading, but they had a clear view of what was happening below.

And it wasn't good.

They could see five large men holding even larger guns standing guard around the perimeter. They were wearing camouflaged gear, even had their faces painted like they were ready for jungle warfare. Looked like Camp Lejeune dropouts. In the center, five others were observing the same mounds and raised earthwork and stones the SEPIO team had explored earlier, probably archaeologists and anthropologists come to explore the lost civilization. They had set up a canvas tent in the middle of the former plaza, as well as the same hammock-netting arrangement the crew had constructed at their camp a klick away. They were clearly preparing to stay for the long haul.

"Wait a minute," Grant said.

He stepped around Torres and descended farther down the embankment a few yards to a large-berthed tree for a better view.

She followed him, coming up behind to his left.

"No way..."

"What is it?" she asked.

Grant pointed to a tall, thin man with a wide-rimmed cream-colored hat holding a long carved wooden walking stick. Light glinted off something hanging from his neck.

"That's Lloyd Kimball!"

"Lloyd Kimball?"

"The lead archaeologist at the Missouri dig." He turned to Torres. "He's the one who found the medallion."

"I thought you found it?"

"I found it, he found it. It's all relative, isn't it?"

"Looks like he recovered his stolen goods. Look." The man turned toward them. Around his neck was the bronze Mormon medallion.

"Damn. Touché, Kimball. Touché"

"I don't get it," Torres said. "What's a Mormon archaeologist's interest in the White City?"

Grant turned around and put his back against the tree. "He probably thought the medallion was a map to the lost tribe of the Lamanites. Like we did. Followed the clues, hoping against hope that 'X' marked the spot."

"But it doesn't, that's the thing. There's nothing here to remotely indicate that it validates the Book of Mormon account. There are zero signs of any sort of connection to Semitic culture. The ruins are Mesoamerican, through and through. They've been here a few hours, so anyone worth their anthropological salt should know that by now."

Grant shrugged. Then he caught sight of Gapinski motioning for them to rejoin him at the top. He tapped Torres on the arm and pointed, then they walked back up to where Gapinski was standing.

Torres said, "What's up, Hoss?"

"Come over here. Something's going on."

They walked around the top of the embankment back toward where they had come. They bypassed the vegetation tunnel they had carved for a path that continued through loosely spaced trees closer to the plaza. A noise rose above the generator sound. It echoed up the embankment toward them, but it wasn't immediately recognizable. They crouched low behind a thicket of brightly colored flowers.

"Look," Gapinski said pointing toward a group of three people crouched around one of the large altars they had seen earlier. Kimball came wandering over as the noise struck up its chorus again.

"What is that racket?" complained Grant.

Kimball leaned over the small group as the sound continued, undulating in obscene tones.

Torres trained her eyes and ears toward the group and noticed a cord snaking away from them and toward the generator.

"No..." she let slip. She clenched her jaw and narrowed her eyes. Her blood was boiling.

She knew exactly what they were doing.

"What?" Gapinski said. "You see something?"

"They're defacing la Ciudad Blanca."

"What are you—"

She waved her hand and pointed forward.

"I knew a guy who had a salvage and excavation outfit in Habana, Cuba. He had garnered an impressive reputation for discovering all sorts of pre-Columbian artifacts throughout Central America. Idols and stoneware and tablets of glyphs. The sorts of things that were small and easily transportable that he could show off. He became a darling among the governments of the region because he gave them back their culture. Even got a cover story on National Geographic. But then some gringos got curious and started doing a little digging of their own into the man and his practices. Then the governments got more curious and forced the man into submitting his artifacts for peer review. That's when everything fell apart."

She turned toward Gapinski and Grant. "The guy developed a technique that could take ordinary stones and turn them into things that looked like ancient Mesoamerican artifacts. He was able to engrave glyphs in a way that made them appear far older than they really were, too. On the surface, the objects and the writings passed the smell test. Damn near fooled the experts, too. But eventually the story came out, and the guy was exposed for what he was. A huckster."

She turned back toward the plaza. "That's what Kimball and his band of hucksters are doing down there. They're manufacturing the history the Mormon Church has always wanted." She turned to Grant. "They're defacing the White City, transforming it into the lost tribes of Israel."

"Over here," someone shouted down below.

Kimball and another man, along with one of the ex-Marines from the perimeter came wandering over to the man who was near the clearing where Gapinski, Torres, and Grant had been earlier.

He was waving his arms around wildly, pointing at the dirt and out into the jungle.

"Crapola," Gapinski said.

"What is it?" Torres said.

"I think we've been made."

"How?" Grant said.

Gapinski continued, "Remember all that digging we did and the objects we unearthed. Didn't really have time to cover our tracks with that chopper coming in hot and heavy, now did we?"

He stood. So did Grant. "Seems like a good time to exit stage left."

Something cracked behind them.

Before Torres could turn around, she heard the sound of a double crack to her left and right. Like the butt of a rifle against two skulls.

Then her world burst unto stars and went black.

CHAPTER 32

SALT LAKE CITY, UTAH.

The elevator deposited Silas somewhere at the top of the Salt Lake Temple. He figured the floor had something to do with the upper echelons of LDS power, as the tenor of the decor changed remarkably toward the ornate and lavish. The walls were still white, but complementing them were red velvet couches lining the hallways, larger crystal chandeliers, and thick ribbons of gold gilding accenting rectangular panels of molding on the walls and lining the ceiling.

He cautiously padded forward, aware he was nearing the end of God's providential rope. Soon, someone would find the bodies in Avard's lair, and the place would be on lock-down. He needed to quickly assess his options for any further intel gathering and figure out how to get back downstairs and out of the Temple to safety. And pronto.

The sound of singing drifted toward him from down the hallway. A hymn. The "Battle Hymn of the Republic," if he wasn't mistaken.

Silas scoffed. How appropriate that Freedom University and the Church of Jesus Christ of Latter-day Saints shared a deep affection for the popular and well-known American patriotic song.

He walked down the hallway and peeked his head around a

corner toward where the muffled song was coming from. No one there, but he could tell the spontaneous number from what sounded like a men's choir was coming from behind closed doors down the corridor.

He looked behind him and down the other hallway, then set out toward the sound. He padded through the cream-colored corridor lit by golden sconces to a set of oak double doors inlaid with frosted glass. Above it was affixed a sign and the words "Apostles Room" in gold-foil script.

Silas had stumbled upon the Quorum of the Twelve Apostles! The elevator must have been a direct access line into the antechamber before the meeting room.

He remembered reading from the dossier prepared by Zoe that the Quorum of the Twelve and the First Presidency met weekly to pray and seek guidance and inspiration from the Lord. They met to discuss the spiritual affairs of the Church and plot the organization's course. Apparently, all decisions made by the First Presidency and Apostles had to receive a unanimous vote, in the spirit of the New Testament apostles being of one accord. Their meetings typically began with a hymn and a prayer, and they partook of the Christian sacrament of Holy Communion, as well.

A tremor worked its way through Silas's body, and he started to feel light-headed. That must be what was happening just beyond those doors, a meeting of the Quorum and First Presidency. If he was going to discover anything during his infiltration mission, it was going to be now.

He pressed his palms against the door, testing its resolve. It was securely shut. He eased his body closer and pressed his ear against its wood. Then he brought his phone up against the door and started recording. Hopefully, its microphone would pick up whatever Silas himself heard.

Someone finished praying and was now leading the group through the Lord's Supper. Silas was disturbed at the thought of them celebrating something so sacred, so holy when they didn't truly believe in its significance for exclusive forgiveness, salvation, and new life.

He looked behind him toward the door to the antechamber. He heard nothing beyond the doors. He hoped it would stay that way.

Someone cleared their throat. The room fell silent.

"The dawn of a new era is beginning to break forth, Apostles. One our holy prophet foretold, that a time would come when the Constitution of our divinely-wrought country would hang as it were by a thread and the Latter-day Saints of Jesus Christ above all other people in the world would come to the rescue. That sacred prophecy is being fulfilled, today, in your hearing and in our midst!"

The men beyond the door cheered and clapped in unison. It must be the Mormon president himself speaking. But what was he talking about?

"Brigham Young," the man continued with a raspy tenor voice, "taught our early ancestors that the governments of the earth were false and should be thrown asunder, and that God had only delegated to the priesthood of his holy people, the remnant of the ancient tribes, the right to set up a government. God promised through his servant Joseph and Moroni before him that he would appoint a ruler, and all persons who otherwise pretended to have authority to govern were usurpers of the glorious intent of the celestial Father. A few days ago we saw firsthand the divine judgment of such usurpers."

Was he speaking of Matthew Reed?

Silas's heart began to quicken, his palms began to moisten. This was most unsettling.

"Brother Young taught that the Constitution of these United States was a divine revelation given to the people of this land by God himself. He also taught that it had fulfilled its purpose, the formation of a government so that the Church of Jesus Christ of Latter-day Saints could be formed and established in order to lead the people in the ways of true enlightened divinity, enjoy the fruitful offerings of the celestial heavenly realm, and attain the fullness of godhood.

"Several decades ago, Brigham Young said that our government, the best government in the world, was crumbling to pieces. He said those who have it in their hands are the ones who are destroying it. I couldn't agree more."

Again, more vocal agreement and applause.

"He wondered how long it would be until the words of the prophet Joseph would be fulfilled. I have wondered the same, myself. Joseph said that if the Constitution of the United States were to be saved at all, it must be done by the people of God, this people—our people! Brigham prophesied that it would not be many years before these words would come to pass. It took a bit longer than he had realized." He chuckled, as did some in the room. "But we are living in the light of those glorious words, beholding the fulfillment of these things. For the Father has raised up a divine conqueror who will save the Republic and humanity itself. Prophet Brigham's great-great-grandson, Amos Young!"

That was news to Silas. Neither Radcliffe nor Zoe had mentioned this crucial information, which led him to believe the Order of Thaddeus was left in the dark, too, along with the rest of America. It seemed as though the boy wonder was walking in the footsteps of the second LDS prophet-president, who had assumed his post after the murder of Latter-day prophet, presidential candidate, and Mormon king Joseph Smith.

Silas stood back and wiped his hands on his pants. This was getting deep. He shifted his posture then leaned against the door again.

"We have just received some very encouraging news from our new friend in the bow tie before gathering with you all. It appears our prospects for capturing the White House are looking brighter every day."

There was that name again. The mystery man in the bow tie Silas had heard about from the two men outside the farmhouse.

Who was he referring to? He and Radcliffe were going to have to get to the bottom of that man's identity. It seemed like an essential piece to the mystery surrounding Young.

"I have just received word that Amos is now leading the national polls, showing he has pulled slightly ahead of the Romanist candidate Robert Santos. In another week we will have attained victory, the vision of our founder realized when he envisioned himself as a king presiding over an empire that would eventually include not only America but the entire world. Through his servant, Amos Young, the Lord of Hosts will establish his church among these native lands upon their repentance by embracing the Mormon gospel. Amos will lead them to such repentance!"

"Amen," a few men said in unison.

"As our prophet revealed, they shall come in unto the covenant and be numbered among the remnant of Jacob, unto whom he has given this American land for their inheritance. And they shall assist his people to build a city, which shall be called the New Jerusalem. And they shall be gathered into it, who are scattered upon all the face of the land. Then the power of Heaven shall be among them, and the Lord will be in our midst! Prophet Joseph's goals of theocratic rule were nascent and went unfulfilled. He had designed to clothe himself with the most unlimited power—civil, military, and ecclesial over these lands for the divine purpose of establishing the dominion of the Kingdom of God forever in the United States and the redemption of these lands!"

The approval was rapturous for the twelve or so seated inside.

"Now, I want to turn it over to one of our own," the man continued over the din of the applause. "What say you apostle?" the president continued, as if turning to someone else in the room.

Silence fell, then there was the sound of someone clearing his throat.

"Fellow apostles. I agree with our illustrious First President."

Silas's mouth went dry. He knew that voice. How could he forget it; it had been playing on every news channel for months.

Amos Young.

Was he a member of the Quorum of the Twelve Apostles?

Young continued, "The Constitution indeed hangs in the balance, as on a thread. This divine document revealed to this land from the bosom of the Father so that this world might be brought back into enlightenment, find salvation from the pitiful existence of the state of nature, and attain the godhood imparted by the celestial realm of glory."

"Amen," someone shouted.

"But I also echo the words of a wise man who had prophesied the downfall of these United States. I believe those prophetic words are fast approaching their fulfillment."

He paused, then began, his voice seeming to change tenor and pitch:

"There will be a complete change of government. Washington, DC, will cease to be the capital. The present national bureaucracy will have its end. The internal conflict will sweep away the current system of governments and will pave the way for the political Kingdom of God and the millennial kingdom through which Jesus Christ will rule and reign. A new government will be established among the saints, and the political Kingdom of God will espouse and uphold the principles of the Constitutional government, rooted in the sacred document revealed by the Divine Messenger, and all the peoples will see the glory of the celestial Father, and come into true possession of the enlightenment sought from ages past. This is the year of the Latter-day Saints, for the truth of our divine messenger Moroni is marching on!"

"Glory, Glory, hallelujah!" the group of men shouted, some joining in by singing.

Silas's head was spinning. Amos Young, the Republican presidential candidate, endorsed and paraded around by evangelical Christians was in cahoots with a member of the highest governing body within the LDS Church hierarchy, patterned after Jesus' own twelve apostles, with equal standing and authority as the First President himself, commissioned with the special calling to be evangelistic ambassadors to the world for the sake of the Mormon faith and the Mormon agenda.

Which apparently included the downfall of the American governing system as we know it and the establishment of Mormon theocratic rule.

The singing abruptly ended, the room on the other side of the door falling silent. Silas furrowed his brow and strained toward the door, placing his palm on its wood surface to listen again. There seemed to be what sounded like movement, shuffling and scuffing on the floor. On the other side of the door, not toward it but away, as if they were leaving out a side entrance. And in a hurry.

Something wasn't right.

Silas stopped recording and shoved his phone in his pocket. Then he backed up, away from the doors and through the entrance to the antechamber into the hallway.

Time to get out of dodge.

The hallway was empty and quiet, eerily so. He half expected a ten-man SWAT team to come barreling down the corridor, but all remained silent.

He quickly padded his way back to the elevator that brought him up to the administrative level. He rounded the corner to his transportation and found it unoccupied and alone. He glanced behind him and ran toward the opened double-doors, his heart beginning to pound in anticipation.

A few feet out they began to close.

He pumped his legs faster and twisted sideways, lunging for the compartment and slamming into the back of the carriage just as the doors slipped shut.

He stood against the wall, breathing hard and waiting.

Nothing happened.

He fished the keycard out of this pocket and slipped it into the slot. Then he pressed his hand against the black glass and waited.

It pulsed predictably blue, then turned red.

No!

He removed his hand and slammed it against the palm reading panel again, then waited.

Blue pulse. Then red.

This time the elevator shuddered to life, the gears far below beginning to carry Silas downward.

He'd been made.

CHAPTER 33

LA MOSQUITIA, HONDURAS.

The pounding between her ears finally brought Torres back into consciousness. She could feel moist dirt under her hands, and the humid smell of rotting debris filled her senses.

She startled, at first not knowing where she was or what had happened. Evening had come, the White City was dimmer than before.

"Relax, Naomi," Grant said sitting next to her. "You're alright. We're alright."

"What happened?" She said groggily.

"They happened," Gapinski said, pointing to two large men with larger necks and even larger automatic rifles slung around their bodies.

Then she remembered the jungle and the White City, the hostiles and the gun butt to the head. They weren't bound, but they were guarded by two of the hired guns huddled together under a large tree off the central plaza where Kimball and his team of archaeologists or treasure hunters or artifact forgers or whatever the heck they were busy working on another set of Mesoamerican artifacts they had unearthed.

She gritted her teeth and started forward.

But one of the guards intercepted her and kicked her backward.

"Hey!" Grant shouted.

Gapinski was about to get up, but the barrel of a gun from behind him was jabbed into his back, reminding him of who was in charge.

"Grant Chrysostom," a man thundered as he walked over to the group boxed in by the base of the tree and the two armed guards. "Never thought I'd see your sorry face again after your little stunt."

"Kimball," Grant growled. "I see you've managed to get ahold of my medallion."

The man grasped the bronze disc in one hand. "You mean this? You mean *my* bronze medallion, my Mormon relic that my man retrieved from your sorry neck? The one you stole from me?"

"Either way, how long did it take you to decode the thing?"

"Apparently, longer than it took you and your illustrious partner to decode it."

"Thanks for the compliment," Gapinski said.

Torres and Grant looked at him. He smirked and looked away.

Then she stood up, going toe to toe with Kimball. "What the hell do you think you're doing here?"

He recoiled at the confrontation. One of the guards quickly grabbed her and shoved her back to the jungle floor. The other guard jammed his gun into Gapinski's back again.

"Hey! You're in my private square, man."

"You're a ripe one, aren't you?" Kimball said to Torres. He crouched next to her. "And who do I have the pleasure of meeting?"

"Naomi Torres. Doctor Naomi Torres."

Kimball leaned back in surprise, a smile spreading across his lips. "*The* Naomi Torres? Mesoamerican extraordinaire who was discredited after pawning off vital artifacts of pre-Columbian culture to the highest bidder on the black market? *That* Naomi Torres?"

She narrowed her eyes, trying to stop the heat from rising up the back of her neck and into her face. She said flatly, "That's the one."

"I hadn't realized you were working for the Order of Thaddeus. But it makes sense that they would put you on such an important religious relic case." He stood. "Just glad we got here when we did."

"You're never going to get away with this," she growled.

"Seriously, Kimball," Grant said. "What are you thinking? I knew you were committed to your religion, but I never took you as someone who would forge history."

The man said nothing. He simply widened his stance, folded his arms, and smiled. After a few seconds, he said, "Let me tell you a story. During the early- to mid-nineteenth century, there was a fevered curiosity surrounding the ruins scattered throughout the Americas. In fact, the biggest selling non-fiction book of the century was a two-volume work on the subject of Maya exploration. Americans were head-over-heels with tales that the New World overflowed with cities and temples and other colossal buildings rivaling the best that Rome, Greece, and Egypt had to offer back in the Old World. Before long, the Mayan civilization and culture came under intense study. Not only by secular scientists, but also the Church of Jesus Christ of Latter-day Saints. They identified the Maya with the lost tribes of Israel. In the 1950s and '60s, there was a fevered attempt by the church to find any archaeological artifacts or settlements that might support the Book of Mormon's claim of early Semitic migration and that the natives of the Americas were in fact lost Israelites. Alongside this search were anti-Mormon pagans who were issuing statements denying any historical or archaeological evidence that would convince them the holy book was anything but a fanciful creation of the mind of Joseph Smith.

"If that wasn't enough, the Smithsonian Institution came along and issued their own statement, refuting the claims of the book's historicity. Claimed their archaeologists saw no direct connection between the archaeology of the New World and the subject matter of the book. Claimed the physical type of the

Native Americans matched the kinds of people from East, Central, and Northeastern Asia, and the evidence suggests they came across the Bering Strait. That the people who visited from the East weren't Israelites but Norsemen, around AD 1000 in Greenland and never reached Central America. They argued that none of the domesticated foods or animals or plants of the Old World occurred in the Americas; they didn't have wheat or oats, horses or chickens before the Europeans arrived. They suggest iron and steel and glass and silk were not used in the New World, as our holy book says they were."

He paused, bending closer. "But we know differently. This site is our proof!"

"Except," Torres said, "there is none nor has there ever been any evidence of ancient Hebrew or other Old World writings in the New World in pre-Columbian contexts. No Old World inscriptions have been shown to occur in any part of the New World before 1492 —including here, in Ciudad Blanca. The only exception being some rune stones found in Greenland which already reflects the history of their having voyaged to that part of North America."

"Kimball," Grant said, "we've spent plenty of time here to know there ain't no Hebrew characters or the Egyptian glyphs Smith claims were etched in golden plates revealing the history of the lost tribes of Israel."

"The White City is the lost Israelites!" Kimball roared, "the Lamanites of the Book of Mormon. Can't you see it? It's just as our holy book describes!"

"Ex post facto, maybe," Torres said sardonically. "You can't discover something and then read it back into your sacred narrative. That's not how historical inquiry works."

"Our faith tells us differently about this holy site. We believe in our hearts the truth of what Joseph Smith recorded after it had been imparted to him from Moroni."

"Yeah, but we know differently," Grant said. "Two anthropologists know differently, might I add. So either you're going to have to lock us up until we die, or you're going to have to kill us. Because we ain't keeping quiet about what you're doing here."

Gapinski jabbed Grant in his side, and mumbled, "Don't give him any suggestions!"

A guard hovering over Gapinski stepped closer.

"Hey, watch it, pal. Private square. Private square!"

Kimball laughed. "I think I'll take my chances, Grant. My people are very good at what they do. Besides, who's going to believe two thieves, one of whom is a professional pariah who was completely discredited for selling cultural artifacts on the black market? No, I think we're going to be just—"

An eruption of gunfire cut him off, coming from the opposite end of the plaza from two separate sources. The bullets were coming in wide and high, meant to distract and provide cover more than anything. But the firepower was definitely not from Kimball and his men.

Had to be the Texas twins!

Gapinski and Grant and Torres immediately hit the ground. Kimball straightened and spun around, then searched for cover. He positioned himself behind the large tree, then ran off toward the tent, crouching low and using one of the raised ruin mounds for cover.

The guard hovering over Gapinski immediately returned fire but was struck by the twin's incoming barrage. It was probably a random stray bullet, but it sucked to be him because it tore a hole through his chest, dropping him cold. The other guard backed up behind the prisoners and started returning fire, leaving no good option for the trio.

They were stuck between two sources of gunfire. Not good.

Suddenly, there was an explosion. A small fireball rose into the sky from near where the men had been carving into the Mesoamerican ruins.

The generator!

Torres smiled. Score another for the twins.

She used the distraction to turn over and kick the bully guard in the groin. He doubled over in surprise and dropped his weapon. Gapinski punched him in the temple, sending him to the ground unconscious.

Grant scooped up the man's weapon, and Gapinski grabbed the one from the guy taken out by the twins.

Two down, three to go.

More gunfire emerged from the jungle, this time from the school bus-like mound they had observed earlier, providing distracting cover for the trio to regroup.

Two archaeologists ran past their tree screaming, trying to seek cover in the jungle. They let them pass, figuring the pair of academics were the least of their worries.

"I'll join in the firefight," Gapinski said, leaning around the tree and taking aim. He released a burst of gunfire from his rifle toward one of the armed men. The man grabbed his leg and cursed loudly before falling to the ground and losing his weapon. He tried picking it back up to return fire but was stopped dead by one of the Texans.

Gapinski smiled with satisfaction, then leaned back and said, "You two go find Kimball. I think the three of us got things pretty well handled."

Torres nodded toward the tent. "Lead the way, Grant."

Gapinski laid down covering fire as the two ran to intercept Kimball. Return fire from the remaining guards sent them crouching behind a mound of earth along the plaza, puffs of dirt and leaves and sod soaring from the bullets.

They heard more gunfire erupt farther up the field. The twins joined in again, which redirected the hostile fire away from their position.

"Come on!" Grant said.

He ran forward, reaching the beige canvas structure first. Without waiting for Torres, he opened the entrance flap, weapon outstretched.

Inside, Kimball was standing over a table holding a radio attached to a transmitter. Grant sprayed bullets into the large electronic box, sending sparks flying and a burst of red from Kimball's leg as he recoiled in fear.

He screamed in pain and fell back against the heavy canvas before sliding to the ground.

"I've already sent a distress call," he moaned. "Help will be arriving shortly!"

Grant aimed the weapon at his chest. "Great. Because you're going to need it."

Torres came up behind him through the entrance flap. She looked from the smoldering box to Kimball who was clutching his leg, hand wet with blood.

"What happened?"

"E. T. was phoning home. Couldn't let that happen now could I?"

She sighed. "If that's true, then we've got about an hour to get out of here and call back for our own reinforcements. Leave him, we should go."

"First things first." Grant walked over to Kimball, reached down, and lifted the bronze disc from around his neck.

"Don't mind if I do."

"Bastard."

"Takes one to know one, pal," Grant said, saluting the man.

He turned to leave when Kimball said, "By the way, your sister says hello."

He stopped short and spun around, his eyes frantic with shock.

"My, my sister...She what? What does she have to do with this?"

One end of the man's mouth curled upward in satisfaction. "Why, she never told you? We wedded this past spring. Sealed in the covenant of marriage by the Church of Jesus Christ of Latter-day Saints. She's already carrying my child. Your niece."

Grant stepped back and aimed his weapon at the man. "Sonofa—"

Torres stepped forward and grabbed his shoulder. "No, wait!"

The gun went off fiercely, its bullets chewing through Kimball quickly at such close range. His body shook with the force of the violence, then fell limp.

She tugged at Grant's arm. "Come on, let's get out of here."

He looked at her wide-eyed, shocked by what he had done. She led him by the arm out of the tent and back into the plaza.

The twins had emerged along with Gapinski. They had dispatched the remaining guards and sent the rest of the hired help scurrying for cover in the jungle.

"You two know how to make an entrance," Torres said to Nick.

He slung his rifle over his shoulder. "You're welcome, ma'am."

He was bleeding from his hand. He said he was fine, only a grazing. But it didn't look like he would be using it again anytime soon. Todd was limping from a sprained ankle. But considering what they had been up against, the Texans called the day a win.

"Let's get back to our gear," Torres said turning toward the main entrance to the settlement site. "We may have company again real soon, and we need to call in our own air support. Especially since the sun is setting."

"Fine by me," Gapinski said.

She hoped Silas was faring better.

CHAPTER 34

SALT LAKE CITY, UTAH.

So not good.

Silas was a caged rabbit who was quickly being hand-delivered to his captors.

No, strike that. He had made himself a caged rabbit when he willingly dashed through his closing cage.

Grey, you idiot!

He paced the elevator cart as it slowly descended to God-knew-where, trying to figure out how to get himself out of the mess he had made.

Think, Silas.

He tried the panel again. Same blue pulse, same red result. He punched it in frustration, only to recoil in pain.

Think, Silas.

He tried prying the doors open, thinking he could climb through them. They wouldn't budge.

He searched around the cabin for anything that could give him a way out. He looked up. What about the ceiling?

He jumped and slammed his fist into one of the tiles. Nothing.

He tried another.

More of the same and the carriage seemed to be picking up speed. Another thirty seconds and it would all be over.

Frustration was boiling. He used it to launch himself higher and send his fist into another tile with more fury.

It didn't move, but he managed to crack it. He jumped and struck it with his fist again, then again. A large chunk of the tile pushed through into the world above, opening a large enough hole for him to push away the remaining pieces and pull himself through.

He jumped and hoisted himself up and through the opening above the elevator carriage. It had just descended past an entrance to another floor. A large number '4' was painted above the opening. He would have to wait for the next level, which would put him uncomfortably close to the waiting posse below.

The ridge of the third level double-doors began to emerge. There was a short lip, about a few inches where the doors were set inside the level entrance. It would be a tight fit and take some finessing, but it was his only option.

Now or never.

Without hesitating, he stepped off into the lip and pressed himself against the doors, his arms taut against the concrete sides. He breathed heavily as he steadied himself, straining with every muscle fiber to keep from falling.

The elevator cart stopped, having reached the bottom. Within seconds whoever and whatever was waiting below would realize their bird had flown the coup. Time to act.

He inched his feet back so that half his foot was hanging off the edge, helping him lean farther against the doors. In one motion, he moved his arms to grasp the crack between the two elevator doors, pressing himself further inward.

Steady, Grey...

He pulled against the doors, straining with all of his might.

They weren't budging.

Come on!

He heard activity below. The doors had opened to his cage. And now there was confusion.

He pulled again, feeling the two metal panels begin to give way. His fingers began to slip inside, and he wiggled them farther in while straining even more to find purchase.

There was more commotion now filtering up through the hole in the elevator carriage's ceiling.

Silas glanced down below and caught sight of a man in a black suit staring up at him through the opening. The man shouted something to someone beside him just as he pried the doors open enough to slip into the hallway beyond.

He fell to the carpeted floor and quickly searched the corridor for signs of hostility.

It was empty, but for the same cream-colored walls, and ostentatious gilding and crystal chandeliers he had seen elsewhere.

He sighed in relief then stood, but had no idea how to escape the giant white temple. He made his way down the hallway, checking doors to see if he could find relief.

That one was locked.

So was that one.

The handle turned on one side of another set of doors. It opened into a massive, darkened theater-style room the height of two floors and length of the temple. Probably the assembly hall for general authorities.

Voices carried down the hallway, sounding frantic and fierce.

He quickly ducked into the room and carefully closed the door so as not to arouse attention, then twisted the lock in place. His footsteps echoed loudly as he ran into the dark space lit only by the moonlight shining through the floor-length windows. He ran past rows of red velvet chairs on a four-tiered platform and underneath large gold light fixtures that looked like clusters of grapes.

He neared the other side when the door jostled loudly as the Danite guards tried opening it. He glanced over his shoulder as he reached another door on the other side of the room. He went to open it, but it was locked. He shook it; it didn't give. This door was locked from the other side.

He turned around as the sound of the door unlocking echoed toward him. No way out!

He ran around to the front of the other four-tiered platform of red velvet couches and quickly ascended the stairs to three high-back chairs he assumed were reserved for the First Presidency.

Tonight they would be cover for a spy.

He ducked down just as the doors at the other end swung open, echoing loudly in the vast space.

In between two chairs, he could see three agents enter the room, at first hesitating, taking in the surroundings. Then they padded through more deliberately. He could see each of them carried a weapon.

Those Mormons meant business.

He tried regulating his breathing as they came closer, sure they could hear his heaving attempts for air.

As they walked past the tiers of rows with red couches, one of the agents stopped. Suddenly, a flashlight flicked on and spread its beam in Silas's direction.

He quickly made himself small, praying to the good Lord that none of him could be seen below the chairs.

The light swung down across the couches and then up toward Silas's chairs again. As the light continued making its sweep, the door Silas had tried jostled loudly. One of the agents said something, and they came back toward the one agent still sweeping with his light.

Then it went dark, and the Danites walked away from Silas's position back toward the original entrance. He heard the door open and close, and the lock clicked into place. Then all went silent.

He closed his eyes and sucked in a lungful of air, not realizing he had been holding his breath. After a few more rounds, he stood and quickly descended the stairs and walked over to one of the windows.

He could see Temple Square below. He assessed the glass and

saw it was too thick to do any real damage quickly enough to make an escape. The drop was pretty far anyway.

Now what?

The only option was the door he had stepped through earlier, the one the Danites had just left through.

He padded carefully toward it. As he neared it, he retrieved his weapon from the small of his back. Just in case.

He paused on the other side of the door, positioning himself to fire. Then he leaned against it and listened.

No sounds, no nothing.

He flexed his fingers around the butt of his gun and waited another minute. He slowly twisted the lock, then grabbed the knob and twisted it as slowly. He held it with one hand and his gun with the other. Then he slowly pulled back the door, training his weapon at the opening. He bent forward to search the corridor.

Empty.

He stepped into the hallway and started making his way toward a door he remembered from the schematics was a stairwell. The plush red carpet squeaked under his feet as he padded toward his exit, weapon at the ready.

He paused at the solid oak door and looked through the beveled glass for any sign of the Danites.

There was none.

He pushed through the door, then started descending the spiral staircase to level two. Then one more, reaching the main level. Through the glass, he could see the corridor was empty. Down the hallway, he knew halfway to the right led to the security checkpoint. Where this whole crazy mission began a few hours ago.

Then it would get interesting.

Silas went to open the door when he heard a noise one floor above. Someone had come through the door on the second floor.

He pressed against the wall on the other side of the exit and trained his weapon up the stairs. He glimpsed a man wearing a bowtie, but his face was turned, and the angle was wrong to identify him.

But Silas could have sworn he looked like...

No. Couldn't be. No way.

The man turned toward the stairs and ascended to the third floor. He took a deep breath and sighed.

Time to get the heck out of there.

He opened the door and stepped through, then padded quickly toward his hallway to freedom.

A man in a dark suit and a scowl to match rounded the corner. He stopped short, surprised as much as disdainful. Glaring at Silas, the man brought his wrist to his mouth.

He began to say something, but Silas wouldn't let him.

He barreled into the man at full speed, leveling him in the middle of the hallway and shoving his forearm into the man's throat. At the other end, the two security guards posted at the entrance were startled, but they retrieved their weapons and aimed for Silas.

He had seconds to act. So Silas leaned back off the man and grabbed him by the chest. Then he twisted him around and put his gun to the man's right temple.

"Don't do it!" A guard shouted. The men had trained their weapons on Silas and were reaching for their radios.

"Drop the radios or I blow the man's brains out!"

"Alright, alright," the other guard said, the man who had originally seen Silas through the security procedures. "Just don't do anything you'll regret."

"No way I'll regret it. I'm ex-Ranger. This is what I've been trained for. So I would advise you to lower your weapons and step aside so I can leave."

The man glanced at his partner who looked as though he wanted to be anywhere but there.

"Do it!"

"Just calm down, sir. We can't let you leave. Not after you answer some questions."

Silas lurched forward and pressed the gun tighter against the man's temple, causing him to jerk his head leftward.

"Hold on, man!" the one guard shouted. "We'll lower our weapons." He nodded to his partner.

"Drop them to the floor," Silas commanded.

The two men looked at each other, as if wondering if they were making the most significant career move of their lives.

Silas shuffled forward a few feet again. "Now!"

In one movement, the two men bent over and tossed their guns to the floor.

"Now kick them to the side."

As they obliged, Silas could hear footfalls echoing behind him. The cavalry had arrived.

He quickly moved forward, still bearing the Danite guard in front with the gun pressed to his temple. He pushed through the two guards then pivoted with his back to the exit. He eyed the men as he leaned against its door to make his escape.

But it didn't budge.

He pushed harder.

Nothing.

Four men rounded the corner at the other end of the hallway, with three more following close behind. All seven drawing their weapons at once at the sight of Silas.

"Unlock the door!" he shouted, pressing his weapon into the guard's temple.

He backed into the door again.

Nothing.

"I'm not messing around. So help me God—"

Suddenly, his body fell through the exit. He stumbled backward, nearly toppling over with the weight of the guard against him. But he recovered.

Silas threw the man forward and quickly padded backward as

the Danite posse came into view. He had kept to a strict regimen of running and weights since leaving the Army, so he figured he could outrun the men.

So he booked it.

He turned around and hustled his way through Temple Square, glancing back to see that the agents had stopped just outside the entrance. They weren't even trying to catch him.

Five blocks later he reached University Boulevard and ran into a parking lot, settling in between a Mustang and Jetta on the far side. When he was satisfied he hadn't been followed, he walked back to the boulevard and flagged down a taxi.

"Where to, pal," the guy said.

"The airport."

"International or domestic."

"Definitely domestic."

He and Radcliffe had lots to sort through.

CHAPTER 35

W hen Silas arrived at the SEPIO headquarters and walked into Radcliffe's study, he was greeted by three familiar faces. Torres, Grant, and Gapinski were all too eager to share what they had discovered.

Radcliffe was much more interested in what Silas had found.

Silas recounted everything: the opposition research on Matthew Reed, his financial records and policy platforms; the folder on the Faithful Majority detailing the financial contributions to the organization members and the organization itself; the letter from Joseph Smith to a group of Mormons in Missouri with reference to his Golden Bible and vision that had apparently been sent along with the bronze medallion detailing the location of the supposed lost tribe of the Lamanites. Then he launched into the revelation surrounding Amos Young himself. That he appeared to be an Apostle with the Quorum of the Twelve. That he had plans to form a theocratic government with Mormon leadership firmly at the helm. That he saw himself as the fulfillment of the Mormon eschatological prophecies concerning the end of America, as well as the savior, come to save the Constitution from destruction and pull its citizens out from calamity.

Then Silas played for them the entire conversation he recorded.

It was a bit muffled, and at times hard to understand, but it was clear enough what they were saying. And who was saying it.

When it stopped the group stood in stunned silence.

"OK, we've got nothing on your adventure," Gapinski said.

Grant offered, "Yeah, you know, we just survived a near-death experience aboard a sabotaged plane, discovered the existence of Ciudad Blanca, and managed to get ourselves out of a sticky wicket involving Nous or Danites or whoever-the-hell they were."

Silas stood stunned and confused, so Torres brought him up to speed on the past few days' events.

"Remarkable," he said. Then he turned to Radcliffe who had remained silent as his operatives shared their stories of adventure. "What do you make of all of this?"

Radcliffe had been seated during the travelogue. He put both elbows on his armrests and folded his hands in front of him. He took a deep breath, then sighed. "It's clear that the Mormons are making an incredible play here, setting into motion events that will force fulfillment of their religion's most sacred prophecies and histories. On the one hand, they are making a move to finally legitimize their sacred book, which historians have dismissed as an outright fraud, let alone Christian theologians as heresy. Then there is the political angle, in which the LDS Church is seeking to fulfill Joseph Smith's prophecies regarding the End Times in America, which anticipates a Mormon savior coming to America's rescue and Mormon Saints themselves enacting the Kingdom of God through theocratic rule."

Torres stepped forward. "Let's set aside the politics for a moment. What do you make of the White City? What about the medallion itself? Is it a legitimate artifact? How could it have been so dead on when it came to its location, yet so dead wrong when it came to its conclusions about what the city actually was?"

Radcliffe nodded. "Good questions. I expect we'll have some answers soon when Zoe completes her analysis of the medallion, finishing whatever she's doing with the thing to make it talk. But let me start by taking us back to the time of Joseph Smith. Speculation ran rampant during Smith's day as to why there were natives in the New World and where they had come from to begin with. It was an especially popular topic of conversation in his neck of the woods in western New York, mostly because of the extensive burial mounds that dotted the landscape. In one article that appeared in Smith's hometown newspaper, it was theorized that the country was inhabited by a race of people who were partially civilized, and who had been eliminated by the current tribes of Indians. Another article appearing in the same newspaper theorized the mounds were descendants of Noah's sons who had crossed the Atlantic Ocean. This reflected one of the dominant contemporary theories at the time linking the native Americans with Israelites."

"Wait," Grant interrupted. "There were legitimate non-Mormon theories that traced the pre-Columbian natives in the Americas to Israel?"

He nodded. "In fact, the very same proposition had been circulated as far back as 1567, when a one Fredericus Luminius suggested the New World inhabitants were the lost Ten Tribes of Israel. Of all of the nineteenth-century theories concerning where the Indians had come from, none was more widely held in Smith's day than the theory identifying Native Americans as descendants of the lost tribes of Israel. Which isn't surprising since mainland Europe had been surmising for centuries where those tribes ended up, the most common explanation being British-Israelism."

"You're kidding," Torres said. "Brits believed they were descendants of Israel?"

"More than that. The most common explanation for the fate of the lost tribes of Israel is that their descendants were the Caucasians scattered across the earth. It was a widely publicized theory with reputable journalistic and scholarly backing. When such a theory migrated to America is unclear, but it was established by the late 1870s. And its related concept suggesting that Israel's lost tribes had migrated to the Americas across the Atlantic and were ancestors to the natives enjoyed similar acceptance. Joseph Smith was the first person to blend both theories into a grand religious scheme. Add to that the fascination with the Mayan ruins scattered throughout the Americas and the intense interest in antiquities of the New World, there was an obvious confluence Smith could mine as foundational fodder for his upstart religion."

"Fascinating history lesson, Padre," Grant said, "but where does the medallion come into play? Is it a forgery?"

"Yes and no," Zoe said, arriving through the double doors and walking to the group.

Torres smiled at Grant, then said to Zoe, "You've got results?"

"Definitely. Here's the thing: the medallion is legit."

Grant crossed his arms and asked, "What do you mean, legit?"

"I mean, the glyphs check out as Mesoamerican, and the characters along the side are accurate, which you already knew. The bronze itself is old. Just not from before the eighteenth or nineteenth centuries."

"Which means what?" Silas asked.

"Which means it's a forgery," Torres answered.

Zoe nodded. "I'd say. And a good one at that. The metal dates to the late-eighteenth and early-nineteenth centuries, which means it was forged at or around the time Joseph Smith was born. My guess is that the guy found some bronze plates and just made himself a medallion. Because it definitely isn't some relic from pre-Columbian times, as the guy was making it out to be."

"But to what end?" Silas asked.

"Legitimacy," Radcliffe said. "And it's no surprise to me that he would have gone to these kinds of lengths to give historical credence to his man-made religion."

"Why not?" Torres asked.

Radcliffe explained, "Apparently, the Smiths were known treasurer hunters, as well as hucksters. Here." He brought out a tablet computer and opened a file. "Listen to this notice signed by fifty-one of the Smiths' neighbors in Palmyra, dated December 4, 1833:

We, the undersigned, have been acquainted with the Smith family, for a number of years, while they resided near this place, and we have no hesitation in saying, that we consider them destitute of the moral character, which ought to entitle them to the confidence of any community. They were particularly famous for visionary projects, spent much of their time digging for money which they pretended was hid in the earth; and to this day, large excavations may be seen in the earth, not far from their residence, where they used to spend their time digging for hidden treasures. Joseph Smith, Senior, and his son Joseph were in particular considered destitute of moral character and addicted to vicious habits.

"Remind me never to piss off my neighbors," Gapinski said.

Radcliffe continued, "There were plenty of other similar testimonies from people who had either watched from the sidelines as the Smith clan plied their treasure-seeking trade or had been taken in by it. Either way, Joseph was well acquainted with the art of deception when it came to trinkets and treasure. Like the medallion."

"So the working theory," Torres interjected, "is that Joseph Smith forged this medallion as a way to bolster his claims in the Book of Mormon about the lost tribes of Israel, merging the existing stories floating around about the Israelites immigrating to the Americas and the discoveries of the Maya. And we theorize he created the disc and then faked the glyphs, perhaps basing them off of existing pre-Columbian native glyphs he had seen or heard about at the time. And then he etched the Hebrew prophetic verses along its edge, which he had co-opted from the King James Bible anyway and put in his fake one."

"Exactly," Radcliffe said. "Smith must have sent it off to a known settlement of Mormon followers in Missouri. To the site where you found it, Mr. Chrysostom. And your finding that letter, Silas, seems to confirm that. As a metallurgist, treasure seeker, and expert huckster, Smith would have been more than capable of pulling off something like this, drawing from his talents from his former life before becoming the prophet of his religion."

"Just think," Grant offered, "he succeeded."

"They *almost* succeeded," Torres corrected. "It was the Mormon Church which tried to desecrate the White City in order to forge it into a lie to suit their purposes."

"And don't forget Nous," Gapinski added. "They're as much behind this plot to legitimize the Mormon religion as the Mormon Church is."

"As well as discredit authentic Christianity in America," Silas added.

The other four nodded in agreement.

He continued, "We haven't even talked about the mother lode I uncovered in Utah. Amos Young is part of the upper echelons of the Mormon hierarchy, for crying out loud! Pretty sure he's an Apostle of the Quorum, maybe even part of the First Presidency, a right- or left-hand man to President Russell Nelson himself. His campaign and the candidate himself is definitely suppressing that info."

"Yeah, Americans would freak," Gapinski said, "let alone the American church."

"And rightly so, given his plans for theocratic rule in America."

"Correction," Grant said. "Mormon theocratic rule."

"Exactly." Silas turned to Radcliffe. "What are we going to do about that? We need to expose the huckster for who he is."

Radcliffe said nothing. Instead, he sat strumming his fingers together, with pursed lips and narrowed eyes.

He finally said, "So what do you propose?"

"We got the guy on tape," Gapinski said. "I say, let it loose into the interwebs!"

The others looked at Radcliffe for confirmation of the move.

"The problem with that, is the recording isn't the best quality. And, while inflammatory, it isn't apparent that it's Amos Young. Yes, we can hear him clear as a whistle, but that's only because we know it's him. Then there is the whole chain of custody issue, regarding how you came to be in possession of the recording in the first place. I'm not sure the Order of Thaddeus would want to draw that kind of precarious legal attention. I'm sorry, but we need to think of something else."

The four were crestfallen. Silas, Grant, and Torres sat down, slumping in their chairs. Gapinski leaned against Radcliffe's desk. They spent the next several minutes in silence.

Someone finally said, "What about a debate?"

It was Grant. Radcliffe turned to him. "What do you mean, Mr. Chrysostom? A debate?"

"Like one of those good-for-nothing, two-hour-long televised events where the two or ten or seventeen knuckleheads say whatever Joe the Plumber and Jane the Stewardess wants them to say without saying anything at all. But in this case, you, Silas, say what everyone needs to hear, but Young won't want you to say."

Silas chuckled. "OK. And what's that?"

"The truth about Mormonism."

"I like the sound of that!" Gapinski exclaimed. "Young and Silas, mano a mano, discussing the finer points of Mormon theology. It'd be a ratings bonanza!"

"I don't know about this," Silas said nervously. "Why me and him?"

Gapinski answered, "Because like it or not, kid, you're the scholarly face of the Order."

Radcliffe smiled and nodded. Silas did not.

Grant continued, "Get that wanker James Maxwell involved. Shoot, have him host the dang thing. But at a neutral location, someplace politically respectable."

"The Washington Press Club," Radcliffe added.

"Even better! Get the national media to cover it and televise it.

I'm sure the Evangelical community would give them a ratings bonanza to hear from the horse's lips what he believes. Not to mention the broader Christian community."

"But how?" Torres asked. "Not to throw cold water on your cozy bonfire, but how do we get him to commit to something like this? What's the incentive for the guy to even do it?"

Silas said, "For one, he needs a boost in the polls. And this could do it among his core constituents."

"Yeah, if they buy what he's selling."

"We've got the recording," Gapinski said.

"Which we can't use," Silas added.

The group went silent.

Finally, Radcliffe spoke. "I think I have the answer."

The four of them turned to hear his strategy.

Instead, he pulled out his phone. "I need the room."

They looked at each other, each registering confusion.

"What's your angle, chief?" Gapinski said.

Then it hit Silas. He answered before Radcliffe could: "The money."

Gapinski whistled. "Questioning a religious organization's skrill is like poking a rattlesnake with a stick. You best watch yourself."

"That's not the only thing Mr. Maxwell and I need to discuss." Radcliffe sat looking at his phone, scrolling through his contacts. "As I mentioned a while back when this whole blasted thing started, James and I have history. And it's bloody well time I tap that vein."

"Brutal," Gapinski said.

He found the number then selected it. It started ringing. "I think it would do us all a world of good to get a good night's sleep. We've still got a long road ahead of us."

Silas nodded, along with Torres, Grant, and Gapinski. The four of them left just as Radcliffe offered Maxwell a greeting.

Silas wished he could be a fly on the wall to hear that conversation.

The others said goodnight and drifted off to bed. Instead of heading for sleep himself, Silas went to the Order's massive underground library.

Sleep could wait.

Time to cram for the debate of his life.

CHAPTER 36

Silas was sweating. And it wasn't just because of the row of klieg lights illuminating the soundstage. His nerves were beginning to fray sitting in his chair across the empty one Amos Young would be sitting in, facing the small studio audience and the cameras and James Maxwell.

For the past day, Silas had been cramming for his one-on-one sparing session with the man who was seeking to be President of the United States. In a few days, the American people would be voting between a Mormon Republican candidate and a Catholic Democrat candidate. The choice was even starker for evangelical Christians: Robert Santos was far more aligned with them theologically and religiously than Amos Young.

Santos was leading Young by only two points, with a margin of error of three. Among Evangelicals, 79 percent were pulling for the Mormon. If he lost a percentage point of that constituency, he would lose the election. He needed to convince them that they had nothing to fear—from either his religion or politics.

Hence the little "discussion," as Maxwell had framed the evening.

Silas was scribbling some thoughts on an authorized notebook provided for him. From stage right, he heard two men laugh. A few seconds later in walked Maxwell and Young. Might as well have been arm-in-arm, like two love-birds, the way they were carrying on.

He closed the notebook, then wiped his moist hands on his pants.

"Professor Grey," Maxwell said smiling, walking over with his hand extended. Silas stood and smiled himself, grasping it firmly.

"James. Good of you to host our discussion this evening."

"Aww, my pleasure. I think it will be a productive evening, a way to reassure the Church of what's at stake in the coming week. Wouldn't you agree?" Maxwell's grin was fixed, his gaze penetrating.

Silas held his gaze. "I agree. There is certainly a lot at stake."

"Good. Good." He let go of Silas's hand and motioned toward Amos Young, still grinning. "Silas, may I introduce to you the candidate, Amos Young. Amos, this is Silas Grey, your sparring partner from Princeton."

"Formally of Princeton," Silas corrected, still smiling and extending his hand. "Pleasure meeting you, Mr. Young."

"Likewise," the man said, his voice firm and grip firmer.

Maxwell said, "Alright, the production assistant has told me we have fifteen minutes until the cameras roll. I like to think of this evening as more of a discussion than a debate. There is surely more that unites us than divides us, namely the name of Jesus Christ."

Young nodded, his face solemn and serious. "Amen."

Silas said nothing.

"We'll open with brief opening statements from the two of you. Then I will launch into a few questions to get us rolling and then open it up for a discussion about our shared beliefs."

Shared beliefs? This guy was high on Beltway Ganja, that's for sure. Intoxicated by the prospect of political power by having his guy in the White House.

Silas wanted to puke.

He also felt terrible for Maxwell. Because his plans were vastly different than the Religious Right figurehead.

Maxwell nodded to a man standing off to the side holding a clipboard and wearing an oversized pair of headphones with a microphone.

"Alright, gentlemen. Showtime."

The three took their seats. The production assistant was giving words to the small studio audience. Cameramen were checking their equipment and getting ready to roll.

Silas's heart was galloping forward. He was grateful he received a final smattering of makeup from a slight man, though he felt he was glistening to the nth degree.

Just breathe...

He felt the future of the American Church was riding on his performance. He knew he was putting way too much pressure on himself, but he wanted to knock it out of the park, nonetheless.

Before he knew it, Maxwell was starting his opening monologue.

"Good evening. My name is James Maxwell, president of Freedom University and chairman of the Faithful Majority, both Christian institutions my late father started with the interest of raising and empowering the next generation of Christians who would unashamedly bear witness to the gospel of Jesus Christ in the public square.

"In a few days, we will be going to the polls to elect the next President of the United States, capping perhaps one of the most consequential election seasons in a generation. Not least of which has been the faith convictions of the candidate for the Republican Party, Amos Young. Many Bible-believing Christians have had questions about what he believes, especially when it comes to Jesus and his death and salvation. So the Faithful Majority thought, why not put those fears to rest and have an open conversation about his Mormon beliefs?

"Joining us this evening is Silas Grey, former professor of Christian historical theology and religious studies with Princeton University, and now a researcher at an ecumenical Christian organization, the Order of Thaddeus. He will bring the perspective of a Christian theologian to bear on our discussion. Of course, joining him is the Republican candidate himself, Amos Young, who will discuss his faith in Jesus and his Christian beliefs."

Maxwell turned from the camera to Young and then to Silas. "Gentlemen, welcome."

"Great to be here, James," Young said.

Silas smiled and nodded at Young. "Yes, great to have this discussion."

Maxwell continued, "We have a lot to cover in the next hour, and I expect this discussion will be wide-ranging, so I want to start off right away and offer you, Mr. Young, the chance to talk about your faith. What would you like to say to American Christians, and to everyone in America who may have questions about what you believe?"

Silas turned toward Young, who was smiling broadly, owning the camera across from him with ease.

"Thanks again, James, for this invitation to express my faith more directly than I have been able to before." He pivoted in his chair toward Silas. "And thank you, Professor Grey, for joining this discussion, as well." Silas smiled and nodded.

He turned back toward the camera. "Now, I'm no theologian like my fellow believer here is, but I have been a faithful member of my church my whole life. I've sought to follow in the way of Jesus and live my life in accordance with his will. And I submit that there is more that unites us than divides us. We are all pro-life, for instance, desiring to care for the most vulnerable members of our society from cradle to the grave, believing all human life is a sacred gift from God. We similarly believe that, when it comes to marriage, changes in the civil law do not and cannot change the moral law that God has established. We also care deeply about issues of justice and equity, and about creation care. So, as people of faith, I see no reason why fellow Christians can't come together in our shared beliefs in order to see the values of God's Kingdom be established in this great society—values like peace and justice, love and respect, which Jesus himself modeled."

Young gave a short nod to Maxwell, indicating he was finished with his monologue.

Silas thought it was interesting that Young framed his faith in political terms. He would correct the mistake, immediately pivoting the conversation back to the theological.

"Thank you, Mr. Young. Now Professor Grey, what say you?"

Silas took a breath and tried to smile, but found his mouth quivering slightly from adrenaline. "Thank you, James, and thank you, Mr. Young, for engaging in this frank discussion about what has always been central to the Christian faith." He paused to gather his thoughts and find his own camera. When he saw a red light off stage right, he assumed it was a camera and began his own monologue.

"Someone once said that the story of Christian theology is the story of Christian reflection on salvation. At the center of this discussion isn't a personal story about faith, it isn't a set of political issues like abortion and gay marriage. What we're here to talk about is what is authentically Christian, and reflect about what Christians have always believed about God and creation, sin and humanity, and who Jesus is and what Jesus has done. Because at the end of the day, the answers we give—" Silas pivoted toward Young. "The answers Mr. Young gives to those questions matter deeply, because those answers are ultimately about salvation. How people can experience rescue from sin and death, from the shame and guilt they so desperately need. Christianity says one thing. Mormons say another."

Silas sat back and nodded at Maxwell, then turned to Young. The man looked like a deer caught in headlights. It was clear this was not the way he imagined the conversation going. Even Maxwell seemed taken aback by Silas going all in from the start.

Yet the discussion was going exactly where he wanted it to go.

"Why don't we get specific," Maxwell said, turning back to Young. "What do you believe about God?"

Before he could answer, Silas said, "Mormons believe there are many gods. Another word for it is polytheism."

"That's neither fair nor accurate," Young responded. "The Church's first article of faith is clear: 'We believe in God, the Eternal Father, and in his Son, Jesus Christ, and in the Holy Ghost. These three beings make up the Godhead.'"

"Yes, but that's the problem," Silas shot back. "It's the heresy of Tritheism, which posits the cosmic divinity of Father, Son, and Holy Spirit are three separate gods. Not three persons with one essential being, as the historic Christian faith teaches."

"You're going to play the heresy card?" Young interjected.

But Silas plowed forward. "Mormonism believes that God and Jesus Christ are glorified, physical beings and that each member of the Godhead is a separate being. That's a blatant denial of the Trinity, which Mormonism has historically rejected. In fact, they teach that the universe is filled with multiple gods, and the god of this planet is an exalted man, Elohim, God the Father with a body of flesh and bones. He has at least one wife, probably more. Isn't that what you believe, Mr. Young?"

Young said nothing, his face transfixed with a weird grin. "I believe what my church believes. I believe in God, the Eternal Father, and in his Son, Jesus Christ, and in the Holy Ghost."

He quickly looked to Maxwell to move the conversation along.

Silas wouldn't let him.

"One of the more interesting aspects of Mormon beliefs," Silas said, "is its understanding of humanity. They teach that every person pre-exists in heaven as a spirit-child, conceived through what they call celestial sex, between Heavenly Father and Heavenly Mother. In fact, Mormons say they are gods in embryo, and they have not yet reached the godhood. 'As man is, God once was: as God is, man may become,' one of their prophets taught. Isn't that right? Which pretty much contradicts Christian teaching on human nature."

Young said nothing, sitting in seemingly stunned confusion with a visible bead of sweat sliding down his forehead.

"And then there is Jesus. Mormonism teaches that he is the first spirit-child of Heavenly Father, which means he is created. And remarkably, he is the brother of another famous spirit-child: Lucifer. According to their teachings, Jesus is only one of many created gods through the union of Heavenly Father and Heavenly Mother. Jesus was a polygamous Jewish male and one of three gods overseeing this planet."

"Wait just a minute," Young said, his voice shaking in irritation, perhaps even fear. "I believe in the same Jesus as you. How can you sit here and deny my belief in Jesus, the man who was chosen by God the Father to die for the sins of the world? Who was resurrected for our eternal life?"

Silas noted his use of Christian jargon but was unconvinced. He needed to tread lightly in order to expose what was factually true about Mormonism.

He faced Young, looking directly into his eyes. "I don't want to presume to know or tell you what you believe. What I'm much more interested in discussing is what Mormons believe, rather than what you believe, Mr. Young. And Mormonism teaches that Jesus was conceived on earth through sexual intercourse between Heavenly Father and Mary."

Maxwell coughed at that suggestion, not seeming to know his own Mormon theology.

"Christianity insists something very different," Silas continued, "that Jesus is not a created being but the Creator—by whom, through whom, and for whom all things were made. I refer you to the Nicene Creed. You know, the one at the heart of authentic Christianity. It says: *We believe...in one Lord Jesus Christ, the only Son of God, begotten from the Father before all ages, God from God, Light from Light, true God from true God, begotten, not made; of the same essence as the Father.*

"Historic Christianity insists Jesus was miraculously conceived and born of the Virgin Mary in fulfillment of the prophecies in the Hebrew Scriptures regarding the coming Messiah. Here's one of them, Isaiah 7:14: 'Therefore the Lord himself will give you a sign. Look, the young woman is with child and shall bear a son, and shall name him Immanuel.' He was conceived without the aid of a man and natural means, but entirely by the power of the Holy Spirit. He is the unique, begotten Son of God with whom no one and nothing else can be compared. Jesus was an unmarried rabbi of Jewish descent and the Second Person of the Holy Trinity. Which means he was both very human and very God, together at once. And, by the way, he has zip, zero, zilch relationship with Satan, who was a created angelic being who rebelled against God."

Young simply shook his head and chuckled, displaying his wide smile again.

"Alright, gentlemen." Maxwell cleared his throat. "We may disagree about the semantics of Christian belief. Shoot, even Calvinists and Catholics can't get along!" he said chuckling, "but we're all Christian. We all trust in the cross of Christ and Jesus' gift of salvation."

Young nodded. "That's right. I believe salvation signifies a covenant relationship with Jesus Christ. Through this relationship with Jesus, followers of Christ are assured salvation from the eternal consequences of sin if they are obedient."

Silas interjected, "But that 'if' is a slight problem. First, according to Mormonism, Jesus' sacrificial death is limited, not being able to cleanse all people of their sins. And ultimately there is no salvation without accepting Joseph Smith as a prophet of God. Within Mormonism, salvation is achieved only by those who do enough good work to merit that rescue. Works of righteousness, maintaining all of the laws of God, earn a person the right to eternal life."

"You don't believe people need to obey the laws of God?" Young challenged, grinning slightly. "That they need to live as a faithful Christian?"

Silas returned the smile. "Of course I do. But Christianity insists that we obey in response to God's gift of salvation, not to earn or merit it. The apostle Paul explains it perfectly in Ephesians: 'For by grace you have been saved through faith, and this is not your own doing; it is the gift of God— not the result of works, so that no one may boast.' Jesus paid for all the sins of the world by being crucified on the cross, offering himself as a bloody ransom payment on behalf of every person. God's gift of salvation from sin and death is not earned or obtained through works, but through repentance, asking for God's forgiveness, and following Jesus by believing in his death and resurrection. That's it. Finally, Jesus alone is the way, the truth, and the life. No one can come to Father to find and experience salvation but by and through him. Not also through Joseph Smith and his teachings and laws. Only through Jesus' life, death, and resurrection. That's a marked difference from the kind of salvation Mormonism offers."

Silas faced Maxwell, who was not looking too pleased. Young sat silent, face flat and looking to Maxwell for similar direction.

"Gentlemen, I believe we're running out of time."

Of course, now that your plans of normalizing Mormon beliefs before a Christian audience went up in smoke.

"I want to give you both a few minutes to offer some closing thoughts for the evening." He turned to Silas, face pained and pinched. "Why don't we start with you, Professor."

Silas smiled. "Thank you, James. And thanks again, Mr. Young. I think this was a productive discussion." He turned toward the camera and looked straight into its lens, talking to it as if he were addressing his own brother.

"The question before us," Silas said more loudly, "isn't, 'Are Mormons Christian?' Instead, we need to be asking, 'Are Christians Mormons?' Do people who call themselves Christians believe what

276 | J. A. BOUMA

Mormons believe? Has the Church of Jesus, the one that has existed for the last two millennia ever believed at all what the Church of Jesus Christ of Latter-day Saints believe—which has only been in existence for less than 200 years? No way, no how. So if Christians don't believe what Mormons believe, and we could never say that a Christian is a Mormon, why would we ever insist on the reverse? That would be like saying a Muslim Christian. Muslims do not believe what Christians believe. Christians do not believe what Muslims believe. Neither of those are controversial statements. They are factual ones. So why would we suggest the same for Mormons? It's unrealistic, pointless really, for anyone who does not accept the beliefs of a religion to claim otherwise. Which is precisely what Mormonism does."

Maxwell went to interject, but Silas plowed ahead.

"What's most troubling," Silas continued more loudly, "is how there has been a relentless attempt by LDS leaders to Christianize their image over the years. They have clouded explanations of Mormon beliefs by adopting Christian terminology and jargon. I remember reading a *Newsweek* article that reported how Mormonism insists that it be regarded as a Christian church, even though its doctrines about God, salvation, and the priesthood differ radically from traditional Christianity. That's a secular, non-Christian news magazine acknowledging that, to the uninformed, the Mormon religion looks more Christian. And yet, it differs radically from the historic, authentic Christian faith. This has happened by placing more emphasis on the name of Jesus without actually changing any of their core beliefs, including about Jesus himself. At every turn, Mormonism contradicts and compromises beliefs that have always been central to the Christian faith. It is truly a man-made religion and bears no resemblance to authentic Christianity, offering a truly American god."

Silas sat back, satisfied with his performance. Now it was Young's turn to respond.

The man looked grim, but he forced a smile. He swallowed

hard, and said, "There's nothing more than I can add, other than to say that I believe in Jesus and try to live my life according to his teachings. I think that life speaks for itself." With that, he sat back.

Maxwell cleared his throat. "Well, gentlemen...I thank you for your time and your candor. I think this has been a rousing, productive discussion about important matters of faith that should give value-voters much to chew on. Why don't we call it a night, shall we?"

He looked at the camera nestled between the two men and quickly signed off. He thanked the viewing audience for participating in the critical spiritual process of seeing God's Kingdom come on earth as it is in heaven through the democratic process.

The outro music played, and yet the room was eerily quiet. Young continued playing for the camera, fixing a well-honed smile on his face as he looked out at the viewing public. Then he stood and turned toward his opponent. Silas joined him, smiling his own performed gratitude, as well. Young nodded and stuck out his hand.

Now was his chance. But he would have to be quick.

Silas grabbed Young's hand and pulled the man toward himself with a tight grip. He leaned toward the man's ear, with the same plastered smile still affixed, then whispered, "There will be a complete change of government. This is the year of the Latter-day Saints. That's what you said, in the Apostles Room the day before last. I was there, I was listening."

He continued smiling, maintaining his grip. Young's face fell, he tried to let go. Silas wouldn't let him.

"I have it all on a recording. I want to meet. Tonight. Lincoln Memorial. One hour. Or I go public."

He let go and walked off stage, hoping Young would take the bait.

CHAPTER 37

A biting wind was chasing the steadily falling rain, lashing the massive white limestone columns and rising marble walls of the Lincoln Memorial.

Silas was leaning against the wall of the yawning entrance just beyond the rain's reach, his back to Honest Abe and facing the expansive National Mall leading down to the People's House at the end. At the center, the Washington Monument was shining like a beacon of hope, flanked on either side by two monuments testifying to the greatness of the nation: the Jefferson Memorial, dedicated to the third President of the United States who was the principal author of the Declaration of Independence, one of the greatest political documents ever conceived; and the White House, the modest two-story Neoclassical home to the President and symbol of America's citizen-power and global leadership.

He checked his watch. Another seven minutes. He better not be late.

A burst of wind sprayed the late-October dousing toward Silas, catching his face and catching him off guard. He jumped back slightly, raising the collar of his gray wool peacoat and wiping his face with his sleeve.

Silas adjusted his posture against the memorial wall, so that he was leaning toward the white presidential residence. Clumps of orange and red and yellow leaves still clung to the American oaks that lined the National Mall basin. He strained to look beyond them to glimpse the gleaming white home, considering the man who was seeking to occupy that palace. America may not have a titular head as in Old World England, but she still had an executive who had grown in power and stature over the last decade, garnering king-like influence that had the power to steer the nation in a way not ever conceived by the Founding Fathers.

Which is why it was vital for the Order to stop Amos Young from being elected President of the United States of America.

A noise caught his attention from behind. He pivoted around the wall, seeing three large men in black trench coats emerge from a door to the right of Lincoln's statue and make their way toward him.

"Mr. Grey," one of them said, "would you step over here, please?"

Silas leaned forward off the wall and walked toward the agent. The man motioned for him to spread his legs and lift his arms. The two other men eyed him as the agent began scanning Silas's chest with a long black wand. He then moved to his arms and legs.

"All clear," he said.

The agent stepped aside and walked toward the middle of the large entrance to the memorial to stand guard. The two others joined him, standing one at each side facing outward.

A minute later three more agents emerged from the same door next to Lincoln, followed closely by Amos Young.

"I didn't think you'd show," Silas said as the man walked up to him, getting uncomfortably close. He towered above him in a soft dark blue, floor-length wool coat, his face hard and eyes cold.

"Shall we?" he said motioning toward the entrance away from the ears of his agents.

He motioned for them to hold back and asked the other three who had positioned themselves a few moments earlier to give them some space. They looked at each other, unsure. It had taken every ounce of authoritative muscle to get them to agree to take him to the unsecured location at such short notice, but they had relented. Now they probably didn't want to be on watch when another presidential candidate was assassinated. But they obliged and moved forward out into the rain, securing the perimeter like good soldiers.

"Talk," Young simply said staring out into the national mall.

Silas took a breath. He hoped Zoe was ready to work her magic. "The night before last, you were at a special meeting of the Quorum of the Twelve Apostles at the Salt Lake Temple. If I were to wager, you're actually one of those twelve ambassadors of the Mormon Church. Or perhaps even a member of one of the special councils to the Mormon President, sitting on the First Presidency. Either way, you spoke of overthrowing the U. S. government and establishing a theocratic Mormon rule. That's what the Constitution calls treason." He paused, letting his revelation sink in.

Young said nothing, continuing to stand, feet apart, staring out into the lashing rain.

"As I said in the studio, I have it all on a recording I made with my phone standing outside the doors."

The man suddenly turned his head toward Silas, his face more hardened, his eyes much colder. That got his attention.

"Remember the sudden pause to your little Mormon pow-wow, the one where you and your brethren were evacuated? Yeah, that was me."

Recognition splayed briefly across Young's face. He turned away.

Silas turned around to face Young as the rain began to pick up speed. "You drop out of the race, or I will release the recording. Say it's for family reasons or a newly diagnosed health problem or whatever the heck excuse you want to give. Just do it in the next twenty-four hours, or I go public."

Young turned to face Silas, rain lapping against the left side of his body and face. "You wouldn't dare."

"Actually, I would. I'm that sort of guy."

The two men stood staring at each other, waiting for the other to blink first.

Young was the first to disengage. He grinned and turned to walk away.

Silas furrowed his brow, worried he had played his hand too quickly, too hard. Was he losing the man?

"I'm serious, Amos," he yelled, his voice echoing back to him off the marble walls. The agents looked toward him. "Drop out by tomorrow night or the world will know of your plot."

"Why?" he shot back loudly. He turned around back toward Silas. "What is the point?"

Silas waited for a beat. "The preservation of the Christian faith."

He stepped closer to Silas. "Excuse me? Th...The what?"

Silas stepped forward himself, not willing to be outmatched.

He said, "Your elevation to the highest office in the land, with the full backing of the Religious Right, would give you a religious platform that would decimate the integrity of authentic Christianity. Your people have already done a wonderful job at muddying the waters over the last decade through a campaign of propaganda and distortion. People are already confused about what is authentically Christian. Your election, and with the help and endorsement of Evangelicals, will further that confusion. And your little speech in Utah made it clear that you want Mormonism to rule the land. The Order cannot let that happen." He paused, then added: "I cannot let that happen."

"You are a psychopath, you know that? A regular tin-foil-hat-wearing conspiracy theorist!"

Silas glanced back over his shoulder. Now to perform for the camera.

"You deny claiming the Constitution hangs in the balance, as on a thread, just like the Joseph Smith prophecies? That there will be a complete change of government and Washington, DC, will cease to be the capital? That the present national bureaucracy will have its end? That the current system of government will be wiped away to pave the way for the political Kingdom of God? That a new government will be established by the Latter-day Saints? That this is, quote, 'the year of the Latter-day Saints, for the truth of our divine messenger Moroni is marching on'? You deny you said all that? Because I've got it all recorded."

Young shook his head. "What does it matter that I said those things? No one will know about it anyhow. And what is it with you people?" He exclaimed loudly. "You Orthodox Christians have been oppressing my people from the beginning. Claiming that we're not legitimate."

"You're not," he interrupted. "You're an American-bred upstart religious sect, crafting an American god born by people heavily involved in the occult with the intent to replace authentic Christianity and subvert Christian churches."

Silas could tell that angered Young. But the man kept his fury at bay and simply turned around, back toward the Lincoln statue. He put his hands in his pockets and stood staring at the monument in silence.

"You know, Abraham Lincoln's own political career led to frequent associations with members of the Church of Jesus Christ of Latter-day Saints. It's rumored he even checked out the Book of Mormon from the Library of Congress and kept it for almost a year during the Civil War. As it raged, he left us alone, we left him alone. Even helped us later secure our Nauvoo Charter. My great-great-grandfather, though, considered Lincoln one of the cursed scoundrels who sought our destruction from the beginning, and he blamed him for doing nothing to stop the persecution of my ancestors. He was especially angered when Lincoln later signed that blasted anti-polygamy law. But Lincoln never really enforced it and he kept the country together, preserving the constitution and the union, which Brigham Young respected."

The man was rambling. Silas walked up next to him. "It's over, Amos. Your candidacy and your religious coup."

Young laughed. "Even if you did have the recording you claim you have, there's no way the audio is good enough to convince the world that I was the man speaking on the other end of a closed door."

"Don't worry about the audio quality."

"I'm not," he interrupted. Then he turned around and started walking back toward Lincoln. "This conversation is over." He motioned toward his agents.

Time for the big reveal. Now or never.

"I don't think you want to do that, Amos."

He continued walking, waving to Silas with one hand.

Silas shouted, "Because that recording isn't the only one I've got."

Young stopped short, turned around, then walked back to Silas. "What are you talking about?"

He said quietly, "We've had aerial surveillance on this site for the past hour."

"What?" Young scrunched up his brow and shook his head. "What are you talking about?"

"Smile," Silas said waving toward the black, rainy void. "You're on candid camera."

Young's face fell as he turned toward the mall. His eyes widened as he searched the darkness for the truth of Silas's claim.

Years back, SEPIO invested in aerial surveillance technology before it became in vogue, outfitting their drones with the best in high-resolution cameras and digitally-enhanced multi-wave audio microphones for such a time as this. Once Zoe had received word from Silas, she sent one of the birds into the sky and hovered it over the Lincoln Memorial, just out of sight range but close enough to get solid footage and audio.

"Why you—" He lunged at Silas, grabbing his neck with both hands. His face was full of fear and fury, his grip murderous.

Silas grabbed both of his wrists, but couldn't breathe. He struggled against the man but couldn't break the hold.

The Secret Service agents quickly coalesced around the fight, confused as to who was attacking whom. Three of them tried to secure Silas, while the other three tried to peel Young off of him.

Finally, he relented, breaking his hold and standing back. "Back off," he barked. "I'm fine!"

The agents quickly obeyed, backing up to give their man the space he wanted.

"You're lying," Young said through gritted teeth, staring back out into the mall.

"No, I'm not," Silas wheezed. He doubled over to catch his breath, then pointed straight out into darkness. "There is a drone with a 4k high-definition, ultra-zoom lens and high-frequency homing microphone floating out there. It's been picking up the entire conversation since you arrived. So whether anyone believes it's your voice on the recording doesn't matter. We've got all we need to expose you and your conspiracy. And if you don't bail from the race by tomorrow night, the Order will release it to the world."

"No, you're not."

Silas startled. His stomach dropped at the sound of the new voice from behind him. Not so much because the invasion caught him off guard, but because he instantly recognized it.

The voice was as familiar to him as his own.

He turned around sharply, disbelieving his eyes.

"Hello, Sy," his brother said. He was wearing a coat similar to Young's. Long and dark. Peeking out from the top was a red bowtie. He was slightly taller and narrower than Silas. But his face was similarly matched, but for blond hair and blue eyes.

"Sebastian?" Silas said breathlessly.

Sebastian folded his arms and said nothing.

"Wha...What are you doing here?"

"Didn't he tell you?" Young said, walking over to stand beside Silas's twin brother. "He's been helping me orchestrate the political win of the century that you're so hellbent on preventing."

Sebastian Grey. Amos Young. Sebastian and Young.

This was not computing.

"I...I don't understand," Silas said stepping toward his brother and looking him straight in the eyes. "What are you doing working for Young? And what does he mean that you've been helping orchestrate his campaign?"

Sebastian stood still, unmoving, hands in his coat pockets. "Let's just say, if you expose him, you expose me."

Silas pinched his eyebrows together in confusion and shook his head.

This wasn't making any—

Unless...

No. He shook his head. No, it couldn't be.

"N...Nous?" Silas said raising his forehead. "But why? How? What reason do you have to subvert and undermine Christianity?"

Again, Sebastian said nothing.

His head was swirling, his legs were feeling weak under the weight of the revelation that his brother was an agent of an ancient organization that had been trying to destroy the Church for two millennia.

"What do you mean if I take down Young I take down you? What is your role in this?"

His brother hesitated. He stood still as one end of his mouth curled upward. Then he said, "Why, because I was responsible for Reed's death?"

Silas stumbled backward, as if the reveal hit him in the chest like the assassin's bullet that took out the former Evangelical candidate.

"No....you didn't pull the trigger. I found the two men responsible."

"I may not have pulled the trigger, but I orchestrated the hit. And if you play the recordings you say you have, I will be implicated. Not only because of what I just revealed, but it will be a matter of time before I'm exposed. That's why I'm calling it. I'm playing the family card, just like you did. Now we're even."

Silas stepped back again and shook his head. "No. You can't do that. Not like this."

"Why not?"

"Because our vow to help one another no matter the cost after Dad died doesn't extend to covering up political conspiracies and assassinations!"

"Oh, but it does cover up religious ones?"

His face twisted in anger at the mention of how he had compelled Sebastian to help him verify the resurrection of Jesus earlier in the year.

"That was different. I didn't ask you to break the law and orchestrate the murder of a presidential candidate!"

"Are you forgetting about the guy we incapacitated and about breaking into that damn church? Just like you to play a double standard, Silas."

"What are you talking about?" he roared. "I didn't conspire to hijack an election and subvert the will of the people. I didn't just commit treason!"

"Goodbye, big brother." Then Sebastian leaned in to whisper into Silas's ear. "Time for you to let go of the fabled Bride of Christ. I know I have. And one way or another, she's going to suffocate to death."

His mouth curled upward and nostrils flared as he stepped back, turning to walk away.

Silas recoiled in revulsion, then shouted, "No, wait!" He stepped forward to intercept his brother, but three Secret Service agents intercepted him. The other three walked with Young and Sebastian out the side door to the memorial.

"Sebastian!" Silas yelled after him. He struggled against the agents, his arms flailing outward toward the only member of his family left—the one who had just stabbed him in the back.

"Sir! You need to calm down and back away," an agent commanded.

He finally relented and walked back from the agents, putting his arms up in surrender. "Fine, fine. I'm fine!"

The three agents stood together like a wall, preventing him from moving forward until their protectee was secure. A minute later, the middle agent put his finger up to his ear and nodded. Then he turned toward his companions and said something. The three turned together to leave, glancing back at Silas as they walked toward the back of the memorial.

Leaving him alone with the bombshell revelation that his brother was working to destroy the Church and undermine the Christian faith.

CHAPTER 38

SANTOS ELECTED FIRST LATINO PRESIDENT
IN HISTORIC LANDSLIDE

That was the headline the day after one of the more remarkable, memorable election seasons in recent memory. One the country gave a collective sigh of relief was over.

The day after Young rejected Silas's offer, a number of mainstream new organizations and one alternative news outlet received a curious digital package: an audio recording from the Salt Lake Temple and drone footage from the Lincoln Memorial. Predictably, the mainstream media hemmed and hawed over what to do. The single alternative news outlet did not.

The Drudge Report posted both recordings with two attention-grabbing headlines above the fold: MORMON REPUBLICAN PRESIDENTIAL CANDIDATE PLEDGES U. S. DOWNFALL; and TREASON: YOUNG THEOCRATIC HOSTILE TAKEOVER. At the top was the site's trademark blue-and-red spinning police strobe light, reigniting its reputation as a first-to-press alternative to the mainstream media reminiscent of the Monica Lewinski scandal that catapulted it to notoriety back in the '90s.

Within minutes, other alternative news outlets picked up the raw footage and posted it on their sites, pinging Drudge with the scoop. From there, the remarkable story instantly went viral through the major social media platforms, which gave the mainstream media coverage they needed to report on the veracity of the original story, rather than the story itself.

In American political jargon, there's a term for what happened that fateful day at the end of October: October Surprise. A news event deliberately created or timed or sometimes occurring spontaneously to influence the outcome of an election, particularly one for the U.S. presidency. There had always been such fortuitous, unplanned news events that swung elections this way or that for one candidate, especially with the rise of broadcast journalism. A conspiracy theory gained ground with the Carter-Reagan election after Iran released its fifty-two American hostages, which they delayed until after the election. In fact, they were released twenty minutes after Reagan was sworn in as president, leading some to allege his team had impeded the hostage release to negate the potential boost to the Carter campaign.

The digital recordings of Young was the October Surprise the Santos campaign needed.

After Maxwell's moderated discussion between Silas and Young, remarkably he was able to hold the five-point lead he had over Santos. Surprisingly, enough Evangelicals had been satisfied with his performance, and he had picked up support elsewhere. However, by the end of the first day of the release of the recording, Santos had pulled ahead eight points, leapfrogging Young and leading him by three. By Election Day, it was more than over: most of the 79 percent of Evangelicals who had been supporting Young decided to stay home, and Santos won the largest margin of victory since Warren Harding defeated James Cox in 1920. What's more: Young himself had gone missing. Probably fled the country, given the precarious, seditious legal position he had placed himself in, what with plotting to overthrow the government and all.

Needless to say, the Order of Thaddeus was pleased. Silas had mixed feelings.

There had been rampant speculation on both the internet and the cable news airwaves surrounding the origin of the recordings. One of the most talked about pieces to the whole mystery was the identity of the other male heard and briefly seen on the drone footage. As of yet, no one had identified Silas. The Order had also yet to be linked to supplying the recordings. They both had wanted to keep their identities a mystery. So far so good.

His brother was another story.

Silas sat in the Washington National Cathedral's nave listening to the boys' choir practice for the coming Sunday morning service, contemplating the revelation about his brother and its implications.

Sebastian, a Nous agent...

For the past few days, he had been trying to wrap his mind around the turn of events. He simply couldn't accept the fact that Sebastian had radicalized into some anti-Christian, pseudo-spiritual operative hellbent on destroying the Church. As he retraced the past year's events, some pieces did make sense, though.

He thought about when his brother had been shot at the Church of the Holy Sepulcher in Jerusalem when he and SEPIO were stopping Nous from destroying the Edicule containing the tomb of Christ. Sebastian had been shot, but in a way that wasn't life-threatening. Was that a ruse meant to throw off Silas so that Jacob Crowley could escape?

Then the random phone call he had received at the Chartres Cathedral asking where he had been, hours before he was intercepted by Oliver Tulu and his henchman. Was that Sebastian's way of tracking Silas for Nous?

And the man in the bow tie. Of course, Sebastian's trademark threads. Silas thought he had glimpsed his brother during his escape from the Salt Lake Temple, but he threw it off as his mind playing tricks. There was no reason to suspect he had been involved.

Now Silas was kicking himself for not seeing or sensing it all sooner.

"So I hear you've managed to keep us out of the dock."

His eyes widened in surprise, and his heart seemed to literally skip a beat. He knew that voice.

Silas whipped around and stood.

"Celeste!"

Celeste Bourne, the director of operations for SEPIO, had nearly been killed a month ago after she and Silas had tracked down and saved the Ark of the Covenant. He hadn't seen her since, as she had been recovering at a SEPIO operations center in France.

She was walking toward him down the aisle, her long hair braided and over her shoulder, her full lips parted with a slight smile. She also had a limp, but otherwise she was looking great. As always.

He embraced her, holding her a little longer than intending to but not feeling the least bit embarrassed or ashamed. He needed her touch.

He let go, and said, "Radcliffe didn't tell me you were coming. I thought you were still living a life of luxury while recuperating at some convent in France."

She giggled. "I'm not sure I would call it a life of luxury, but the good sisters did take good care of me and fixed me up right."

"Come, sit," Silas said motioning toward his row of wooden chairs. "Take a load off that leg. How is it healing?"

He slid inside, she followed on his left. "Better every day. Was worried I would be taken out of commission for good, given the severity of the leg wound. But between the wicked therapy of Sister Helga—"

"And your own resolve, I'm sure," he interrupted.

She smiled. "Yes, that and her therapy has almost brought my leg back to full use. Can't quite run a marathon yet. But I'll get there."

"I know you will."

Silence fell between them as the boys' choir began another number, their supplications rising high toward the heavens. The two sat side-by-side listening to their serenade, their souls being fed by the angelic melody.

"So," she began, putting her hand on his leg, "sounds like you had yourself quite the adventure! Full of the usual conspiracy and treachery I'm sure you've come to expect from the Order."

He looked at her, smiling weakly. She kept her hand there as they continued listening to the choir. "You could say that," was all he said.

What Silas didn't say, what he could not say, was that his brother was involved in the conspiracy and treachery. That he had gone to the dark side as an operative for Nous, the single greatest threat to the Church and the Christian faith. Not only had he not seen it coming, it happened right under his nose. None of his pleading and witnessing and arguments had done a lick of good. His brother was an apostate, he had rejected the Christian faith. Not only that, but Sebastian had told him he wanted the Church to die!

When he had left the Lincoln Memorial, Silas hadn't spoken a word of his brother's involvement to Radcliffe or Celeste or anyone at SEPIO. He was too afraid of what might happen to him, too ashamed of what he had allowed him to become. So the mysterious third man remained just that. A part of him knew he should share the vital intel of Sebastian's involvement, but he couldn't bring himself to do it. Another part of him wondered why it would matter anyway. It was far from clear how deep he was in with Nous. Probably a one-time gig to vent his animosity toward the Church.

Regret still pinged his gut, though, sitting next to Celeste. But Silas said nothing, his heart and mind enraptured by the canticle of praise acting as a balm for his soul.

"Sorry to change the subject," she said, "but have you given more thought to working for the Order?"

He turned toward her, draping his arm behind her on the chair. He smiled, and said, "Are you offering me a job, Celeste Bourne?"

She turned toward him and leaned back with a serious face. "Well, what are your qualifications, Mr. Grey?"

"Qualifications?"

"You didn't think I was going to hire you without a formal interview, did you? Besides, I understand you were just sacked from your previous place of employ."

He laughed at her playfulness, then he transfixed his own serious face.

"Alright, let's see. Qualifications. Ahh, yes. I've got this piece of paper from a university on the East Coast. Maybe you've heard of it, Harvard University. Says I'm a doctor or something of church history and religious studies."

"Hmm," she said contemplatively. "That's helpful."

"And then I did two tours in the Middle East with the United States Army Rangers, receiving commendations from both."

"So I can imagine you can handle a gun when called upon. How's your aim?"

He leaned back and cocked his head in contemplation. "Precise."

"Good answer. Anything else I should know about?"

"Well, I managed to help save the Shroud of Turin from doom and destruction."

"I heard a rumor that it was your better-looking female partner who tracked down perpetrators fleeing in a van, managing to single-handedly bring it to a halt and rescue the ancient relic."

Silas twisted his face. "Oh, yeah. But then I single-handedly caught the villain in a crypt at the Church of the Holy Sepulcher."

"While your illustrious better-looking female partner managed to save your hide and shoot him before he blew your head off."

He smirked. "I could have taken him down."

"But I will give you credit. Because I also heard you did happen to dismantle a bomb that almost leveled the holy church and Christ's burial tomb."

He snapped his fingers. "Yes! I knew there was something. And don't forget my painstaking research that led to locating and saving the Ark of the Covenant."

Celeste cleared her throat.

"Along with my illustrious better-looking female partner, of course."

"Good lad."

"You have to give me credit for single-handedly taking down a Republican presidential candidate, though. And, no offense, but I'm pretty sure I did that one without my illustrious better-looking female partner."

She grinned slightly. "'Tis true. I do have to give you that one."

He leaned in closer, though not quite touching the woman. "It wasn't nearly as fun, though, without you kicking ass and taking names alongside me."

She leaned away slightly and offered him a wry grin. "Are you flirting with me, Silas Grey?"

He quickly leaned back, his face reddening with embarrassment.

"Because I'm not sure how you Yanks land jobs in the States, but that's definitely not how us Brits do it. And, for the record, it was you who was kicking ass and taking names alongside me."

He almost apologized until Celeste let a giggle slip. Then she grinned and offered him her hand.

"You're hired. That is, if you want the job."

He looked at it, then his mouth curled upwards slightly. "And what job is that?"

"Why, assistant director of operations for SEPIO, of course."

He recoiled slightly and furrowed his brow. "But aren't you the director of operations? Wouldn't that make me your assistant?"

She propped her arm on the back of her chair. "Hmm. I guess that would, wouldn't it?"

He smiled and took her hand. "Then sign me up."

Celeste smiled and nodded, then stood. "Good. Because we've got work to do."

Silas stood and followed her down the aisle toward the secret entrance to the operation center below.

"Do you people never rest?"

She shook her head. "Not when the future of the Church and the Christian faith is at stake."

Good answer.

He had dedicated much of his adult life contending for and preserving the once-for-all faith entrusted to God's holy people by Christ himself. As he descended into the nerve center of the Order of Thaddeus, he was thankful for the chance to enter that fight again.

With her.

AUTHOR'S NOTE

THE HISTORY BEHIND THE STORY...

When I wrote this story, I recognized people would probably either love it or hate it, given the two dicey topics it addresses: politics and religion. But I was fine with that, because both are near and dear to me given my own personal experiences with them. Rather than an anti-Mormon screed, I hoped to start a conversation about Church-State dynamics and authentic Christianity by using the alternative Christian sect's history and beliefs as a dialogue partner.

As with all of my books, I like to add a note at the end with some of the thoughts and research that went into the story. So, if you care to learn more about the foundation of this episode in the Order of Thaddeus, here is some of what I both experienced and discovered that made its way into SEPIO's latest adventure.

The Politics of Church and State

First of all, this is a political thriller with a religious edge. While it centers on the Religious Right, the same commentary on its involvement in the political arena could easily be said of the Religious Left. It was just easier to use them as the springboard into the conversation given its more overt history with playing politics—as well as my own history with the movement. Let me explain.

298 | *Author's Note*

I spent half a decade working in politics. First as a congressional aide to a U. S. Senator, then as a sort of pastor to politicians serving the spiritual needs of Members of Congress and their staff. No, we weren't lobbyists for Jesus. We were a nonpartisan, nonpolitical organization that sought to serve the spiritual needs of those serving in America's capital. (Although, our group was part of a larger entity founded by someone who was intimately involved with the Religious Right). I led prayer groups and Bible studies for those serving in our government for Christians and others interested in spirituality. It may surprise you, but there are over 20,000 congressional staffers working to support the 535 congressmen and senators and their committees. And get this: the average age (at least when I worked there over a decade ago) is 27. It's a tough environment with long hours and short tempers, and so we sought to be a safe place for them to receive counsel, prayer, and support in their important roles. It was a great vocational gig that afforded me super-cool opportunities to attend a State of the Union Address and presidential election party.

With that said, I also saw the seedy underbelly of the relationship between Church and State, and how Christians from both sides of the political spectrum vie for power—spending money and doing what is necessary to secure a seat at the table. One poll conducted shortly after the 2004 election put this relationship in perspective: a number of Members of Congress were asked which political group they would ignore if they didn't have to worry about the political ramifications. At the top of the list for Republican members was the Religious Right. Which told me that, in many ways, the Church of Jesus Christ has been reduced to a lobbying group on par with the NRA and AFL-CIO. I saw, up close, how the Church whores herself to either political party for the lowest bid—and how both Democrats and Republicans use the Bride of Christ to further their own political agendas. What I saw then, over a decade ago, has continued to play itself out on the American political scene—most recently in the 2016 presidential election.

I wrote this story in the summer of 2017, after a tumultuous election year. Yet again, the Church leaped into bed with the State—creating confusion about what is authentically Christian and sullying her reputation and integrity. And so, I wanted to tell a story confronting this tendency in a way that might encourage people to ask the questions Silas and Radcliffe and the rest of the Order were asking. The reason I chose Mormonism as the catalyst for the conversation is for a few reasons.

First, I asked myself the same questions when a Mormon headlined the Republican ticket in 2012. The same "What does it mean to be Christian?" questions rose to the surface as some parts of the Church threw millions of dollars at his campaign to gain a seat at the table. The candidate seemed like a fine fellow, much like Amos Young. But I wondered what sort of spiritual confusion it might cause in America with the renewed talk about Mormonism's relationship with Christianity if he were elected to the highest office in the land. Plenty were insisting that his Mormon faith was merely a sect of Christianity—much like Presbyterianism or Catholicism. The statistics Radcliffe offered in chapter 5 accurately represent the broader public's perception of this relationship.

The second reason, however, is rooted in history: all of the apocalyptic prophecies by Joseph Smith and Brigham Young mentioned in the story concerning the United States and the End Times are accurate. Much of the language from the "letter" Silas found and speeches he heard at the Quorum of the Twelve meeting in chapters 30 and 32 respectively were borrowed from direct quotes given by these two founders. Smith indeed predicted that the time would come "when the Constitution of our country would hang as it were by a thread, and the Latter-day Saints above all other people in the world would come to the rescue." And while languishing in a Missouri jail, Smith seems to have decided that a political Kingdom of God would precede an apocalyptic one, in which the former would be "the kingdom militant, struggling against a hostile world," while the later would be "the kingdom victorious, having subdued all its enemies." In his famous White Horse prophecy, Smith pronounced certain judgment and destruction upon the United States, and he organized a sort of shadow government, the Council of Fifty, which was created as "the Municipal department of the Kingdom of God set up on Earth, and from which all Law emanates, for the rule, government & control of all Nations, Kingdoms & towns, and People under the whole Heavens." According to one former Mormon president, Wilford Woodruff, this Council was to "organize the political kingdom of God in preparation for the second coming of Christ."

Now, does that mean there is today a conspiratorial cabal within the Church of Jesus Christ of Latter-day Saint hierarchy waiting to overthrow the American government and set up a Mormon theocracy, as was the case in this story? Who knows! What is known, however, is that such an impulse was a deeply historical component of the founding of the Mormon religion based on the words of Mormonism's founders, and that it was a crucial part of its eschatology—its theology of the end of the world. They believed the Latter-day Saints would be the saviors of wayward America.

My hope is that exploring this Mormon impulse in this way, combined with a similar impulse within certain sectors of the Church to leverage the secular government to establish God's Kingdom, will spark some conversations about whether we believe Jesus is Lord, or Caesar is Lord. That was the choice of early believers—and they paid for their belief in the former with their lives by denying the latter. The Church is the hope of the world—not Congress, or Parliament, or the Supreme Court, or any other government institution. We also don't need to rely on a particular political party to accomplish what Christ has commissioned us to do. Because as Jesus himself promised: "All authority in heaven and on earth has been given to me. Go therefore..." (Matthew 28:18–19).

The Church doesn't need the government to do its job; we have all we need: the authority of Jesus himself! So let's get to our mission: making disciples of Christ, baptizing them into the faith.

Mormonism and History

Authentic Christianity is thoroughly rooted in history and entirely historical. Meaning: it openly makes historical claims and invites all who are interested to examine and assess those claims. For instance, either Jesus rose from the dead, or he didn't (see first book in the series, *Holy Shroud*). Authentic Christianity rises and falls on that claim. In fact, one of the chief apostles of the faith, Paul of Tarsus, says as much in a letter he wrote to Christians living in Corinth (see 1 Corinthians 15). This historicity of authentic Christianity is one of the main reasons why Mormonism isn't Christian.

Chapter 6 recounts the Book of Mormon's tale about the early settlers of the Americas. And chapter 30 recounts Joseph Smith's tale about how the Book of Mormon came into existence. Both rest on historical claims, and both fail the test of history. Not only is the so-called "history" of the Lamanites a complete fabrication with zero anthropological or archaeological credibility, institutions like the Smithsonian Institution have flat-out denied its history. For instance, in a statement on the book in 1965, they wrote: "The Smithsonian Institution has never used the Book of Mormon in any way as a scientific guide. Smithsonian archeologists see no direct connection between the archeology of the New World and the subject matter of the book." The statements made by Lloyd Kimball concerning this newfangled history of the New World in chapter 33 reflect the rest of their reasoning.

Which brings up the Mormon medallion Grant Chrysostom uncovered in Missouri, and the map it held to the so-called White City. The medallion is a fabrication of my imagination, but the treasure-seeking history surrounding the Smith clan covered in chapter 35, as well as their nefarious deeds and hucksterism, lends a degree of credibility to the fictitious element; it's not too incredible to suggest Smith could have created a fake medallion to bolster his claims. However, the mystery surrounding Ciudad Blanca is real —not only the city itself, but its connection to Mormonism.

Douglas Preston wrote a splendid book on the subject, *The Lost City of the Monkey God*—which I used to inform the adventure of Torres, Gapinski, and Grant in Honduras. I read it before I started writing this story, because I've always been an Indiana Jones junkie at heart and was intrigued by the story it told about finding the lost White City. There's also a connection between Mormonism and the kinds of ruins known as Ciudad Blanca: Mormons were certain the Mayan civilization was the lost Israelites told in the Book of Mormon, and they explored their ruins throughout Mexico and Central America in the hopes of finally gaining historical credence to the Book of Mormon's claims. It is true that a well-funded group of LDS archaeologists tried to confirm those stories. But in the end, those ruins disproved the Mormon view. Some of the archaeologists lost their faith, some were even excommunicated. So I merged these parallel accounts from history to inform my tale.

Then there is the so-called Golden Bible, itself a historical fabrication that virtually plagiarized the King James Version of the Bible. The Hebrew inscription etched into the Mormon medallion Grant discovered in Missouri that Rowan Radcliffe later translates in chapter 6 represents several similarly lifted verses from the KJV that Joseph Smith wrote into the Book of Mormon, in addition to several passages that mirror the Apocrypha. Furthermore, in recent years it has come to light that Smith seems to have drawn considerable inspiration from contemporary works linking Native Americans to Israel, even going so far as to copy whole portions from such works as *The Wonders of Nature* (Josiah Priest) and *Views of the Hebrews* (Ethan Smith) and use them in his religious text.

From a historical perspective, it appears Radcliffe was right: Joseph Smith was the first person to blend the theories circulating at the time concerning the origins of Native Americans into a grand religious scheme. Add to this his borrowing of material from the KJV Bible and Apocrypha, and you have yourself a truly American-made religion offering an American god. As Mormon scholar Thomas Stuart Ferguson wrote: "Mormonism is probably the best conceived myth-fraternity to which one can belong. It's a refinement of Judaism...and a refinement of the Jesus story." He also concluded, "the Book of Mormon was produced through Joseph Smith's own creative genius and through his use of contemporary sources, including Ethan Smith's *View of the Hebrews*." I am indebted to Richard Abanes's masterful book *One Nation Under Gods* for the fascinating history of Mormonism and the Book of Mormon that I weaved throughout this story.

(In case you were wondering: yes, the Danites are a thing!)

Mormon Theology vs. Historic Christianity

This brings us to the heart of the book: a discussion on what's authentically Christian. I decided to use Mormonism as a catalyst for this broader conversation, because of how it has been thought of within popular culture in recent years as a Christian sect.

The issue of authentic Christianity—what Christians have historically believed and taught since the apostles—is an important one to me. Not only because I am a historical theologian by training, having earned a Master of Theology in historical theology in addition to a Master of Divinity in the Bible. But also because I myself have been on a personal quest the past decade to understand the essential beliefs of Christianity. So this discussion about what is authentic to the historic Christian faith, and how Mormonism differs from it, is as much personal as it is professional.

Everything mentioned in this book regarding Mormon beliefs, particularly the back-and-forth dialogue in chapter 36, is accurate to Mormonism. You don't hear about those believes frequently, because the alternative religious sect has made it a point to focus on Jesus and its allegiance to his teachings. And yet, these are the core doctrines from foundational Mormon theological texts and teachers. Here is a brief summary of those beliefs, and how they contrast with authentic Christianity, presented by several helpful charts in Richard Abanes's book.

First consider a number of central contradictory tenets of faith between Mormonism and authentic Christianity (*ONUG*, 382):

Central Mormon Beliefs

- *God*: There are many gods, which is polytheism. The god of this planet is an exalted man with a body of flesh and bones. He has at least one wife, probably more.
- *Pre-existence*: Humans have pre-existed in heaven as spirit children conceived via celestial sex between Heavenly Father and Heavenly Mother. Our actions in the pre-existence determine our race on earth.
- *Human nature*: Mormons say they are gods in embryo, and they have not yet reached the godhood. "As man is, God once was: as God is, man may become."
- *Jesus*: Jesus, the first spirit-child of Heavenly Father, is the spirit-brother of Lucifer. Jesus is only one of many created gods.
- *Eternal Life*: There are three levels of eternal life, the highest level being godhood, which is available only to perfected Mormons.
- *Salvation*: Salvation is achieved only by those who do enough good deeds and obey all God's laws, which amounts to works righteousness.
- *Holy Spirit*: A third god, like Heavenly Father and Jesus, with a spiritual body only, rather than a physical body.
- *The Bible*: It isn't infallible, inerrant, or inspired. It is also incomplete, not containing God's full revelation.

Central Christian Beliefs

- *God*: There is only one God, which is monotheism. God is not a man, nor does God have a body. God is not married, which is not even hinted at in the Bible.

- *Pre-existence*: Christians are children of God by adoption to sonship and daughtership through faith. One's spirit is formed on earth as they begin life within the womb. God is no respecter of persons and the Christian faith does not favor a single race; there are no racial distinctions within Christianity.
- *Human nature*: We are created beings created in the image and likeness of God, whom he longs to be in covenanted relationship with. However, we are separate from the Creator; we do not become God(s).
- *Jesus*: Jesus is not a created being, but rather, is the Creator—by whom, through whom, and for whom all things were made. As the central Christian creed says, the Nicene Creed: *And in one Lord Jesus Christ, the only Son of God, begotten from the Father before all ages, God from God, Light from Light, true God from true God, begotten, not made; of the same essence as the Father.*
- *Eternal Life*: There exists no other gods, nor can any person become a god, no mater how dedicated they are to the church. All people will be separated at the end of the age: some granted eternal life through faith in Jesus; others damned to eternal death through rejecting Jesus.
- *Salvation*: Salvation is not achieved or obtained through good deeds and works of righteousness, but by simply asking God for forgiveness of sins, trusting Jesus' ransom payment for personal sins on the cross, and submitting ones life to God in faith and obedience.
- *Holy Spirit*: The Holy Spirit is God, the Third Person of the Trinity, co-equal and co-eternal with God the Father and God the Son. He is not a separate entity, but one being with the Father and the Son.
- *The Bible*: It is infallible, inerrant, and inspired. It is also complete, containing God's full revelation and complete gospel of salvation.

The contradictions between Mormonism and authentic, historic Christianity become starker when it comes to Jesus (*ONUG*, 378).

Mormon Beliefs about Jesus:

- A literal son (spirit child) of a god (Elohim) and his wife.
- The elder brother of all spirits born in the pre-existence to Heavenly Father.
- A polygamous Jew.
- One of three gods overseeing this planet.
- Atoned only for Adam's transgressions by sweating blood in Gethsemane.
- The literal spirit brother of Lucifer.
- Jesus' sacrificial death is not able to cleanse every person of all their sins.
- There is no salvation without accepting Joseph Smith as a prophet of God.

Christian Beliefs about Jesus:

- The uncreated, eternally existent, unique incarnation of God as "the Son."
- The unique Son of God, with whom none can be compared.
- An unmarried Jew.
- The Second Person of the Holy Trinity.
- Atoned for everyone's personal sins by being crucified on the cross.
- No relation to Satan, who is a mere angel.
- Jesus' sacrifice on the cross is able to cleanse every person of all their sins.
- Jesus alone is the way, truth, and life. No need to recognize or follow a prophet.

The conclusion, then, is that Mormons do not believe what Christians believe; Christians do not believe what Mormons believe. But why does this matter?

Silas opened his monologue in chapter 36 by quoting Roger Olson, who said "the story of Christian theology is the story of Christian reflection on salvation." It's true, which is why discussing the finer points of these theological beliefs is so vital, because nothing less than the salvation of humanity is at stake. Christianity says one thing about salvation, Mormonism says another.

His closing statement differentiating between the questions 'Are Mormons Christian?' and 'Are Christians Mormons?' was borrowed from Abanes's book. It is a helpful distinction, for it gets to the heart of the matter: do people who call themselves Christians believe what Mormons believe? Has the Church of Jesus, the one that has existed for the last two millennia ever believed at all what the Church of Jesus Christ of Latter-day Saints believe—which has only been in existence for less than 200 years? As you can see from the brief survey of Mormon theology and Christian theology above, the answer is a resounding "No!"

So if Christians don't believe what Mormons believe, and we could never say that a Christian is a Mormon, why would we ever insist on the reverse? As Silas said, that would be like saying a Muslim Christian. Muslims do not believe what Christians believe; Christians do not believe what Muslims believe. Neither of those are controversial statements; they are factual ones. So why would we suggest the same for Mormons? The core tenets of the Mormon faith contradict the core tenets of the Christian faith. Which is precisely what Joseph Smith had in mind in the first place.

Interestingly, he founded the alternative religion in direct response to historic Christian orthodoxy, which he saw as the "Great Apostasy." As the official Mormon version of Smith's supposed First Vision states: "I saw a pillar of light exactly over my head...I asked the personages who stood above me in the light, which of all the sects was right—and which I should join. I was answered that I must join none of them, for they are all wrong, and the personage who addressed me said that all their creeds were an abomination in His sight: that those professors were all corrupt." All other churches, he insisted in the Book of Mormon, were founded by the devil and representations of the "great and abominable church" of the satanic world system. He wrote: "Behold there are save two churches only; the one is the church of the Lamb of God, and the other is the church of the devil...the whore of all the earth" (1 Nephi. 14:10). And as Abanes reveals: "Mormons have repeatedly confirmed that their church is 'the only true and living church upon the face of the whole earth' and that 'the power of God unto salvation—(Rom. 1:16) is absent from all but the Church of Jesus Christ of Latter-day Saints'" (378).

Add to this the occult angle of Joseph Smith and his family documented in chapter 16 (which was drawn from primary sources quoted in Richard Abanes's resource, leaving little doubt that Smith Junior was deeply entrenched in occultism along with his family), and the entire foundation of the upstart religion is questionable. At every turn, Mormonism contradicts and compromises beliefs that have always been central to the Christian faith. It truly is a man-made religion offering an American god, bearing no resemblance to authentic Christianity.

Aside from the conversation about Mormon beliefs, there is growing confusion within the Church about what is authentically Christian. I hope this story will help others better understand this confusion and what Christians have always believed, in addition to considering how the Church compromises the integrity of those beliefs by aligning so closely with the State—for it is only in independence from the State that the Church can bear prophetic witness against it. And as Saint Jude Thaddeus insisted in his letter to Christians living in Asia Minor, there is a once-for-all-faith that has been entrusted to God's holy people. It is our job—the Church's generally and Christians' specifically—to contend for it.

Research is an important part of my process for creating compelling stories that entertain, inform, and inspire. Here are a few of the resources I used to research Mormon beliefs and history (Abanes and Palmer) and the White City (Preston):

- Abanes, Richard. *One Nation Under Gods: A History of the Mormon Church*. New York: Four Walls Eight Windows, 2002. www.bouma.us/mormon1
- Palmer, Grant. *Restoring Christ: Leaving Mormon Jesus for Jesus of the Gospels*. Self-Published, 2017. www.bouma.us/mormon2
- Preston, Douglas. *The Lost City of the Monkey God*. New York: Grand Central Publishing, 2017. www.bouma.us/mormon3
- Statement from the Smithsonian Institution regarding the Book of Mormon: www.bouma.us/mormon4

ABOUT THE AUTHOR

J. A. Bouma is an emerging author of vintage faith fiction. As a former congressional staffer and pastor and bestselling author of over thirty religious fiction and nonfiction books, he blends a love for ideas and adventure, exploration and discovery, thrill and thought. With graduate degrees in Bible and theology, he writes within the tension of faith and doubt, spirituality and theology, Church and culture, belief and practice, modern and vintage forms of Church, and the gritty drama that is our collective pilgrim story.

He also offers nonfiction resources on the Christian faith under Jeremy Bouma. His books and courses help people rediscover and retrieve the vintage Christian faith by connecting that faith in relevant ways to our 21st century world.

Jeremy lives in Grand Rapids, Michigan, with his wife, son, and daughter, and their rambunctious boxer-pug-terrier Zoe.

www.jabouma.com
jeremy@jabouma.com

facebook.com/jaboumabooks

twitter.com/bouma

amazon.com/author/jabouma

THANK YOU!

A big thanks for joining Silas Grey and the rest of SEPIO on their adventure saving the world!

Enjoy the story? Here's what you can do next:

If you loved the book and have a moment to spare, **a short review is much appreciated.** Nothing fancy, just your honest take. Spreading the word is probably the #1 way you can help independent authors like me and help others enjoy the story.

If you're ready for another adventure, you can get a full-length novel in the series for free! All you have to do is join the insider's group to be notified of specials and new releases by going to this link:
www.jabouma.com/free

GET YOUR FREE THRILLER

Building a relationship with my readers is one of my all-time favorite joys of writing! Once in a while I like to send out a newsletter with giveaways, free stories, pre-release content, updates on new books, and other bits on my stories.

Join my insider's group for updates, giveaways, and your free novel —a full-length action-adventure story in my *Order of Thaddeus* thriller series. Just tell me where to send it.

Follow this link to subscribe:
www.jabouma.com/free

ALSO BY J. A. BOUMA

J. A. Bouma is an emerging author of vintage faith fiction. You may also like these books that explore the tension of faith and doubt, spirituality and theology, Church and culture, belief and practice, modern and vintage forms of Church, and the gritty drama that is our collective pilgrim story.

Order of Thaddeus Action-Adventure Thriller Series

Holy Shroud • Book 1

The Thirteenth Apostle • Book 2

Hidden Covenant • Book 3

American God • Book 4

Grail of Power • Book 5

Templars Rising • Book 6 (March 2019)

Faith Reimagined Spiritual Coming-of-Age Tetralogy

A Reimagined Faith • Book 1 (January 2019)

A Rediscovered Faith • Book 2 (January 2019)

A Ruined Faith • Book 3 (June 2019)

A Resurrected Faith • Book 4 (September 2019)

Made in the USA
San Bernardino, CA
12 March 2019